MONSTERS, MOVIES & MAYHEM

MONSTERS, MOVIES & MAYHEM

KEVIN J. ANDERSON, EXECUTIVE EDITOR

Editorial Team
Elizabeth Drisko, Kelly Lynn Colby, Angela Johnson,
Ashley King, M. Scott Lee, Tracy Leonard Nakatani,
James Romag, Kailey Urbaniak, Carol Wyrick

WFP
WORDFIRE PRESS

MONSTERS, MOVIES & MAYHEM
Copyright © 2020 WordFire Press
Individual Copyright Information Available at End of Book

EBook ISBN: 978-1-68057-106-6
Trade Paperback ISBN: 978-1-68057-105-9
Hardcover ISBN: 978-1-68057-107-3

Kevin J. Anderson, Executive Editor
Editorial Team: Kelly Lynn Colby, Elizbeth Drisko, Angela Johnson, Ashley King, Scott Lee, Tracy Leonard Nakatani, James Romag, Kailey Urbaniak, and Carol Wyrick

This anthology was made possible with assistance from Draft2Digital and Western Colorado University

Kevin J. Anderson, Art Director
Published by
WordFire Press, LLC
PO Box 1840
Monument CO 80132

Kevin J. Anderson & Rebecca Moesta, Publishers

WordFire Press eBook Edition 2020
WordFire Press Trade Paperback Edition 2020
WordFire Press Hardcover Edition 2020

Printed in the USA

Join our WordFire Press Readers Group for
sneak previews, updates, new projects, and giveaways.
Sign up at wordfirepress.com

❧ Created with Vellum

CONTENTS

INTRODUCTION

This anthology came about as a group project for my Publishing MA students at the Graduate Program in Creative Writing at Western Colorado University, where I teach. During the summer residency, the nine students brainstormed ideas for an original anthology, and they came up with *Monsters, Movies & Mayhem* as their favorite. They wrote up their pitch for the book, defined exactly what kind of stories they were looking for.

The students sent out a wide call for submissions and received over four hundred stories in the slushpile. They waded through them, weeded out the ones that weren't ready for prime time, chose the best, and wrote up publication contracts. The wrote rejection letters for all the others. With generous assistance from Draft2Digital and support from Western Colorado University, we were able to pay professional rates for these stories.

They waded through them, buried under stories not formatted properly, or that had nothing to do with the anthology subject (one guy sent us a list of tourist sites in Manhattan...and then resubmitted the manuscript after we rejected it!). They needed to weigh hard and visceral stories against light and funny ones, balance the number of werewolf stories against zombie stories or haunted theater stories. After several iterations, they weeded out the ones that weren't ready for prime time, chose the best, and wrote up publication contracts.

They worked with the authors to copy edit and proofread their individual pieces. They designed the cover and the interior, produced the book, and published it in hardcover, paperback, and ebook as their graduation project.

Much more than just a class project, though, *Monsters, Movies &* *Mayhem* is filled with remarkable stories, some terrifying, some funny, some heart wrenching. Let the lights go down, lean back in your seat, and enjoy them like popcorn.

—Kevin J. Anderson, Director, Publishing Program
Graduate Program in Creative Writing
Western Colorado University

GAVIN FUNKE'S MONSTER MOVIE MARATHON

MARATHON

(Bring the Whole Family!)

JONATHAN MABERRY

GAVIN FUNKE'S MONSTER MOVIE MARATHON

-1-

Gavin Funke sat in the dark and watched his monster movies. One after the other.

All day.

Well into the night.

He had the theater mostly to himself. The popcorn was fresh and the smell of it filled the entire theater with buttery goodness. The Coke was cool, not cold, but that was okay. Making ice was a luxury, and he needed as much juice as the generators would give him to run the projectors and the air conditioning.

The theater was nearly quiet. A few people made some noise, but there was always a little of that. Over in the corner, in the darkest and most private spot in the auditorium he could hear soft moans.

Gavin didn't care about that. He was not that kind of voyeur.

He sat with his feet wedged between the backs of the two seats in front of him, his sneakers parted in a Vee so as not to obstruct his view. On the screen a black man in a stained white shirt was hammering boards over the windows of a farmhouse. There were banging sounds on the doors as clumsy fists pounded on the doors and walls. Anyone with half a brain could tell those boards weren't going to stop anyone. Even if Gavin hadn't seen this movie a dozen times he'd know that. They were nailed

3

crookedly and in haste. And they were straight-nailed, not toe-nailed. Not screwed securely. Wouldn't take much at all.

"Dumbass," he yelled at the screen.

But the actor playing the guy in the movie with the monster didn't listen. None of them ever did. They did stupid things because they were stupid characters. And they died. A lot of them died. Sometimes all of them died.

But not Gavin Funke.

No sir.

He was the star of *this* movie and he was not going to make any mistakes at all. Not one.

Sure, there had been a learning curve, but the point was that he *did* learn.

He dug into the tub and pulled out a fist of popcorn, not caring that some of it fell onto his shirt or lap, or onto the floor. That was what brooms were for.

A foot kicked his chair but he didn't bother turning and instead hissed, "Mom! Shhhhh!"

Another kick.

"Mom, *c'mon*—how 'bout it?"

Kick.

Gavin abruptly stood up, shot his mother a lethal glare, and moved to the row in front. Not the perfect distance, but still good. And no kicking.

He ate the popcorn more slowly, and it lasted all the way up until the hero got killed. He kept hoping the movie would—just for once—end differently. But it stubbornly refused to do so.

-2-

Gavin slept in because he hated morning. That's why he arranged the movie marathons to go well past midnight. Last night was zombie night. From one yesterday afternoon until the last credits rolled up a minute after five a.m.

He was bloated with popcorn and Milk Duds and Night & Day and some shady off-brand beef jerky because, hey, he needed protein and all the good stuff was gone. Marathons were good for the soul but hard on the colon, and he spent a bad hour in the chemical toilet out by the dumpsters. Gavin was wise, though, and daubed Vicks on his upper lip to kill the smells. He read nearly three chapters of an autobiography by an actor with a huge chin. It was pretty funny, and laughing helped his colon do its business.

Then he went inside, took a shower, dressed in new clothes that came from JCPenny. The belt was a tighter fit than it should have been and he wondered if all that candy was nudging him up a size. That could be a problem because all he could manage was off the rack.

"No more Milk Duds," he promised. But that was a low bar because he didn't have that many boxes left anyway. No way he'd cut out the Night & Day because the licorice helped him move things along.

Gavin turned the house lights up and cleaned the theater floor. Nothing worse than walking on all that sticky mess. As he worked he listened to Tom Waits songs on his Bluetooth earbuds. He liked Waits's older stuff, back when it was more dramatic and melodic. Currently *Tom Traubert's Blues* was breaking his damn heart, like it always did. Gavin had his own theories on what the lyrics meant. They were timeless. People leave, things end, hearts get broken. Hardly mattered what the singer intended. That guy was dealing with his own blues. While he knelt down to fish under a chair with a dust brush, he wondered if Tom Waits was still alive. Probably. Guy like him would find some way to figure things out. He'd get his crap sorted. Gavin was sure of it.

Maybe one of these days he'd take a drive north to find out. He thought Waits lived in Pasadena or someplace like that. Up that way. But the singer had been raised right here in San Diego, Gavin thought.

The song ended and Gavin paused to push the buttons to play it again, but then he stopped, looking down at the debris his last brush sweep had gathered. There was some of his own popcorn, and a stray Milk Dud that still looked good.

And a ring.

Gold. Slender. Very pretty. With delicate, old-world Viking tracery that twisted all the way around the band. He picked it up and sat back on his heels. The ring was dusty, as if it had been there a long time.

Had it? Could he have missed it the other times he cleaned the floor?

It made his heart hurt and the tears ambushed him. He didn't even feel them coming but suddenly they were there. Shoving their way out of him, choking him, kicking at the walls of his lungs. He caved forward so suddenly his forehead banged against the floor. It hurt but he didn't care. Not one bit.

He closed his fist around the ring and tried to push the fist into his chest. If he could have managed that he'd have buried the ring in the tear-moist soil of his heart.

"Mom ..."

The single word escaped his lips. He blubbered it, and the word slipped free and fell onto the dirty floor.

-3-

It took a lot for Gavin to get up off the floor.

It took so much more for him to return the ring to his mother.

He didn't know how he actually managed it, but he was aware of the cost. It was more than he was able to afford.

Getting to his feet would be like jacking up an unloaded truck. He was only five-nine and stocky though not yet fat, but his body felt like it weighed three or four tons. Even lifting his head away from the dirty floor was almost too much, and for a while he knelt there, stupid with pain. His nose was thick with snot and it ran, diluted by tears, over his lips and chin, hung there in pendulous strands, and fell unheeded to his chest.

"Mom ..."

He felt something on his face and brushed at it, and watched bits of popcorn and a strand of half-chewed red licorice whip fall away. He frowned at the red candy. How long had *that* been there? He couldn't remember the last time he'd had any, and yet it had been swept into the light by the same brush that discovered the ring. What the hell was under that chair? A black hole? The Bermuda Triangle of lost theater stuff?

The ring was tiny but heavy in his hand.

"Mom," he said again. His voice sounded a little less broken to his ears, and that gave him the courage to try and stand.

Standing. Yeah. Jesus.

That took forever. He braced one hand on an arm rest of a seat. The wood was polished and cool and only mildly sticky. He fixed his eyes on the red fabric that covered the seat and back. Did every theater everywhere in the world use that same stuff? Was it a rule? A regulation? He didn't know.

He flexed the muscles in his arm and shoulder and chest and pushed.

His body resisted, as if it and gravity were conspiring to keep him down on his knees. The traitors.

But ... no.

This was not an act of betrayal. It was a mercy. To help him in this

6

GAVIN FUNKE'S MONSTER MOVIE MARATHON

effort was to be complicit in more self-inflicted harm. Finding the ring was bad enough. Looking too closely at it was foolish, because seeing meant *knowing*. Knowing meant understanding and accepting.

He wanted to scream. To hurl a string of the most obscene words he knew—and after all the movies he'd seen, Gavin knew them all—but that would be wrong. Mom would hear him. She never liked it when people cursed. The only time she'd ever hit him growing up was when he'd dropped an f-bomb by accident after stubbing his little toe on the edge of his bedroom door on a Christmas morning when he was nine. He'd come bolting out, all happy and filled with Yuletide greed, having already peeked after his weary parents had gone to bed. There was a mountain of brightly wrapped boxes stacked like a city of goodness around the base of the glimmering tree. Gavin hadn't been able to sleep a wink, then when he heard his parents' door open, he'd whipped back his own and rushed into the hall. His little toe hit the corner and folded sideways with a sharp *crack*. Mom hadn't heard that, though. All she heard was him howling that word over and over. And she'd given him a hearty slap.

As he knelt there, preparing for another attempt at standing, he thought about that morning. Instead of opening presents, he'd fallen, clutching his foot. The toe was standing out at the wrong angle and the whole foot was starting to swell and darken. With a shock of horror, Mom understood what had happened. She screamed. Dad came running. Then there were hugs and kisses and apologies. They bundled Gavin into the car and drove straight to the urgent care, leaving every gift unopened and forlorn. When they'd returned around one-thirty in the afternoon, Gavin was half dopey with painkillers and his foot was swathed in protective gauze, with the broken toe buddy-taped to the next one.

Mom had been so contrite and embarrassed for having hit him that his own infraction for the use of that word was never spoken about. Then or ever again. She never hit him again. In retrospect, he realized that she'd simply been exhausted by sitting up until three a.m. wrapping all those presents, and then been startled by the dramatic opening of his door and him rushing out and curses filling the hall. A perfect storm that made the morning a disaster, but became a much sanitized anecdote for years and years after. It was even told at the reception at Aunt Joan's house after Dad's funeral.

It put a small smile on Gavin's face. He could feel it, but the fact that it was a smile—given the circumstances—made him angry. He ground his teeth together and pushed.

Gavin tottered over to where Mom sat. Her eyes were alert, but they always were. They watched him approach with unfiltered anger. More like hate.

It had become hate, born of resentment and disappointment. He knew that but tried to build layers of personal misdirection over it. She'd had a hard life. Five kids. No chance at a job until the last one, Jimmy, was in school, and by then she was in her forties. Always jostling for crappy jobs with kids not much older than her oldest. Twenty-something managers at temp jobs who really didn't give a crap about her or anything. Dead minds overseeing numb employees in a nowhere job. The economy kept tanking, and then all that political stuff. More wars killing young men and women from town who went to serve and came home in boxes. Or, if they lived, came home damaged in body or soul. More diseases to be afraid of. Mom used to joke that her life was as frustrating and complicated as George Bailey's in *It's a Wonderful Life,* except that there were no adorable guardian angels and no heartwarming third act where everyone who was a pain in the ass came to save her.

Gavin could see echoes of all of that in Mom's eyes. Even now.

He raised the ring and showed it to her, angling it to catch the glow of the house lights.

"Look what I found under the seat," he said.

Mom said nothing. She glared.

He sighed.

"I'm sorry, Mom," he said.

Nothing.

Gavin took a half step toward her and she bared her teeth. Or, tried to. The gag didn't really allow that. She tried to reach for him, but her thin wrists were snugged tight to the armrests by turn after turn of duct tape. Her ankles were similarly bound, and more of the tape held her torso to the chair-back and crisscrossed her body. He'd found pink duct tape. For her. For Mom.

Her fingers were free, though, and they flexed and twitched and clawed at the armrest. It took Gavin nearly five whole minutes to capture one of those desperate fingers, clumsy the ring onto the proper finger, and snug it in place. She was not at all cooperative. She thrashed and cried out and stabbed him with those hateful stares.

He sagged back, sweaty, gasping.

Crying.

He looked down the row to where Gavin's youngest brother and sister —Jimmy and Allison—sat, with Aunt Joan next to them. Uncle Pete was next to her, and their twins—Abby and Deedee—at the far end of the row. Gavin had not yet caught up with the rest of the family. His other two sisters, Connie and Gail, and all the various and assorted cousins, nephews and nieces. There were a lot of Funkes in San Diego County. It was a Funkey place, his dad used to say. This was all he had now. Each of them tied there. Each of them his guests, however unwilling, for his nightly movie marathons. Each of them trying to break free and escape. Each of them wild with hatred.

Gavin turned away and sat on the step beside her row, put his face in his hands, and wept again. Not as hard this time, but longer. The minutes crawled over him like ants.

-5-

As soon as he trusted his legs to carry him, he got up and staggered out of the theater and stood in the concrete yard out back. The big dumpster was near to overflowing and he could hear rats moving inside of it. He heard them crunching on discarded popcorn. They were movie-house rats, though, and he didn't mind. If they ever snuck in, though, he'd catch them and then they'd be sorry.

It was a bright day and the sun seemed nailed to the blue sky. He had plenty of time before he had to be back at work. Gavin walked around the dumpster to where his big white commercial van waited for him. It was gassed up because he always did that before he came home. And, because he was anal and was okay with it, he opened the back doors and made sure he had everything he needed. On the left-hand wall was a pegboard covered in hooks from which his many rolls of duct tape were hung. Below those were knives, clubs, brass knuckles, hatchets, a sledgehammer, bone saws, a scythe, a fire axe, coils of rope, and several canvas hoods with Velcro neck bands. On the righthand side were sturdier hooks and some eyebolts, along with a huge bundle of plastic zip-ties for restraining bound wrists and ankles. There were boxes of big black industrial trash bags, a stack of rubber body bags, and a pile of precisely cut pieces of cloth and leather belts. He always wrapped the leather belts in T-shirt cotton because he was mindful of comfort. Gags did not have to be nasty.

He also had a wheelbarrow and a decent hand-truck, both of which were fitted out with bungee cords. He'd learned from experience on that. As he had with all of it. Everything was a work in progress for Gavin. But he was smart and patient and diligent and focused.

The last thing he checked was his toolbox. It was a big red Craftsman, stocked with excellent tools for any task. Drills, hammers ... all of it.

He closed the doors, patted them for luck, got behind the wheel, used the remote to open the gates, and drove out. Being careful. Always careful. Last thing he wanted to do was get caught.

The city was always quiet on Sunday mornings. He saw some people, but even though they looked at the big white van he just kept going. He didn't know any of them, and had no interest in inviting total strangers to one of his marathons. He had a big one planned for Wednesday. Wacky Wednesday, as he thought of it. Always a hodgepodge of movies. He had a totally eclectic blend in mind. Start off with trailers and a bunch of cartoons. Even the cartoons were a blend—old Woody Woodpecker, an episode of Lippy the Lion and Har-de-Har-Har; then a Porky Pig one, some Disney stuff, and wrap it up with one of the earliest Popeye shorts he could find. It was a good thing his theater had been renovated a few years ago to show high definition Blu-ray DVDs instead of actual film. There were two big multi-disc banks. That was great for archived funnies and old trailers. But the real heart of his projection room was the digital streaming capabilities. He had thousands of hours of movies on an Apple MacBook Pro networked to an eight terabyte external drive. Plus software that would keep the movies playing endlessly until he turned it off. Gavin could play movies until the cows came home.

After the trailers and cartoons, he'd start soft, with kind of a retrospective of cinema history. First up was a digitally remastered and ultra clean version of *The Gold Rush*, Charlie Chaplin's masterpiece. After that he'd jump to an early Marx Brothers flick, then onto *Abbott & Costello Meet Frankenstein*. From there it was John Wayne in *She Tied a Yellow Ribbon*, and the Gene Kelly, Donald O'Connor and Debbie Reynolds classic, *Singing in the Rain*. He had a lot of variety after that. Comedies by Mel Brooks, one of Orson Welles's lesser-known pieces, a John Houston adventure, and on to William Friedkin and so on. The marathon would be an education as well as a celebration. The monster movies wouldn't start until sunset, and would again go silent with 1927's *Nosferatu*, through some of the Universal and RKO catalog, onto the Hammer flicks, more of the George Romero oeuvre, and through the darkest hours of the night. He had *Silence of the Lambs* inserted in the block of horror rather than mystery because Gavin considered it a horror film and could go toe-to-toe with any film history snob who argued otherwise.

He smiled to himself, and his heart thumped happily as he thought about the marathon. It was going to be the last word in such showcases of cinematic artistry.

Gavin put in his earbuds, turned up the music—Adele this time—and went about his business.

-6-

Gavin drove up Route 5 to the Shell station in Carlsbad. The day before he'd rigged a small generator to power an electric siphon. He checked to make sure no one was around, then got out of the van and went over to view the gauge on the single-tank truck. The needle was buried in the green and the generator was silent, its automatic shut off triggered by the anti-spillover float in the tanker. He climbed up onto the truck and double-checked with the big stick he'd set there for that purpose. The whole tank was filled to capacity. Three thousand gallons.

Smiling, he climbed down and uncoupled the vapor and fuel hoses. He went over the whole truck to make sure every setting and fitting was correct, then climbed in and drove it back to the theater, waited until the street was clear, opened the gate, and backed it in.

He took his mom's old Honda back to his van. She wouldn't need it again, so he left the keys in it and got back into his old vehicle.

It didn't take long to get to Solana Beach, where his two sisters lived in a beach cottage. Connie owned it and rented a room to Gail. They called the place Party Central and it was indeed that. A steady stream of buff surfers or bearded hipsters. The kinds of parties Gavin would never have been invited to. The kind he only ever saw when he peeked through windows. Connie was the most promiscuous, but Gail was hardly a nun.

He spent an hour looking for them. They were not at home. Not at the Starbucks down the block. Not in the taco bar on the beach. They were nowhere. It saddened him. He was hoping they could join the movie marathon. He wanted the whole family there. He sat in his van and stared at their cottage, feeling the loss of them. Connie and Gail were always a bit silly. Flighty, Mom often said. But he loved them. They both seemed to find something funny in any situation. They even shared some giggles behind their hands at Dad's funeral, which had made that afternoon somehow bearable.

"Damn," he murmured. The pain and weariness in the sound of his own voice hit him like punches. Not jabs, but deep blows to the chest and stomach. Fresh tears tried to burn their way out of the corners of his eyes, but he pawed them away. He didn't want to cry again. Gavin was afraid he might not stop this time.

He realized that it was Gail more than Connie that did this to him. She was the baby. She was the one who seemed to be filled with life and sunshine. As a little girl she was always smiling. At everything. A falling leaf, a snoring dog, a hummingbird. She wasn't beautiful but she'd always been pretty. Gavin understood the difference. People didn't necessarily fall in love with her, but everyone wanted to be around her. Strangers wanted to know her. You felt good when Gail was around, and when she laughed, everyone laughed. Even the real sticks-up-their-butts types had to smile. Gail was always alive. Gail *was* life.

If she was gone—then there was always going to be a Gail-shaped hole in the world through which sunshine and happiness and optimism would be slowly sucked away.

He sat there for a long time. Hands locked around the steering wheel. Fingers constrictor tight on the knobbed leather. Eyes burning as he stared and tried not to cry.

Gavin sat there for a long, long time.

And Gail was not there.

-7-

Until she was.

-8-

It took a lot for Gavin to drive back to the theater.

Too much effort.

Too much pain.

Too much time.

The sun had somehow rolled across the table of the sky and then tumbled off behind a wall of twilight clouds. There were shadows seeping out from under every car, and leaning out from the sides of homes and stores. The streetlights did not push back against this tide of darkness because they had lost that fight more than a year ago. Instead, they stood in a silent vigil as the day burned down like a dropped match.

Gavin knew that he'd lost time. Hours.

It was like that sometimes, but never as bad as this. No. Not even with Mom.

Gail, though.

As his mental circuits came back online with great reluctance, he turned to look behind him, into the bay of the van. With the doors closed everything back there was muted to vague shapes.

He could see Gail, though.

He could hear her.

She was strapped to the hand-truck by a dozen bungee cords. Her wrists and ankles were secured with duct tape. Not pink. He hadn't been able to think things through enough for that. When he saw her simply walk up to his van, Gavin lost most coherent thought. He'd managed to grab her, though. To wrestle her down to the ground, put the hood over her, tie her up, attach her to the hand-truck, and get her into the van. The hand-truck was locked in place against one wall, held by industrial metal clips. It wouldn't fall over. He didn't want Gail to get hurt.

All of that had been done, but it must have been sheer autopilot because Gavin could not remember any of it. Not one bit. There was nothing in his head from the moment he and Gail locked eyes through the windshield of the van and now, waking up out of whatever it was. A fugue? Maybe. He thought that was the word. Even now he wasn't entirely back to himself. Not even close.

He was almost all the way back to the theater before he realized that he was hurt.

Gavin slowed and stopped for a moment in the middle of a side street and looked down at his hand. It was covered with dried blood. Not actively bleeding, though, which was something. But Gail must have fought. They always fought. Even family. Or, maybe especially family. Aunt Joan had really put up a fight. So did Mom.

He hadn't expected it from Gail, though. Not her. Not sunshine-and-smiles Gail.

He flexed his hand. It hurt, but everything seemed to be working. The bite wasn't bad and it hadn't bled that much. No major arteries cut. Or, maybe there were no arteries in the hand. He wasn't sure. But the bones weren't broken and the muscles didn't seem to be damaged.

So, Gail had fought back, had gotten him —probably when he was trying to get the gag on. He had to accept that the smiling, laughing mouth had turned savage in defense. Maybe in his fugue state he hadn't been able to reach her, to explain what he wanted from her. Maybe he'd been so messed up that he forgot to tell her that Mom was there, and Aunt Joan, and the others.

"Damn, Gail ..." he said, and heard the whine in his voice. Like how he used to say that when she played a prank on him when they were little. Before her smile made him smile back.

The sun was almost down now. He should have started tonight's movies already.

But he lingered a moment, resting his forehead on the steering wheel. She'd *bitten* him. *Gail* had bitten *him*.

It was so unfair. So wrong.

She'd never once been mean to him her whole life.

The bite, though.

That was very mean.

"That wasn't very nice, you know," he said, and the words rose to a shout.

Gail thrashed and howled and definitely would have done worse to him if she could.

"No," he said as he lifted his foot from the brake and pressed on the gas, "that wasn't very nice at all."

He drove the rest of the way to the theater, feeling the hurt burn through him, like acid in his veins.

That wasn't very nice at all.

-9-

He parked in back and had one hell of a time getting the hand-truck down from the van. His hand was hurting now, and it was starting to throb.

Crap.

He nearly dropped her, and it would have served her right for what she did. But Gavin was quick and caught the handle of the hand-truck just in time, steadied it, and saved the day. Then he wheeled her inside.

There was some real drama getting her into a good seat. Gail was a lot younger than either Mom or Aunt Joan, and even though she lived like a slacker, she had surfer muscles. Gail fought him every step of the way. He tried to reason with her but gave it up and saved his breath for the task of getting her from the hand-truck to the seat. It took forty minutes and about a gallon of sweat.

Then he staggered over to an empty seat and collapsed into it. He was aware that every eye in the place was on him. Including Gail, now that the hood was off. Those big blue eyes. Even the spray of sun freckles across her nose and cheeks looked somehow angry, despite how pale she was. Her suntan was faded to a pale yellow.

"Not exactly a bronze sun bunny, are you?" he yelled, then felt immediately ashamed of himself. That was unkind. She couldn't help that. Not anymore.

None of them could. Mom was so pale she looked gray. Or ... maybe *was* gray. The house lights in the theater were too weak to show clearly. Aunt Joan looked positively jaundiced. The rest were a mix of milk white, ash gray, pee yellow.

Gavin looked down at his hand. Wrestling with Gail had opened the wound and it bled sluggishly. He lifted his arm and angled it into the spill of light. The blood wasn't exactly red. Too dark, and too thick. Brick-red at best.

Even though he knew what Gail was—what she had to be—it was a shock.

Or, maybe it was the last thread holding up his denial. His hope.

He looked around the theater. There were eleven members of his nuclear and extended family here. And about thirty other people. His favorite teacher from the eighth grade. His neighbors—the nice Muslim couple from upstairs who were always sweet to him. The two guys from the game store. The cute girl who ran the concession stand in this very theater. Others. The people who mattered to him. The people who filled his world. All of them seated in chairs. Held in place. As comfortable as he could make them.

But ...

Not all of them.

Connie wasn't here. Some of his favorite cousins weren't here. His niece, Emma, wasn't here. He missed her a lot. So tiny. Seven weeks old when this all happened. There wasn't enough of her left to bring to the theater. Not after Aunt Joan had ...

Well.

He'd hoped to find more of the family.

To keep him company. And for the marathon.

The marathon.

Damn.

He looked at his hand. There were small black lines radiating out from the bite. At first he thought it was just lines of dried blood, but now he knew. Gavin fished around inside his own feelings, looking for evidence of the change. It was there.

A small thing, but there. His hands and feet were cold, and he was never cold. He rarely even slept with blankets. But they were like ice.

Is that how it would be? Just getting colder and colder until there was no warmth left in him? He hoped not. This was sunny San Diego and people came here because it was warm year round. Not really hot, just nice. Gavin didn't want to be cold forever.

He got up and stood there, swaying a little, feeling sad and lost.

Everyone looked at him.

He saw the same hunger in their eyes that was always there. But now, for the first time, he thought he understood it. A little.

Gail tried to snap at the air between them, but the gag didn't permit it. Would she chew through it eventually? Mom did that once. She even ate part of the leather. It was cow, after all. Maybe they'd all have a last meal together. Leather. Cotton, too, but so what?

An ache opened up in his stomach. That was the best way to describe it. Opened. As if his whole body was a mouth. He thought about the popcorn and the Milk Duds. No. He didn't really want those anymore. Maybe not even the beef jerky.

He knew what was happening. Gavin understood what he was getting hungry for. It was happening so fast, though. Or ... was it fast? How long had it really been since Gail bit him? Hours. He closed his eyes and in the darkness behind his lids he saw his veins drain of their redness and go dark. His face was starting to get cold, too.

He felt two tears break and roll down his cheeks, but when he wiped them away and looked at his hand, he saw red-black smears.

The hunger was getting bigger. It was becoming insistent.

Gavin looked at his family and friends.

"I've got some stuff to do," he said thickly. "I'll be back as soon as I can."

He turned and hurried out, and he only fell twice.

-10-

It was dark out, so he turned on the exterior lights. He rarely did that because it drew other hungry people. That didn't matter anymore, though.

Gavin worked as fast as he could, attaching the hoses from the tanker truck to the line of generators he'd networked together. They chugged and hummed and poured electricity into the cables that ran like snakes across the ground and into the back of the theater. A lot of power to operate the industrial projector. He tested the system and checked the redundancies. Everything was working perfectly, and he managed a smile. Or, thought it was a smile. It felt weird, though, and his teeth clacked together.

As if biting.

That frightened him, so he hurried. His fingers were so cold, and his feet were blocks of ice. Walking was getting hard because the cold was in his knees and hips now. It hurt, too. All his joints did.

Gavin set up the laptop in the projection room, opened the master file and started the software running. Then he peered out at the house, seeing the screen display appear, announcing a few trailers. Another smile. Another *clack*.

"Hurry," he told himself, but the word didn't sound like a word. Just a sound. A moan.

He double and triple checked everything, then he dimmed the house lights and shambled down to the theater. He picked up one of the big rolls of duct tape. Blue. Nice. His favorite color.

Gavin shuffled sideways along the row and sat down in the empty seat next to Mom. She stared at him but now her eyes were different. No hate anymore. It startled him and he looked around. Everyone was studying him. No one was glaring. No one was thrashing as if trying to lunge at him. No one was trying to bite.

They just *looked* at him.

He stood there, watching them watch him.

"Mom ...?" he said tentatively.

There was no reaction. At least nothing like what she'd done every other time since she'd died and he brought her here. He raised his hand— the one with the bite—and held it close to her nose. She sniffed at it. And that was all. No anger anymore. No hostility. Sniffing his hand as if sniffing his newest cologne, or a bunch of flowers he brought her on Mother's Day.

Something else opened in his chest. Not a hungry mouth this time, but something beautiful. She was Mom again. Okay, not really, but as much Mom as she could be. More than he ever expected her to be.

Gavin bent and kissed her cheek. Not even a flinch.

The coldness was growing inside of him, and despite the lovely glow inside he knew that the hunger was going to take him soon. It would make him want to go outside looking for something to eat.

17

"No," he said, forcing him to shape that word. To make it sound like a real word and not a moan.

Gavin sat down. It took so much of what he had left to peel off strips of the duct tape. So much to bind his ankles together. So much more to wrap it around and around his stomach and chest and the back of the theater seat. He looped zip-ties around each wrist and bent to use his teeth to pull them snugly. The left was a little too tight, but he knew that soon it wouldn't matter.

On the screen the trailers ended and the cartoons began.

He made it all the way through them. He thought he even laughed once or twice. But he wasn't really sure. The rest of the family and friends sat with him. They were all watching. The last time he looked around he saw that they were staring at the screen. Entranced by the people moving there. By Charlie Chaplain.

Gavin settled back to watch the movie marathon.

It played for hours.

For days.

For weeks.

As far as Gavin and his family were concerned, it played forever.

Jonathan Maberry is a *New York Times* bestselling author, five-time Bram Stoker Award-winner, and comic book writer. His vampire apocalypse book series V-Wars is now a Netflix original series. He writes in multiple genres including suspense, thriller, horror, science fiction, fantasy, and action, for adults, teens, and middle grade. His works include the Joe Ledger thrillers, *Glimpse*, the Rot & Ruin series, the Dead of Night series, *The Wolfman, Ink, Mars One,* and others. Several of his works are in development for film and TV. He is the editor of many anthologies including *Aliens: Bug Hunt, Don't Turn Out the Lights, Nights of the Living Dead, The X-Files* anthologies and others. His comics include *Black Panther: Doom War, Captain America, Pandemica, Highway to Hell, The Punisher,* and *Bad Blood.* He is a board member of the Horror Writers Association and president of the International Association of Media Tie-in Writers. He lives in San Diego.

FLICKERING DUSK OF THE VIDEO GOD

LUCIANO MARANO

FLICKERING DUSK OF THE VIDEO GOD

A fresh burst of white noise roars through my head and jittery tracking lines wiggle and squirm through my vision again, even worse this time. The world stretches and distorts like in a mirror in a funhouse that's no fun at all.

The girl behind the bar pushes my pizza and a sixer of sweaty beers forward, a look of disgust on her small-town pretty face. If this were a movie she'd be played by Lori Petty, circa a few very hard years after *Free Willy*. She was nicer to me yesterday, even nicer when I first came in four days ago. I know how I look, enacting this, our daily routine, in the same wrinkled clothes again. I know what she's thinking.

I desperately shove my fingers into my eyes until pain stars flare up and drive away the other stuff, blink hard. Things are normal again, and I realize I know this girl. I've seen her before, and not just in the bar.

She's on the tapes.

For a second, even though it's stupid and doesn't matter, I want to defend myself. It's a reflex. I want to tell the pizza princess that I'm not nuts, that she's not so hot. A Rust Belt eight's an L.A. two at best, baby. Back home, I've kicked hotter than you out of bed for snoring, for hogging the blankets. Ask my ex-wife. I'm still someone who matters. But I've been away from the house too long already.

Money down, sustenance acquired, I go back outside into the dishwa-ter-gray afternoon, into my dad's rattly Buick, down the only real road in

21

this dead-end western Pennsylvania town I thought I'd escaped half a lifetime ago.

The world warps again. It's happening more often. The ragged staticky lines do their awful dance and I pull over into the gas station lot, jamming my fingers back into my eyes until I begin to cry.

A knock on the window makes me jump. Fred—hardware store swami, bestower of king-size Crunch bars at Halloween—leans over me with an enormous CinemaScope smile. If this were a movie Fred would be played by Brian Cox circa *Super Troopers*. He smiles and raps again on the window, insistent. I roll it down a crack, but just a crack. He's on the tapes, too.

"You all right, Davie?"

I nod, wiping away tears with my sleeve.

"Sure is a shame about your old man. We're all real sorry."

His face is doing a strange twitchy thing, movements all herky-jerky like a movie watched in fast forward. His eyes don't match up with his smile, words don't match his lips. The soundtrack for this scene is out of synch.

"Need any help up at the house?" he asks, words coming a full second after his lips cease to move. "Going through their things can be real hard. And your old man, well, he never did throw nothing away, did he?"

I put the car in drive.

"Did he, Davie?" Fred's smile is gone, his face too close to the window. "Did he keep... everything?"

I start to laugh as I drive away, leaving Fred behind. He looked so painfully earnest, so awesomely dramatic. If this were a movie—not one of mine of course, a good one—such a display would never fly, it's too operatic. But in real life people in crisis often behave like bad actors. Life imitates camp, so maybe my stuff's more realistic than the critics say. I mean, just look at me. Behaving like one of the characters in my own trashy films instead of doing what I know I should: Get the hell out of here.

Past the old white church, abandoned and covered in peeling paint. Stained-glass windows shattered by vandals. Other than that, though, things look shockingly great around here. Aren't places supposed to be worse in reality than memory? Isn't it the real world that comes up short, not time-tinted recollection?

I drive past the grocery store, marquee promising a sale on organic juice. Gone are the discount notices for Mountain Dew by the case. The parking lot is free of young mothers with too many screaming babies clinging to them. I don't see a single obese form straddling a scooter puffing Pall Malls. Gone are the slouching junkie kids, and the shambling homeless drones with filth clouds in tow. The sidewalks are even and unbroken. Lawns are clear and mowed. Houses are freshly painted. Good God, is that a jogger?

It's as if a Mayberry filter's been applied to footage of my hometown, and that's what I'm seeing projected on the car's windows instead of actual passing scenery. What happened here? I drive past Dad's shop and the familiar neon Video Realm sign, darkened now for good. No point going back there again. All those tapes are just movies.

Four days ago, it was the first place I went. Took a cab from the airport, a two-hour drive and a hefty fare, to find the door wide open, locks busted, tapes scattered all over and the sheriff (a pudgier young William Hurt, if this was a movie) already there, too eager to help me straighten up and figure out what had been stolen.

"Kids," he said, greedy eyes scanning the scene, looking everywhere but at me.

"Meth heads?"

"Oh no." His face was full of condescending civic pride. "We got none of that around here, thankfully. Not anymore."

Maybe he was right. Nothing was missing. In fact, only the VHS section had been touched at all. The few DVDs and Blu-rays the old man had tentatively begun to stock, the only stuff in the place worth any money, were arranged just as they should be. Nobody cracked the register. Hell, there wasn't even any candy taken. What kind of thieves break into a dead man's movie rental shop to riffle VHS tapes and don't even take any?

I came back and went through the entire inventory the next day. Every copy of every title was accounted for. Of course, by then I'd already found the tapes they'd been looking for. They were at Dad's place the whole time. Safer there, he must have thought. And he was right.

I began to see what happened. Even a Z-grade schlockmeister like myself, the infamous David "Hacksaw" Holland, can put a plot that obvious together. There was no way they could have known I was in New York for a convention, no way they could have known I'd be home in hours instead of days. I surprised them, and nobody had time to check Dad's house before I got there. Now I have the tapes, and they know it, too. But what does it all mean? What's happening and who is involved? I'm only halfway through the tapes and already—

Tires squeal as I slam the brakes, jerk the wheel. A huge stag stands in front of the car. Dark charcoal, with an enormous ornate antler spread, eyes shiny and black. It appeared in front of me as if inserted somehow, out of nowhere. I watch it begin walking away, moving too slowly and then too quickly, like the fast forward thing is happening again. Like frames of this movie are missing.

The buck looks back once as it bounds away and out of focus. Not out of sight. Not into the woods that line the state road. It just gets blurrier and blurrier until it's gone, worn-out film that's been rewound too many times at last dissolving to nothing.

When I get back the door is open. Someone has been inside, but it doesn't matter because the tapes and ledger were in the trunk of the car. I bring them in, along with the pizza and beer, and get back to it, my own little private film fest.

My father had still lived in the same small shabby two-story structure I grew up in, a glorified cottage crouching at the end of a short gravel drive, nearly impossible to see from the paved road if you don't know what to look for. I'm bivouacked in the den, semi-unpacked duffel bag in the corner spilling clothes. I rearrange the VHS tapes in their clear cases into small stacks before the enormous widescreen television—the nicest thing he ever owned—like a miniature plastic Stonehenge.

Bottles of scotch stand ineffective guard around the room, the only thing the old man loved more than movies. He had good taste in both. Authentic classic posters adorn the otherwise drab walls. He was a cineaste of the highest order, my dad, which only made my discovery of the prominent David Holland display at the shop all the more shocking. Two or three copies of all my films—even *To Serve the Devil's Favor*, hard to watch even for me—sitting by the register. Each one had a detailed synopsis attached, written in a tight professional script I know well. I didn't think he'd even seen any of my movies, let alone that he'd promote them.

I'm only more certain he didn't kill himself.

The store was somehow thriving. Even in the age of Redbox and streaming services, Frank Holland was the movie man in Pritchard County. In this part of the country yesterday is sacrosanct and tomorrow is suspect. Being the patrons of quite possibly the last video store in America would have been seen as something to be proud of, another fine tradition being upheld. And poor people are weirdly obsessed with customer service. Rich folks enjoy automation; they don't want to hear the lawn boy at work. But these people, *my people*, know they'll only ever be the boss when they're exchanging cash for momentary privilege. They liked knowing somebody was there at the video store waiting to serve them.

Also, half the kids who grew up around here worked in the shop at one time or another. I spent most of my young life there. It worked out for all involved. Dad got cheap help, the kids got free rentals, and everybody in town either worked, had worked, knew or was related to somebody who worked there. Hence, the video store was an institution. Hell, more than an hour's drive to the nearest theater, it was practically Hollywood.

It doesn't make sense. Mom died more than a decade ago. He was as over that as he'd ever be. I suppose I can't be certain he wasn't sick. When was the last time we even spoke? I can't remember. I ignored so many calls, deleted how many voicemails unplayed? I left him here, all alone. Would I have even believed him, would I have believed any of this, if I had bothered to answer?

He hated guns anyway, never owned one in his life. So I find it hard to believe my old man would have chosen to go out chomping on a pistol, like the sheriff said, even if I could picture him punching his own ticket—which I can't.

I eat little, drink more—two, three beers rapidly. Plastered is my preferred state of mind to work in, nobody sober could have made *Nasty Nuns Tame Sasquatch*, but these are strange waters in which I can take no chances. I stop at three for now, select the next unwatched tape from the nearest wobbly stack, push it hesitantly into the bulky VCR.

The cool feel of plastic, the smooth electronic sound of the tape being accepted, the closing of the little front door, the whirring as it begins to play: familiar reassuring things I did not realize I missed. I am comforted. The glaring TV screen is the only light in the house and I huddle before it like a campfire, a man lost in the woods, clutching my father's ledger.

Then, the images begin.

I'd thought myself desensitized to violence. Hadn't all the panic-ridden shrinks and parental groups promised that would eventually happen if only we watched enough? I'm a professional provocateur, a connoisseur of atrocities, but this is different. This is real.

In a large empty barn, three men are wrestling with a struggling young girl. She's wearing an oversized T-shirt, hair wild from fitful sleep, eyes wide with panic. Her bare feet and legs are kicking, fighting desperately. If this were a movie—a real movie, I mean—the girl would be played by some unknown. Somebody cheap with great legs.

Over the girl's mouth, muffling her screams, is a thick patch of duct tape. One of the men grappling with her is Fred, good old smiley Fred.

The men never speak. It's clear they don't know about the camera, never once even look in its direction. They tie the girl to a large wooden post and leave. She sobs into the gag. The picture is black and white and grainy, clearly recorded on video with a cheap camera. The sound is scratchy and clipped. A lantern is hung near the girl cutting out a section from the surrounding dark like a theater spotlight. The contrast of the picture is high, making the edges of the room impossibly black.

My father began to rent video recording equipment along with VCRs at the shop years ago, back when I was still around. It never caught on, but became something of a hobby for him. All movie buffs are frustrated, would-be filmmakers. Our home movies had title cards. Clearly, Dad had found a new project to dedicate his talents to late in life.

I do not see the thing in the corner until it moves.

After, I don't know how I missed it. Rewinding the tape, I cannot determine the exact moment it appeared. Maybe it was always there.

Long, thin fingers reach out slowly from the dark. The girl sees what is coming and becomes hysterical. Slowly, the thing comes into the light, flesh the color of neutral gray on a photographic color card. Two long gangly arms, and legs ending in strange clawed feet, snake out from it's grossly swollen torso. A pendulous belly droops over its lap, obscuring the thing's gender. I cannot look at it for long. It shimmers and blurs as if it's moving too fast for the tape to capture, even while seeming to be reaching out in slow motion. Tracking lines pull its shape this way and that. My head hurts.

Before, in the other tapes, I'd only glimpsed it. A hand reaching, a blur in the corner, an out-of-focus gray *something* standing near a ritual, observing a sacrifice, lording over a frenzied orgy and watching the bodies mingle, stroke, fondle, squeeze—always on the edges, though. Like a director. Like me. Now, I see it all.

These people, I realize, the people on the tapes, the people of my hometown, they're performing for this thing. They aim to please it, to entertain it. They serve it. And now I understand, numbly watching as it embraces the squirming girl and begins to sloppily devour her, they also feed it.

Her blood on the hay-strewn floor is too dark, too thick. Romero's

Bosco chocolate syrup ichor straight out of '68. It doesn't look real. For a moment the gag comes free and the girl's screams fill the room. I stare saucer-eyed at the glowing screen, crouching still in the dark, ledger forgotten. Quickly, the shrieks die in a wet gurgle.

Christ, Dad. What did you find out here?

The gore-streaked thing shuffles silently back into the dark in that same eerie, sputtering way it moved before. Soon, the men return and begin to clean up the scene of the sacrifice. The sheriff is among them this time, along with Fred and several others I recognize. The men of town going about a hard, unpleasant task with the usual stoic determination of rural workers the world over. Blood's just business here. Not unlike any other harvest season, judging by their faces. Some are even smiling.

I review Dad's annotations. He recorded dates, times and the places where he filmed these things. Camera settings, tape brands. Dozen of locations. He'd been at it for months.

Fast forwarding to the end proves there is little more to see. The men finish and leave in a speedy rush, and the light of dawn floods in through the open door to fill the empty barn. Finally, the camera is moved, taken from its hiding spot. I see a brief flash of my father's tired old face before he turns it off.

Dad and I talked about movies the way other fathers and sons talk baseball or cars. After Mom died, it was all we had. My memories of my father are all in Technicolor, the good times echo through my brain in Skywalker Sound. His ghost smells like popcorn.

If my life was a movie, he'd be played by Martin Landau or somebody else really good. He deserves somebody good, somebody who'd never be in one of my movies. I know the power of pictures, and so did my old man. This documentary project would have seemed to him the best way to combat something he did not understand. It's what I would have done.

I eject the tape and stand in the cold light of the blank blue screen, sipping his scotch from the bottle. I scan the walls of my father's favorite room: *Gentlemen Prefer Blondes* and Gene Kelly's *Singin' in the Rain*. Orson Welles stares down at me from a vintage *Citizen Kane* poster. The curdled prodigy's final bitter performance was voicing the planet-eating baddie in *The Transformers: The Movie*. I think of my film school degree, ambitious dreams buried somewhere in L.A. beneath a mound of scripts with titles like *Lesbian Vampire Hobos* and *Revenge of the Jurassic Octo-Sharks* and recipes for fake blood and vomit. I also know something about wasted potential. Guess nobody ends up where they think they will. Ask my second ex-wife.

Outside, a car is trundling down the driveway. Through the window shade I see headlights growing in the darkness. If this were a movie I'd know what to do. God, I wish this were a movie. I also wish my father had felt differently about guns. The biggest knife in the kitchen will have to do.

I stash the tapes hurriedly in my duffel bag, toss some clothes over them and move to the door, bottle of scotch in one hand, enormous knife in the other. I flick on the light above the small front porch, prepared to greet my most unwelcome guest.

It's the pizza princess. Climbing out of a Ford Taurus more rust than red, carrying a fresh six pack and a pizza box. She looks better than she did earlier. A fitted black T-shirt hugs her best assets and her jeans are tight enough to make me concerned about her circulation. She is smiling until she sees the knife. Then, she starts to laugh.

"It's a peace pizza," she says. "I promise."

"I already ate. You know I did."

"It's for tomorrow. Thought I'd save you a trip."

"Who says I'll still be here tomorrow?"

She walks slowly closer, stepping more into the light. I remember the gray thing on the tape, the way it snuck out into the lantern glare, bit by bit then all at once.

"Stay right there."

"You can relax." She stops walking. "I'm just here to talk. They thought you might listen to me."

"Why?"

She looks sad for a second, then pushes it away. "I didn't think you recognized me. We went to high school together. My name's Heather. You remember?"

I shake my head, eyes on the dark behind her. The sound of crackling static is in my ears again, nagging and distracting.

"I'm not surprised. Two years of meth is like ten years of regular life. Sometimes I don't recognize me either."

"Funny, the sheriff was just telling me how clean this town is."

"He's not wrong, not now. Used to be real bad."

"Guess quality of life around here depends on which side of the camera you're on."

"We just want the tapes, Davie. We want the tapes and we want you to go home. You don't belong here anymore. No hard feelings."

There doesn't seem to be anyone else in the dark, but I'm starting to feel foolish posing under the spotlight. A classic Hollywood victim. "Come inside. Slowly."

She follows me in, putting her offerings on the coffee table next to empty bottles. "Nobody wants to hurt you."

"Is that what you told my dad? Was it you who blew his head off?"

She looks around the room with a hint of wonder, like someone walking through Graceland or the White House, like she's amazed to be there at last. "That was unfortunate, but it was required. Your father was going to close the shop and take the movies away. He didn't understand."

"That's why you killed him? So he wouldn't close that stupid shop?"

She looks at me, eyes flickering as if lit from within by phantom film projectors. Or maybe it's my eyes that are flickering. Either way, the static is getting louder.

"Your father was killed because the God of the Screen wished it so."

"I've seen the tapes."

"All gods demand sacrifices, Davie."

"You think that's God?"

"He's a god." She shrugs. "The one that's here. He's the one that cares, anyway."

She began walking around the room, running her hands over the furniture and the posters as if they were sacred relics in an Old-World cathedral. I suddenly feel far too sober for this conversation.

"The house of the Purveyor," she says reverently. "It was in your father's films that the God of the Screen appeared to us. Flickers at first, like glitches. We did not yet know how to look. Later, as we learned, He became clearer, His wishes more obvious. But only ever through your father's films could we see Him, never in any others. We tried. We tried to find Him elsewhere, but we could not. Then, when your father learned what redemption required and could not understand, when he threatened to take the movies away, we did what we had to. We must visit the Realm and conduct the renting ritual. It pleases Him."

She pauses before the television, head bowed slightly. Bathed in the cool blue light, she looks dead. "He saved my life, Davie. I was lost and He found me. I had nothing and He gave me purpose. He saved me, saved the town."

I adjust my grip on the knife's handle. "Did he save that girl in the barn? Or how about the kids, the ones on the missing posters my father collected? What did he do for them?"

She smiles, a quick flash of teeth. "He made use of them. It was more than they'd ever do for themselves."

"Time for you to go, Heather."

"Just give me the tapes, Davie. Give them to me and leave. You did it before. You, like so many others, abandoned your home as quickly as you could. All we ask is that you do it again. Go back to California. Go make more movies. We still walk the old roads, still worship the old gods."

"You *rent videos*," I say, sneaking a quick gulp of booze. "Not exactly forgotten lore, is it?"

"Nobody reads anymore." She gestures to the tapes, the movie posters. "This is the new ancient. We must have the tapes. Then, we will take them, plant them in whatever other rental shops remain, and in rummage sales and secondhand stores and spread His gospel. We will make the world over again, Davie, so much better this time. We'll get it right."

I think of the car accident that killed my mother. Not a drunk. Not an epic pileup. Just a wayward deer, a buck on the road—dark charcoal, eyes shiny and black. Just a plain old everyday life-changing, life-ending accident. It would make a lousy movie.

I think of my father sitting alone in this room with his movies and his booze and a son who ran half a world away to make great art. A son who failed, who didn't answer the phone when it mattered.

I think of *Hacksaw*. Gritty, authentic: The one time I got it all perfect. Someone's remaking it, I hear, updating my best work already.

Heather turns, begins peeling off her shirt.

"What are you doing?"

"I am for you," she says, undoing her belt. "Tonight, you can do what you like. I am His messenger, meant to please you. To show He wishes you no harm. Tomorrow, you will give me the tapes and go away. We won't hurt you, Davie. You make movies."

She's suddenly naked. There's a black garter tattooed on her left thigh, something a wannabe bad kid would have done. The kind who couldn't afford to run off to California, who didn't have a proud papa waving bon voyage with one hand and dishing out tuition checks with the other, so proud of his aspiring auteur, his little future Fellini. It made me sadder than I thought possible.

"But I make *lousy* movies."

"Oh, no." Her eyes are big as IMAX screens and filled with that hypnotic flickering again. "He loves all movies, even yours. Especially yours, in fact. He has often come to us in your work. He favors you, David, Son of the Purveyor. He's in you already."

She's nearly pressed against me. Maybe it's the booze, or the strange pulsing lights in her eyes, or the increasing noises in my head—sounding more like voices all the time—but she is undeniably appealing. If this were a movie you might be screaming at the screen right now, telling me to get out of there. My father always hated people who did that. So do I.

She reaches out to stroke my face, whispering. Her words are like the rumbling of surround sound thunder. I feel them and want to believe the things she says. The television screen begins to strobe behind her. I watch it ignite and die again and again. She leans in to kiss me, so obviously a trap.

If this were a movie, I might even fall for it.

I bring the bottle down over her head. It shatters, covering her hair and face with bits of glass and liquor. But it wasn't how the movies promised me it would be. The sound, the feeling, her reaction—it was all so disappointingly real.

Then, suddenly it wasn't.

She looks up, wide eyes full of static. Her gashed face drips spilled scotch, but no blood. She opens her mouth to scream, but only white noise explodes out. She's a dead channel turned to max volume. She grabs for my neck with both hands, and I shove the knife forward into the taut muscles of her stomach. Her skin stretches and splits apart like cheap cellophane. The knife, then my fist, is swallowed. Her insides are dry and smooth and cold.

I shove, and she falls limply to the ground like a zombie shot through the head. The knife is tangled in the long black tendrils of her film-strip guts, plastic entrails that shine in the quickly strobing light. They stretch out from the void in her stomach like the tentacles of a parasite Cronenberg would dream up, unspooling further as she crawls away to lean against the wall.

She looks from the hole I gouged in her, up from her own dangling celluloid parts, to me, test pattern eyes brimming with tears. "I was all used up, Davie. I was dead and He began my life again. He *rewound* me."

I pull the knife free of the shimmering strips, move quickly to stand over her. Raising it high, knowing already what I'm going to do.

"I hate remakes."

The blade went in easily through her eye, nearly up to the hilt. Light spills from the gash, filling the room. I stab her again and again until that light goes out at last, until she lays down and is good and still and stays that way.

There's no blood. The television goes dead. Fade to black. Roll credits. That's a wrap, people.

Except it's not.

In my business we call this part the Third Act. The finale. If this was a movie there'd be very serious music playing over a quick series of cuts showing yours truly hurriedly getting things together. An awesome '80s-style montage of getting packed up and into the car. I've got the bag full of Dad's tapes, three bottles of that fine scotch, and a tank half full of gas. The cigarette lighter in Dad's junky old Buick still works fine, one of the only parts that does. And I've got a neon-crowned chapel to burn.

Speeding back down the state road toward town, the headlights show flickering glimpses of something large and gray on the shoulder always just ahead of me, out of focus. But I know what it is: The God of the Screen is angry. But that's okay. So am I.

The world is again stretched and distorted by tracking lines. *He's in you already,* that's what Heather said. If that's true he's in good company, slinking around with the Wolf Man and Godzilla and a horde of vampires, mutants, and masked killers. I've been dreaming of monsters my whole life. I've seen all the movies. I know what to do.

I drive through the dark, remembering how it feels to live a dream, why I loved the movies so much back before it became a grind. Just a job. A way to meet women. I see why Dad never stopped. It can be a drug as powerful as any I ever found in L.A.—and I searched thoroughly.

I'm Han Solo, back to cover Luke and see the Death Star explode.

I'm the Duke, sniping Liberty Valance from across the street.

I'm Rocky, still on his feet in the fifteenth round.

But then I'm just me again, a scared guy in a crappy Buick. It's tempting to hide in the comfy haze of nostalgia, to make our lives fit the stories we love. I've made a pretty decent living at it. But life has no end credits, no second takes. And remakes suck, almost always. I'm old enough to know that. I've paid my respects, but the old gods had their day.

Behind me, I see red and blue lights flashing. The sheriff must have been nearby, chaperoning my time with the pizza princess. An insurance policy, in case I didn't respond to sweet talk and seduction. Everybody speaks bullets. I can't outrun him, not in this heap. But that's OK, too. I don't have far to go now. I never did.

I think maybe I've always been working my way back to the shop. A part of me never left. I don't know if torching it will have any real effect. I don't know if these people can be saved, if they deserve to be saved. Because in many ways things here are better than ever.

Not for Dad though, are they? Not for the girl in the barn, either. Not for those missing kids, and who knows how many others? Nobody came to help them. Failing a better contender, it seems I turned out to be the hero of this strange little saga. It's a new role, against type for sure, but I'm getting comfortable with the idea.

Nearing the shop, I see the Mayberry filter fade. The grocery store's sign doesn't actually advertise a healthy sale at all. It's broken, missing most of the letters. The church windows are shattered—that was real. But the houses are just as decrepit as I remembered. The yards are patches of weeds. The homeless shapes slump against crumbling walls. These special effects are cheap and actually pretty easy to spot if you know how to look.

I depress the cigarette lighter.

Did you see the truth too, Dad? I think it's a matter of taste, like a tolerance. Maybe our preferences made us harder to trick. It certainly made him harder to please, cranky old snob. Maybe he was saved by that snobbery? His standards were too sterling. And me? Well, I never minded a little squalor. High class, poor taste—our educated eyes imbued us with resilience to this, whatever it is. Not immunity, I think. Maybe we just know what we like.

If that thing is in my mind he should be the one afraid. He should have already seen there was only one way this would end. Because maybe I was a lousy son, maybe I have squandered my talent, maybe I don't treat people very well, and I sure do hate a lot of things—not least among them myself. But I like a big dramatic ending. Just ask my last wife.

The lighter ejects.

I touch the glowing tip to the pile of tapes on the seat beside me. It goes up quickly, as I thought it would. On the floor is the booze, bottles uncapped, sloshing onto the carpet. Pedal to the floor, I aim the Buick at the large front window of the Video Realm. One hand on the door handle, I prepare to bail.

Hope this is as easy as the movies make it look.

I don't know what it takes to topple a god, even one grasping so tenuously to power as the God of the Screen. My occupation is the creation of myths. But I do know one thing: There's a California sunrise waiting for me on the other side of this nightmare. If I die, I'm a tragic artist, gone too soon and awaiting rediscovery. They'll call me a genius. And if I live, maybe it's not too late for me after all. I do hate remakes. But sequels? Well, I like sequels. Redemption stories are what great cinema is made of. And if I live through this, mine will make one hell of a movie. My best work yet.

I think I'll play myself.

Luciano Marano is a journalist, photographer, and author. His award-winning nonfiction, both written and photographic, has appeared in numerous national and regional publications, and he was named the 2018 Feature Writer of the Year by the Washington Newspaper Publishers Association. His short fiction has been featured in several anthologies, including *Year's Best Hardcore Horror Vol. 3*, *Crash Code*, *Breaking Bizarro*, and *DOA III*, as well as the podcasts *Pseudopod*, *Horror Hill*, and also *Chilling Tales for Dark Nights*. Originally from rural western Pennsylvania, he now resides in Seattle, WA. A U.S. Navy veteran, he enjoys movies (especially horror and documentary films), jogging, craft beer, haunting used bookstores, and would choose Wolverine-style healing abilities if he could have any superpower. Luciano-marano.com.

MICHAEL THINKS THE HOUSE IS HAUNTED

DAVID GERROLD

MICHAEL THINKS THE HOUSE IS HAUNTED

I t's an old house, older than me. It creaks in the wind. It groans in the
heat. It settles back into itself at night. It shivers in the winter and
aches in the summer. It has its own set of rustling noises everywhere. The
chimneys whistle, the windows rattle, the floorboards squeak. The house
has a voice.

So Michael thinks the house is haunted.

It's not just the noises, although they're very convincing. It's all the
other things.

It's the basement door that he closes tight every night and comes back
in the morning to find it open again, as if something that lives below
comes out and prowls the house at night. It's the drapes in the front room
that he opens every morning and then comes back to find them mysteri-
ously closed. It's his little Catholic statue of the Virgin Mary on the shelf
in his bedroom—someone or something keeps turning it to face the wall.

Michael isn't my first roommate. He's just the latest one. I'm not that
easy to live with. I like playing jokes on people.

Michael has only been living here a few months. He knows all the
stories about the house, of course. The house has a reputation, because
people like to believe things, so they tell stories.

Some of the stories are pretty good. Four generations of Morrisons
lived here—and died here. One of the best stories involves a young woman

whose lover fell into the well and drowned; she locked herself in the attic and slowly went mad; she chanted all day in a language nobody understood and sometimes scribbled arcane notes and drawings in a thick journal.

And of course, there was the murder. Or maybe it wasn't. Nobody knows for sure. Maybe it was a staged suicide. But that's one of the reasons why it's hard to find renters. Who wants to sleep in a room with a ghost? Especially an angry ghost.

Sometimes Michael sets up cameras; sometimes he prowls around with his ghost-hunting equipment. He makes videos too, long involved discussions of ectoplasmic concurrences. He has a blog and a podcast and several thousand followers. He's sure he's going to find something. They're sure he's going to find something. Michael is determined to prove the house is haunted. He makes me laugh.

Sometimes I follow him around, making jokes the whole time about how silly this is and how he's wasting his time. He ignores me, of course. He's so determined to find out who or what is opening doors and closing drapes and turning the virgin that it's turned into an obsession. He goes from room to room, from attic to basement, from maid's quarters next to the kitchen, all the way upstairs to the far corners of the nursery.

I think Michael is silly. He's never going to find any ghosts. I'm the one who opens the basement door and closes the drapes and turns the Virgin Mary to the corner. I do it to tease him. I do it for the joke.

I know this house. I know it better than anybody.

It's old, yes. It's tired and creaky. But haunted?

I don't think so.

I've lived here nearly two hundred years—and I've never seen anything.

David Gerrold is the author of over fifty books, hundreds of articles and columns, and over a dozen television episodes. He is a classic sci-fi writer who will go down in history as having created some of the most popular and redefining scripts, books, and short stories in the genre. His TV credits include episodes from *Star Trek*, *Star Trek: The Animated Series*, *Babylon 5*, *The Twilight Zone*, *Land of the Lost*, *Tales from the Darkside*, *Logan's Run*, and others.

His novels include *When HARLIE Was One*, *The Man Who Folded Himself*, The War Against the Chtorr septology, The Star Wolf trilogy, The Dingilliad young adult trilogy, the Trackers duology, and many more sci-fi classics. His newest novel is *Hella* (June, 2020). The autobiographical tale of his son's adoption, *The Martian Child*, won the Hugo and Nebula awards for Best Novelette of the Year and was the basis for the 2007 movie *Martian Child*, starring John Cusack, Amanda Peet, and Joan Cusack.

ATROPOS GREEN

JESSE SPRAGUE

ATROPOS GREEN

The final message I received from Earth haunts me, yet I play the video one more time, carefully watching my granddaughter's face as she speaks those unforgettable words.

"Old people always say that, Grandma Dini. Just because we're different than your generation, that doesn't mean society is going to implode."

My granddaughter's voice crackles in my headphones, sounding a million miles away. In fact, the distance back to Earth is far greater than that. After more than nineteen years in space, our ship is just six months from returning home.

I stare into her eyes, bright green, as if she's wearing colored contacts.

Harri's expression—the same rebellious sneer that's been sported by teens since the dawn of time—melts away. "I promise," she says with menacing sweetness, focusing those green eyes directly into the camera, "we'll be here waiting when your vessel returns home."

I jab at the red button below the monitor. Pulling off my headphones, I hear the common sounds of the women's dorm, where I've lived for all of my fifties and most of my sixties. Rhi, a woman from the Tech Team, lies immobilized in a containment chamber. Tubes feed her and keep her unconscious. The hiss of energy from that and the soft snores of the only other woman on board make a low drone in the white and gray room. I haven't left the dorm since waking even though it's hours past "breakfast time." The definitions of day and night surrendered long ago to the unremitting darkness of deep space.

With the video turned off, I stand and lean against the nearest bed— stacked in tiers on all walls of the room. The only decoration in our space quarters is the center console, where three monitors—each with privacy screens and headphones—play the home movies we receive from Earth.

The waves sending the videos travel at the speed of light. That's twice as fast as our ship moves, so what we see on our screens are scenes from Earth's past. I don't know what we will find on Earth when we inevitably arrive. The ship can't even stop but must continue to follow the pre-programmed course home.

I don't understand all the science of our mission. Unlike almost all the other people chosen for this voyage, I'm not an astronaut, a scientist, a soldier, or even college-educated.

Fifty of us were selected for travel to the Alpha Centauri system. Earth was swiftly becoming unlivable, with climate change bringing on far worse storms than anyone had predicted. Global temperatures were continuing to rise and new studies showed that it would not stop. The expedition was a last-ditch effort to save humanity. We went to find a new home, a world to colonize.

I wish I'd never gone. But I can't claim my presence was luck; I auditioned to be here. I pull up that video and queue several more to watch after. There are many more videos I could play from the voyage, but I don't need to watch all of them. I wait for the selected series to play.

Year 0

AUDITION TAPE: Dini Kemper: 2029-02-01

My face fills the screen minus two decades of wrinkles. My smile is too bold. This is a problem I've always fought on screen. It all goes back to my start in show business as a magician's assistant. My employer, Harry Whoo, became famous with his magic act. Then Hollywood scouted me for movies and Harry swiftly fell out of favor without his "Dini." The only thing I have left from those days is my stage name and that darned smile.

"When I first heard about the Alpha Centauri mission," I say, "I was proud of our scientists for figuring out a potential solution to Earth's decline. Traveling as part of the *Moirai*'s crew was a mission for heroes; being an actress who once played an astronaut's wife didn't qualify me." I laugh—a warm, velvety sound. My laugh is better suited to film than my smile.

"Then the positions for Earth correspondents were announced. I knew I had to go. Being one of two faces to report back to Earth's masses is a huge responsibility. But I believe that the citizens of Earth, especially the children, will need to learn about any habitable world we might find to help them adjust to leaving Earth when the *Moirai* returns."

On the screen, I run a hand over my dyed brunette hair. The salon-made color hid a dozen gray hairs, but even that was too much in an industry obsessed with youth. Still I am a *real* movie star, not like the YouTube sensations invited to fill the other spot. I'll never comprehend how eating odd foods on dares, pranking people on camera, and taking baths in random substances adds up to fame.

My younger self holds up a picture of my granddaughter, Harri. "And I have her to inspire me. Harri is barely eleven months old now. She and her mother Cici mean everything to me. I can think of no better way to safeguard their futures than to help find a new home for humanity. And then to expose them to the place that will someday be their new home."

YouTube: THEEVERS channel: 2029-09-05

Everett and Everly don't look like twins. She's a petite blonde, and he's a lanky goofball with wild tufts of brown hair. But they act the way I imagine twins should act. Despite the video being labeled as TheEvers announcement of their roles in the Alpha Centauri mission, the first minute of the video is them bickering about some "challenge" they are planning to do later.

This is the future of the entertainment industry? I shudder to think what this says about the decline of society.

When they start talking about the mission, it comes without warning and rapid-fire as all their videos seem to be.

"If you didn't watch our last video—" Everly says.

"Where we discussed our upcoming mission to Alpha Centauri—" Everett says.

"Then you should go back and watch it before continuing on," Everly says.

"We'll wait," they say together.

There's a brief pause where Everett makes faces behind Everly's head, stopping whenever she glances over.

"Back?" Everett asks the viewers.

"Well, last video we talked about the woman we'll be 'co-hosting' with on the voyage aboard the *Moirai*, Dini Kemper. But we also—"

"Announced that today we'd do a coin toss to choose which of us would go to Alpha Centauri and which of us would be the Earth correspondent and post—"

"All the videos to our YouTube channel—"

"TheEvers," they say together. "The only YouTube channel that broadcasts from the stars."

Everly pulls out a coin and holds it out to the camera. Then she rotates it in her fingers showing both sides. Everett grabs it from her hands.

"Heads," Everett says.

Everly thumps her hands on the table in front of them like a drumroll and after a few false starts Everett tosses the coin in the air. He catches it. There are a dozen ways to cheat on a trick like this. Given my past profession, I know a lot about magic tricks, even the new type of sleight-of-hand that is all the rage on YouTube. I find it hard to believe that anyone would really decide their fate by a coin toss.

The twins look at the coin. They speak at the same time once again. "And I won the toss!"

"I get to travel on a *spaceship*," Everett says, beaming his toothy smile.

"And I get to eat real food for the next twenty years!" Everly pokes him in the ribs.

Year 10

SENT from the Moirai: *2040-05-22: PUBLIC MESSAGE: Author: DINI*

The video starts with Everett and me outlined by the starscape shown in the window at our backs. I look as young as I ever do beside Everett, which is to say not at all. His brown hair is starting to turn gray and there is no hair dye on the ship, but Everett still exudes the presence of a teen. It was cute when he was twenty and the voyage started; at thirty he should have matured. Most days I want to smack him. At this crucial moment, I am as excited as he is, though my calm, bemused expression doesn't show it.

We both face the camera, eager to send our news home to Earth.

"We've been putting off making this report until we were sure," Everett says. "Or Dini has ... I've been dying to send out a message since we reached the Alpha Centauri system. It's crazy. I, uh ..."

"Six days ago," I say, picking up on his trailing voice naturally after a decade of sending broadcasts to Earth. "We reached a green planet, and the scientists gathered samples. After much debate, we decided to follow the long tradition of naming celestial bodies after ancient Greek gods. Our ship, the *Moirai*, was named after the three fates of Greek legend. It seemed fitting to choose one of the fates for the planet. To honor the idea of one life coming to an end in order to begin anew, we've dubbed the planet Atropos. She was the fate who snipped the thread of life to—"

"Aaaaand, enough boring Greek mythos ... moving on to what people actually care about," Everett says. "Yesterday we sent down a settlement team!"

My too-bright smile masks my annoyance at being interrupted. "That's right! A settlement team. Atropos should be able to support life."

Everett thrusts his fists upward in triumph, as if he found the planet and saved humanity single-handedly. "Most of the crew has been sent down already. And in the morning, I'll be *joining* them."

"From here on out, Everett and I will be recording separately, because I will be one of the ten people staying with the *Moirai*." There didn't need to be many of us to return, since the only real purpose was to deliver the samples we'd collected. There were forms of analysis available on Earth that the *Moirai* simply didn't have.

"I've been trying to talk Dini into a celebratory drink, but she's being a ..." Everett makes a raspberry sound with his mouth.

"I'd have *a* celebratory drink with you," I say. There's real sadness I can't quite mask in my eyes. Despite finding Everett a bit much at times, he is the only friend I have on board the *Moirai*. The ten-year voyage back to Earth will drag without him. "I'm too old to deal with the hangover that goes with your sort of 'celebratory drink'."

"You're not old, Dini," Everett says, winking. "You're just seasoned."

"I'm not a chicken."

Everett shrugs. Personal discussions on camera are something I avoid. I give so much of me to my audiences, but I have to keep a bit for myself. Everett doesn't understand that. I guess that's what his type of modern celebrity does—broadcasts their own lives.

After a moment of looking at me, Everett returns his goofy smile to the camera. "Enough of us ... time for what you want to see: my expertly cut footage of the crew and what they've discovered so far about this planet."

The video cuts into a montage of samples and scientists explaining the samples, namely that everything points to habitability. Despite the fact we'd hoped for a habitable planet, the odds hadn't been good. Nothing mattered more than the fact that Atropos was capable of supporting human life.

The factoids are interspersed with shots from the ship's outer cameras of Atropos. The planet nearly glows in an unbelievable green, with lush forests and frozen icecaps of a luminescent, milky jade color. We found no evidence of intelligent life on the land, but the video flashes several captures of the scarlet-scaled creatures that seemed to be the most advanced lifeform.

Then come pictures of the basecamp for our ground team. A group of scientists in suits, but without helmets, give a thumbs-up.

The pictures of their camp contain little more than the spacecraft they landed in and a wide area they cleared for crops. But the ground team also sent pictures of the white-trunked trees that surround the camp. The shadows in all of these pictures seems exaggerated and dark. Of course, differences are to be expected in a new world.

The video finishes with a shot of the distinct Atropos green forest spreading out toward an ocean white-capped with wind and rain. After the dingy gray of the spaceship, and the faded colors of Earth before that, the view assaults the eyes with its brilliance.

RECEIVED from Atropos: 2040-06-15: Author: EVERETT

There is no picture, but the audio of Everett's voice comes through fine. He talks for a while about how gorgeous Atropos is and how they are finding new foods. He spends a solid five minutes blabbing about some fish that he swears tastes like strawberries. But at the end, there is a message specifically for me.

"Dini, nothing to worry about so I don't want it in the communication to Earth. Or the one to Everly. She would worry. But we're having a few little problems here. I'm sure you've noticed that there is no video. What I said before about the team working on a fix is true, but not the whole truth. One of the technicians seems to have 'lost it.' She keeps staring off into space at things that aren't there. Yesterday she destroyed a chunk of our video equipment before we could stop her. It may be a while until it can be fixed because our focus still has to be on survival. The 'brains' are trying to find out what went wrong. They think maybe it's an allergy to a food ... or some poison she ingested. But I thought you should know."

I hear Everett swallow hard and little puffs of breath follow as if he starts to say something and then stops. After about ten seconds of silence, he speaks. "On a lighter note, it really is gorgeous here, the green is just ... its everywhere, Dini. I'm trying to convince some of the astronauts to do a food challenge with me. But they are almost as grumpy about that stuff as you. So ... I guess there will be no video of me puking up that weird moss that they've decided is edible!"

Year 15

RECEIVED from Earth: 2045-01-13: PRIVATE MESSAGE: Author: CICI

My daughter's brown eyes crinkle at the corners. Wisps of mousy brown hair fall from her ponytail. She's sitting in the office of my home in Hollywood. Behind her on the wall are a series of pictures of me, her, and Harri. There are no shots of Cici's deadbeat ex-husband.

"Our last viewing party went well," Cici says. "Everyone here is super excited about you finding Atropos. I don't think I've seen so much green since ... well, since you took me camping as a kid. Heck, maybe not even then! Everyone is talking about what it will be like to live on a new planet ... and how old we'll be when we get there."

"Probably the only downside to the party was ..." Cici's eyes sparkle and she leans toward the camera, "You guessed it, Everly! She got drunk on the champagne toasts."

Cici gives a small humorless laugh. "I think you got the easier twin; I really do."

The monologue is easy to watch. I almost miss the man-shaped shadow hovering behind her. From the angles, whatever cast the shadow should have been on screen, but there was nothing there. Cici seems not even to notice it exists. I wonder if that shadow is a new stain on the wall behind her, or perhaps caused by some damage the video received in transport. Cici talks about Harri and her obsession with magic. Cici thinks that Harri will grow up to be just like me.

The video cuts to a fifteen-year-old Harri demonstrating a magic trick. My granddaughter wears a sparkling gown that I recognize as an old stage costume of mine. She sports star stickers under her brown eyes. One of the stickers has half peeled off and flaps a bit as she moves. A shadowy shape lurks in the back of the room. There is nothing anywhere near it, and no logical explanation for a shadow to be there. Again, Harri, like Cici, seems not to see it.

SENT from the Moirai: *2045-01-13: PRIVATE MESSAGE: Author: DINI*

With the make-up I use for public broadcasts wiped away, I look old. Still, there is a vestige of a movie star in my face. I first recorded this video directly after watching Harri's magic show and noticing the shadow man hovering in the background.

"I know Harri's probably on to bigger and better things, what with the time delay," I pause but am unable to calculate the current time lapse between videos. It'll take two years for my message to reach her but calculating in how long her message took to reach me goes beyond my skills. "But regardless of any delay, I wanted to tell you that I loved that bit with Harri performing."

I force a smile. I usually don't have to fake joy with Cici, and she can spot my "acting" smiles. She says I never look that happy when I really am. "It's nice to see her have such an active interest. So many kids don't."

I try to go on and say nothing to worry her. However, the odd shadow has me worried for reasons I don't entirely understand. My face freezes in the video as I wrestle with the information. In the end, the worry and curiosity overcome my desire not to frighten her unnecessarily. "But, Cici, there was an anomaly on the film. It looked like a shadow man in the background, and it was in all of the shots. It's probably just some damage that the film took in transit or something gone awry with our ship's receivers. But ... it worries me. I guess, just be careful. As much as finding a world to colonize means to me, bringing you two hope means more."

RECEIVED from Atropos: 2045-04-05: Author: EVERETT

Everett flops back on his bed with his hands linked behind his head. Without his YouTube persona, he actually seems to fit his thirty-five years.

"Time to record?" he asks someone off-screen. Then he turns his gaze to the camera. Most times since staying on Atropos, he talks directly to me and on occasion to Everly. "Dini! Good news this time. The ground team has found a few new edibles ... and they are speculating that the air might have some kind of euphoric effect because some of the team members have been acting oddly."

He lifts a hand to cover his face and sighs. "God, I'm not in the mood today."

There is a group of photos on his lap and he sifts through them. Then rather than show them, he stands up and looks outside the window. "Earth has left us behind, Dini. Everly is the only link I have and ... she seems distant recently."

Watching him behave so uncharacteristically melancholy, without any of his usual flamboyance, creates a heavy weight in my gut.

"She got married ...," he sighs. "But that isn't it. Some of the changes can be chalked up to me being gone so long, like we used to be able to finish each other's sentences, but now I can't even figure out what she means half the time."

He drums his fingers on his legs and looks behind him, swiftly, as if checking if he's being watched.

"The clips she sends to me from our fans are even different. The videos are all just ... odd. I wish I could say that's what's got me so down, but the truth is ... what they want me to call a 'euphoric' effect, isn't at all. It's like something foreign is getting inside us, Dini. If Everly is changing, the people here are changing more. People keep saying they see *shadows* around camp."

My heart flinches at that word. My mind recalls the shadow in Cici's video. There's no reason to think they are related, but my adrenaline rush doesn't care about reason.

"They start turning to look at things that aren't there ... and after that happens"—he snaps his fingers—"they alter."

SECURITY FOOTAGE the Moirai*: 2045-04-05*

The security cameras don't record in color, leaving the shot a slightly fuzzy gray. I walk from a distance toward the technical labs. I move like an old lady. Part of that is age, but part of it is how heavily Everett's video weighs on me, especially where he talks about shadows.

My image is clearer in the camera when I stop and Rhi walks out. The view only shows the back of her head. She's the only technician still aboard the *Moirai*. We sit together on two stools just inside the tech lab's entrance and she waits quietly for me to state why I'm there.

"There was this shadow in my latest few videos," I say. "Like a man lurking in the background, only there was no man. Have there been any irregularities in our incoming transmissions?"

Rhi grips the arm of her chair and glances around, double checking that no one else is in earshot. "You've seen her?" Rhi whispers. "You've seen her too?"

Her? If the videos are warping, it should be the same image for everyone and mine was decidedly male. But it could be a camera trick too, like some bit of video magic Harri is trying out on me. Only then it wouldn't be showing up for anyone else. "Could it be a flaw in our system? You know, like equipment breaking down or something?"

Rhi shakes her head. "I've searched and searched for damage or any anomaly in the equipment. And I've checked outgoing transmissions—nothing. I asked my son to send me one of my messages back. I want to see if the image was being added in transmission."

"Was it?" I ask.

"No reply yet."

"So, what is that shadow on the videos?" I ask. "Do you think it's related to what's happening on Atropos? Everett has been saying they see shadows."

"I really don't know. There are a lot of explanations for what could be happening on the planet."

"We have to do something."

"I will continue to study it. I don't want to cause a panic, but the others on board will notice something is off in the videos soon. The image is getting clearer every time."

Year 16

RECEIVED from Earth: 2046-3-23: PRIVATE MESSAGE: Author: CICI

The dark, shadow man is there in the background of Cici's video. He seems closer to her, maybe, or maybe Rhi put that idea in my head. I hardly hear what Cici says—I'm watching him. Very swiftly, Cici transfers over to a video of Harri.

Observing my granddaughter shuffle a deck of cards with an abundance of flair, I'm reminded of why this voyage matters. Now seventeen,

Harri is a vision of humanity's future. Saving her is why I went to Alpha Centauri in the first place.

Harri is performing a card trick for Everly and her husband. It's a trick I've never seen before and I can't figure out how it works. Normally, that would take all my attention, but the shadow man is standing behind them.

His eyes open. Glowing green stares out at me, a vivid color, a shade I swear I've never seen earthbound—but it was all over the vegetation on Atropos.

He is still watching me with those eyes when Harri finishes. Everly and her husband applaud. But Harri stands by the green-eyed thing, smiling at it. As far as I can tell, she is the only one who sees the creature.

And I recall what Everett said about people who look at the shadows.

SENT from the Moirai: *2046-11-08: PRIVATE MESSAGE: Author: DINI*

Lines crease my face and bags hang under my eyes. When I lift a hand to run through my hair the knuckles are thicker, arthritic.

"It scares me that the delay on these videos is so long. I don't know how things stand with you as I record this, or what they will be like when you get the message." I flinch, recalling that it would be more than a year before Cici even sees the video. "Don't think I'm crazy. Something is happening in our videos, Cici. There is a green-eyed shadow standing behind you. He's not fully defined yet, but there is a similar creature around Harri. And she has been seeing it in the last few videos."

Year 17

RECEIVED from Atropos: 2047-07-05: Author: EVERETT

Everett stares at the camera. His eyes glow green. He smiles. "Things are going great here. We're just loving our new home."

SECURITY FOOTAGE the Moirai: *2047-09-30*

"My son's reply came back," Rhi says, stalking up to where I sit in front of one of the *Moirai's* video recorders.

"Reply?" I ask before I realize what she must mean. He sent her back one of the videos she sent to him to see if the same creature existed on the film.

"He said that he didn't see any shadow form on the image, but when I looked at the take, it shows a green-eyed woman laughing, a taunting, mocking sound."

"Can I see it?" I ask.

"No," Rhi says, her eyes are dark rimmed. "Haven't you noticed? All the people who watch our videos on their initial screenings are changing. I'm afraid that viewing the movies is somehow tied to those changes. Until I know more, we shouldn't be watching them."

"I don't understand ..."

"Somehow that shadow creature, thing, she is riding on the video transmission," Rhi said.

"It. We cannot assign it a gender," I say.

"What does it matter?" Rhi snaps. "As best I can calculate, this process must have started with the transmission we sent from Atropos. And the videos from Atropos have shown the same changes. Which means, whatever it is, *we* sent it to Earth."

Year 18

RECEIVED from Earth: 2048-02-07: PRIVATE MESSAGE: Author: CICI

Cici cries. She is not a pretty crier and her face looks puffy and red. The shadow man still stands behind her, but so close now, his fingers folded over her shoulder. "I don't understand it, Mom. Harri did this magic trick yesterday. She made Everly disappear ... only Everly never came back. Harri just laughs when I ask her about it. And there isn't anyone to report it to. It feels like half the city has gone crazy. Everyone I know has lost their minds."

Cici's arm moves through the shadow's chest and she doesn't appear to feel it or note his presence. "Then Everly came back and she laughed too. They say that next time, it'll be me who disappears."

Cici rubs at her eyes.

"It's not just them either, some of the reporters who watch my screenings have been arrested. It's all over the news, they just laugh as if they know something we don't. And their eyes ..." She pauses, as if unsure. "There's no biological reason Harri's eyes would change, right? I tell myself it's something she is wearing, but this green, it's like no color I've ever seen. The color just burns out from her. And it's not just Harri, or the reporter, or the news. I swear, Mom, I think I saw Everly's eyes do the same thing."

SECURITY FOOTAGE the Moirai: *2048-02-22*

Rhi's eyes flare green from the otherwise black and white picture. She stares up at the security camera and then walks down the hallway to enter the cafeteria, where she faces the small group gathered there.

Her eyes glow, as green as the trees on Atropos. As green as Everett's eyes on his last transmission.

"You came to colonize us, but you see, we beat you to it." She begins to laugh.

SENT from the Moirai: *2048-02-22: PUBLIC MESSAGE: Author: DINI*

"Given what I've seen," I say. I'm not even looking at the camera. I choke on the next words. What is there really to say? "Watch out—we sent something to Earth. It's some sort of creature and I think ... I think it's using you as hosts. It happened to one person aboard our ship and quarantining her has worked so far, but we don't really know yet. Maybe you've done the same down there. I hope you have, or that there is still time."

Unlike for the people on Atropos. I don't say that, though. "You've got to stop people from changing. Somehow. They'll destroy humanity."

RECEIVED from Earth: 2048-10-25: PRIVATE MESSAGE: Author: HARRI

Harri looks out at me with a sneer sported by all teens since the start of time. Her bright green eyes twinkle as she leans toward the camera, as if we are face to face instead of being separated by a six-month time delay.

"Old people always say that, Grandma Dini. Just because we're different than your generation, that doesn't mean society is going to implode." Then her sneer melted. "I promise—we'll be here waiting when your vessel returns home."

Jesse Sprague has been writing dark speculative fiction as a way of exploring ideas that don't fit neatly into our world since her college days as an English Literature major. She has published a novel, *Spider's Kiss*, and several speculative short stories, including stories in the *Once Upon Now* anthology from Gallery Books, *Seattle Crypticon's Decompositions* and other anthologies. Jessesprague.com.

LAST SUNSET HOME

C.H. HUNG

LAST SUNSET HOME

Kids these days don't understand the value of hard work, of grit and determination and pulling themselves up by their bootstraps. They don't know what it's like to get kicked in your teeth when you're down, and still find the gumption to stagger upright and spit in the face of death and say, damn you, you ain't got the best of me.

Hell, how many young'uns even know what a bootstrap is? The world's goin' to hell in a handbasket, and no one even knows it. No one but me.

I should know. I was created there. In hell.

Yeah, I probably should've gone back ages ago, but I like it too much up here. This theater don't look like much from the outside, overrun with the same beige stucco that coats this entire shopping center, but it's got twelve screens, and that ain't nothin' to sneeze at here in Monterey, in a state full of strip malls. There's not much better 'n the smell of popcorn poppin' and the fizz of Coke pouring from the fountain, the softness of velvet cushions under your ass instead of the worn leather of a saddle, and the falling darkness welcoming you into the evening feature. Like the wise ones say, a man with money in his pocket is a man full of peace, and working at that movie theater sure brought me more peace than I deserved.

But you didn't hear that from me. If word got out what I was doin'—or not doin'—Boss would find me and devour my *chi*. I ain't no good to Boss if I ain't out there causin' trouble.

I'd been sent to deliver righteous damnation to these poor souls who don't know better, oh—I dunno, maybe fifty years ago? Sixty now? I'd just graduated with papers, you see. Highest circle and everything. Made Ma proud, even if she was too busy in the European theatre to do much more than send me off with a congratulatory firebombing of Dresden. Yeah, that's my mama, all right.

I was what you'd call one of those traditional demons. Heard of Dante? The pope? Crosses and such? Yeah, most have. That's what Ma is. One of those hell-spawned demons. She'd done good on assignment in Europe 'cuz folks there, they're proper terrified of demons. We get real respect over there.

But I ain't one of 'em. Not anymore. We change depending on the slant of the weather, if you get my drift, and the weather in Monterrey was such that nobody gave a crap what flavor of evil you were as long as you weren't a corporate, anti-environmentalist asshole. Which doesn't eliminate as many candidates as you'd think.

Watching all those Westerns and samurai and kung fu movies as I did ... well, I didn't know exactly what flavor I was no more. But I didn't belong in no ninth circle of hell, I knew that much.

Which is why I stayed here, in an ordinary theater in an ordinary beachside coastal town where nothing more exciting than electing a movie star as mayor ever happened. Nobody would look for a retired gremlin here.

So when I spotted the kid standing in line at the concession stand, saw the way she was thumb-tapping on her phone like she was tap-dancing with her fingers, felt the way I was drawn to her like a mosquito to sweat-stank skin, I knew trouble had finally found me.

For one thing, the kid was some flavor of Asian, with straight black hair that fell down to her waist like a dark velvet curtain. Old enough to be a first-time bride, young enough to not be widowed of her naiveté.

She wore a puffy parka that covered her down to her knees, even though it was only 50 degrees outside, about average for this time of the year. It made her look fat and thick around her middle. Some kids behind her were snickering none too quiet-like. One of them made a joke about Eskimos that had the kid flushing like she had the fever, but she ignored them.

Even if this kid weren't the *right* kind of Asian, I knew that I looked different enough that she'd notice me, just like others had noticed her. I, too, was dark-haired and darker skinned than most folks 'round these parts. I could've changed to a lighter-colored mask that would've helped me blend in better, but it also would've helped me forget why I was there in the first place.

And if there was one thing I couldn't do, it was to forget myself. Nobody needs that kind of trouble, not even a critter like me. So the mask I wore was the one closest to my true self. I can pretend that I'll be able to ride off into the sunset when my time's up, but I can't pretend I'm someone else, no matter how badly I want to. It would negate me.

So I knew how the kid felt, looking different, pretending she wasn't. She couldn't change masks like I could, and it's hard being the black sheep in a white herd. Predators can spot you a mile away.

I grabbed a broom and a dustpan in one hand and a rolling trash can in the other, and headed toward the nearest theater, the one that I was supposed to clean after the last showing. Best way to avoid trouble was to run like hell at the first sign of it.

Sure enough, she glanced up when the line shuffled forward, and saw me hustling off. Her stare made the spot between my shoulder blades itch somethin' fierce. Her little bow lips parted and she almost put her phone down.

But then she saw the kids snickering as they whispered and stared at her, and she stuck her nose back into her phone.

Dammit, she *was* the right kind of Asian. And she knew who I was, all right. I hadn't been fast enough on the draw to slip on a mask she wouldn't recognize and disappear into the shadows.

I made a show of brushing a non-existent gum wrapper into my dust pan, then dumping it into the trash can while the kid paid for her soda and oversized tub of popcorn. I sized her up out of the corner of my eye. She wasn't much, just a little ol' slip of a thing, but better slingers than me have been felled by less, so I didn't dare underestimate her. Not one bit.

Especially not after catching the way she sprinkled salt onto her popcorn at the condiment stand, her lips barely moving. Whispers gathered around her, the protection of her ancestors, and I kept my mask on tighter than a sticky jelly jar.

In this day and age, it wasn't often I ran across someone who'd been taught how to protect themselves. But this kid had. It showed in the strength of the protection that hovered over her, fed by regular prayer and offerings at an ancestral altar. Whoever her ancestors were, they'd been kept close.

"Hey," the kid said. She looked directly at me, making sure I knew that she knew exactly who she was talking to. She shoved her popcorn tub toward me. "You look hungry. Eat." Her English was fluent, like she'd grown up here.

"I'm working," I retorted, and shuffled into the empty theater as much to work as to get away from her and her ancestors.

There wasn't much to tidy up after the last showing of an overrated sci-fi flick that'd flopped in its opening weekend. I flicked trash into my dust pan and dumped it. Swish, dump, swish, dump.

The kid set her soda in a cupholder and her popcorn tub on an empty seat, then marched up and down the rows, collecting the few discarded tubs, half-filled paper bags of popcorn, candy wrappers, abandoned drinks. She emptied her arms into my trash can.

"You don't have to do this," I growled. Her presence set my nerves on edge, and I just wanted her to get the hell out already. "Go enjoy your movie."

"It hasn't started yet," she said, calmly and patiently and perfectly reasonably. Her irrefutable logic made me want to strangle her even more. "And you look hungry." Again, she held out the tub. "Eat."

It wasn't a prayer at an ancestral altar, but I couldn't keep resisting her, not with the power of her ancestors compelling me to obey. I took a kernel of popcorn and chewed. Salt and oil threaded through me like fish hooks to keep me anchored to the kid.

"Done," I snapped, and headed out of the theater. I'd forgotten the trash can, but I didn't want to go back. My will was slipping from me, tied to the food offering and anchored by my reluctant acceptance. But I could still fight. I wouldn't go down without my guns blazin', that's for damn sure.

The kid called, softly, *"Mo gui."*

I stopped. Turned.

Not because I wanted to. Because I had to.

Because I'd accepted and ate her damn offering.

She'd picked up her popcorn tub, hefting it with the crook of one arm as if she were carrying a squalling babe. My hands itched to draw my guns from their hip holster, but of course I carried none. I was in a goddamned theater, not the wild west.

"What do you want?" I snarled.

"I want you to do your job," she said. She picked a popcorn kernel off the top without disturbing the other kernels and crunched it. "Your *real* job."

The dread sharpened into a stomach ache that reminded me of that one time I was so desperate, I ate some cow that'd gone off ages ago. I looked hard at the kid.

"I *am* doing my real job," I said.

The kid ate another piece of popcorn. Chewed it slowly. Thoughtfully. Swallowed.

"No, demon," she said. "You're not."

I squinted at her, putting the pieces together and wondering what kind of asshole she had to be for Boss to have set her on my tail and finally tracked me down like the low-down, good-for-nothing that I'd turned into.

"Took Boss long enough to find me," I said.

The kid scrunched up her nose, all cute-like, and asked smartly, "Huh?"

So. Not one of Boss's underlings then. That opened up all sorts of interesting possibilities.

"Who're you working for?" I asked, genuinely curious now.

The kid turned into the brightest shade of guilty I'd seen in a long time. I could feel the thrum of her ancestors pulling close, lassoing her tight like a rodeo calf, snarling me off louder than a cornered dog.

Whatever the kid was up to, her ancestors had come armed for bear, ready to protect her. They powered up, spinning 'round and 'round her like a silkworm hunkerin' down for the long sleep. And the kid had anchored me to her will with the popcorn, so I couldn't run.

I gripped my broom as if it were a bo staff, wishing I had bigger guns. I'd been fightin' the good fight for a lot longer than she'd been alive. Still, for the first time in a very long time, I felt outmatched. Like I could be in danger of coming undone. Torn into oblivion.

I'd forgotten what that felt like, that uncertainty about yourself. The feeling that everything is spiraling out of your control too quickly for you to, well, *control*. That you were caught at a high noon showdown without a gun at your hip.

I didn't like it, not one bit. But my favorite actor, Ben Grady, wouldn't have backed down, not in any of his million cowboy Westerns, so neither would I.

"I'm not working for anyone," the kid said. She pulled her phone out of one of her puffy jacket's pockets and held it up, its bright screen facing me. Some sort of social media feed was displayed, but I didn't know two hoots about that stuff so I couldn't tell which one was loaded. "I'm here for myself."

I nodded toward her phone. "Sure, kid," I said. "You and a hundred thousand followers. Who you puttin' on the show for?"

"It's not just show," she snapped, and the voices of her ancestors screamed their defiance. She shook her phone-sized fist. "*They* made this happen. All of them, with their trolling and their stupid arguments on the internet that go nowhere. Everyone thinks that they're on the side of good, but are they really? How can you tell who's good and who's evil?"

I gripped the broom between both hands, imagining it was a samurai sword. As the natives say—they don't like being called Injuns no more—today was a good day to die.

"Look for the cowboy," I said. "The outsider who rides into town and saves it from the gang harassing the townspeople before riding off into the sunset. He's always the good guy. The bullies are the bad guys."

The kid flinched, as if I'd slapped her.

I remembered how she'd looked, standing in that concessions line. Alone in a crowd. A crowd that stared and whispered. She hadn't a friend with her. I wondered if she had friends.

Cautiously, I lowered the broom. "That's you, isn't it? The outsider?"

"And you. Whoever heard of a *mo gui* who didn't cause trouble? Who didn't harass and threaten and create chaos everywhere it went? Why are you here, if not for that purpose?"

I shrugged. "Maybe I *want* to be here."

My answer seemed to amuse her. She raised an eyebrow, as if daring me to prove it.

I lowered my broom, and tipped the brim of my imaginary hat. "Welcome to *mi casa*, darlin'," I drawled. "Come in and put your boots up a spell. We ain't got nowhere else we need to be."

Once I opened the door, the whole picture came spilling out from the kid faster than coins from a drunkard at the bar. I leaned against the plush wall of the theater, arms crossed, nodding and murmuring every so often to let the kid know I was listening. I'd encased the theater in an aura of forget-about-me so that no one would remember the sci-fi flick was supposed to have started 10 minutes ago.

Her story weren't nothing unusual. I'd seen it before, in my line of work.

The job weren't all that bad, at first. It weren't all that hard to nudge here, give a little push there, guide folks in the right direction when you wanted to create a little mischief every now and then. Enough to separate some souls from their corporeal bodies and along their way to the next realm, where Boss can sort them out later.

Sure, maybe some of that mischief wound up in the morning paper or on the 5 o'clock news, but if it weren't for me, the news folks wouldn't have jobs.

Then I found the movies.

It struck me something solid, when I figured out how the good guy was always the one fighting for change, even if he were the quiet type or the loner type or the drifter type or—more likely than not—all three. It was okay if he didn't have no friends either, 'cuz he'd usually have some by the end of the film—friends that he'd walk away from for the greater good. Or for his own good. Or for the good of the people he'd saved. Probably all three.

The bad guys were always the ones trying to keep things the same. They liked the way the world ran just fine the way it was, and they didn't want no change. Why would they? The world took care of them, and that was just fine. I supposed if I were them, I wouldn't want nothin' to change, either.

By that logic, the kid was the good guy. She wanted something to change, and that something had everything to do with the reason she was bundled up in a parka in 50-degree weather and nothing whatsoever to do with the fact that she was no bigger than a hungry tick on a cattle dog.

"Look," she said finally, unzipping her parka just enough so that I could see the black polymer grips of the handguns she'd shoved into the waistband of her jeans. "I know how this works. I know about Eventide, and how the perp almost got away with it. I came prepared."

And even though I'd seen this play out before, countless times in countless realms by countless tortured spirits, I couldn't help straightening from my slouch and pressing back against the wall as if I could disappear into it.

It was a bloody showdown, and I'd been caught in the open without my guns.

"Nobody," said the kid, dark eyes gleaming, "can ignore me after today. Nobody can joke about slanty eyes or smelly food or broken English and expect me to laugh along with them because they think it's just harmless fun." She zipped the parka back up with a quick, decisive jerk. "Because they think it's my patriotic *duty*," she spat out, "to be a good girl and a good citizen and laugh along with them. I'll even honor you with the chaos, *mo gui*—all the honor you could ever need. Just grant me the protection I need to do this."

I shook my head. I didn't want to believe what I was hearing.

But I'd already heard it before.

She couldn't know, of course, that I'd been there. That Eventide Cinemas had been my first real success. One disgruntled kid, a backpack full of arms and ammo, and a theater packed even fuller with movie-goers. Boss had been so damn happy that I'd done so well, cloaking that red-headed loony in an aura of dismissal so strong that I had to just about physically trip the cops into the kid outside of the emergency exit to make them take a second look at him. Afterward, Boss promised to bring me home for an early retirement if I could pull off one more assignment.

"Doesn't even have to be a theater," Boss had said. "Try a shopping mall or dance club."

I'd said the only thing that I could think of. "Some movie soundtracks cover up the sound of gunfire really well."

"Fine," Boss said, generous and expansive. "Stick with what works. You're not far from hitting your quota. Then you can come home and get promoted to the big time."

Here and now, confronted by someone who remembered Eventide, who wanted to re-create it, no matter her reasons ... I felt like a mule had kicked me in the chest.

It'd been easy to do my job when I hadn't been around to witness the aftermath. I'd work an assignment, see it through, then moved on. Each success increased my honor, each failure decreased it, a perpetual seesaw. It's how Boss keeps everyone workin', you see. You can't beat the system. You can only survive.

Eventide was supposed to be my ticket out. Create one big success so massive that it would permanently tip the scales in my favor, and I could retire, away from the chaos that made me feel as if I would never gain one modicum of control over my life. Over *my* choices. Ma and her crew in Europe had made it to retirement, never mind the fact that the Other Side had won that war. We didn't care about victory. We just wanted the collateral damage.

But it was that damage that'd shown me the cost of chaos.

The eyes of the survivors, of their families, of folks surrounding 'em with prayer and support ... by then, I recognized that look.

I'd seen that look in the townsfolk when Ben Grady's loner cowboy would stroll into the scene—that look of defeat, of resignation, of surrendering to the capricious fates because nothing more could beat you down further than life had. I'd seen that look when the damsel in distress grasped at the solo samurai because throwing yourself at the devil you didn't know was better'n giving in to the devils you already knew.

I saw that look now, in the kid standing before me, fists raised as if she could take on the world with a handful of magazines and her quiet, unending rage.

It was always the quiet ones who broke hardest.

I didn't want to relive this scene. Not in this theater. Not on my watch. Not again.

I grabbed the kid's arm and ignored the pain shooting up mine from her ancestral guardians clawing at me, protesting my violation of her personal space.

"Trust me, kid," I snapped, "you don't want a repeat of Eventide. What the hell are you thinking?"

She jerked her arm away and glared. "Because they deserve it. Weren't you listening?"

"All I heard was some bratty, no-grit kid complainin' about how the world works," I said coldly. "So bullies are picking on you for being different. Boo frickin' hoo. Fight back with something besides bullets. Thinking you're gonna change anything by shootin' up all these innocent folks ain't gonna change nothing for you, but it'll change everything for them just 'cuz they were here, in the wrong place at the wrong time. They don't deserve this." I shook my head. "It ain't right. Not for them, and not for you. There's no call for this chaos you want. I ain't gonna do it."

The kid's jaw dropped. She pointed an accusatory finger at my chest. "I thought that of all the monsters in the world, you'd understand."

"Why? Because I'm a chaos demon?" I rolled my eyes. "That just because I look like a *mo gui* and was created to be a *mo gui* and was sent here to do *mo gui* things that I'm stuck acting like one?"

Her eyes narrowed. "But Ah Ma said you would. She said you were spirit-bound to do what we asked, if we fed you from our altar."

"Sure, kid. That happens." I leaned forward and jabbed a finger back at her, deliberately mimicking her. "But you didn't offer enough to bind me. Because, let me tell you, kid, when I did my job, I was *good*." I summoned the scorn I needed to shed the ties that bound me. "Good enough to build up the honor to resist your paltry offering."

The kid stumbled backward. I felt the hiss of the kid's ancestors as they released my will from their bonds, stunned by my disdain for their offering. They couldn't hold me, not with *popcorn*. Back in my day, offerings came piled up with fruit and smelling of incense, flavored with the earnest prayers of the devout.

"I'm pretty damn good at my job," I said, "but I didn't feel real good about it. I've had a *long* time to think, and I've come to realize—there's always a chance to do better, you know? No matter how much of an asshole the cowboy was in the past, or what type of bad stuff he did to get by, or how much he don't want to care about no one because he don't want to keep losing, he always gets a chance to prove he's changed. That, deep down, he's got the grit to risk everything for one more shot at happiness. And if it ain't his happiness he wins, it's at least someone's. It's a chance to set things right. To leave the town a better place than the one he rode into."

I crossed my arms to show that I wouldn't draw on her, even though I weren't armed. "This is me now. I ain't no ordinary *mo gui*, and I ain't at your beck and call, no matter what you offer me. I might be all hat and no cattle, but I'm here waiting for my last ride into the sunset, and I ain't gonna do nothing to jeopardize that."

"Don't you want to go home?" she asked.

I shot her the Ben Grady look—that narrow, squinting scowl that had withered dozens of black-clad villains where they stood on the silver screen. She didn't so much as quiver.

There was some semblance of a backbone, somewhere in there. Maybe the kid had a chance after all.

I pretended to take a cigarillo from my mouth and flick it onto the ground. "Maybe you didn't hear me the first time." I touched the brim of my imaginary hat. "I'm where I need to be. I *am* home."

She stood silent and still, fists clenched at her sides. I waited for her fingers to uncurl, her shoulders to relax, the anger to fade. Then the trembling started.

I caught the kid before she collapsed.

She shook so bad I thought she was laughing, until moisture soaked through my uniformed shirt and I realized she was crying. I'd heard plenty of tears before, wails and lamentations from the dead and living alike, but I'd never heard nothing like this—this deep, gut-wrenching, body-twisting sobbing that sounded and felt as if she was turning her guts inside out for the world to pick through.

I didn't know what to do. But I'd seen how in the movies, sometimes folks just held on to each other for no good reason while they cried. So I wrapped my arms around her parka-puffed shoulders and held her until the shaking stopped, and she could talk again without hiccupping.

"I'm sorry," she whispered. She scrubbed her face with her parka's sleeves, leaving slimy trails of snot and tears. "I just don't know what else to do when they make fun of me." She sniffled. "When they make me feel like I'm nothing, just because I don't look or act like them."

I grasped her by the shoulder. "You can't change the way you look, but you can change the way you act. The way you react. That's all on you, kid. That's all you've got control of. Change. Become something better than those hooligans. Be the cowboy."

She mulled it over. "Leave the town a better place."

I chucked her under her chin. "You've got it, kid."

It took damn near forever. But her answering smile, when it came, beamed like sunshine bursting through after a storm.

I took her guns, of course. She didn't tell me where she'd gotten them in the first place, and I didn't ask. The point was, she didn't want 'em no more. I disintegrated them so that they couldn't cause trouble, and lifted the aura of forget-about-me from the theater.

When the kid left, I felt the shift before I saw it, the sighing whisper of power gathering and coalescing. The digital projector flickered on and a movie began playing on the big screen.

A lone cowgirl stepped through the screen, spurs jangling and thumbs hooked through her belt loops. Her hat was slung so low that I couldn't see her eyes, but I saw through her mask anyway.

"Boss," I croaked.

This was it. I'd been caught in disgrace, hell-deep in dereliction of my duty. Hell, I'd even let the kid leave without helping her create the chaos Boss demanded of me.

Boss had every right to obliterate me.

She glowered, her hands hovering dangerously near the pistols riding low on her hips. "You were showing such promise," she said. "What happened?"

I didn't answer. It's hard to talk back when the other person has the right of it, and I couldn't think of anything to say that didn't further condemn me.

She spat near my feet. "I thought so," she said, and then added for good measure, "Coward."

That did it. I'd felt guilty she caught me not doing my job, but she had no right calling me names. Especially when she was dead wrong.

I straightened my shoulders and raised my eyes to meet hers, scowling back, my lip curled. "It takes more balls to admit when one's done wrong," I said, "and to stick around trying to make amends, than it does to strut around like a cockamamie doodle boasting about how big or how fast yer guns are."

She flinched. "What did you say?" she asked, slowly, as if she couldn't believe what she'd heard.

I don't think anything or anyone had ever made Boss flinch. But I just did, and seeing that uncertain look come over her eye, it built steel into my spine and I held my ground, just like Ben Grady would've.

I spread my hands at my sides, palms open, like I'd seen some of those bald monks do in kung fu Westerns. Showing my inner peace. Showing acceptance of my fate. Showing Boss that I was done – done creating her chaos, done reaping souls for her benefit, done *working* for *her*.

I was my own demon. Just another loner passing through, looking for one last shot at happiness. For redemption. For forgiveness, for what I'd done, at Eventide and elsewhere.

For that, I'd risk everything. I'd risk oblivion.

"I said," I told Boss quietly and deliberately, "I quit."

Gunshots rang out in the theater. Startled, I jerked my head up to look at the screen.

It wasn't showing the sci-fi flick. It was showing one of my favorite movies, the one where Ben Grady saves the town from the gang of ranchers threatening to run all the townsfolk out so that they could buy up their homes for a pittance and turn the land into grazing land for a giant profit. At the very end, Grady swings into his saddle and tips his hat to the adoring gazes of the newly saved.

"Don't ask me to come back," he says. *"There ain't no place for me here."*

Boss snarled. "Oblivion is too good for you." She flourished an arm toward the screen, but she still didn't seem to notice the movie. "Go. Get lost, and never come back. Suffer as the mortals do, in loneliness and despair, without a place in the world, without purpose."

I watched Grady's rugged visage as he nods at the far-off sunset, burnished a deep, burnt orange.

"My place is out there," he says. *"There ain't no other place for the likes of me."*

"You're banishing me from demonkind?" I asked Boss, slowly, to make sure I understood.

"For eternity," she confirmed, her expression grim and uncompromising. She thought she was punishing me.

She didn't know she'd just set me free.

Like I'd told the kid, I *was* home. And I had a purpose greater than the one I'd been created for.

There were more folks out there, livin' in towns that needed a cowboy. A former demon. A hero to help 'em rise up against their foes.

I meant to ride into every last one of them.

My heart soared, thumping faster than a wild mustang's. I didn't have a horse—not yet—but I weren't worried. I'd find one eventually. The weight of two pistols settled comfortably into the gun belt slung around my waist.

I tipped the brim of my hat to Boss, and sauntered off into the sunset, a *mo gui* redeemed.

C.H. Hung grew up among the musty book stacks of public libraries, where she found a lifelong love for good stories and lost her 20/20 vision for good. She possesses a stubbornly rational soul intersecting with an irrational belief in magic, which means her stories are often as mixed up as she is, melding the plausible with myth and folklore.

Her genre-spanning short fiction has appeared in anthologies published by WordFire Press, LMBPN Publishing, Camden Park Press, and WMG Publishing, and will soon appear in *Pulphouse*. Read more at Chhung.com.

LOVE YOUR MOTHER

KEVIN PETTWAY

LOVE YOUR MOTHER

M aita picked over the larger of two yard sale tables in the student housing parking lot, searching for an appropriate murder weapon at a reasonable price. While the sun pressed down on the mostly young and summer-clothed Los Angeles deal hunters, a steady, cool breeze tried, and failed, to whisk the heat away.

"You don't need a machete," Lidia said in her thick Cuban accent. Her steel-gray hair lifted in the breeze, and she scowled up at her daughter through oversized sunglasses. "You're a lawyer. Lawyers don't need machetes." A frown pulled at her wrinkled features, heightening a thin scar that ran in a smooth arc down her right cheek. Maita had given her the scar while an infant, when she'd gotten her tiny hands on a broken jar of pureed carrots.

"I told you, Mom," Maita said as she reached across the table, "it doesn't have to be a machete. That was an example. I just need to be able to kill someone with it."

"My *daughter* doesn't need a machete." Lidia banged her fist on the table, making both the assembled tchotchkes and the two girls hosting the yard sale jump. "Even forty years after you run away from home and leave me alone, you are *still* the only one who can hurt me."

"It's only been thirty-five years, Mom. More like a long weekend."

Other yard sale patrons cast sidelong glances at the short, elderly cubana and her tall, statuesque daughter. A few whispered and pointed at Lidia.

"I heard that," Lidia said with no small amount of aggression, glaring at a pair of boys in swim trunks and sunglasses. They grabbed each other's hands and moved to the opposite side of the sale.

"It's true," Maita said. She smiled at the boys and shrugged. "She hears everything. Most annoying superpower ever."

One of the two boys jerked his head away and made a *tsk* sound with his tongue. The other scowled at Maita.

With her fiftieth birthday barely a week behind her, Maita had long ago stopped putting up with other people's stupid crap.

"If anyone's carrying a sword-bladed bayonet, early 1800s or so, I'll fight you for it." It paid to know your weaponry in her line of work.

The immediate area around Maita and Lidia drained of people.

"My daughter should be making good money at a good job," Lidia went on. She pushed Maita's bushy black hair—with more than a few strands of Lidia's own dark silver creeping in—behind her daughter's shoulders where it wouldn't blow in her face. "Do you ever think ahead? What about your retirement? Eh? How are you going to take care of me when you have wasted all of your money on monsters and murdering?"

Well, she had stopped putting up with everyone's stupid crap except for her mother's, anyway. Some dynamics died hard.

"Please don't make me sorry I invited you out here." In the time since Maita had run away from home, she had put herself through law school by cashiering at grocery stores, built a successful career as an entertainment attorney, and parlayed that into a less lucrative but far more rewarding job as writer, director, and producer of B-horror movies. Along the way, she briefly married the father of her own daughter, Artemia, before his alcoholism forced their divorce.

Her mother would *never* find out about Artemia.

"You live your life without me. I don't even know you anymore." Lidia frowned up at her daughter. "We need to talk. About when you left."

"Maybe so, but we aren't doing it now." Maita turned away and cast her gaze over the rest of the yard sale offerings. Beyond the two tables, in the open bay door of a cluttered cinderblock garage, handles poked out of a battered plastic trash can. Not wanting to lose any possible treasures to the milling crowd, Maita sped toward it.

Lidia followed.

"You were just a little girl, *mija*. You couldn't know what you saw. You don't know what you heard."

Maita pushed aside the rusted golf clubs and dented wooden bats, and spied unexpected booty in the back. She came up with a corroded blade, some two feet long plus the grip. It curved forward a bit and was heavier toward the end, so the user could chop as well as slash.

Or just swing it around and try not to hit anyone because they ran out of money for fake props.

"Falcata," Maita whispered. She held the rusting sword up in front of her and admired it. Hannibal used blades just like it against the Romans in the Punic Wars. This particular sword looked old enough to have seen those conflicts first-hand. It would be perfect for the monster's weapon in her movie, and just in time for tonight's shooting.

Even if it *did* look a little bit like a machete.

Bright studio lights illuminated the unconcerned blonde girl lounging in the cushions of a soft brown loveseat. Behind her, a picture window took up the entire wall and looked out on a nighttime suburban street, while below her and to the side, a round piece of white foamboard reflected soft light into the shadows of her face.

The room smelled of potpourri and stale french-fries.

Outside the window, a shadow stalked closer. It glided out of the gloom under the old oaks on the even lawn, a silent silhouette cut from a distant streetlamp.

Black passed into black and, for a moment, nothing moved. Had anything been there at all?

The girl picked up a magazine and flipped through the pictures of celebrities and sexual positions guaranteed to keep that man in your life forever. She sighed and pulled at her baby-blue tank top, where the couch cushions drew it too tightly around her middle.

On the lawn, a face caught the glow from the key light and reflected it back, twisted and horrible. The huge countenance bent and curled in a tangle of protruding scars, a permanent mask over the soul buried within. An enormous body towered in the window, covered in bloodstained over-alls that might once have been white, but now displayed all the colors of violence.

The figure raised an ancient sword, curved and pitted with rust. In the dim corners of the room, people clung to the shadows, holding booms and secondary cameras.

"Stop, that's enough."

"What now?" the girl on the sofa asked. Her name was Kayla, and she'd been picked because she was a "social influencer." The fact that she turned out to be a very good actress was why she had not been fired.

Repeatedly not fired.

Maita pulled off her headphones and stepped from around the camera. She pushed a lock of wavy black hair behind one ear and shoved the sleeves of her gray hoodie up her arms.

"Reggie, can you come in here? I still have a problem with this blocking."

Outside, in the window, Erik-the-monster lowered his sword to his shoulder and raised several parts of an eyebrow in befuddlement. Below him, Kayla rolled her eyes and muttered under her breath.

Reggie, plaid flannel over a T-shirt that read *Make an Assessment*, strolled out of the kitchen and into the hall just outside the little room, potato chip bag in his hand and crumbs in his beard. His glasses reflected the bright white key light.

"These are stale," he said.

"Are there any locally sourced apples?" Kayla peered over the top of her magazine at Reggie. "Craft-Lady said she'd get me some."

Maita closed her eyes and pinched the bridge of her nose. She loved making movies. She really did. But it would be so much more enjoyable without the actors.

"Erik isn't going to look scary clambering over a cushy loveseat." Maita said to Reggie. "This room is too small for both of them, the sofa, and the lights."

"Sorry, boss," Reggie said with a shrug. "I thought it would work. That's my bad. We can move it into the dining room if you want. It's bigger. Then he can come out of the hall here."

Kayla interrupted the conversation with a shriek.

"Jesus *Christ*," she shouted as she came to her feet from the loveseat. "It's just standing there, *looking* at me. Someone needs to put a fucking bell on it or something. That face is so *gross*." Kayla flitted across the room and pushed past Reggie into the hallway.

Reggie leaned in Maita's direction. "She does know that's his real face, doesn't she?" he whispered.

"Take twenty, everyone," Maita said, raising her voice over the conversations beginning around her. She dug in her pocket for keys and tossed them to Reggie.

The room emptied of crew. Erik, his expression unreadable, walked away.

"Reg, take my van over to my apartment and get Arti to help you bring back the TV chair. The one with the flowers. It won't fit in your car."

"Sure. Don't break my mom's house while I'm gone." Reggie hesitated. "Is Arti gonna wanna come? She scares me a little."

Maita's lips quirked up in a brief smile. "She'll come. She's been dying to meet Erik."

"She likes guys who fell into lawn mowers?"

"No," Maita answered. "She likes reruns of old sitcoms between trips to the bookstore. Erik used to be that kid on *The Lights Are Always On.* Before the face thing." The face thing was saving them several thousand dollars in make-up and prosthetics.

"Now be a good AD and go. I have to fix this. I want to get this shot tonight."

"Chair and daughter." Reggie gave Maita a thumbs-up as he backed out of the room. "And some fresh chips," he added as he stepped out of sight.

Maita played with her necklace while she thought about how the scene would play out. Building the film in her head like this was one of her more favorite activities. It let her leave her other worries behind for a while and left her feeling in control.

The smaller chair would allow Erik to crash through the window and land on the floor, then they could move the bounce closer to Kayla for close-ups. She could run right, out of the bounce light and into the dark. Easy.

She shook her head. Overall, she considered Reggie to be an excellent assistant director, *and* he knew how to cast breakaway plastic windows and other props. But there was a back door in his skull that his brain fell out of whenever he was around overly pretty girls like Kayla.

With a loud sigh Maita shoved her hands into the front pocket of her thin gray hoodie and flopped down on the comfy loveseat. She closed her eyes and sank into a mental picture of the room around her.

Innocent-ish girl here on the sofa, horrifying monster creeping up behind. She's preoccupied with her magazine, doesn't see him until it's too late. He crashes through the window there ...

Maita shrieked. Her phone started vibrating in her back pocket.

She answered it. "Holy crap," Maita said, her breath ragged. "You just about scared me to death."

"Like mother, like daughter," Artemia replied. "Think I have a career in movies?"

With a wide grin, Maita stretched sideways on the sofa and folded her legs up in front of her. Artemia, just fifteen-years-old, was a tonic to her mother. Maita felt her stress dissolving, leaving her back and shoulders warm.

She loved that kid.

"Whatcha need?" Maita asked.

"I don't know," Artemia said. "You said you wanted to talk to me about something important. Oh shit, I'm sorry. I'm not supposed to call when you're shooting. Did I mess everything up?"

"Oh, no, not at all." Maita breathed in deep, and sent her tension out on the exhale. "We're on a break. Oh, hey, I sent Reg to the apartment to pick up the living room chair. If you want to come back with him, you can meet Erik ..."

Maita held the phone away from her face until Artemia stopped squealing.

"Done now?"

"Done," Artemia answered, not done at all. "Thank you, Mom. Thank you, thank you, thank you, thank you! I'm sorry I said your job was stupid and that L.A. sucked and you didn't know anyone worth a crap and I hated all your movies. This is the best thing *ever*!"

"What did you say about my movies?" Maita asked, one brow raised.

"Ooh, do you think he still hangs out with Jennifer and Rudy and all the others?" Artemia asked, ignoring her mother's question.

"I don't think so," Maita said. "I think he pretty much keeps to himself these days ... since the thing with the lawn mower. But, hey, I did need to tell you, I'm going out of town for the weekend. With your grandmother."

Artemia calmed like a match dropped into a pond.

"The grandmother you invited here and won't let me see?" she asked.

"That's the one," Maita said. Some of the tension returned to her shoulders and her grin faded away. "We have some ... stuff to work out. Easier for us to talk alone. Away from distractions. Always was."

"I imagine a secret granddaughter would be distracting." Artemia sounded calm, but what kid would not want to meet her grandmother? "Can I at least know why I'm not allowed to see her?"

"It's mostly for your protection," Maita said. "Your grandmother can be kinda mean. And, if I'm being honest, it just makes everything easier. If I tell her now, then I have to deal with her being angry because I didn't tell her before, and then that will be all she and I will talk about, and the whole thing will be for nothing."

"I don't think I need protection from a seventy-year-old woman," Artemia said. "There's no way she's meaner than my algebra teacher, and you make me see *her* every day." She blew a dramatic sigh through the phone. "But I'm sure I can find something to do while you're gone. I just got a new book about these aliens that inject *their* eyes into *your* eyes and make you see things that aren't there, so you go around killing everyone because you think they're giant lizards and stuff."

"Do the infected people think they're killing people in lizard costumes, or CG lizards?" Maita asked. "CG lizards are way more expensive."

"It's a *book*, Mom. Not a movie." Another sigh. "They're totally costume-lizards."

Mother and daughter laughed, said goodbye, and hung up.

Artemia embodied all the best parts of Maita. Fearless and strong, intelligent and trusting. Those parts that Maita would most want to live on after she was gone.

If Maita was being especially self-serving, it was almost like being immortal.

Her faint smile vanished as Maita considered her own mother. Paranoid concern jumped to the front of her brain, pushing out more reasoned thoughts.

Did Lidia know where they were shooting? Was it a good idea for Maita to ask Artemia to come back with Reggie? If her mother discovered Artemia, all of Maita's planning would come crashing down like ...

A scream came from within the house.

Kayla.

Again.

Kayla shrieked every time she saw Erik's face. Good for the film, but crazy-making for everyone else. Maita was pretty sure Erik hated her for it.

Maita frowned and pushed herself off of the loveseat. She walked into the hallway and looked left into the empty kitchen. No one was making dinner. Craft Services must have gone to the all-night grocery.

Reggie better bring enough chips for everyone.

Up ahead, Reggie's mother's dining room glowed a dim yellow. Using the AD's mom's house to shoot saved a ton on sets, but made lighting and blocking a continual hassle. There were always trade-offs.

"Kayla? Everything okay?" Maita walked around the dark wood table and chairs and put her hands on her hips. The single hanging lamp with its goldenrod shade lit the center of the table well enough, but left the walls and their framed photos of family members at sports or school events in shadow. She peered closer.

Teenaged Reggie looked like a dork.

Dark bedrooms lay ahead, and Maita turned right again, toward the front door. Where was everyone? She stopped just before stepping through the archway and took in the scene.

The windowed door stood at the end of a small foyer; to the left sat a metal canister with a colorful Norman Rockwell print on it, holding several folded umbrellas. Against the door itself lay Kayla, face turned into the wood, a hole in her back still oozing blood down her spine and into her cut-offs. Above her a thin puncture in the door allowed a sliver of bluish light from the streetlamp into the tiny space.

The hole was perhaps three inches high, and a quarter-inch wide. Big enough for a strong man looking in the door's window to shove an ancient sword through the door *and* the girl on the other side.

Maita's cellphone found its way into her hand, and 9-1-1 was already ringing by the time she consciously acknowledged it.

"9-1-1, what's your emergency?" The voice sounded older, female, and efficient.

"Oh, um ... I'm sorry. Crap. You know what, I meant to call 4-1-1 and I forgot which one was which."

Maita watched the blood pool beneath Kayla's body.

"Name, please."

"Maita Lamiana."

"Thank you. Phone number where you can be reached?"

Maita gave the woman her cell phone number. She knew how this process worked. It had been in her last movie.

There was a pause on the other end.

"Are you sure everything is all right?"

"Yes, I'm fine." Maita smiled to give her voice a lift. "I'm just a dummy. Good night."

After she hung up, Maita stood with her phone in her hand and waited.

Things were going to happen faster than she'd planned, but she couldn't rush it.

This was her shot.

The phone rang and Maita answered it. She assured the 9-1-1 operator a second time that all was well, thumbed the off switch, and replaced the phone in her pocket.

Not the plan, but she would adapt. It was the theme of her whole life.

Crap! Reggie and Artemia would be back with the chair in fifteen minutes. She couldn't even call Artemia back now without risking her daughter's safety further. Having a time limit wasn't part of the plan either. She needed to move.

Maita carefully hauled Kayla's cooling corpse away from the door. She stood straight and pulled on the doorknob. Tall bushes to either side of the door made a sort of darkened hallway into the front yard. To the right lay Erik, his oversized muscular form torn open from his neck down to his navel.

Blood dripped from everything.

While sorry for the big man, Maita wasn't surprised. As a potential threat, Erik would have been among the first to go. The stink of a freshly ruptured digestive system wafted up and into Maita's face.

"Oh, boy. You do *not* smell good," Maita said. She placed one hand over her nose.

She knew horror and fright were the appropriate emotional reactions here, but her immediate needs overrode those feelings. She could be terrified later.

This kind of thing had always been a possibility.

On a hunch, Maita pulled aside the branches from the left-hand hedge and spotted the falcata in the dirt and leaves. She snatched it up and returned to the house. It wasn't likely to help—Maita knew her horror movies—but it made her feel better anyway.

Almost a foot of the rusty blade glinted red with smeared Kayla.

A frightening crash shuddered through the house and a deep voice, like a mountain sliding off the world, shrieked, "All dead, all dead. No more friends, my little *mija*."

If this were one of Maita's own movies, the rest of the crew would be scattered around the house in gruesome displays for her to find while the horrifying monster chased her down. Better to go ahead and jump to the end.

"I guess we're not waiting until Saturday to have our talk?" As soon as the question left Maita's lips, the grinding crash began again at high speed, tearing down walls and furniture alike in its haste to get to Maita. The house shook as if ready to pitch itself to the ground, and clouds of shattered plaster billowed out from the kitchen.

Maita fled into a shadowy bedroom, taking just enough time to open the slatted closet door a half-inch before rolling beneath the bed.

Clothes covered the floor and obscured her vision but did nothing to disguise her mother's flowery perfume when the gigantic clawed feet, covered in scales like stone, scraped into the room. The creature's throaty chuckle vibrated along the base of Maita's spine, and its claws *click-clacked* on hardwood flooring as it moved toward the closet door.

The perfume's odor shifted from too-sweet flowers to rotted urine, and Maita grimaced against it. Worse, now that the stench was in her nose, she couldn't recall it ever smelling any different. Every memory of her childhood home was drenched in that stink.

Seems about right, she thought.

The creature that had been her mother smashed at the closet doors above Maita's line of vision, bringing whitewashed wooden slats and a considerable amount of drywall bouncing to the floor. At the same time, Maita slashed out with the falcata. The blade dragged clothes and tumbling slats in a low arc before cutting into Lidia's hind ... paw?

A rough scream sliced through the room and the bed flew away from Maita into the far wall, crashing into the dark. Before Maita could draw a breath, a taloned hand grabbed the front of her hoodie. It clawed at her chest and lifted her into the air.

Then Maita screamed, too.

"What the ever-loving Christhole?" A gruff woman's voice shouted from the dining room.

Maita jerked sideways and shifted her torso inside the hoodie so she could see the doorway of the bedroom. The Craft Services Director, her short, stiff hair dark against the swinging golden ceiling lamp behind her, stood there with a full paper grocery bag in each arm.

Lidia shoved Maita into the ceiling and cackled like exploding glass in a wildfire.

Craft-Lady—Maita couldn't have recalled her name now if there were a gun to her head—dropped the bags at the same time Lidia dropped Maita. As she hit the ground, Maita crawled toward the door, but jumped sideways when the muscular woman slipped an enormous revolver out of a back-holster and raised it.

The first *BOOM* illuminated Craft-Lady's faded denim pants and white cotton shirt. Her eyes, wide with fright, reflected the muzzle-flash.

"Center mass," Craft-Lady shouted.

The second *BOOM* lit up the four-legged monster that scraped the ceiling. Fangs protruded from a human face with a thin white scar on one cheek, and dark green scales hissed against the floor and walls. A whipping, serpentine tail struck long gouges in the walls where it hit.

"Headshot."

Maita closed her eyes after that.

BOOM.

"Shoulder."

BOOM.

"Center mass."

BOOM.

"Gut shot."

When Craft-Lady screamed, Maita opened her eyes.

Lidia's tail wrapped around Craft-Lady's throat and then through her back, curling out of the center of the woman's chest. With a flex and several audible pops, the Director of Craft Services' head fell to the ground.

Maita grabbed the revolver.

The creature rushed out of the dark, grabbed Maita by one foot, dragged her from the bedroom, and flung her with a *bang* onto the dining room table. Maita's vision swam, and the lamp hanging above the table swung in uneven circles, haphazardly spotlighting teenaged Reggie's baseball games and outdoor church services.

The ankle-drag. A staple of horror movies everywhere. Maita should have been ready for that.

"Now we will have our talk, eh, *mija?*"

The voice ground her mother and the monster together, all the more frightening because of its familiarity. Maita pushed herself up and sat straight-backed, looking her mother in the face.

"You killed my father," Maita said, her words a husky rasp. "You burned the house down with him in it."

"He discovered what I am," the monster answered. "He could have ruined our lives."

"What the crap?" Maita asked, her anger batting down her fear. "How have *you* not ruined my life?"

The creature placed its scaly hands between its very-human breasts and managed to look offended. "You have a blessed life. Blessed by the same gods who cursed me. Blessed *because* of me. You want to be a lawyer; you are a lawyer. You want to make movies; you make movies. All of this comes from me."

"I *wanted* to make another movie, but *you* killed all my crew." She fought against the grief that threatened to well up within her. There would be time for that later. "So, thanks for that blessing."

"You are so cutting with your words." Lidia's tail flicked, slicing a wide gouge in the wall behind her. The breeze from it sent the smells of gypsum dust and old urine throughout the room.

"It is hard to believe you are even my daughter." Powder from destroyed drywall coated Lidia, sticking in clumps to the blood where Maita had injured her foot with the falcata.

"Because I'm not horrible? Because I'm not like you?" Maita's anger gave her the courage to say the things she'd been thinking for decades. "Well, I'm not you, and I never will be. You're toxic, and even when you were just a mother, you *murdered* our family."

"But, *mija*, you *are* me." Lidia whispered.

"I heard your argument with Dad that night," Maita said. "I heard him call you Lamia—the monster. I guess you want to try and deny that now, too?"

"I am a good person," Lidia answered.

At that, Maita burst out with a small, half-hysterical laugh.

"This answers so much about my childhood." Maita shook her head and felt the heavy weight of Craft-Lady's gun in her lap.

Oxford. They used to call the woman Oxford. That couldn't have been her real name though.

Not relevant. Monster now.

"You have Googled Lamia on your computers, I am sure," Lidia said. The scales at her throat shuddered, producing a weird trilling noise. "You know what was done to me, by Zeus and his bitch-wife? You know I am cursed to grieve for eternity for all of my children?"

"I did my research." Maita did not say how long she had planned for this day. "How many of your children have you murdered to get this far, Mom?"

Lidia waved a long-taloned hand. "I don't know. Hundreds? Thousands? I just don't want you to think I won't be sad after I kill you."

Confronted by this creature, Maita could not help but be curious. It was still her *mother*. She took control of her breathing and centered herself.

Her mom would never kill anyone while there was an opportunity to talk about herself.

"As comforting as that thought is," Maita said, "how exactly does this work? You just take over my body when you die? Do I follow along inside? Do I ... go to heaven?"

"There is a little ceremony." Lidia clicked her claws. "Then I eat your soul and take your body. I never would have waited so long except you ran away from home like a selfish brat. I never raised such a thoughtless girl."

"Do you only take daughters? I never read anything about a male Lamia."

"I have had to take a son or two when accidents happen." She frowned and a thin whip of a tongue flickered out and vanished. "I do not like the way they smell."

"I only hope when you eat my soul and possess my corpse that you can smell your*self* the way I do." Maita wrinkled her nose. "All that stuff about wanting me to concentrate on law instead of movies—that was just so you could have a fortune ready and live off of my money."

"I have always planned for your future," Lidia said.

"You know, I only invited you to California so I could kill you." Maita checked the chamber of the revolver to be sure. One more bullet.

"And what do you think of that now, *mija*? Now that you have seen with your own eyes that I cannot be killed."

Maita lifted the big revolver. Five shots, point-blank, and her mother was still walking, clawing, and bitching.

Good thing there was a Plan B.

Even if it sucked.

"That's true," Maita said, "I can't do anything to *you*, but you need me to survive." Maita raised the barrel of the gun to her forehead. "And you don't have me anymore."

Lidia's tail raked back and forth at a frenetic pace, shredding the wall behind her to pieces. She reached out, then withdrew her hand, seeming unsure if she could cross the distance before Maita could pull the trigger.

"Must you hate me so?" Lidia wailed. "You wish for my death so much you would kill yourself?"

"Yeah," Maita replied, lips curled into a knowing smile, "I guess I do."

"Selfish, brutish child! Ungrateful child! You should love your mother. After all of it, you are *still* the only one who can hurt me." The monster slowed, ceasing its frantic motion and coiling its muscles, a huge, unnatural snake preparing to spring.

"I cannot even sleep. I am cursed to lie awake and cry for the children I have lost. I only wanted to kill you to spare you an eternity of torment." She lowered her hands and sighed. "But you may pull your trigger. I will mourn you. Just as I will mourn poor Artemia after I dine on her soul and take her beautiful young body."

A wave of fear washed across Maita, obliterating her thoughts and plans. How was this possible? Lidia should not even know about Artemia. More than anything else, this was the thing she had tried to protect. This was the reason she hadn't called her daughter back on the phone.

This monster heard everything.

Through the door window, Maita saw the headlights of her van enter the driveway, carrying Artemia and Reggie into the jaws of the beast. She heard the engine stop.

"Guests?" Lidia asked with a snakelike flick of her head. "We can do the ceremony later. I will take your body and your soul now."

She glided across the floor on hissing scales and clicking claws.

Maita's head shot up. It made sense. The scar on her mother's cheek from the broken jar, the ineffective bullets from Craft-Lady's handgun, and the gypsum-crusted blood covering Lidia's injured foot.

Maita really *was* the only one able to hurt her mother.

She whirled the handgun at her surprised demon-mother's face.

"I never loved you."

The last bullet flew through her mother's skull, just above her left eye.
BOOM.

The hasty fires were beginning to lick against the ceiling when Maita ran out the front door and into the arms of a frantic Artemia. Reggie had yanked the skinny teenager back into the van when he spied Erik's corpse, and called the cops. Tomorrow he would have the bruises to show Artemia's difference of opinion.

Maita was already planning a tale for the police, and the fire would obscure the details enough for it to fly. That would be the easy part.

"Oh, Mom, I was so scared you were hurt." The girl babbled.
Stupid child.

The sirens arrived and policemen flooded the scene. Maita and Artemia were ushered to the back of an ambulance and given blankets.

No, the hard part—as ever—would be planning Artemia's future. Ensuring she made something of her life. Something a mother could live on. And that the brat had a child of her own.

Preferably a girl.

Kevin Pettway is a long-time fan of good fantasy as well as being a smartass. He brought together these two burning passions to create the Misplaced Mercenaries series, the first of which, *A Good Running Away*, is available now.

Kevin lives in Florida with his wife of twenty-six years and two *Firefly*-themed dogs—Book and River. He probably spends too much of his time worrying that he will someday be introduced to the world as "Florida Man."

You can find Kevin on Facebook or his own website at www.kevin-pettway.com. Fair warning—he is a smartass there, too.

PROGRESS GROWS OUT OF MOTION

A Drowned Horse Chronicle

DAVID BOOP

PROGRESS GROWS OUT OF MOTION

Arizona Territory

Retirement from bounty hunting didn't suit Hal Turk too well. The part about not getting shot at was fine with him, but the challenge of knowing a man; predicting his actions? Of pursuing him wherever he went? That part he missed.

In the three years since his left eye had gone fuzzy, Turk tried to fill that void by taking up big game hunting in Maine, but found that animals —even the biggest and smartest—were too dumb to be much of a challenge. He tried his hand at gambling, but decided he'd much prefer being the house. He even took out one last, small bounty, but that nearly cost him his other eye. Luckily, Diaz, who, despite being a lousy shot, distracted the prey long enough for Turk to get the upper hand by shooting off six rounds without hitting nary a thing. To top it off, the money they got for that swindler weren't nothing like he was used to.

So, Hal Turk, freshly re-retired, figured it past time to head back west on the Topeka & Santa Fe Line. He and Diaz had chased men throughout the territories, and even so far as up into the Canadian Rockies, that it would be almost like going home—if such a thing existed for Turk.

He'd only heard rumors about the town of Drowned Horse, located in the nicer part of the Arizona territory. Sure, it'd been doing fine thanks to a large copper strike in Jerome, least according to the papers, but many a failed settler returning East had spoke nonsense about the place having demons.

Everyone had demons, Turk especially, but he'd never known a town to have one that didn't come from the people who lived there.

That was also something familiar to Turk: people and what drove them to do evil. As a newly christened faro and poker dealer, Turk could work with that.

In the seat next to him, Diaz annoyingly fiddled with a new compass Turk had gifted him.

"I think it is broken, Señor Hunt—I mean, Señor Turk."

Diaz still had the nasty habit of calling Turk "Señor Hunter." Even after five years together, Turk's translator and tracker occasionally slipped and called him that damn nickname. While they hadn't started out as friends, escaping countless near-death experiences had won over the tired bounty hunter, who'd never really had a friend before.

"What makes you think so?" Turk responded.

"The compass, it keeps pointing to the east, when we are clearly heading west." Diaz directed Turk's gaze to the cabin's window with his index finger. "It should be pointing that way, no?"

"That might be my fault," came the voice of the third person in their compartment.

The older gentleman had not said more than an occasional greeting since they'd switched trains in Indiana. He mostly slept, but seemed cordial enough during their comings and goings for dinner.

"How so?" Turk asked.

The man lifted his cane, something he always had by his side, and lightly rapped the large spherical, silver end against his head.

"Metal plate, you see. Got it from a carriage crash. Lucky to be alive, they say. Others say it caused me to go crazy, but I tell them that I was already crazy before the accident." He laughed in a way that suggested more truth behind the joke than he let on. "I find that, occasionally, after waking from sleep, I've created some sort of electric charge in it. No idea what causes it, but I bet Edison could figure it out."

"Yeah, maybe," Turk replied.

Diaz moved the compass closer to the old man's forehead and, sure as anything, the compass pointed right at it! Satisfied that his new toy was not broken, Diaz put it away. "What takes you to Arizona, Señor ...?" Diaz let the question hang.

"Eadweard Muybridge." He extended a hand to Diaz and then to Turk.

"I'm heading to San Francisco to pick up some equipment I left before returning to Chicago in time for the Columbian Exposition."

That interested Diaz, as he'd traveled through most of South America. "I have read about the upcoming World's Fair in the papers. They will have replicas of Columbus's ships. I heard even Little Egypt will perform." Diaz blushed at the thought of the belly dancer. "It sounds *increíble*."

Turk, however, thought it all just a money grab as bad as a bank robbery. The organizers had denied Buffalo Bill a place in their precious faire, and that irked him. Bill was a friend.

"It certainly will be *increíble*, my good man." Muybridge leaned forward conspiratorially. "In fact, because of my time exploring *America de Meridianol*, they've designed a whole hall in honor of me."

That sounded too *increíble* for Turk. "So what does one do to warrant such an honor? Capture wild animals?"

Muybridge stroked his long, white beard and grinned in a mischievous way. "Well, one could say that I have done that, after a fashion. I'm a photographer, and I've captured such creatures in a way no one else has ... with photographs."

Photography wasn't new anymore. It'd been around since before Turk was born, and he said as much.

"Oh, but not *my* photos, mind you. My photos move. People, animals, even a train like this—captured forever—in motion."

Hal Turk no longer just *thought* Muybridge crazy—he reckoned it to be so.

"Ah, I can see the skepticism in your eyes, Mr. Turk. Let me show you. Mr. Diaz, would you kindly draw the shades?"

Muybridge reached up to the luggage rack for a large container as Diaz drew the blinds. The shades allowed enough light for the old coot to set a box upon a small tripod. Taking out a candle, he lit the wick and placed it inside the box. The light from the candle shone upon the wall across the compartment.

Muybridge motioned Hal and Diaz to join him on his side as he installed a disc-shaped object into a slot in front of the candle. A photo of a horse projected onto the wall.

Muybridge cranked a hand lever on the side of the box. As he did, the horse photo was replaced by similar one; the horse in a slightly different stance.

And then another one.

And another.

As Muybridge spun the crank faster, the photos blurred together, making the illusion of a running horse. So simple, and yet Turk had never seen anything like it. A tiny horse ran in place on the wall. He and Diaz slumped back in the seats, flabbergasted.

Having proved his point, Muybridge stopped cranking and re-opened the curtains.

"This is the traveling version of my *zoopraxiscope*. The much bigger version I left in San Francisco will be able to show my moving pictures on a much larger scale."

The "less-than-crazy old man" put his equipment away. "And what do you gentlemen do?"

Diaz answered for them. "We have just taken up table stakes in a town called Drowned Horse. They were very happy to offer us five tables."

Too happy. It worried Turk.

"My, that is a fascinating endeavor," Muybridge said. He stroked his long beard. "From what I hear, gambling takes a fast and steady hand. Do you have such a thing?"

Diaz shook his head. "No, but Señor Hun—um, I mean Senior Turk, he does. Very fast hands."

Turk didn't like it when Diaz bragged about his skill. It gave people ideas.

Muybridge studied Turk in an appraising way that unnerved Turk. He certainly hoped the man had no interest in drawing on him.

"Could you show me?" Muybridge finally declared.

"How?"

Muybridge thought on this. "How about dealing cards? We can use the zoopraxiscope stand as a table."

Resigned to his fate, Turk nodded.

Diaz got out the deck of cards Turk used to teach his partner card tricks.

Hal was no magician, but having skill in sleight-of-hand came in handy as a gambler—more so as a hunter.

Turk dealt the cards and then showed Muybridge a few simple tricks, like three-card Monte, and such. He didn't however, demonstrate the best techniques he'd acquired from other dealers. Those cheats. Those subtle movements which would allow him to keep an edge over the people at his table. The type of cheats he and Diaz had to watch out for, or be victims themselves.

Seemingly impressed, Muybridge clapped. "You do have an amazing hand, sir." Then sitting back, he pronounced, "I have a proposition for you. In the freight car, I have my cameras for taking zoopraxiscope pictures. I would love to capture your skill on film. I think it would be an amazing addition to my library."

As Diaz put the cards away, Turk steeled himself to decline just as Muybridge added, "And I'll pay well for the honor."

How could Turk say no after that?

As it turned out, Drowned Horse was not nearly the boomtown Turk and Diaz had heard. Quite the opposite. The notion that "word travels fast" didn't factor in the distance from Arizona to Pennsylvania. The Jerome mines had indeed taken off, but so had the new town of Jerome, reneging on promised prosperity of Drowned Horse. Others, such as Cottonwood and Clarkdale, had also sprung up in the area, siphoning off potential growth.

Plus—as Turk and Diaz discovered soon after arriving—there *was* the curse.

"Curse?" Turk asked the owner of the Sagebrush Saloon, the only saloon still open in the town. He hadn't gotten the man's name, but everyone around the bald man seemed to call him Owner.

"Yeah, I shoulda probably mentioned that in the letter I sent ya." Owner's head was as smooth as a river rock. A long, graying mustache draped down to either side of his mouth, which currently held a smile. "But I'd inquired about you before replying to your request, and it seemed like you were the sort to be able to handle a touch of the dark in your life."

Indeed, Turk had run across more evil than was to be believed.

Diaz crossed himself upon Owner's initial proclamation, but seemed to have settled in with the notion. "In what way, Señor Owner? How does this curse behave?"

Owner, who wiped the bar and talked about the macabre as if it was just bad weather, explained, "Oh, we get the occasional demon or mythological monster from time to time. Hell, we recently even had ourselves some aliens from Mars or some sort. Can't remember rightly where they said they was from. Cost our current sheriff his right arm, but he shoots with his left, so no worries there."

Turk looked at Diaz who looked back at his partner with an incredulous expression.

"Why would anyone *come* to this town, let alone stay?" was the only response Turk could think of.

Owner tilted his head slightly, and with a straight face, answered, "The challenge, of course. Haven't met a settler that didn't think he was smarter than the devil himself."

As if that said it all, Owner asked if Turk and Diaz still wanted the offered table stakes, as originally planned.

Turk considered his options. He and Diaz could leave for another town nearby, or maybe continue on to California where they would also have the ocean to their backs. Or go south to Tucson or Tombstone, each of which came with their own set of troubles.

But then Turk thought of Owner's promise of the potential for danger. Being in a cursed town and all, could be a hook he could use to his advantage. Maybe this was destiny calling, giving him what his soul sorely needed.

Turk leaned over to Diaz and whispered an idea, which made his partner chuckle.

"We're going to need to increase our share," Turk finally told Owner. "And, we want to advertise in such a way to draw miners back into town. 'Gamble at the Sagebrush! Where the winnings are worth betting your life on!'" Turk waved his hand as if his words were written on a banner.

Owner reached down and pulled out a contract that already had Turk's adjusted share filled in. "I thought you might say that."

Diaz sucked in breath. "Señor Turk. We should have asked more."

Zhu Jun, known to the people of Drowned Horse as John Chew, because *gweilo* did not bother with pronouncing his name correctly, carried an armful of clothes he'd gathered from the line outside. The young man felt grateful the weather had been mild enough to dry clothes outside. His wife, Ling, hated having Westerners' clothes draped over every surface of their apartment which sat above Jun's shop. She understood that working for greedy *gweilo* rail bosses had given Jun enough money to bring her over to America. She also accepted that washing disrespectful Westerners' clothes kept food on their table. But that didn't mean Ling had to like any of it.

Jun, on the other hand, liked most of the citizens of Drowned Horse. He had heard stories of how immigrants were treated in other towns, especially the bigger cities. His people were called many derogatory names and spat upon. However, the worst thing he was called by his neighbors was "Chewy," which was not too bad.

Jun climbed the back stairs to the room they had to themselves. His wife had not produced any children in their time together, which suited Jun. While he would have appreciated the eventual extra helping hands, or someone to leave the business to, their small room was crowded enough with ironing boards, extra wash tubs, and supplies for the shop below.

The one thing that seemed to please Ling was Jun deciding to open a stable behind the shop. It only housed three horses, but, as a child back in *Zhōng Guó*, Ling had ridden horses. She had been the daughter of an influential and wealthy politician. Despite Jun being a commoner stable boy, Ling fell in love with him like a story told in books.

Unfortunately, Ling's father married her to a horrible man. Jun knew she could not be happy. He came to America to make money to bring her over, knowing the risk he was taking. Finally, when he had enough, he found her and stole her away. He knew one day, Ling's husband, or her father, or brother, might seek them out, but for now, they were happy.

"Ling?" He called from the top step. "Can you open the door?"

"Jun!" She cried out urgently. Jun had never heard her so scared. "Come quick!"

Not knowing what to do with the clothes, he tossed them over the railing and rushed inside.

Ling sat on their bed, a scroll and an arrow lying on either side of her.

"This was on the door to the shop," she explained.

A broken wax seal remained intact enough to see the insignia. He expected to see the crest of Ling's husband or father, but it was not.

"From your brother?"

Ling nodded. "He says that our father has chosen to work on improving relationships with the *Rìběn*, but instead made things worse."

That did not surprise Jun, at all. Everyone knew that war between his country and the one Westerners called Japan was only a matter of time.

"Brother says word reached Emperor Meiji that I had fled to America, and that he has sent his *akuma* to capture me, in hopes of weakening my father's position."

Just the sound of the word sent chills down Jun's spine. The legends surrounding the Japanese Emperor's secret assassins, known also as *Shinobi*, were terrifying. Their mystical powers were unrivaled.

If they had chosen Ling as their target, Jun did not know what to do. Ling's brother had taken a great risk sending a messenger to warn her.

Jun knelt by his love. "I will get help from Sheriff Patrick. He will know what to do. He has faced many such demons. He will protect you, even if I can't."

Ling nodded.

As Jun got up to leave, he could not help but wonder how Ling's brother had found her so easily, and were Meiji's demon assassins close behind?

It didn't take long for word to get out about the new tables at the Sagebrush, and though there were others in the area, the chance to meet and play against the infamous bounty hunter Hal Turk brought enough business to make a decent living.

At night, Turk and Diaz had a packed house, with many players waiting in the wings. During the day, Ed Muybridge set up his cameras and took photos of Turk dealing cards.

Turk did not think himself a handsome man, but the eye patch certainly helped him with the ladies. They sat spellbound as he spun his tales of how his eye had been lost, each time a different—and completely fabricated— yarn.

And yet, the thought of being in pictures—multiple pictures—moving pictures—made Turk nervous and a bit shy. He dressed up, got a shave and haircut, and even trimmed his thick mustache until he could see his smile in the mirror.

Turk didn't like it. The smile.

He didn't do it often enough for it to look natural on his face, despite the steady flow of money coming in. But a deal was a deal, and he would uphold his end.

Muybridge's zoopraxiscope set-up was just like taking ten photographs at once. Muybridge positioned several cameras in a line and set them off in a succession using a control mechanism, capturing each of Turk's movements. He had Turk deal slow, and then fast. The camera flashes blinded Turk, and he found himself blinking away stars from his eyes after each session.

During the exercises, the old man seemed happy, but at night, after he developed his prints, he came back down dejected.

"They are not coming out the way I hoped. I need a better angle to film from."

Muybridge asked for, and got, permission from Owner to hang the cameras from the rafters, which turned out to be quite the endeavor. After each round, Muybridge asked Turk to deal faster, with the photographer adjusting his cameras to activate quicker. Finally, Muybridge seemed satisfied. He left the cameras hanging there as he rushed up the stairs.

"I'll let you know if this worked after I develop them tonight. Maybe I'll show everyone the finished moving pictures here on the stage."

Owner thought that a fine idea, knowing it would bring in more customers than even the chance to play faro against Turk.

Later, in his room, Turk waited for Diaz to return from Chewy's with their laundry. He turned as the door creaked open slowly.

"Hey, Diaz. That crazy old man might've finally—" His partner's face stopped him short. "What's up, Amigo?"

Diaz sat down on his bed. "It's Chewy, Señor Turk. He's dead."

Chewy had been a good man. He and his family not only ran the laundry, but he stabled Turk's horse, Armageddon. Chewy washed Armie's saddle blanket without ever charging Turk, because he was honored to have such a fine horse in his stalls. Turk also knew Chewy must've been slipping Armie treats, because the warhorse had never taken to someone so fast. Even Diaz still got bitten occasionally.

"What happened?"

Diaz shook his head. "No one is certain. As he walked down Main Street, there was a sudden breeze, and next thing anyone knew, Chewy's head lay on the ground next to his body."

Turk thought Diaz might cry, and Turk would've joined him, were he not so angry. He raced downstairs, just as the buzz of the murder reached the Sagebrush.

Turk and Diaz had met Sheriff Theodore Patrick upon arriving in Drowned Horse. It was part of the town's ordinance that all guns be surrendered during your stay. Normally, Turk would've turned them all in, but considering the job he'd just accepted, and the type of money he'd be carrying around, the good sheriff agreed to let him kept his sidearm.

Under normal circumstances, a one-armed lawman would be a risk to any he protected, especially against things that defied belief, but Turk's instincts told him Sheriff Patrick wasn't a person he should be on the wrong end of a gun from. Turk's biggest surprise had been Patrick's age, as most men to carry a badge didn't live long past thirty. At the ripe old age of thirty-seven, Patrick's reputation had gained legendary status even before he'd come to Drowned Horse.

When Turk arrived at the scene, the sheriff was squatted down near the two parts of Chewy's body. Patrick raised an eyebrow and, with a touch of amusement in his voice despite the gruesome sight, said, "Figured you'd come. Still retired?"

"Depends. Know who killed him?"

"Not 'who,' but 'what.' And yeah, I do. You ain't going to like it."

Turk's palms suddenly grew moist, and his heart thumped in his chest. It was time, he realized, for him to face one of Drowned Horse's infamous curses.

Turk hadn't felt like this since his first bounty.

Is this what I've been missing in my life? A dance with Death? Is that the only way I'll ever be happy?

A scream tore Turk from his thoughts.

Ling, Chewy's wife, raced down the street as fast as she could in her dress. Patrick moved faster, getting up and meeting her before she could get any closer to the body.

"Ling," he said, taking her into a hug and turning her away from the scene. "You don't want to see. I don't want to see it either."

She tried to get around him, but Patrick held her firm until she broke down in sobs.

Turk stood himself between them, trying to be another screen from the sight on the ground. But he knew there was too much blood creeping down the packed-hard street to soak into the dirt. No matter where you looked, Death made sure everyone knew it'd come to town.

After Ling had been taken to the town's church by the pastor's wife for comforting, which the sheriff said would also include communion wine to calm her nerves, Turk sat in Patrick's office listening to the man recite a list of swear words even Turk didn't use.

"Fond of him, were you?" Turk asked.

"No. I mean, yes. But I'm not cursing about that." Patrick dropped into his chair. "I'd tried to stop this very thing from happening."

"Do tell."

"Chewy came to me a few days ago, saying that the Emperor of Japan had sent some sort of demons to kidnap Ling. 'Shinobi,' he said. Ling called them 'akuma,' which I guess means devil in Japanese."

"Like this town didn't have enough demons without having to import them?"

Patrick glared at him, but then sighed. "That's the risk everyone who lives here takes. The evils of the world are drawn to Drowned Horse, like bees to a flower. But we had warning this time. Ling had gotten a letter, and I did my best to keep an eye out for anything ... well, demonlike. I asked every Oriental I could find between here and the mines what we were up against, only to discover that their bastards don't act like good ol' American demons, or even the ones the Indians worship. They're practically invisible and good at killing without leaving a trace."

While Turk was curious what 'good ol' American demons' acted like, he knew that story was best told another day over drinks. For now, he wanted to move fast, while he was still riled.

"So, what then?"

Patrick pulled out some papers filled with notes and sketches.

"I found some Japanese miners who'd brought scrolls and such from their homeland. I copied what pictures I could find. Shinobis, or akumas, or whatever, usually work in the dark, blending in with the night. But when they do work during the day, they ain't any easier to spot. They disguise themselves as any normal person. They also disappear in a puff of smoke, but it don't smell like sulfur, though."

"Hmmm." Turk looked over the sketches. The expression each demon wore looked as though they smiled, or laughed. In Turk's opinion, nothing was more effective at creating fear in prey than a laughing predator. Just ask any hyena.

Their horns were also longer than the Catholic version of the devil he'd been warned of back in the orphanage.

That had been the last place Turk had ever called home, and due to the way he had been treated there, he'd never wanted to lay down roots again. The people who ran the place were monsters of a different sort, promising hellfire and brimstone—and beatings—to keep Satan away.

The sketches also had the Shinobi carrying swords, knives, and ...

"What are these things? The stars?"

Patrick shrugged. "That's exactly how they were described to me.

Little metal stars the demons shoot out of their hands with such force, they can stick in just about anything."

"Or anyone."

Turk's instincts went off. Something about these drawings didn't sit right, but he couldn't say what.

"Right. But how'm I supposed to catch, let alone shoot, something I can't see. Especially if it moves that fast? At least five people saw Chewy die, right there in the street, but no one saw how. One moment, he was looking around nervously. Next thing anyone knew, his head rolled down the road as his body sagged to the ground, blood gushing everywhere."

The sight would have unnerved anyone, even the hearty people of Drowned Horse.

"Why'd they kill him? Didn't you say they were after his wife?"

Patrick nodded. "Yup. Her father got mixed up in some Chinese-Japanese mess, and this Meiji guy sent his demons to take Ling back to Japan as leverage against her father."

"So, why haven't they taken her yet?"

Patrick thought on that. "Maybe that's how they work. Distract the guards with some sort of—"

Both leapt from their seats and reached the church steps just as the sounds of chaos erupted within. Drawing their pieces—Turk just a hair slower than Patrick, he noticed—they busted through the front door.

Four smoke funnels rose up from various places in the room, and from each cloud, a demon jumped out. The Shinobi wore normal, everyday clothes. They were not scaly, or demonlike, at all.

No cloven hooves.

No forked tail.

But each had a face just as Patrick had drawn from people's accounts of them. No two were alike, though, and yet, somehow, they all implied a primal fear instilled into every child. These were the demons that parents warned their brood about.

Ling and the preacher's wife cowered, while the pastor bravely held up his bible, yelling words to cast out sin. Without any noticeable movement from the Shinobi, three metal stars embedded in the pastor's good book. Luckily, it was wide and thick enough that none of the stars reached the reverend himself. He dove under a pew and prayed, loudly.

The demons each wore a blade at their side, which struck Turk as odd even on the sketches.

Why does a demon need a sword?

Before he could pose an answer, one of the four demons batted the preacher's wife aside and grabbed Ling. The other three, having seen the new arrivals, turned and made motions with their hands. Turk pushed Patrick down just as several metal stars embedded in the wall behind where they'd just been.

Using the pew for cover, Turk and Patrick sat up and began shooting—the blast of their guns deafening in the normally tranquil room. Each shooter tracked a different Shinobi, but the demons moved so fast neither man hit what they aimed at.

The Shinobi drew their swords and leapt pew over pew towards the place Turk and Patrick had made their stand.

Suddenly, more voices came from outside. A group of heavily armed citizens of Drowned Horse flooded through the open doors, led by Owner.

Turk growled. "What about that ordinance? You told me I was an exception."

Patrick sheepishly grinned. "It's a cursed town. Think I'm gonna leave these folks unarmed?"

They shot the demon nearest Ling, catching it in the shoulder but not killing it. It let her drop to the floor before turning to see the whole room.

The Shinobi apparently didn't like the odds, and more smoke funnels arose around them to cover their escape.

Sheriff Patrick quickly directed everyone to the Sagebrush. There, tending to the party's superficial wounds, he swore again. "They move too fast. We caught them by surprise this time, but they'll be ready next."

Owner agreed. "If only there was a way to slow them down."

At that moment, Muybridge, who had not been a part of the cavalry charge, shouted from the top steps, "Eureka! I did it! I managed to capture your lightning-fast hands on film, Mr. Turk!"

As everyone looked up at the old photographer in sudden awe, Muybridge squinted down at his gawking audience. "Did I miss something?"

Owner closed the Sagebrush and sent word around. This type of warning was all too common from Owner, and other towns knew that whatever Drowned Horse faced, it was best to stay away if you valued breathing.

The saloon remained as dark as night itself inside. And despite being secured, Turk suspected that whatever magic the demons had would not only get them inside, but allow them to see in the dark. That part of their legend seemed true of every person Patrick interviewed.

"You know what I would do?" Diaz whispered to his partner.

"Let me guess. Create another distraction?"

"Si, Señor Hunt—Turk. Draw everyone outside."

Turk nodded, but then realized they sat in pitch black, so he said, "Yeah, we figured on that. That's why most of the townsfolk are scattered around the town, laying low, while we're the stupid ones inside with Ling."

Ling Chew sat at a table in the middle of the room. All the other tables had been pushed to the sides, and used to barricade the windows and doors. A single candle remained lit in front of her.

Turk respected that, despite being scared, Ling remained defiant. She would see her husband's killers fail at their mission and fall before her. Her chin held high, she waited, as did Turk, Diaz, Patrick, the reverend, Owner, and several of Drowned Horse's finest men.

As is on cue, an alarm sounded outside.

"Fire! The livery's on fire!"

Sheriff Patrick called out in a loud whisper, "Go!"

Several volunteers got up as one and pushed aside the tables blocking the front door. They ran out into the night, as planned, making it appear as if Ling would be left alone, or at least only weakly guarded.

Turk and Diaz moved quickly to push the doors closed and replaced the tables, but before they could, a breeze whooshed by them. Something faster than a falcon had rushed into the Sagebrush. Turk barely had time to turn around as shapes of four demons surrounded their bait.

Ling didn't scream in fear. Instead, she stood and shouted, *"Now!"*

The room burst into full daylight as all of Muybridge's cameras went off at the same time. The Shinobi stumbled backwards, blinded. They threw their hands over their eyes to block what must be the million after-flashes that Turk knew oh so well.

With that, Owner turned up all the gaslamps.

Ling drew a large knife from the back of her dress, and leapt onto the table. Her cry of rage echoed through the saloon as she launched herself into the air, both hands on the hilt and brought it down on the closest demon.

Even stunned and blinded, her Shinobi moved just in time to avoid a death blow.

Ling had cut through its face, though, which ... fell into two pieces!

Behind it, a very stunned Oriental man shot panicked eyes around the room.

Sheriff Patrick called out, "They ain't demons. They're just men!"

The pastor cursed. "Dammit! I blessed all your weapons for nothing?"

Not wanting to waste their element of surprise, Turk shot the closest Shinobi, catching him between the shoulder blades. "They die like men, too. Sanctified bullets or not, padre!"

Patrick grazed the next "demon" in the leg as the assassin tried to escape upstairs. He was finished off by more of Patrick's impromptu deputies, who'd been hiding in the second floor rooms.

Turk spotted motion above him. Muybridge jumped from rafter to rafter, belying his age, replacing powder in each of the camera's flashes.

Two of their number gone, the remaining Shinobi did what Turk thought they would do. They pulled out the pellets that they used for making smoke, and threw them to the ground, creating a large, obscuring cloud.

Ling's muffled cry reached Turk just as she was grabbed by one the demons.

"Ed? Anytime now!"

Muybridge replied, "Ready! Go!"

As they had before, each of Patrick's men prepared for the flash by covering their eyes. Turk and Patrick, however, waited with wide open. When the multitude of flashes went off, they could clearly see the silhouettes of all three people in the smoke. Lawman and hunter both fired taking the two taller shapes down

When the smoke cleared, Ling knelt in the center of the room, stabbing the lifeless corpses of her husband's murderers, inflicting curses on them that Diaz wouldn't translate even if he spoke the language.

In the end, Ling Chew decided to go back to her homeland and fight beside her brother and father in the coming war. She promised she would bring the curse of Drowned Horse with her when she did. At least ... in spirit.

Before collecting his equipment, Muybridge agreed to accompany her to California and make sure she got on her ship safely.

"I want to leave my small zoopraxiscope with you," he told Owner. Muybridge had debuted the images of Turk dealing cards to a packed house. "A gift, for giving me the adventure of a lifetime. Plus, I still have all the pictures I took of the fight with the Shinobi on my undeveloped plates. Not sure how that's going to look as a moving picture, but it will be interesting to see."

Diaz agreed. "To think that maybe you captured enough of the battle to show it all over again. It *is* magic."

Turk patted his partner on the shoulder. "Don't get ahead of yourself. The idea of recreating a gunfight in moving pictures? Well, that's even more magic than this town could handle."

Diaz sighed. "Sí. You are probably right, Señor Turk."

Turk noticed that Diaz had lost the "Señor Hunter" thing, as if the town wasn't just about curses, but also cures.

As Muybridge and Ling left by coach, Patrick and Owner stood on either side of Hal Turk, former bounty hunter and would-be casino boss.

"So, you gonna stay now that you've had a taste of the curse?" Owner asked.

"They weren't no real demons, were they? Does it still count as the curse?"

Patrick reached into a pocket on his belt and drew out a freshly rolled cigarette. Turk obliged him by lighting it. "Maybe not this time. But a good man died by strange and unusual circumstances, and that means evil won another hand."

Diaz finished waving at the departing carriage and asked, "So it will get worse, Señor Patrick, sir?"

The lawman nodded. "There's a storm coming, gentlemen. That's why I asked Owner here to find me a warrior tougher than the darkest night. And he did what he always does. He found me someone." Patrick took in Turk with a steel gaze. "Did he find the right man?"

Turk thought about it. He spat on the ground and answered the question he'd been asking himself for going on three years.

"Yeah, he did. I think I could grow to like it here. Feels like there's a job to do, and I just might enjoy doing it."

And with that, Hal Turk finally found someplace to call home.

David Boop is an author, screenwriter, and award-winning essayist. He has worked as a DJ, film critic, journalist, and actor. His debut novel, sci-fi/noir *She Murdered Me with Science*, was published by WordFire Press.

David edited the bestselling weird western anthology, *Straight Outta Tombstone* (Baen Books), followed by *Straight Outta Deadwood* and *Straight Outta Dodge City*.

David's many short stories include his weird western series *The Drowned Horse Chronicle* (of which this anthology story is part). He also writes a flash fiction mystery series, *The Trace Walker Temporary Mysteries* on Gumshoereview.com. He has gotten to play in the worlds of *Predator*, *The Green Hornet*, *Flash Gordon*, and *Veronica Mars*. His hobbies include film noir, animé, and Mayan history. Davidboop.com.

WHEN THE SHIFT HITS THE FAN

JULIE FROST

WHEN THE SHIFT HITS THE FAN

Y ou want me to do what now?"
I planted my fists on my hips and stared up at the director in consternation. He'd invited me into his trailer for a private meeting before the day's filming, but I hadn't expected, well, this. We hadn't even sat down yet when he sprung the suggestion on me.

"Shift on camera," Munroe said.

Nope nope nope. Hit the brakes, flip a one-eighty, and get *off* the road to Crazytown.

He raised a conciliatory hand. "Please, Janni, have a seat and hear me out. Drink?"

"Sounds like I'll need one for this conversation." I pushed a drift of scribbled-on script aside and sank onto the couch, which was softer than it had a right to be. My heart beat a trapped-bird tattoo against my ribcage, and I glanced at the clock. Early, but werewolf constitution meant alcohol meant the rules of gentility were more like guidelines. "Comfort and Coke, if you have it?"

"Coming right up." He mixed a generous one from a well-stocked bar, and I wasn't sure if that put me more or less at ease. After pouring himself a scotch, he sat across from me in a chair and tilted his head earnestly, resting his elbows on his knees and leaning forward. "Look, Janni, the accidents on set have wreaked havoc on our budget. If I can shave a few bucks off by saving on CGI in post, that's all to the good. Plus it'll look more authentic."

I sipped my drink, when I actually wanted to gulp it down. "And that will out me as a werewolf to literally everyone present. I told you, and you alone, because of moon scheduling, Kev, and I hope to God you didn't tell anyone else. But this isn't something we do in public unless, you'll pardon me, a situation has gone completely to shit."

Half his scotch disappeared down his throat. "Well, it hasn't gone *completely* to shit. But I'm in a tight spot right now, and it's getting tighter. These accidents are killing us."

The movie's plot was "rookie werewolf cop whose training officer doesn't know she's a werewolf." The lead actor—who was a household name—was carrying the thing nearly singlehanded. He was a renowned action star and a genuinely nice guy, signing on because Munroe was an up-and-coming friend.

But the production was getting a reputation as a bad-luck show. The accidents had started small: Munroe's chair breaking under him the first time he sat in it, a mix-up in on the call sheet that meant necessary cast and crew for a scene were nowhere to be found because they thought they had the day off, a distinctive classic car—a cherry-red 1970 Boss Mustang that the star's character drove—that wouldn't start, sending us scrambling for a spare while the mechanics hired suddenly by the Unit Production Manager scratched their heads. Minor events, so far, but movie people were a superstitious bunch, and we were all waiting for something truly awful to happen.

I wasn't sure if the definition of "something truly awful" included shifting on camera, but it was on a list of things I'd never expected to be asked to do. It was almost like a nude scene—something spelled out in the contract beforehand, not sprung on me in the middle of shooting.

"I'm gonna have to run it by some people, Kev, and think about it on my own account even if they say it'll be okay. My husband, my alpha, and the Protectorate will all have input. This isn't a trivial thing you've asked of me. Even if I say yes, it'll have to be a closed set with minimal crew."

"Let me know soon. We're shooting that scene in less than a week."

I drained my drink.

It wasn't like me to show up on set with booze on my breath, and the lead looked down at me with worry creasing his brow. "Everything all right?" he asked. He was over a foot taller than me, and nearly three decades older—though like most leading men, he wore it well, with a full head of floppy dark hair and a distinctive salt-and-pepper scruff. Brown eyes under bushy brows regarded me kindly. We'd taken to calling him "Temp" as a good-natured joke, since someone had suggested early in his career that he change his name, and "Templeton" was one he suggested. It was roundly rejected, and now no one could imagine him with another name.

"Munroe threw me for a loop this morning is all. He offered me a drink and I took it after he asked me to—" I paused, considering how to phrase it. "Do something I'm not sure I'm entirely comfortable with."

Temp's brow creased further. "Do I need to have a talk with him?" He'd do it, too. "It's not that scene we axed when we decided to keep it PG-13, is it?"

"Oh, no, not that, at all." I smiled at him. "I'm gonna run the notion past a few people and sleep on it."

"Okay," he said slowly. "But I'll talk to him if you want."

"I'll let you know. Thanks for being a gentleman, Temp. We don't always get that in this business."

"Go to one, everybody!" Munroe had shown up. Today's scene was an extensive foot chase in which my character outran her training officer and tackled the perp on her own, much to the training officer's surprise and consternation, filmed with drones so we could do it in one continuous shot.

The initial confrontation with our perp worked as scripted, and Taylor, the actor, bolted down an alleyway after leaving Temp pretend-wheezing on the street. My rookie character froze for a bare second, and then took off after him, with the training officer shouting after her uselessly. But I knew this reaction down in my bones—prey ran away, and I wasn't really acting, except inasmuch as I held back my native speed for the sake of the scene.

Taylor used a conveniently placed dumpster to propel himself onto a fire escape, leaping it with the agility of a monkey. But I was hot on his heels, and he improvised a kick that grazed my cheekbone and snapped my head back. Eyes wide with shock, Taylor stopped dead. "Are you okay?" he asked.

"Run, sugar," I answered, all business. They'd fix it in post.

"Keep rolling!" Munroe shouted, and we resumed.

My character caught the perp on the roof and subdued him after a brief fight that he surprised himself by losing. But he hadn't taken were-wolf strength, speed, and agility into consideration, and the rookie had him down and cuffed before he quite knew what hit him. "How the hell are you so strong?" he protested. "You're tiny!"

"I work out." As my character, I hollered into my cop shoulder mic for my training officer, who showed up a few moments later, panting and pissed off.

We reset the scene to get everyone in place. Munroe pulled me aside to ask if I was all right, and I brushed him off. "Wolf healing. It's realistic, leave it."

"It's your face. Roll," Munroe said.

The training officer got down into the rookie's face. "That was rash as hell, Diggs. You could have been killed."

"I caught him, didn't I?" she shot back.

"You're bleeding," he pointed out, which wasn't in the script, and sure enough, there was a trickle from the already-healing scrape the perp's boot had left on my cheek.

"So is he." Taylor wasn't, but a few well-placed squibs had done their job. We were off the reservation, but it was good, natural dialogue and probably wouldn't end up on the cutting room floor.

"We'll discuss it further back at the station." And now we were on script again as he jerked the perp to his feet.

"Cut," Munroe called. "Great work, guys. Meet back downstairs."

Someone uncuffed Taylor, and he came over to me. "Janni, I am so sorry," he said. "I didn't mean to connect with your face like that."

"Don't worry about it," I said. Make-up wouldn't even need to put the scrape back on my cheek for subsequent scenes—I'd wear a band-aid, on set and off, and that would cover it. Maybe we could write it into the script as a clue that my character healed fast. Yet another accident. We were racking them up pretty good.

"You should have the nurse look at that," Temp said. "It's pretty nasty."

"My husband's a private eye. He says face wounds bleed a lot. It looks worse than it is." I shrugged. "But I'll go see her right now if it'll make you feel better."

"You're a trooper, Janni." Temp gave me that famous smile. I'd thought I was immune to it, but ... not so much. My stomach did a funny little flip-flop. However, I was a married werewolf who mated for life, and he was still broken by a relationship that had ended in the worst possible way, so I smiled back at him and headed toward the medical trailer.

... Until I was out of his sight, and then I turned toward my own trailer instead. I scowled at my face in the mirror, wet a washcloth, and cleaned the blood away. The cut was already healed, leaving a livid pink scar against my dark skin that would disappear in less than half an hour. What a pain in my ass. I stuck a band-aid over it as a nod to appearances, fluffed a hand through my wild mop of curly black hair, and decided to hunt down some lunch.

Upon exiting the trailer, I nearly crashed into the new gaffer, who had replaced the old one when he quit "over these bad-luck shenanigans." Jay Barnson stood at the bottom of the steps, left hand upraised to knock, right hand in his pocket, with an expression that was anything but pleasant.

I took an abrupt step backward, nostrils flaring. He smelled of wild that was all human—along with silver and wolfsbane.

Hunter.

I kept claws from sprouting by an act of sheer will, but my vision sharpened, telling me that my eyes had gone amber. Crap.

"Something I can help you with?" My voice came out in a strangled growl.

The look on his face changed from hostility to puzzlement like a switch had been thrown. "Miz Lockwood?" He had a soft southern accent. I didn't expect that.

"That's what it says on the door," I said tartly, forcing my eyes back to their normal brown.

"Oh, I—hell, I didn't even look at that," he confessed. "Tunnel vision, I reckon."

I crossed my arms. "What in the world are you on about, sugar?"

"I tracked a werewolf here," he said, like that explained any-damn-thing.

"Clearly, you found one." I lifted an eyebrow. "Now what." It wasn't inflected like a question. "Because I'm not advertising, and you'll excuse me if 'tracked' sounds more like 'hunted down to put a hurt on.' I can smell what you are."

His lips compressed. "Is there another wolf on the set?"

"Probably," I admitted. I didn't know for sure, but the chances were good. "Like hell am I gonna aim you at any of them."

"You should. This string of accidents you're bein' plagued with isn't accidental."

"Oh, honey, please. You and I both know Taylor didn't kick me in the face on purpose."

"Maybe not that one. Nice band-aid, by the way. But there's a wolf on this set playin' merry hell, and I aim to hunt him down and put a stop to his bush-wah." Barnson's eyes narrowed at me. "Unless it's a 'her' I'm looking for."

I snorted. "This is a breakout role for me. Sabotaging this show would be stupid. Do I look stupid to you, sugar?"

"No, ma'am, I suppose you don't," he allowed.

"Good. Glad we got that straightened out." I took a breath. "That being said, if you've got evidence that some wolf's wrecking stuff on purpose, bring it to me and I'll help you find him. Meanwhile—" I locked the trailer door behind me and stepped down the stairs, and he moved out of my way, for a wonder. "I need to feed myself and make a phone call, and I'm sure you have lighting to arrange for the next scene."

"You're not wrong." He fell into step beside me. "I hope you don't mind if I keep in touch."

"I suppose. Sabotage isn't good for anyone, and now I'm interested. The producers know what you're doing?"

"They hired me," he said.

Official sanction. That made me sit up and take more notice. He wasn't haring off on his own—someone high up thought there was something to it.

"Well, then. I'll see you around, and let you know if I notice anything or anyone suspicious."

We separated at a junction, him heading off to do gaffer stuff and me looking for craft services. I pulled out my phone and called Megan while I walked.

She sounded harried, but that was a given, considering who she was married to. "Hi, Janni, what's up?"

"Munroe wants me to shift on camera."

A pause. "What."

"Yeah, that was kind of my reaction. I told him I'd have to run it past a few people, and you were first on my list."

"This isn't something we should talk about over the phone. And I'm thinking maybe Claire Wellington should be there too. Have you asked Ben what he thinks?"

"Not yet. Like I say, you were first on my list. You know he'd just say 'whatever makes you happy, honey,' leave it up to me, and back my play if he needed to." My husband was awesome that way. Claire Wellington, on the other hand, was an agent with the Protectorate—supernatural law enforcement—and might get stuffy about it. They'd surely want input, and would probably fall on the side of "absolutely not." But I wasn't sure they were the boss of me, so I'd take their advice and warnings into consideration before I decided—and then maybe do it anyway. It depended on the consequences.

"Text me your schedule, and I'll work around it in the next day or so." Megan was the personal assistant to our own private mad scientist, who worked a manic schedule and played harder than he worked. It kept her on the jump, but she apparently thrived on it, since she'd married him not long ago.

"Sooner is better. That scene is coming up in less than a week. Tonight would be ideal, honestly."

"I'll get with Claire and let you know."

"Super. Thanks, Megan." I texted her the information and signed off.

Craft services had laid out a sumptuous lunch spread. Huge meaty sandwiches and fresh green salad greeted me as I followed my nose to the table and filled up a plate. After finding a seat, I settled in for some serious snarfing.

Munroe sat down next to me with his own laden dish. "Sorry about Barnson. They just told me. How's your face?"

"Already healed. Make-up can have fun with it, if they even have to," I said after swallowing a mouthful of turkey and roast beef. "I don't like getting accused of sabotaging the production, Kev. But Barnson and I came to an understanding, and I've got wheels turning for a meeting that'll help me decide if I'm gonna do that thing for you."

"Do you need permission?" he asked.

"Not as such." I stabbed a forkful of salad. "But I'd like some advice from people who've been doing this longer than I have and know the ramifications better. I've been given to understand that torches and pitchforks weren't so long ago, and we'd all like to avoid a repeat, I'm sure."

My phone chirped, and I glanced at it. "Okay, meeting tonight at seven-thirty." He opened his mouth, and I pointed at him with my fork. "No, you are not invited."

I found time to call Ben, and his answer was exactly as I'd predicted. He had a surveillance job, so he couldn't join us at the restaurant. I slid into the booth beside Megan and across from Claire.

Megan was tall, blonde, and willowy, while Claire was a no-nonsense brunette of average height. We were all werewolves with corresponding appetites, and the steak house was a place we'd picked because it was quiet and didn't overload our sensitive ears. Also, it smelled good. I'd walked out of more than one eatery because my nose told me the food would be terrible.

"So," I said after we exchanged pleasantries and ordered dinner. "The director of this movie has asked me to shift on camera because of budget constraints. I'm not real comfortable with the notion, myself, but I wanted to run it past you two. I could be talked into it."

"We stay hidden for several very good reasons," Claire said. "A movie budget is not worth outing us, and your director is a jerk for even asking."

"Would it be outing us, though?" Megan asked. "The audience will just put it down to special effects."

"How many crew have to be there to see you do it?" Claire countered. "Ten? Twenty? The more there are, the more likely it is someone will blab. Probably several someones."

"Munroe already knows. So does Barnson, the gaffer, because the producers think there's werewolf causing trouble on the set and hired him as a hunter." I glared at my soda. "He was a nasty surprise. Ben's last encounter with a hunter didn't go so hot."

Claire looked at me sharply. "What happened with Ben?"

My chin lifted. "The hunter was after a couple of rogues, there was some collateral damage, the hunter tried to murder Ben. And Ben took him out first." I gave her a look that had sent a billionaire mad genius scurrying for cover. More than once. "Is there an issue?"

Claire grumped into her daiquiri. "Since we never found out about it, seems the tracks got properly covered. So I suppose not."

"Good. I like to think that self-defense is something even a big bad wolf gets."

"It is, most of the time. But, Janni, I still don't like the idea of you shifting on camera. It's one thing for your director and a hunter to know— they need to. The guy who brings the coffee manifestly does not."

"This role is a huge step up for me, Claire, and I don't want to botch it. I'll talk to Munroe and find out exactly how many people need to be there for that scene. We'll go from there?"

"We'll go from there," Claire said. But she still looked grouchy about it.

Running feet accompanied by shouting and sirens woke me up the next morning. I stuck my head out of my trailer to see everyone racing in the direction of the set. I slipped on a pair of shoes and joined them, still clad in my penguin-patterned flannel pajamas.

Barnson stalked furiously up and down, not quite shouting into his phone. "Yes, it was sabotage! You think I don't know my job and what it looks like when someone's deliberately tampered with the lighting on a set? And now Andrea's hurt. I think her foot's broken."

Our best boy, who assisted the gaffer, was actually a girl, and I inhaled and grabbed a passerby. "What happened?"

"One of the lights fell off the ceiling and hit Andrea. Someone yelled a warning and she barely dodged in time for it to miss her head."

No wonder Barnson was so hot under the collar. The lights were his responsibility, and someone had screwed around with them. Not cool. He spotted me and stormed over.

"I need your nose," he said without preamble. "I want to know every damn wolf on this set, right now."

I crossed my arms and glared up at him. "'Damn' wolf? I know you're upset, Barnson, and so am I." Andrea was a perky kid in her very early twenties, cheerful and enthusiastic about her job. Everyone liked her. "But you'd better check yourself."

He scrubbed a hand over his face and took a deep breath, blowing it out slowly and nodding. "Sorry. I'm sorry. You're right."

"We don't even know for sure that it's a wolf causing the accidents." I looked down at the cartoon penguins on my pajamas. "And I should put some clothes on before I go sniffing around."

"Do that. I'll wait here for you."

I wasn't scheduled to film until the afternoon, so that gave me a little time to help Barnson find the other wolves. After taking a quick shower, I threw on some shorts and a T-shirt and met Barnson at the site of the accident. No one had touched the light, and I knelt beside it and let my nose go to work. A few seconds later, I sat back on my heels, frustrated.

"Whoever it was used heavy leather gloves. I can't get a human or a wolf scent through that." I stood up. "What about your crystal thing?" Hunters had a detector that worked via a hunk of moonstone on a string.

"It keeps pointin' at the nearest werewolf," Barnson said sourly. "That'd be you right now."

"Maybe we should split up, then. Call if we find anything."

"You take the north side, I'll take the south." He stalked away, shoulders stiff. I hoped he wouldn't cause me any problems. We had enough of those.

Any wolves were keeping themselves to themselves, and I had no luck finding one other than an errant whiff that disappeared nearly as soon as I caught it. Munroe caught up to me next to the craft table, during a break in filming while they reset the sound stage. "Have you thought any more about shifting on camera?" he asked.

"Trust me, other than the sabotage on the set, that's all I'm thinking about." I sipped from a cup of fresh coffee. "The Protectorate doesn't like the idea, and neither does my alpha. I'm not seeing the upside, Kev."

"I might be able to finagle a bonus for you. I'd still be saving a ton on the budget, even with that."

"It's not about the money. It's about my privacy, and the repercussions if we suddenly get outed to God and everyone." My lips compressed. "How many crew would need to be there when I did that? How are you going to break it to all of them beforehand? People tend to freak if you throw a sudden werewolf in their faces. And how would you make sure they kept their mouths shut afterward?"

"Nondisclosure agreements. I've been asking around, discreetly. There's a few on the crew who already know about werewolves, though not you in particular." That was worrying, but not surprising. Werewolves weren't thick on the ground, but in a close-knit community like this, secrets were hard to keep. "We'll use them for the essentials and close the set to everyone else, just like you wanted. That leaves your two costars."

I raised a skeptical eyebrow. "Sure. Those guys will just take it in stride."

"Maybe. This place isn't called Hollyweird for nothing, right?" He snagged a chocolate donut with sprinkles. "You'd be doing me a solid on this, Janni."

"I'm still thinking about it. It's not a *definite* no at this point." The coffee was good. This wasn't a given on a movie set. "Let me get used to the idea, Kev."

"Okay." He took a bite of the donut and swallowed before continuing.

"We're filming that gunfight in a little while. Be sure and get a good vantage point. You know how Temp likes to do his own stunts, and he's really good at shootouts." This was an understatement. Temp was famous for researching his parts with live ammo at actual gun ranges.

Ben would be jealous, even if they were shooting blanks. "Wouldn't miss it," I said. My character wasn't in this scene, so I could relax. My own gunfight came later.

Munroe finished his donut and headed back to supervise the set-up of the scene. I snagged a sandwich and followed him a few moments later, and he waved me into a tall chair nearby. This particular shootout took place between my training officer and the bad guy's lieutenant. I hadn't had much contact with that actor, Roberts—he was an older guy, oddly avoidant of me, and a well-known character actor. We hadn't had any scenes together.

"Places," Munroe called. Everyone nodded. The training officer and the lieutenant crouched behind cars on the opposite sides of a city street, and the script called for the lieutenant to die, while the training officer escaped unscathed.

It was a fairly standard shootout scene. The training officer was off duty and not in uniform, and the lieutenant had ambushed him. They exchanged gunfire and verbal barbs across the hoods of the cars—

And then blood sprayed from Temp's bicep and he fell backward with a pained shout.

I exchanged a wild glance with Munroe. "That wasn't a squib," I stated.

"No it was not," he answered, coming off his chair with wide eyes.

My head swiveled nearly of its own accord to spear Roberts with my gaze, and I leaped from my seat hard enough to send it flying backward. The set armorer never allowed live ammo anywhere near his precious guns, and yet somehow a real round had ended up there anyway. Only one person could have done that, and I was looking right at him with eyes that had gone amber.

Purely on instinct, I ran toward Roberts. From the other side of the set, Barnson did the same.

Roberts dropped his gun and booked it, maneuvering around café tables and other obstacles on the set's sidewalk, pulling them into my path. But I was more wolf than woman at that point and hurdled them with contemptuous ease. He burst out of the set and into the back lot, and I chased him around golf carts, craft tables, crew, and rolling props, more and more furious with him and the entire situation.

I didn't even realize I was half-wolfed until I tore out of my clothes and completely shifted, tripling my mass while still running. The shift was practically instantaneous, smooth as a stream flowing downhill and just as painless, though stretchy and weird until you got used to the sensation. And then the chase was truly joined. Roberts glanced over his shoulder, let out a yelp, and put on a burst of speed that did him no good whatsoever. He didn't shift; maybe he had better control than I did.

He skidded around a corner with me hot on his heels—and bounced off Barnson. I landed in the middle of Roberts's back and smashed him to the ground, with my teeth fastened into the back of his neck, growling like a chainsaw.

If I crunched down, he'd be finished, and he froze under me. "Okay, okay, I give up, don't—" He choked and swallowed hard.

I was fortunate. Most male werewolves had a visceral aversion to hurting women, and I used that to full advantage, pressing a paw into his back and holding him down. I rolled my eyes to look up at Barnson.

His silver-loaded gun pointed at *my* head. I spat Roberts out and shifted back to human, naked, glaring up at him.

"Are you serious?"

Barnson blinked, looked sheepish, and aimed the gun toward Roberts instead. "My apologies, Miz Lockwood." So maybe all hunters weren't jerks after all.

I bitchslapped Roberts on the back of his head. "What the hell is the matter with you?" Not quite shouting, but ... emphatic.

"Your part was written for a man," he said, sulking like a child instead of a grown-ass adult. "I should've gotten it, not this bone they tossed me instead."

"I got this part because I nailed the audition, asshole." He wasn't wrong about it being written for a man, but it wasn't the first time I'd gotten a role not written with a woman in mind. Hopefully it wouldn't be the last. "So you decided to sabotage the production, and then to put a *cap* on it, you thought *shooting Temp* was a good *idea?*" I was emphasizing words and should probably stop. Maybe I'd picked that habit up from my husband. "You could have *killed* him! Are you out of your tiny *mind?*"

"Janni," Barnson said. "The Protectorate will deal with him."

"Oh, yes they will." I shoved myself to my feet, not being either gentle or particular about where my knees pressed into his spine. "Get him out of my sight, Barnson."

We'd drawn rubberneckers by that point. A giant wolf chasing a guy through the film lot wasn't something we saw every day. I lifted my chin and stared everyone down in a challenge, and most of them dropped their eyes.

"Someone wanna get me a robe or a blanket or something?"

"I guess the wolf's out of the bag now, at least as far as anyone who was there is concerned," I said. Claire and Megan had met me at the steak house again. I stabbed a piece of medium-rare meat with more emphasis than I needed to. "So that's awesome."

"Is Temp all right?" Great, now Megan was calling him that.

"Fortunately, only a flesh wound. But that could have gone way south. Roberts is an idiot."

"I suppose shifting on camera is a moot point now," Claire said. She didn't look happy about it. Honestly, I wasn't either, but plenty of the people who'd seen me shift to wolf hadn't believed their own eyes, and no one but Barnson and Roberts had seen me shift back. Small mercies.

"The extra money will come in handy, and I might as well. If I have to. I guess."

"You don't have to," Megan said, taking my hand. She still hadn't come completely to terms with her own lycanthropy, and held a lively horror of wolfing in front of strangers. "You don't, Janni, and if he's putting unwanted pressure on you, Alex can have a word with the producers." Alex didn't throw his billionaire weight around very often, but was singularly effective when he did.

My voice grew thoughtful. "No, you know what, it's okay. It's fine. I can do this." It would be a hell of a thing to put on my résumé, anyway.

"Are you sure?"

The steak had disappeared without me noticing. I smiled. "As sure as I want dessert."

"Ready?" Munroe asked.

"As long as someone's got a robe handy." I rubbed my arms nervously. "I didn't sign up for nude scenes."

"Yep. Okay, then. Places."

Temp and I hit our marks, and when the call for action sounded, we started a foot chase after the lead villain. The training officer was soon huffing—we'd written his injury into the script, and he wasn't faking all of it—and my character glanced back at him, glanced at the bad guy ...

And shifted in mid-run. I heard a soft "whoa" from Temp that wasn't in the script.

I'd only taken a couple of strides before I heard "Cut!" We all stopped in confusion, and someone settled a robe across my shoulders. I shifted back to human and pulled it around me while Munroe came trotting up with a hangdog expression.

"Is that all it is?" he asked, clearly disappointed.

"Yeah, Kev," I said. "It's not like in the movies. It doesn't even hurt."

"Oh." Munroe pinched his nose. "I thought it would be more ... dramatic. Than that." He scrubbed a hand over his face. "Well. I guess we gotta go CGI and rubber masks after all. Emote for me, would you, Janni? Reset!"

Julie Frost is an award-winning author of every shade of speculative fiction. She lives in Utah with her family—a herd of guinea pigs, her husband, and a "kitten" who thinks she's a warrior princess—and a collection of anteaters and Oaxacan carvings, some of which intersect. She enjoys birding and nature photography, which also intersect. Her short fiction has appeared in *Straight Outta Dodge City*, *Monster Hunter Files*, *Tales of Ruma*, *Writers of the Future*, *The District of Wonders*, *StoryHack*, and many other venues. Her novel series, Pack Dynamics, is published by WordFire Press. She whines about writing, a lot, at agilebrit.livejournal.com.

HYDE PARK

SHANNON FOX

HYDE PARK

Cassian drummed his fingers against the steering wheel of his car as he waited for the gate that blocked his long private driveway to fully slide back. When the way was clear, he pressed his foot against the accelerator, and the Ferrari F430 shot forward with a growl.

Dusk was falling, and as he crested the top of the driveway, the sun had already slipped below the horizon, its light painting the ocean below in a wash of red and pink hues.

After parking his car in the garage, Cassian hurried up the short flight of steps to the house's main level. His footsteps echoed through the front hall as he strode towards the kitchen. When he had first toured this house with his mother, she had described it as "cold." Even the jaw-dropping ocean views hadn't been enough to soften her distaste for all the concrete and glass. But to Cassian, it was perfect. The sterile surfaces and hard edges lent a particularly masculine energy to a house that had been specifically crafted to take advantage of the incredible panoramic views.

In the kitchen, Cassian poured himself a finger of whiskey and took a sip before walking down the hall to his bedroom. His guest would be arriving soon.

The sun had fully set by the time Cassian entered the master suite. He stood at the floor-to-ceiling glass windows, drinking whiskey and watching the last of the light drain away as night descended.

"Cassian," a voice rasped.

He didn't turn. He knew who was in the room with him and didn't care to look upon his face.

"The new film premieres tomorrow night," Cassian said, swirling his glass. "At the El Capitan. They're calling it the blockbuster of the summer. I think the studio will green light the next film by week's end."

"You should be proud," the visitor said.

"I am." And he was. The miniseries he'd pitched and produced just six years ago, *Hyde Park,* initially attracted a small but mighty following that soon exploded as more and more people began tuning in. Now it had become a cultural phenomenon that had spawned two feature-length films, the second of which debuted tomorrow night.

"You don't sound like it."

"You still haven't told me what you want in exchange for your help on the next film. I assume that's why you're here tonight."

His guest chuckled, a sound that never failed to make Cassian's stomach twist in fear.

"The woman," the visitor said.

Cassian felt ice enter his veins. "What woman?" he asked, though he had a feeling he already knew.

"The blonde. Veronica."

The room tilted, and for a moment Cassian wondered if the big earthquake they'd all feared had finally struck Los Angeles. But when he placed a hand against the window to steady himself and took a deep breath, the room snapped back to normal. Cassian closed his eyes.

"No," he said. "Not her."

"You asked me what I want."

"But you can't have her," Cassian said, putting as much force as he could muster into the words. "She's not like the other ones. She'll be missed. Someone will come looking for her, and when they discover what you've done ... no, it can't be her."

"The price is the price," the visitor said.

Cassian opened his eyes and stared out into the inky darkness. "She's the star of my new film. Not an addict or a streetwalker. If I bring her here, or anywhere really, someone will remember seeing her leave with me. And when her body is found ... it just can't be done. I won't be able to get away with it."

"We have an agreement, and the agreement must be fulfilled. What happens to you after that is not my concern. This city is full of thousands of young men just like you, who would do anything for success, to have what you have. I can find another." The visitor chuckled. "I don't think you can say the same. Unless you've found a way to create your films without my help?"

Cassian swallowed hard. He'd tried with this last film. He really had. But without the inspiration the visitor provided him, without watching him hunt and kill ... Cassian's writing felt hollow. Stilted. Unremarkable. He doubted anything had changed in the intervening time.

"Bring her here after the premiere," the visitor commanded.

"Tomorrow?" Cassian's voice sounded strangled to his own ears. "It hardly gives me time to plan."

"That is not my concern. If you wish to have my help in the future, you will bring her here tomorrow night. But if you want to return to the man you were when I found you, you need only say so."

Having witnessed the viciousness with which the visitor killed, Cassian doubted he would let him walk away from their agreement so easily.

Cassian brought the glass up to his lips and drained the last of the whiskey, allowing the taste of it to flood his senses as his thoughts spun out into the abyss of his future. Even if the visitor somehow let him live, his life as he knew it was over. He was utterly incapable of creating at the same level without the source material the visitor provided. He could try, he supposed, but he knew he'd gone too far down this road, dug himself in too deep. The studio, his crew, the actors, they would notice something was amiss. Would wonder where Cassian Charles, the genius writer-director, the wunderkind of Hollywood, had disappeared. Would wonder who this hack was that had taken his place.

He lowered the glass and leaned his forehead against the window. If he wanted his career, his life, to continue, then he only had the one choice.

"I've never been up this way before," Veronica Zeismer said, from the passenger seat of his car.

Cassian tightened his hands on the steering wheel and stole a quick glance across the car at her. Veronica's gaze was focused on the landscape outside as the Ferrari hurtled past towering gates and dense foliage cloaked in darkness. She was no doubt trying to catch a glimpse of the homes that lined one of the most exclusive streets in Pacific Palisades.

"Not many people live up here," Cassian said. "It's what attracted me to this area."

Out of the corner of his eye, he saw Veronica smooth the fabric of her dress. He reached across the car to place a hand on her knee. He could barely bring himself to touch her, knowing what was going to happen as soon as they got to the house. But Veronica was smart, at least as far as beautiful young actresses went. When he'd asked her to come back to his house after the premiere, he was sure she'd formed an idea of what was really behind the invitation. Indeed, she didn't stiffen or pull away from his touch, but placed her hand over the top of his and gave it a soft squeeze.

Her skin felt warm, the flesh of her palm smooth and pliable like a ripe peach. He had a sudden vision of it splitting open under the light pressure of a knife and tried to shove the thought away.

"Are you all right?" she asked. He realized, to his embarrassment, that he must have made a sound.

"I'm fine," he said, shooting her a quick smile. "Just had something in my throat."

Silence hung heavy over the car as they continued to climb toward his house.

"Can I ask you a question?" Veronica asked.

Cassian felt him stomach twist. "Sure."

"I've always been curious how you came up with the idea for *Hyde Park*. I mean serial killers are nothing new. There are plenty of TV shows and movies about that. But the killings are so ... inventive. So detailed. It almost seems like you witnessed it for yourself."

He licked his lips, allowing himself a moment to collect his thoughts. To step fully into the practiced lie he'd constructed for just this purpose. "History is full of stories of serial killers and their crimes. It wasn't hard to repurpose some of the details. But to answer your question, I've always been fascinated with the story of Jack the Ripper. I've read lots of different theories about the murders and who was behind them. So one day I started to wonder what it would be like if modern-day Los Angeles had its own Ripper. And the story kind of evolved from there."

"That's why the Hyde Park killer's victims are all prostitutes and drug addicts," Veronica said. She nodded as if suddenly connecting the dots. But Cassian knew she was only flattering him. He'd told her nothing that he hadn't already repeated on every late-night talk show over the past six years. "You were copying the profile of the Ripper's victims."

"Exactly," he said. That, and it was the kind of prey he'd been told to go after.

132

"How fascinating," she replied. "So who do you think the Ripper really was?"

Cassian glanced at her. "You really want to talk about this?"

"I told you in my audition that I have a healthy interest in the macabre." Her tone was light, teasing. "I wasn't kidding about that."

The car shot around a bend in the road, and suddenly they were at the foot of Cassian's long driveway. He hit the brakes a bit too hard, and Veronica let out a yelp as the seatbelt no doubt contracted tightly across her chest, as his own had done.

"Sorry about that," he said. "The entrance still kind of sneaks up on me."

Veronica let out a weak laugh as they waited for the gate to roll back. The car's headlights illuminated part of the driveway beyond, but were no match for the thick tangle of bushes and trees that lined the road up to the house. Cassian might have found it spooky if he didn't already know what the night had in store for them.

Veronica cleared her throat as Cassian steered the car up the driveway. "You didn't answer my question," she said. "About who you thought was behind the Ripper killings."

"There was a man who drowned in the Thames. His body was found not too long after the last murder. Even though there was little to connect him to the killings while he was alive, it always made sense to me. That as monstrous as the murders were, there was still just a man behind them. It doesn't seem that far of a stretch to imagine that perhaps he grew remorseful and decided to end it."

By Veronica's silence he wondered if she was disappointed in his answer. After all, that wasn't the kind of killer who was behind the murders in *Hyde Park*. That man was utterly evil. Devoid of every last shred of humanity. Perhaps that was the sort of response Veronica had been hoping to hear.

As he pulled up to the house, Veronica let out a gasp.

"This is your house?" she asked.

"Yes," he said, his hand already on the handle of the door. Though he too felt a bit awed at the sight of it. He'd forgotten how impressive the house looked when it was all lit up. He usually did not leave the lights on while he was out. But tonight, he'd hoped that in doing so the house would appear welcoming. Inviting. That if he'd managed to make Veronica feel ill at ease on the drive over, it would help cloak his true purpose in bringing her back to the house.

Cassian darted around the front of the car to open the door for her. He watched as she unfolded her lithe body from the car. Veronica had dressed in a figure-hugging red dress for the premiere. Though he was sure the gossip columns might call it plain, he thought she looked stunning.

She lingered for a moment, staring up at the house until Cassian gently pressed a hand to the small of her back.

"Shall we go inside?" he asked.

Lacing her fingers through his, Veronica allowed him to lead her through the front doors and across the foyer. Her heels echoed in the cavernous space.

In the kitchen, he took down two wine glasses from the cabinet and set them on the oversized island. "Red or white?"

She fastened her incredible blue-gray eyes on him as she replied. "White. Red wine gives me a headache."

"Me too," he said. "I was only going to drink it to be polite."

Her lips curled mischievously. "Trust me, you don't have to worry about being polite with me."

Cassian forced himself to chuckle, to give her his most flirtatious smile. "I'll be right back," he said.

He strode down the hallway, past the temperature-controlled wine room, to his bedroom at the end of the hall. He kept his stride even, unhurried, though his heart was hammering in his chest. Only once he was safely inside the bathroom did he allow himself a shaky breath as he sagged against the closed door.

The visitor would be here soon. Somehow Cassian always knew when he was on his way. Which meant he only had to entertain Veronica a little while longer. To pretend that everything was normal.

He caught a glimpse of his reflection in the bathroom mirror. Though he was not yet thirty, dark shadows had taken up permanent residence beneath his eyes. His normally pale skin looked bloodless, even for him. He smiled at his reflection and wondered how he'd convinced Veronica to get in a car with him. He looked as unstable as he felt.

Cassian staggered toward the sink and turned the faucet on. He splashed some cold water on his face, the shock of it jarring his brain to action.

Was he really going to do this again? Was he actually going to allow another woman to die in service to his art? And in his own home no less?

He grabbed a towel off the sink and rubbed his face with it. The answer, he knew, was yes. Because, as the visitor has clearly spelled out for him the night before, he really had no choice.

Cassian gripped the edge of the sink with both hands as he forced himself to take deep breaths. It would all be over soon. Very soon.

On his way back to the kitchen, he stopped and selected a bottle of his favorite white wine. He doubted Veronica would get to drink very much of it, so he might as well choose something he enjoyed.

As he stepped back into the hallway, he heard the sounds of the piano drifting from the great room. A tune he recognized but couldn't quite place. He listened for a moment as the notes tumbled out from beneath Veronica's skilled fingers. He hadn't realized she played.

The wine glasses were on the counter where he'd left them. But Veronica had helped herself to the block of Havarti cheese he kept in the fridge. It, too, was on the counter beside a long, serrated knife.

"I'll pour you a glass," he said, popping the cork on the wine bottle.

"Not too much," she called from the piano.

Cassian ignored her, filling her glass nearly to the top.

The sound of the piano died away, and he heard the scrape of the bench against the concrete as she stood up. Her heels clicked across the floor as she approached.

He looked up and flashed her his most charming smile as he handed over her glass.

She pretended to pout. "I told you not to pour me too much. Now I'll fall asleep on your couch for sure."

He forced himself to chuckle. "Trust me, you falling asleep on my couch was never the plan."

The lights of the kitchen picked up the golden tones of her honey-blond hair as she tilted her head to the side. Her eyes drifted to his lips and then back up again, settling on his eyes.

And despite the sick feeling in his stomach, the sense of dread that had been his constant companion that night, Cassian found himself wanting to kiss her, too.

He took a step toward her and slipped a finger under her chin, lifting her face up towards his. Veronica set her wine glass back on the counter and closed her eyes, surely waiting to feel his lips brush hers.

But all at once, Cassian became aware that they were not alone and dropped his hand. He stepped back from Veronica and looked to the left, already knowing what he would find there.

"I knew you wouldn't be able to walk away from it," the visitor said. "Just like all the others before you."

"Cassian?" Veronica asked. "What's happening?"

He forced himself to look back at her, his cheeks burning with shame.

"I'm sorry," he said.

Her brows knitted together in confusion. "Sorry for what?"

Cassian shook his head, unable to get the words out. It had been easier with the other women. He hadn't known them. So it'd been easy to tell himself that they didn't matter, that the world was better off without them. That their deaths were no great loss.

"Cassian," Veronica said. "Look at me."

Tears pricked his eyes as he stared at the window over her shoulder. He knew he couldn't look at her face. If he did, he wouldn't be able to give her up.

He could hear the visitor already moving toward them. All Cassian had to do was hang on for a few moments more and it would all be over.

Warm fingers suddenly gripped his jaw as Veronica grabbed his face and forced him to look at her.

"Tell me what's happening," she said, her eyes scanning his features, seeking answers that he was unwilling to give.

But as he stared back at her, he felt the last bit of his resolve crumble. He couldn't do this to her. Couldn't stand by and watch her die.

Before he could talk himself out of it, he broke free of her grasp and reached for the knife on the counter.

As he turned to face the visitor, Cassian was gratified to see that he seemed taken aback by the turn of events.

"Think of what you're doing, Cassian," the visitor said. "Think of what you're giving up."

"I have," said Cassian. His voice shook as he answered. "And it was never really mine to begin with. The success, the house, the car ... all of it. I should never have walked down this monstrous path with you. But tonight, it ends."

His hand trembled as he raised the knife above his head. But as he brought it down towards the visitor's heart, the fear fell away and his grip tightened on the weapon. Cassian let out a cry as he drove it in as deep as he could. He was dimly aware of Veronica screaming in the background.

Suddenly exhausted by the effort, Cassian's knees buckled, and he collapsed to the floor. Pain bloomed through his body as he hit the concrete.

Staring up at the lights of the kitchen, he heard Veronica talking to someone. She sounded as if she were deep under water.

"Hello, yes, I'm at the home of Cassian Charles in Pacific Palisades and there's been a stabbing ... he stabbed himself I mean. Please hurry, we need help. There's so much blood ..."

Shannon Fox is a San Diego-based writer whose fiction spans multiple genres. She grew up in the foothills of the Colorado Rockies before relocating to California to attend UC-San Diego, where she earned a B.A. in Literature-Writing. She misses the rugged natural beauty of Colorado, but definitely doesn't miss the insane wind. Her short stories have appeared in *Cursed Collectibles, The Copperfield Review, The Plaid Horse Magazine, Black Fox Literary Magazine, The Fat City Review*, and more. Besides writing, Shannon has a passion for horses and has competed at the international level in the sport of dressage. Shannon also owns a digital marketing company that works primarily with small businesses and real estate agents. For more stories from Shannon, visit her at Shannon-Fox.com.

MAKE ME A STAR

BRENDAN MALLORY

MAKE ME A STAR

The demon Salazar leaned back in his chair and put his hooved feet up on his desk as he leafed through the third script for the day with his long, clawed fingers. It was a standard supernatural action movie—pretty much the only genre he ever got to read anymore. The macho, brooding hero comes across a teenage orphan girl with amnesia and goes into protective-daddy-mode, blah blah blah, turns out she has magic powers, blah blah blah, Mafia bosses trying to open a portal to Hell for some reason, everything explodes, orphan girl dramatically sacrifices herself to save the world, hero goes back to brooding, the end. Salazar sighed and flipped the script closed, then pulled a red pen out of the decorative mug on his desk and scrawled out a couple of notes:

Page 18: The "magic words" you used were gibberish. Please use real Latin incantations. They aren't that hard to Google.

Page 54: A real demon would not "bite someone's head off." We have standards. Maybe decapitate using a bladed weapon.

Page 107: The Mafiosi using his grandma's old crucifix to repel Satan himself is not going to fly. Either use a more powerful religious artifact or excise this scene entirely.

General: Demons don't use swear words like "Jesus" or "Goddamn." Remove any instance where these words appear.

Everything else looks fine. Please fix these issues and resubmit for approval.

Salazar flopped the script unceremoniously onto the "done" pile next to his desk, snuck a glance at his watch, and let out a long, beleaguered sigh. I wasn't even three in the afternoon yet. Two more hours of reading this crap before he could go home for the weekend. He reluctantly slid his hooves off the desk and reached for another script.

"Please," he muttered under his breath. "Please, just this once let it be a rom-com or something—"

Salazar heard the door to his office creak open and immediately jumped to his feet.

"Yes, hello?" he blurted out quickly. Anything to distract him for another couple minutes before he got back reading—he glanced down at the title page—*Zombie Cannibal Strippers from Hell Part IV: The Strippening.* Ugh ...

There was a young woman half-hiding behind his office door, sheepishly peeking out from behind it. She was wearing a beat-up backpack covered in patches with various indie band logos, and barely looked a day over twenty.

"Um, h-h-hello," she stammered. "Is this the studio's Hell Liaison Office?"

Salazar's expression fell. He glared at her for a moment, then silently gestured up towards the large, curved horns sticking out of his forehead. As if the bright red skin wasn't already a giveaway.

"R-right," the woman said, slipping into the office and closing the door softly behind her. "I understand this isn't *really* my job, but I need help with something ... *supernatural*, for lack of a better word, and I didn't really know who else to—"

"Fame or youth?" Salazar said flatly.

The woman stopped and blinked several times. "What?"

"Kid, please. I've been working in Hollywood since before your grandpa was eating solid food. Someone in this town wants a favor from a demon, it's either gonna be fame or youth."

"I don't want either of those things!" the woman said. "Well, I mean, yeah, they'd be *nice*—but that's not what I'm here for!"

"Well, that's good," Salazar muttered, lowering himself back down into his chair. "'Cause I can't do any of that crap."

The woman suddenly turned pale. "You can't?"

"No! Of course not! What do you think I—" Salazar's eyes narrowed. "Do you even know what the Hell Liaison Office does?"

She didn't answer, but her eyes drifted to the side and she bit her lip. Salazar lowered his face into his hand and sighed.

"A lot of low-budget horror movies want to use actual demons in their production in order to save on special effects costs," he grumbled. "Hell is amenable to this, but naturally, we require approval of any and all scripts that are intended for business with us. That's my job. I read three or four awful screenplays a day and determine if there's anything in there that'll piss off Satan. If there isn't, I give the go-ahead to use our services. I'm a bureaucrat, kid." He smiled thinly. "Soul-sucking in its own way, but not how I think you're looking for."

"Oh," the woman said, glancing down at the floor dejectedly. As her posture went slack, it looked like her entire body was beginning to deflate. "Okay ..."

She slowly turned around and started shuffling back towards the office door, but stopped when she heard Salazar clear his throat.

"Uh, hold on a sec, kid," he said, glancing down momentarily at the script he'd have to get back to reading as soon as she left, then back up at her. "Just because I can't help you, doesn't mean I don't know someone who can. Why don't you sit down and tell me what your problem is anyway?"

She suddenly brightened again, just a little. "Oh, okay!" She scurried over to the moth-eaten old armchair adjacent to Salazar's desk. "Well, um, I—"

"Start with a name, kid."

"Oh, right! My name is Andi Springfield, my uncle got me a job as a PA on one of his movies, so this is the first time I've ever worked on an actual film set—"

"Wait," Salazar said. "You mean your uncle is Robert Springfield? The director?"

Andi blushed and sunk down a little into her seat. "Yeah ..."

Salazar rolled his eyes and threw his hands up into the air. "I've been trying to get that guy to return my calls for weeks!" he said. "Do you know how many strings I had to pull to get the exorcism scene in his last flick to work right—ugh, anyway, not your problem. Continue."

Andi gulped. "Um, so, my uncle's been trying to cast his latest movie," she said, "and he's just been holding audition after audition, and he keeps saying none of the guys who come in are right for the lead, none of them have 'the look' he's looking for."

Salazar had one of his elbows propped up on his desk, and was resting his chin in his hand. "Okay," he mumbled.

"But he keeps describing the kind of actor he's looking for," Andi continued. "Someone with Gene Cullen's eyes, he said. But with Alan Fineworth's hair. And Jack Grayson's chin, and Don Garcia's physique, and, well ... the list went on. And I just ... this is my first gig, and I really wanted to do a good job, I really wanted to make my uncle happy ..."

"Okay," Salazar said slowly. "So what happened?"

Andi hesitated for a moment, then reached around, unzipped her backpack, pulled out a pickle jar, and leaned forward to set it on Salazar's desk. There weren't any pickles left in the jar, but it wasn't quite empty. As the contents stopped bobbing and sloshing around, Salazar could make out two milky white orbs floating in the brine.

His gaze abruptly locked onto the girl in front of him. "Andi," he said sharply. "What are those?"

She gulped again, and gave him a nervous smile before softly murmuring, "... Gene Cullen's eyes ..."

Salazar was on his feet, and his hands were flat on his desk as he leaned over and glared down at Andi.

"What did you do, girl?" he hissed as she tried to sink deeper and deeper into her chair. *"What in Creation's name did you do?"*

Andi pulled open the back door on the rented film truck and then stepped aside, gesturing for Salazar to take her place and peek inside. Deep down, he knew he didn't particularly want to, but he'd already followed her out to the parking lot (and it was still an hour and change until he could clock out for the weekend) so there was no point in chickening out now. He took a deep breath, leaned into the back of the truck, and saw ... more or less what he'd been expecting to see. He couldn't decide if that was a good thing or not.

The back of the truck contained a partially constructed human being lying on the type of gurney that one might find in the back of an ambulance. The body was crossed back and forth with lines of thick, black stitching, and the various parts of it had different skin tones. The right arm and right leg looked like they came from the same person, but the left arm didn't match, and the body didn't have a left leg at all yet. The right leg had a foot, but neither of the arms had hands. And the body didn't have a head, which was probably why Andi was still carrying its eyes around in her backpack.

Salazar just stood behind the truck and stared at the body for a couple seconds. Then he turned his head to the side and stared at Andi. Then back at the body. Then back at Andi.

"You did this?" he finally said, pointing weakly at the body.

Andi just nodded.

"All on your own?"

She nodded again.

Salazar went back to staring at the body. He hadn't blinked once since the back door had been opened. "I don't know if I should be horrified or impressed," he finally muttered.

Andi shrugged. "I mean, so far, everything has been constructed from bodies that were already dead," she said. "I've got a couple friends in med school, and one or two who are studying to be coroners. Between them all, I've got a pretty good selection to choose from. Just sneak into a morgue when nobody's looking, hack off the bits that I like. Don't even have to take the whole body." She looked pensive for a moment and stroked her chin. "I've only had to dig up one actual grave so far ..."

"But those eyes," Salazar mumbled, gesturing vaguely towards her backpack. "Gene Cullen is still alive."

Andi blushed.

"Yeaahhh," she said, letting the word out slowly and carefully. "That's why I was putting off the head for last. The rest of the body's not going to be on-screen much, you know, so it's okay for the parts to be a little more generic. Any number of bodybuilders would be able to give him the right physique. But Uncle Robert was *very* specific about whose facial features he wanted, and most of those guys are still alive—"

"Wait," Salazar said. "Does your 'Uncle Robert' know that you're doing this?"

Andi's blush deepened, until she was almost the same color as Salazar.

"I wanted to surprise him," she said quietly.

"Crap," Salazar muttered. "I was hoping I could blackmail the bastard." He shook his head. "Anyway, you were saying?"

"Oh. Well, um, I was still a little queasy about, you know, taking parts from *living* people, but then Gene Cullen came to do a cameo in the movie I was PAing for, and I knew this was probably the only chance I'd get, so I snuck back to his trailer after the shoot, and, um ..."

"... gouged his eyes out," Salazar murmured, still staring at the body. Then, abruptly, his gaze turned to her again. "How did you do that, anyway? It looked like you got 'em out real cleanly, without any damage."

She met his gaze and stared back at him, dead serious. "I am very good with a spork."

"Right ..." Salazar muttered, taking a subtle half step back from her. "So what's the game plan now that you're walking around with Gene Cullen's peepers sloshing around in your backpack?"

Andi shrugged again.

"Work on getting the rest of the head," she said. "And hope I can finish before Gene Cullen notices."

"Before he notices that *his eyes are missing?*"

"He was *very* drunk the last time I saw him," Andi muttered.

For an eternal couple of seconds, neither of them spoke. Salazar took in a long, deep breath through his nose, and let it out slowly through his mouth.

"Okay," he finally said. "So you've gotten yourself into a mess of trouble that could come back to bite you in the ass in ... any number of ways, honestly. What is it, exactly, that you need demon help for? Are you in too deep and trying to get out of this, or do you need help collecting the last couple body parts, or what?"

"Oh, no, I think I've got that covered," Andi said. "But when I was about halfway through constructing him, I realized had no way of bringing him to life once I'd completed him."

"Ah," Salazar said. "Yeah, that could be a problem."

"I mean, I could try getting him struck by lightning," she mused, "but I have no idea how to make that happen, and even if I could, I don't even know if that would work or not."

"It wouldn't," Salazar muttered nonchalantly.

"Right," Andi said. "So I was kinda hoping a demon might be able to use black magic to animate him, or 'give him the spark' or whatever. Even just have another demon possess the body and walk around in it for a couple hours—"

"Hold on," Salazar said. "Yes, one of us *could* do that, in theory—in fact, I might even know a guy—but it would have to be worth our while. What kind of movie is your uncle making here, anyway?"

Andi clenched her teeth and hugged herself a little as her entire posture tightened.

"You're not going to like it," she said, just barely over a whisper.

"Try me," Salazar said evenly. Andi gulped.

"It's, um, it's kind of a side project he's been doing lately," she said, conspicuously avoiding eye contact with him. "My uncle, um ... he's just partnered up with this company that produces faith-based entertainment ..."

Salazar immediately doubled over and burst out laughing, so loud and raucous that Andi scurried over and slammed the back of the truck shut in case he brought them any unwanted attention. He was going for a good thirty seconds before the demonic chortles finally settled down into light, gasping chuckles, and finally into silence as he had to catch his breath.

"Oh my gosh," he finally said, wiping a tear out of his eye. "This is unbelievable."

"Yeah, I know," Andi muttered, staring dejectedly at the ground. "Guess I'm kinda out of luck."

"Are you kidding?" Salazar said. "Of course I can get a demon to help you with this! Can probably even get 'em to do it *pro bono*, so you don't have to sell your soul!"

"Wait?" Andi said. *"Really?"*

"Yeah!" he paused for a second. "I mean, you just mutilated a dude in his sleep and stole his eyes, so you're probably going to Hell anyway, but it won't be because of me."

"Right, right ..." Andi muttered. "But why would *demons* want to help a *Christian* movie get made?"

"Are you kidding?" Salazar said again. "Nothing makes the Big Guy Upstairs look more ridiculous than those flicks. Satan has a whole collection of them in his condo, and sometimes he does public screenings of them in Hell just for laughs!" Salazar chuckled a little more, then cleared his throat and straightened his tie a little. "Anyway," he said, "I'm gonna go call my people, see what I can get lined up for you." He put his hands together and pointed at her with both index fingers. "You just work on finishing your little arts and crafts project in there. I don't want to rush you or anything, but we should *probably* get this done before your guy starts to smell."

"Right!" Andi said enthusiastically, running off into the parking lot. Just before she was out of earshot, she called back over her shoulder, "I'll come by your office on Monday to touch base."

Salazar nodded, smiled, and gave her a little wave, then discreetly checked his watch. Mission accomplished: it was five o'clock on the dot.

"Sal?" said the demon Griswold, his head perking up as Salazar approached. "Sal, is that you?"

Salazar smiled and held his arms open as Griswold got up and jogged over to him. Griswold was a warrior-class demon, meaning he was significantly larger than Salazar—about eight feet tall, with the muscular build of a gorilla—and had olive-green skin, along with curling, ram-like horns on either side of his head. Like most warrior-class demons, he also wore little more than an old, tattered loincloth, since it was a lot harder for someone of his stature to find a sharp three-piece suit that fit him as well as Salazar's.

"Griswold, my man!" Salazar said as the demon physically picked him up and pulled him into a crushing hug.

"Man, I haven't seen you in forever!" Griswold bellowed as he set Salazar back on the ground.

"Aw, c'mon," Salazar said. "It can't have been more than a century or two. But what did I tell you? Was I able to get you into the movies, or what?"

Griswold rolled his eyes.

"Yeah, but look at this!" he said, waving his script pages in Salazar's face. "Demon Number 4? I'm a glorified extra, man!" He tossed his script pages into the air, and folded his arms, pouting as they rained down around his head. "There's a rumor goin' around about this new movie version of *The Tempest*—you know how Hollywood goes on this Shakespeare kick every couple years—and I *know* I got the acting chops to play Caliban, but it's so hard to get people to notice you, you know? Especially in this town ..."

"Hey," Salazar said, putting a hand on Griswold's shoulder (which required him to get on his tippy toes). "I've got some pull in this town. As long as people want to use real demons in their movies, I'm the ass they've gotta kiss. I can ask around, see who's producing this thing, see if I can't make a couple 'suggestions' regarding casting."

Griswold's fanged grin spread ear to ear. "Aw, you'd really do that, Sal? That'd be great!"

"Of course, buddy!" Salazar said. "But if I'm gonna do this for you, I might need *you* to do *me* a favor first—"

"Coming through!" a human crewman shouted as he barged through, carrying an authentic Hell battle-spear—one of the many other props and services supplied by Salazar's department. Salazar saw it moments before it was going to happen, but there was nothing he could do to stop it: as the crewman rushed through the set, his foot caught on a loose cable and he stumbled forward, losing his grip for a moment and juggling the spear in the air in front of him for a second before catching it again and regaining his footing.

"Hey!" Salazar shouted. "Be careful with those things!" He jogged over and grabbed the spear out of the crewman's hand. "This spear was designed to take out an angel! You know what it takes to kill a non-corporeal being? If this thing sticks you, there's no afterlife—that's it, you're just *gone*."

"Nah, don't worry," Griswold said as he lumbered over, took the spear away from Salazar, and pushed the palm of his hand harmlessly down against the tip of the spear for effect. "These are the old, beat-up ones that have been in battle a few too many millennia." He smiled, and tossed the spear back to the original human crewman, who had to catch it with both arms. "They know what kinda idiots humans are. They don't hand *these* puppies out unless the point is so dull it couldn't cut through cheese."

"That's a comfort ... I guess," Salazar muttered, watching the crewman slink away.

"Besides, you shouldn't just grab a prop out of a crew guy's hand like that," Griswold said. "They got rules about these things on set. I spent ten thousand years burning in the Lake of Fire, but even *I* ain't gonna screw with IATSE." He shook his head and sighed. "So, anyway ... what was this favor you wanted?"

Salazar smiled. "Do you still have that knack for animating inanimate objects?'

"Yeah, sure," Griswold said. "Haven't used it in a while, so I might be a little rusty, but I'm sure it'll come back to me."

"Great," Salazar said, clapping his hands. "Think you could work your magic on a dead body?"

"What?" Griswold grumbled, looking genuinely peeved for a moment. "You serious here? That's, like, the easiest self-locomotion spell you can do. Any idiot can animate something that's already got all the guts and muscles and stuff ready for you. That's almost insulting." He leaved his fingers together and stretched his hands out, loudly popping the joints. "Now animatin' a statue or something, makin' solid stone move and talk and act like it's alive, *that* takes finesse ..."

"Just the body will be fine for now," Salazar said, reaching up to pat Griswold on the shoulder again. "Think you can stop by my office after the shoot?"

"Yeah, sure," Griswold grumbled, turning to lumber back to the craft services table. "But you better come through with that *Tempest* gig."

By the time Salazar got back to his office, Andi was already there waiting for him, sitting in the same plush armchair across from his desk, staring at nothing in particular with a haunted, dead-eyed expression. Her face was pale and gaunt, and her hands were stained crimson as she clutched her backpack protectively on top of her lap. The same shade of red speckled and splotched her clothing practically from head to toe, and after a couple seconds' examination, Salazar realized that a dark, wet stain covered the entire bottom of her backpack.

"Um ... do I even want to know what's in there?" he said, gesturing idly towards the bag in her lap.

"No," she said quietly, without looking up at him. "No, you really don't."

"Fine," Salazar muttered, shuffling over to his desk and slumping back down in the chair. "Anyway, you're good to go. I've set you up with someone who can bring that thing to life."

"Wait," Andi said. *"Really?"* Without thinking, she stumbled to her feet, and her backpack landed on the floor with a subdued *squish*. Salazar winced. This carpet was a pain in the ass to clean. "Oh my gosh, thank you so much—"

"Hey," Salazar said, holding up a finger to silence her. "Just 'cause I don't want your soul doesn't mean I'm doing this for free, *per se*. Are you still in contact with that famous uncle of yours?"

Andi swallowed. "Y-yeah ...?"

"You tell him to get his ass into my office before the end of the week," Salazar said, lowering his hand onto his desk. "We've got business—like, actual, above-board Hollywood business—that he's been putting off for way too long."

Andi's expression brightened again. "Oh, okay!" she said cheerfully. "Is that all?"

"Yeah," Salazar muttered, leaning back in his chair. "Now you should go finish up whatever else you need to do on your monster. His body needs to be whole and complete before my buddy comes and works his magic."

"Oh, yeah, of course!" Andi said, grabbing her backpack up off the floor. She turned and marched toward the door, but stopped just before leaving and hesitantly glanced back over her shoulder. "Uh ... Salazar?"

"Yeah?"

"When I was out collecting the last set of, um ... *parts*, the ones I was taking from *living* people, tracking down the ones I needed like I was some kind of ... *big game hunter* or something ..." Her gaze lost focus for a second, like her mind was drifting elsewhere, then she forced herself to snap back. "I, um ... I kind of *enjoyed* it." She gulped. "Is, um ... is that a *bad* thing?"

Salazar shrugged. "Only if you think actors count as human beings," he said. "I've been working in this business for over a century, and as far as I'm concerned, the jury's still out."

"Oh," Andi said, trembling a little. "Well, um, okay. I guess I'll just—" Her phone started ringing, and she quickly fumbled it out of her pocket with her less-bloody hand and glanced at the screen. "Oh, crap," she said. "It's Gene Cullen's lawyer. I should probably take this ..." And without another word, she scurried out the door and let it close behind her.

Salazar just sat at his desk, slowly shaking his head for a couple seconds, then let out a long sigh and pulled the next script off of his "To Do" pile. He still had another hour and a half before he could quit for the day. This particular masterpiece of cinema was titled *Lesbian Werewolves on Campus Part II: That Time of the Month Again!* Lovely.

Salazar was halfway through reading the third draft of *Swamp Beast in Cleveland* when the door to his office creaked open again and Andi poked her head in with a beaming grin. As usual, Salazar would take any excuse to put his script down for a second, even if this one was surprisingly not terrible.

"Yes?" he said.

Without saying a word, Andi pushed the door open the rest of the way to reveal the tall, newly-animated figure standing behind her. And to Salazar's shock, Andi's creation actually looked ... *good*. Griswold's life-giving spell had fused the flesh together and evened out the skin tone, making the scars and stitching holding the creature together almost invisible. And the whole idea of taking a bunch of features that were individually handsome *a la carte* and fusing them together had actually kind of worked. Gene Cullen's pale blue eyes gazed out at them from under Alan

151

Fineworth's long, golden mullet and overtop of Jack Grayson's perfectly cleft chin. The rest of the face seemed to be taken from that teen heart-throb kid, Tundifer McCloud, and however Andi had patched the rest of the body together, he now looked like a realistically buff California beach hunk.

Salazar immediately got to his feet. "Well?" he said expectantly. "Has he met your uncle yet?"

"Yes!" Andi squealed. "And Uncle Robert said he was *perfect!* I told him this was 'Jerry Cruz,' a friend of my cousin, and that he just got off the bus from Oklahoma—"

"Oh ... kla ... ho ... ma ..." the creature droned out.

"Right, Jerry. And Uncle Robert signed him for the part immediately, without even auditioning him!"

"Congratulations!" Salazar said. "What part does Mr. Springfield want this guy to play, anyway?"

"Isn't it obvious?" Andi said, glancing back up at the creature, beaming. "He's casting Jerry to play Jesus!"

Salazar started laughing so hard it didn't even register when Andi said she had to get Jerry back on set and led the creature out the door. At first, Salazar was supporting all his weight on his desk, until he finally rolled onto the floor and lay on the carpet for a while gasping for breath in between bouts of giddy giggling. He wasn't sure how long he had been on the floor by the time the laughter finally ceased, but a bolt of realization flashed across his mind, and he scrambled back to his feet.

"Hey, wait!" he shouted at the empty room. "Don't forget your side of the bargain! Tell your asshole of an uncle that he still owes me money!"

Andi hunched down next to her idling pickup truck as she rolled the dead body into the muddy ditch at the side of the road. It was pouring rain in the dead of night, but even that had not been able to wash the red stains off of her jacket. The tears streaming down her face mingled with the rain-drops splattering her from above. It had all started with that damned monster she created; that's what had given her the taste for it.

It had seemed so innocent back then—well ... relatively speaking, at least. Back then, she hadn't been killing people just for the thrill of killing them, she was collecting raw materials for a Very Important Project, some-thing that would help her uncle's career.

Except ... she had liked it. Not just liked it ... she had begun to *crave* it, that brief hit of absolute euphoria she felt every time a human being's life drained out between her fingers, like nothing she ever felt, better than sex, better than *God*, followed almost immediately by the growing urge to do it again. After she had finished the monster, she had made it almost a month before killing someone again, just for fun this time. Then two weeks after that. Then only one week.

Now, she could barely make it two days.

Her heart was already pounding in her chest, but she felt it lurch into double-time when she saw headlights suddenly appear in the distance. Another car was coming. *Breathe,* she told herself. This back road was pretty far out of the way, but it was by no means abandoned. It could easily be just some schlub from the suburbs coming out for a late-night beer run. They had no reason to suspect she was out here disposing of a body, or doing anything else sinister. Hell, the driver probably couldn't even *see* the body from their vantage point as they passed by the truck—

The car slowed down as it drew closer and closer, until it finally pulled to a complete stop parallel to her truck. Andi told her legs to move, to just run off down the road like a madwoman and disappear into the rain, but her muscles wouldn't obey. The door swung open, finally revealing the mystery driver. It was Salazar.

"Get in," he grunted at her. She quietly obeyed.

"H-h-how did you know I was here?" she stammered, as soon as the passenger's-side door was closed behind her. Salazar just rolled his eyes as the car started back down the road.

"Please," he muttered. "Your little late-night excursions are the worst-kept secret in Hollywood. If your uncle wasn't rich, you'd be in prison a dozen times over by now."

Andi only barely heard what he was saying as she watched her truck—and the body—disappear in the rearview mirror.

"But that's not what I'm here about," Salazar continued, keeping his eyes locked on the road ahead of him to avoid making eye contact with her. "Your little science fair project worked *too* well."

Andi gulped, then glanced over at him. "He ... he *what?*"

"You never gave your monster a personality or identity," Salazar said, "so whenever a director gives him a role, he literally thinks he *is* the character."

"Dear God," Andi whispered. "I've created a ... a ..."

"A method actor," Salazar grumbled. "Which would be bad enough on its own, but do you happen to remember the first role your bouncing baby freak was assigned to?"

Andi thought for a second, and then her eyes went wide.

"He thinks he's *actually* Jesus?"

Salazar nodded gravely. "Or close enough," he muttered. "The mad bastard's been going around telling everyone he's the messiah, and since you made him to be a bloody *actor*, he's charming and persuasive enough that people are actually believing him. He's already got his own cult with thousands of followers—here, listen, they play his speeches on Christian talk radio almost twenty-four seven."

Salazar clicked the car radio on, and the monster's eerily recognizable voice immediately came drifting out of the dashboard.

"... I am a created being," he said. *"Created by God Himself! In His image! As are all of you! And I am here to tell you that—"*

"You get the picture," Salazar grumbled. "Listening to that crap for too long makes me start to itch."

"I-I-I had no idea," Andi stammered. "I was so caught up with —with my—"

"Turning into a serial killer?"

Andi's face turned bright red. "Well ... *yeah*."

Salazar sighed. "Well, the good news doesn't end there," he said. "See, because he's a false messiah brought to life by demonic power that originated in Hell, he *technically* counts as the Antichrist. Kinda-sorta. It's a bit of a stretch on the original wording if you ask me, but the boys upstairs are taking it as gospel ... so to speak."

"Oh," Andi said quietly. "Um. That's bad."

"Oh, this passed *bad* a couple miles back," Salazar said. "See, there are some contracts—some very old, very powerful contracts—that say as soon as the Antichrist appears on Earth, that's it, game over, gentlemen start your engines for Armageddon."

Over the course of seconds, Andi's face went from bright red to pale as a sheet.

"So ... we've ... just ... ended ... the ... world ...?" she said slowly.

"Hey, where'd this *we* come from?" Salazar snapped. "It was *your* idea. Mostly. I mean, I only helped a *little* bit—And you *still* never put me in contact with your uncle!—but you know what, that's not important now!" Still keeping one hand on the steering wheel, he turned around and started fishing around for something in the back seat. "What's important is ... we didn't end *anything*." He found what he was looking for—the broken-off end of a Hell battle-spear that he'd pilfered from one of the film sets—and dropped it into Andi's lap. "I don't care what kind of demon mojo is keeping him alive, we stick him with one of these things and we're golden. No more Antichrist, no more Armageddon."

Andi just stared down at the shabby, worn-down weapon lying across her knees. "This thing looks like it couldn't kill an earthworm," she said.

"Well, yeah, that's why you're here," Salazar said. "The only way we're gonna get that thing in his gut is if we jam it into one of the seams where you sewed him together. And you're the only one who knows exactly where those seams are. So I figure you ought to be the one to do the actual stabbing."

"What?!" Andi sputtered. "I can't—I can't just walk up and kill him!"

He just glared at her evenly. "Andi, our most *conservative* estimate is that you've killed at least two dozen people in the months since you created that son of a bitch. How is this any different?"

"Well—those were always in private!" she said. "If he's a celebrity, this is probably going to have to be, like, a public assassination-type deal, and, like ... I can't do it with people watching me!" She sniffed and lowered her head. "And ... and *I'm scared.*"

Salazar reached over and put an arm over her shoulders, still keeping the other hand on the steering wheel. "Hey, hey, don't be scared!" he said. "I'm with you, and I know you can do this. *We* can do this."

Andi glanced up. Something had changed about the rain splattering the windows of the car. It was heavier and thicker, and the droplets left a translucent film behind them as they trickled down, and—

It was blood.

The skies were raining blood.

She looked at Salazar. He had a wide, rictus grin in what was probably his attempt at a reassuring smile, but she could see the bags under his eyes and the worry lines creasing his face and the sweat trickling down his forehead. In the rearview mirror, Andi could see the clouds starting to clear and the sun rising behind them. The sky was bright red. And except for a thin layer of corona, the sun was pitch black.

"This ... this is *fine*," Salazar said, his smile twitching, and his voice cracking just a little as the two of them sped back towards Hollywood. "*We can fix this!*"

Brendan Mallory is a writer and cartoonist based in Los Angeles, CA. He's had a lifelong affinity for the film industry (it's kind of unavoidable when you grow up that close to Hollywood), and majored in the film program at California State University, Northridge, but eventually decided that his writing talents were better suited to prose, comics, and other print media. A number of his short stories have appeared in various issues published by Ahoy Comics; he currently publishes the webcomics *I Think I'm a Penguin* and *Perverted Napkin Doodles* through Line Webtoon; and he recently released his first novel, *The President's Head Is Missing!* You should check them all out. They're really funny.

ALIEN PIZZA

LINDA MAYE ADAMS

ALIEN PIZZA

The aliens didn't mean anything, really. They just wanted pizza.

It was our third month after opening the gluten-free pizza parlor. Actually it was more of a shoebox. The storefront wasn't very big so we called it Pizza Shoebox. My ex Hank wanted to name it after me, but I couldn't see my name on the sign. I mean, who'd want Fizzy Pizza? Sounded like indigestion.

We'd done up the restaurant nice. Added a big plasma so we could run old movies. The kind from the 1950s, mostly monster flicks and shoot-em-up Westerns, since we both liked those.

But the restaurant still looked like what it had been in its last incarnation: a Chinese restaurant.

Sometimes it still smelled like soy sauce.

The store had landed in our lap. Hank had won a boatload of money on one of those cooking shows ("Never again," he said afterward), and then a friend suggested this place. It was in a strip mall with four other stores in walking distance of one of the movie studios. The rent? Dirt cheap for Los Angeles.

But we hadn't asked questions, not even when we had to draw on our savings. Maybe we hadn't wanted to.

I stood at the window, wistful as people walked by, glancing in, but not coming inside. The day dimmed into evening. The streetlights flicked on.

A police car pulled into one of our slots. Like everyone who had stopped by, they all avoided the closest spot to the entrance. That spot had been paved and repaved over so much that it looked like a body was buried under it.

The wind chimes on the door tinkled as the lone officer entered. Behind the counter, I heard Hank sigh.

He came out, smoothing out his apron. Even on that food show, he'd dressed nice like he was now: dress shirt, nice slacks, and Oxfords. Thin hair neatly trimmed. No weird piercings or tattoos. He believed in original parts only.

"What can we do for you, Officer?" he asked, his customer service hat on. "I'm Hank, and this is Fizzy."

We knew the officer wasn't here to buy food, given the six previous visits from other officers, but we didn't want him to think we were rude.

The officer took off his hat and looked around. He paused to watch the movie playing on the plasma. A monster was chasing the heroine across a swamp.

He was older than the last one, with skin the color of an old penny and eyes that were friendly for a cop. His name badge identified him as Ruiz.

"Gluten-free pizza? My wife's gluten-sensitive. She'd kill for a pizza." He pressed his lips together. "I think I would, too."

A smile spread across my face. I liked that he ate what she did even though he didn't have any problems.

"What would she like?" Hank asked.

Ruiz' mouth worked as he studied the menu on the wall. We had a lot of pictures of pizza up. "The works. No anchovy."

Why did people always say that? Pizzas didn't come with anchovies by default.

Hank got to work right away. Get the dough, spoon on the chunky sauce, then shredded mozzarella.

Ruiz arched an eyebrow at me. "Fizzy? That a nickname?"

"Nope. Both my parents were actors." Actors lived in their own world, even when it came to naming babies.

"Ah. You two married?" he asked.

Ruiz seemed to be making conversations, which was quite odd. The other officers had been perfunctory, almost to the point of being rude. I hoped he wasn't sweetening us up for worse.

"Divorced," I said.

Surprise lit up his eyes. "And still workin' together?"

Hank said, "We figured out that we get along better divorced than married."

He slid the pizza and pan into the oven.

Of course, now, it was too much for me to wait any more ... I had to know. Hank was pretty good at reading me and came to the counter to watch.

"I'm sorry, Officer ... I have to ask you something. Officers have come in here a lot. They tell us not to call them. What are they talking about? What if we get held up? We don't call for help?"

Ruiz glanced away for a moment, composing his face.

"The landlord didn't tell you," he said finally. "It seems like there's always a new restaurant here. They don't stay long."

"This isn't a bad location," Hank said. "What is it—this place cursed?"

Ruiz stared at his feet, then stared at the pizza pictures on the wall.

"It's because you're going to be visited by aliens."

Hank and I didn't know what to make of what Ruiz told us. It seemed like pure silliness. If there were aliens out there, surely it would be all over social media.

We came in the next morning to get everything set up for the lunch crowd (we hoped there would actually be a lunch crowd). It was already getting to be pretty hot out, pressing down on the yellow haze of smog that laid over the valley.

As we got out of the beat-up minivan, a flash of movement made me stop. The parking spot rolled, like a wave.

"What the hell?" Hank said.

"Maybe something to do with the aliens?" I asked.

Almost in answer, the spot gurgled again. Rotten-egg smell made me recoil.

The asphalt was squishy like I was walking on ground saturated with water.

Gurgle.

I screamed and jumped back. Would've lost my balance and flashed the world if Hank hadn't grabbed me. I smoothed out my skirt. My hands were shaking like crazy.

We walked gingerly around the spot and went inside. Should we close off the spot? What if it ate people?

Maybe I was watching too many movies.

We were yawning throughout the evening. I put on a DVD of one of those movies where the monster was created by atomic power. More monster power to stay awake.

We'd had a bit of a rush at dinner time—some people from the set of a film picking up a stack of pizzas—and then it was like a switch was shut off. No one came in.

Heck, no one even walked by.

Hank sighed and folded his arms on the counter, shifting his weight. "It's discouraging, Fizzy. You know, you imagine that when you open the door on your first day, people will be lining up. And then they don't."

"You could always get on another cooking show." I gave him my best smile.

"No. Never. Again."

I ran my hand through my hair, pushing it away from my face. It was hard not to think about all the money we put in. What would happen if business continued to be so poor? It was bad seeing Hank demoralized.

"Do you want to do something else?" I finally asked.

Hank pressed his lips together, which he did when he was doing some deep thinking. "No. I like cooking. I like making pizza."

"Well, maybe that movie crew will pass our name around."

Word of mouth was probably going to be the best way to get business. People just didn't look at ads anymore.

Blue strobes flashed across the store.

Hank groaned. "Not more police again."

"Maybe they want pizza."

We both laughed at that. Pizza should be cop food because it was fast and portable.

But when I looked out the window, ice gripped me. The blue light wasn't coming from the street.

It was from the parking spot.

A door opened up in the ground, and the light was coming out it. The rotten-egg smell was back, too.

Hank crowded against me, peering over my shoulder. His nearness helped warm me up.

"Is that the aliens?" he said.

We hadn't believed Ruiz, not really, thinking it was some kind of joke. But now, my stomach was tightening into knots. If there were aliens, what were they going to do?

Shapes silhouetted against the bright light walked up what appeared to be a set of stairs under the parking lot. There were three shapes, human only in the sense that they had two arms, two legs, and a head. Two looked like they were wearing—top hats?

Then the light cut off abruptly, and the rectangle of land became a parking space again. The three figures walked to our door.

"They're coming in here!" My voice was a squeak.

The wind chime on the door tinkled as the aliens entered. The first one turned, gazing at the wind chimes like a child making a new discovery.

The aliens were quite slender, so much so that I wondered how they got internal organs to fit in their bodies. Their skin was a pale, pale violet, topped with a waterfall of white hair. It was quite striking, really. Their eyes were purple marbles.

And they were dressed up in formal wear. Two were in tuxedoes and top hats. One had a sparkly cummerbund, and the other had a gold sash stretched across his chest. The third was a woman, dressed in a shimmering silver evening gown, a vibrant red wrap draped over her shoulders.

Just like they were going to the Hollywood red carpet.

Hank and I drew back toward the counter, both of us trying to remember to breathe. What were they going to do? Were they invading Earth? Were they going to shoot us with laser weapons?

On the plasma screen, a woman in a white bathing suit screamed. The aliens gathered in front of it. They gasped as a monster surged out of a river and snatched up the screaming woman.

Good? Bad? Did they think the monster was a cousin?

Continuing to glance at the movie, they moved to the menu on the wall. They had the liquidity of cats as they walked.

Their voices were musical as they discussed something. I tried to make out the words, but they slipped from my ears.

Then Gold Sash pointed at one of the pictures and cocked his head questioningly.

Wait—pizza? They wanted pizza?

"One sausage and pepperoni pizza coming up!" Hank said, bursting with nervous energy. "Why don't you show them a table, Fizzy?"

His words unstuck my brain. Customer service instincts kicked in. Aliens were customers. Okay. I smiled and pointed to one of the tables, the one that had a good view of the plasma. Sparkly Cummerbund pulled out one chair for Lady Alien and bowed to her. They all adjusted their chairs so they could watch the movie.

I put out glasses of water and retreated back to the counter. It was hard not to jump around. Fear had turned into electricity in my body.

Hank arranged rings of pepperoni on top of the cheese. His hands were shaking so bad that he dropped some of the pepperonis. Shredded mozzarella was white confetti around his feet.

"You okay?" I asked. Heck, I wasn't sure if I was myself.

"They really just want pizza?" Hank said.

All I could do was shrug and give them pizza.

Fifteen minutes later, I brought out the hot pan with the steaming pizza and three plates. Lady Alien leaned over the pizza, inhaling deeply. Her small mouth broke out in a smile.

So far so good.

Gold Sash added a slice to each plate. All three bowed their heads, and their voices drew down into a sing-song murmur. They stopped at the same time and then began eating.

Hank and I both watched the aliens for the next two hours. I was trying not to worry ... what if they didn't like the pizza ... what if it made them sick ... what would we do if that happened?

And then it became amazing watching them eat. Their eyes lit up as the melted cheese stretched out. The woman swiped a piece of crust off Gold Sash's plate (and he let her), biting it for the crunch.

They discussed the food at length ... couldn't understand a word, but it was about the food.

At least they finished, right down to the last glob of cheese and crumb from the crust. All three stood up. Gold Sash came over, and he was smiling. He pressed a small pouch of sturdy but soft material into my hand.

The wind chimes tinkled as they departed, and a moment later the parking space opened up to the blue light again. It was only after the light cut off that Hank and I finally unstuck ourselves.

"What did they give you?" Hank asked.

The bag was heavy. I shook it. Metal rattled inside. I poured the contents on the counter.

Gold coins. We'd just made a profit.

Human business trickled in during the day. Mostly from the nearby studios. Gluten-free was considered by some to be a trend; therefore every actor was following it like a religion. We also got a business traveler staying nearby who had been desperately looking for gluten-free.

Alien business came late in the evening. Always two men and a woman, always dressed in formal attire, bearing gold coins. They watched whatever movie we were playing.

They liked shoot-em-up Westerns and monster flicks, just like us.

We could tell when they were coming because the parking spot would be extra squishy and smell like rotten eggs.

It was Thursday, about forty-five minutes before the aliens usually arrived. Our last human customer left with a whoosh out the door, mumbling angrily.

Filming nearby must have broken late because we got a rush of people when it should have been quiet, including the star of the film.

Jason Broadman blew in, wearing arrogance the way everyone else wears clothes. He had a face that would make teen hearts flutter but by thirty, no one would know who he was.

He demanded Hank remake the pizza twice because the slices weren't exactly the same size, then complained about the movie we were showing.

"C'mon!" He glared at the plasma. "You can tell that's a guy in an ape suit."

He still hadn't been satisfied with the third pizza, though Hank had done an admirable job at cutting the slices. There just wasn't pleasing some people.

After the door closed, I said, "You were more polite than I would have been."

"Believe me, I was about to hit my limit when he started fussing on that third pizza," Hank said. "But he would've bad-mouthed us to the film crew."

He took off his apron and tossed it on the counter. His back cracked as he stretched. His gaze flicked to the clock. Every night it was the same. We looked at the clock as the evening drew to a close and felt both a flutter of excitement and trepidation.

"What do you think of the alien thing, Fizzy?" he finally asked.

We'd avoided the question for days, though it was the elephant—or alien—in the room that we were all stepping around. The aliens paid well, very well. We were turning a profit now, entirely because of them. But they were ... well, aliens.

What if they turned on us one day because they didn't like the pizza? What if SWAT busted down the door and came in armed, ready to shoot? What if we went viral on the internet?

I considered my words carefully and what came out surprised me.

"I enjoy it when they come in here. They're ... you know, respectful. We get too many people like that guy who just left. Rude and nasty."

Hank dunked his head, embarrassed. "I like watching them. They just have so much fun with the pizza and watching the monster movies. But still—"

Yup. They were aliens.

Headlights flashed across the window, and an engine cut off. Officer Ruiz sauntered in a few minutes later to the tune of wind chimes. From the set of his eyebrows, he was surprised to see us still here.

"They didn't scare you off?"

Hank shrugged. "We're still thinking about it. They can't be all bad. They like pizza."

"My wife liked it, too," Ruiz said. "She wants another one. She's a make-up artist, so she's been telling everyone about your restaurant."

Hank beamed. "The works, right?"

"The works. No anchovies."

Hank retreated to make the pizza, leaving me to ask questions.

"How long have the aliens been coming here?"

Ruiz's eyebrows came together. "Over a year. Not the only place either. They showed up at a movie theater. Didn't like the movies."

I glanced up at the movie playing on the plasma screen. The ape stalked a team of explorers through the woods.

"They like ours," I said.

Ruiz watched the movie for a few moments. "I watched those when I was a kid. Hollywood doesn't make movies like that anymore."

The lights flashed outside, and a few minutes later the three aliens came in. This time the woman approached me with a big smile and handed me a DVD.

They wanted us to play it? I pointed at the plasma. She shook her head and all three turned to the menu to order their pizza. They settled in to watch the ape movie. The DVD was apparently a gift. I wasn't sure what to make of it.

The next morning, Hank and I plugged in the DVD and watched while we prepared for the day. The aliens had made a movie!

The location was a beach with ruddy sand. Majestic cliffs stood watch in the background. Might be anywhere on Earth, except for the two moons hanging over the cliffs.

The woman alien wore a blond wig and a filmy white dress. She was being chased by an alien in a rubber sea monster suit. The hero was in cowboy clothes and carried a sword.

Heroine did a dramatic scream, going limp in a faint. The wig nearly fell off. Cowboy lunged at the sea monster with the sword. He obviously missed, but the sea monster clutched his chest and dramatically died.

It was so bad. But the aliens were having so much fun that we both enjoyed it.

So we played the DVD during the day to the human customers. Most seemed to enjoy it. Some asked about it. We just said, "It's an indie film."

Over the next week, the aliens came back every night at the same time. It wasn't always the same ones, but always two men and one woman, and always in formalwear. They always bought another DVD movie they'd made.

Then they pointed at pictures, and we made pizza.

But I felt a niggle of worry. I didn't tell Hank, though I'm sure he figured it out, too.

What happened if they stopped coming?

On Thursday, Officer Ruiz returned, half an hour before the aliens were due. It was a new moon out, so the only light outside was from the street lamps.

He gave me back the alien video he borrowed and got another one. Bribery works. He'd gotten the other officers to stop bothering us and got to watch fun films.

A high-powered engine growled outside. The driver had parked in the alien's spot.

Hank tensed up with alarm. "We need to tell him to move. I don't know what'll happen if the portal opens—"

"Got it," Ruiz said.

But before he reached the door, it bounced open and Jason Broadman strode in like he owned the place. He ordered a pizza and got on his cell phone to argue with someone while it baked in the oven.

Ruiz and I watched the parking spot, hoping the aliens would be a little late. So far, no rotten-egg smell, no glow.

I didn't realize I'd been holding my breath until the actor was back out in the car. Only he didn't pull out right away. He was still on his cell phone.

Light glowed under the car.

No, no, no. Hank and I rushed outside to do ... we weren't even sure what.

The portal opened.

It ate the car.

Officer Ruiz warned us not to say anything. If anyone came by about Jason, we'd tell them that he bought his pizza and left.

Hank and I were beside ourselves. Three days crawled by. No Jason, no aliens.

The silence made it worse.

We got through the days mechanically, terrified the police would barge in and arrest us. We didn't know what they would arrest us for, but we were certain it would happen.

After the lunch rush had vacated, Hank leaned on the counter wearily, watching me prop open the front door.

Between the heat of the day and the lunch rush, the restaurant was frightfully hot. Of course, we were both avoiding the elephant—alien—in the room.

"Maybe we should have left when the aliens first started showing up," Hank said.

I couldn't really answer him because I didn't even know how I felt. My stomach hadn't been right since Jason had disappeared. Every time I saw a news alert about the disappearance, I wanted to crawl back into bed and hide.

Since I didn't say anything, Hank said, "I've been thinking that we should close up the Pizza Shoebox."

I knew what I thought of that. I rushed back to the counter. "No, no, Hank. We had this discussion. You like cooking. You like making pizza."

Hank slammed a pizza pan on the counter. "What are we supposed to do, Fizzy? I don't want to be looking over my back forever!"

His anger caught mine on fire. "We did not do anything!"

"The aliens took a man. What did they do with him?"

Of course, I didn't have an answer to that.

What were they doing with Jason?

That night, Ruiz came back. He'd lost some of the grimness he'd had over the last few days. He'd been afraid, too.

He ordered a pizza and waited for a couple to leave before speaking. "We found him."

"Jason Broadman?" Hank and I both came to the counter to gawp.

"Wandering around on Melrose. His car was out in Simi Valley."

"They didn't do something to him?" I asked.

"Does he remember what happened?" Hank asked.

Ruiz leaned in close. More glances over his shoulder. "I had a talk with him. It took a few days for the aliens to work out how to get the car back. The aliens treated him like royalty. Asked him for autographs, took pictures. I told him he can't tell anyone. They'd think he was nuts. Official story is that he got drunk and had a blackout."

A weight lifted off me. Tension drained out of Hank, too.

We knew what we'd really been arguing about. We knew the aliens were good people. They just liked pizza, and we liked serving it to them.

That night, they came back. Their gestures were apologetic, and they left us extra coins.

We changed the name from Pizza Shoebox to Alien Pizza. Jason recommended us as the spot to be.

He still stops by, always when the aliens arrive. Poses for pictures with them. He's been different since the accident. More thoughtful, more focused on having fun in his film roles. His reputation went from a difficult actor to one everyone wanted to work with.

To be on the safe side though, we marked the portal parking spot with a sign "For aliens only," with a picture of the gray ones off the internet. On our sign for the hours, we have "11:00 am–10:30 pm, Human Customers. 11:00 pm–1:00 am, Alien Customers."

It's fun to watch people walk past the store, then return to look at the sign. They always come in and they get to watch alien monster movies while they wait for their pizza.

Maybe aliens are good for business. We're not telling.

LINDA MAYE ADAMS

Linda Maye Adams was probably the least likely person to be in the Army —even the Army thought so! She was an enlisted soldier for twelve years and was one of the women who deployed to Desert Storm. But she'd much prefer her adventures to be in books. She is published in *Red, White, and True: Stories from Veterans and Families, World War II to Present*. She is also the author of the military-based GALCOM Universe series, including the novel *Crying Planet*, featured in the 2018 Military Science Fiction Story-Bundle. She has also been a three-time honorable mention winner in *L. Ron Hubbard's Writers of the Future*. lindamayeadams.com.

WHOEVER WRITES MONSTERS

SAM KNIGHT

WHOEVER WRITES MONSTERS

There is nothing so alone as a man without a woman, yet there is nothing more miserable than a man with one.'"

Carolyn raised her hands, fingers spread wide. "Fade to black. Credits roll." She held her melodramatic gaze skyward until applause broke out around the boardroom. Stepping back, she took a half-bow. Long red hair fell forward, covering her face as she bent. Straightening, she pointed to Mike, seated in one of the extra chairs against the back wall.

Addressing the room, Carolyn spoke over the applause. "I think that is the most powerful message in a monster movie since King Kong, don't you?"

One of the board members rose, still clapping. Others followed. Soon everyone stood, clapping for Mike.

Flushing, Mike nodded and waved, wishing it was all over. Carolyn motioned for Mike to stand, and he knew she wanted him to talk. It was all he could do not to glare at his agent. Talking was the thing Mike did *not* want to do.

But the ovation continued until he was unable to resist without looking like an ass.

"Thank you," he said, standing. "You know I am a writer, not a talker, so I'll be brief." A smattering of laughter echoed around the room. Mike was notoriously reclusive. "I want to thank the board, and everyone here, for everything you've done. For helping make the world a more *monstrous* place." He waved again and then sat, tossing Carolyn a look that said she'd better take over.

Taking the cue, Carolyn began wrapping up the presentation. When she finished, the chairman of the board stood and singled Mike out again.

"Before we adjourn," the gray-templed woman said, "I would like to again offer our thanks to Mr. Michael Bernard, known to some of you as the famous Mike St. Bernard." She waited as people chuckled. "We are enjoying a new golden age of monster movies, unrivaled since the early days of Universal Pictures' classic monsters, and we are on the verge of usurping the age of the superheroes. Without Mike, and his wonderfully terrible monster stories, this would not have happened, nor would this company exist. I would not be here. You would not be here. I know you all know how he and his partner started this studio from a produced-in-their-basement MyChannel show, but I think sometimes we forget we owe all of this to Mike, Glen, and their wonderful nightmares. So, I wanted to say thank you, Mike. Thank you, and may you always have nightmares."

Mike smiled, nodding graciously as everyone applauded, then he headed for the door at the earliest opportunity.

The elevator door slid shut. Carolyn slumped her shoulders and blew out through puffed cheeks. "That went really well," she said, unbuttoning her top button and fanning her face. "You know, you don't need me. Your stories sell themselves."

Mike, leaning against the elevator wall, didn't answer.

"I know you and Glen disassociated from the company as best you could to make sure there was no favoritism or appearance of impropriety, but, honestly, this company lives off your stories as much now as when you started it."

"Are you trying to talk your way out of a job?" Mike asked.

"Hardly." She bounced on her toes like an excited teenager. "You know I love this! I came to you, remember? What I'm saying is you've made a big enough name for yourself that any company would pay through the nose for one of your screamplays. I think we should consider putting your next one up for auction and see what we can get."

The elevator jerked to a stop as though the look on Mike's face had startled it still.

"You heard what Chairman Miller said," Carolyn told him. "None of them would be here without you, yet they pay you less than five percent of what they make off your movies. They make hundreds of millions off each movie. They are pushing *billions*, and you get thousands."

"I get hundreds of thousands," Mike countered, stepping into the building's lobby.

"Barely. If it hadn't been for the cost of Glen's treatments—" Carolyn stopped herself when she saw the look on his face. She tucked a wayward strand of red hair behind one ear. "I'm sorry. I shouldn't have said that. But truth is, this isn't your company anymore. Working for pittance no longer benefits you in the long run, and you shouldn't have all your eggs in one basket. We need to get you diversified. We need to have your stories everywhere!"

Mike, farther down the entrance steps, stopped and turned, looking back up at her. "You're right. But you're wrong. This company—these people were there for me when I needed them to be. Now, they need me to continue to be there for them. Going somewhere else would be like spitting in their faces."

"I get that. But you deserve a lot more than what you're getting. Just look at the merchandising sales—"

"You're the agent, Carolyn. If you don't like what we're earning, then go renegotiate."

She nodded as if that had been what she wanted to hear all along. "In order to do that, I need to know what you're working on next."

Mike shook his head and continued down the stairs to his waiting ride.

"I know you don't like to talk about your screamplays before they're done, but I need something."

He shook his head again.

"At least tell me what *kind* of monster! Supernatural? Ghost? Cryptid? Alien?"

Mike got in the car and waved goodbye to her with a pinched smile.

Standing in front of the fireplace, Mike's gaze flickered between the portrait and the urn on the mantle. He was never sure which to talk to. Between them, they represented the best and worst days of his life.

The portrait, Mike sitting while Glen stood behind with one hand on his shoulder, had perfectly captured Glen's gentle smile and loving nature. It been their big splurge when they crossed the million-dollar mark, when they left their day jobs and went full-time with their tiny production company.

The urn, small, white, and simple, contained all that was physically left of Glen in this world.

Mike talked things out with Glen, even now, but today he didn't know what to say. The bottomless inkwell had run dry. No more ideas came from out of the ether, and he'd run out of unfinished projects to work on. Memories of how much Glen loved the monsters had carried Mike through the last few screamplays, as he re-worked old ideas they had bandied about but discarded. Now Mike had used up all those ideas.

Every last one.

Throwing himself into his work at a record pace, he'd cranked out ten full-length screamplays in the year since Glen's death. Two had already been made into films and were successful—unexpectedly so. Another four were in production. Three were being adapted into series. The last, as of today, was in the queue, waiting for resources to free up so it could be made. It was the best position Mike, and the company, had ever been in.

But it meant nothing without Glen.

Mike turned from the portrait and looked around his smallish house. Glen would have loved it. Cozy yet open, it carried the white-picket-fence feeling while still being modern. It was something Glen had died thinking Mike would never be able to afford again.

The experimental treatments had cost them their home, their savings, and their ownership of the company, and it had put them deep in debt.

Worst of all, it hadn't mattered.

Just as the treatments seemed to be working, just as Glen was getting better, he had a heart attack. More specifically, he suffered from takotsubo syndrome, also known as broken-heart syndrome—a heart attack induced by massive amounts of emotional stress. The doctors couldn't know if it was related to the experimental treatments or not.

Mike poured a whiskey, breaking his own rule about not drinking alone. He held the glass tumbler under his nose and inhaled the biting scents of caramel and Earth, trying to ground himself in them. Breaking another rule, he threw back the shot instead of sipping it.

He grimaced and set the tumbler down, fighting the urge to throw it across the room and scream.

"Damn it, Glen," he mumbled at the portrait. "I was writing them for you. Envisioning what you would think I was going to write and then figuring out how to surprise you. What would make you laugh, what would make you scream ... How much you would love the monster ..." He dropped into the chair and sank his face into his hands. "It wasn't so hard when you'd already seen at least a peek at them, when I knew something about what you thought of them. But now all I see ... is you're not here. That you don't laugh anymore. That you don't scream anymore."

Mike choked out a laughing sob.

"I don't have any more monsters without you."

"Sooo ... when will it be done?" Carolyn asked, eyebrows raised as high as her expectations. She nearly vibrated with enthusiasm.

"When it's done." Mike shrugged, not looking at her.

"Wine?" an approaching waiter asked. He placed a basket of bread on the table and held out a bottle of red.

Carolyn immediately covered her glass with her hand. "No thank you. Sparkling water, please."

"Just water, thank you," Mike said. The waiter nodded and turned away.

The clinking silverware in the restaurant around them reminded Mike of the time Glen had suggested a story about aliens made of crystal fighting aliens made of metal. The company still sold a collection of hand-blown wine glasses and metal shot glasses shaped like the little beasties.

"Mike, you were cranking out a screamplay a month. I couldn't keep up. Now, I've got nothing to do. It's been six months. You gotta give me something. We gotta ride the wave! Heck, there's a tsunami of interest in Mike St. Bernard monsters right now. We've gotta take advantage while we can! The world is alive with your monsters! There are so many markets we could—"

"Maybe," he picked up a roll from the breadbasket and tore it open, "you should add another writer or six to your stable?"

"Are you kidding?" Carolyn stopped bouncing in her chair and leaned in, face clouding. "You don't have anything, do you?"

Mike shook his head.

"Nothing at all?" Her voice quieted. "This is why you refused public appearances, isn't it? You didn't want anyone to figure it out."

Setting the pieces of roll on his plate, Mike met Carolyn's eyes. "I'm out of ideas, Carolyn. All out. I've written wolfmen, wolfwomen, vampires, mummies ... lizard men, aliens, ghosts, giant every kind of freaking animal there is, not to mention all the shapeshifters ... I am out of ideas."

Carolyn's face darkened.

"Do you have any ideas?" he asked. "Seriously. Name a monster that hasn't been done. Hell, name one *I* haven't done."

She opened her mouth, then closed it.

"Let me try to trigger an idea for you," Mike said. "Swamp monster, desert monster, mountain monster, sea monster, snow monster, jungle, lake, river, basement, attic, backyard, barn ..."

Carolyn sat back in her seat, fidgeting with the napkin in her lap.

"Giant monsters?" Mike continued. "Tiny ones? Bacterium that eats you from the inside out? Flying? Invisible? Only in the dark? Only in the sunlight? The ghost of a monster? The man who is a monster? The monster who is a man?"

He picked up the roll again and, reaching for the butter, said, "It's all been done already, and I'm all out of ideas."

He ate the roll in silence as she stared at the table.

"What do I tell the studio?" Carolyn finally asked, her voice barely audible over the babble around them.

"I don't know. Tell them I have writer's block?"

Sitting across the table from Mike, in the little breakfast nook just outside of his kitchen, Carolyn looked tired and a little desperate. "It's been a year," she said. "Don't you think it's about time to at least try?"

The house, bright and full of springtime whites and yellows, was nothing at all what most people thought a horror writer's house should look like. To Mike, it felt dead anyway. Abandoned. Like no one actually lived in it. Although he did. All the time.

Somehow, it felt even more dead with Carolyn in it.

"Money is starting to get tight." Carolyn added milk and honey to her tea then picked up her spoon and stirred absently as she tried to get him to meet her gaze. "And I don't mean just for me. Without genuine Mike St. Bernard screamplays to produce, the company is slowly imploding. Their other stuff just isn't as good, and the infighting is getting out of control. People are starting to wonder if the age of monsters is over.

"What I am trying to say, Mike, just in case you aren't getting it, is that if the company you're so worried about betraying goes bankrupt, or out of business, or gets bought out, we may not have any royalties coming in anymore."

Mike shook his head. "Putting pressure on me doesn't help, you know. I've tried everything. Every writing prompt I could find, every weird news article, every murder in the news, every new scientific breakthrough. I even tried a story about an actual writer's block that lived off ideas of writers, sucking them right out of their heads," Mike stood and started pacing. "I've got nothing. None of it comes together anymore!"

He found himself in front of Glen's portrait. He only ever saw Glen in the image now, never himself, and lately Glen's kind eyes had started to feel ... accusing. "I'm sorry," he said in a soft voice. "Our company, our baby, is falling apart. All those people who helped us grow, who we gave jobs to, who helped us when we needed it, are now at risk. Because I ran out of monsters."

"Maybe we could revisit your early works? The internet shorts? Revamp them. Sell them to new places. Remakes are common in the film industry. Your name is still strong. We can keep things rolling if—"

Mike took a deep breath and turned to Carolyn, still sitting at the table. "You should go, Carolyn."

"You know I have your best interests at heart, right Mike? I'm just trying to help. You worked so hard to build up this momentum. We shouldn't lose it."

"Yeah, I know. I just need to be alone right now. I need to—" He shook his head. "I'm sorry."

"I'm here for you, Mike. We're in this together. You're not alone." Carolyn picked up her briefcase and let herself out.

But I am alone, he thought, watching the door close. *I am all alone.* He turned back to the portrait. *Without you, Glen, I don't have anything.*

Glen blinked. The eyes of his image becoming uncharacteristically hard as they turned to meet Mike's.

Mike stepped back, horrified as Glen's fingers turned into claws and dug into the shoulder of the Mike sitting in the portrait. The image of Mike didn't move, but the real Mike gasped, and his knees buckled from the pain flaring in his shoulder. Blood soaked through the jacket of the Mike in the portrait, and Mike felt hot wetness dripping down his own, paralyzed arm.

Terrified, he looked to his shoulder and found the blood to be real.

He looked at Glen, gaping at the cruelty he saw in the eyes of the man he loved.

"You're not Glen," he gasped. "What the hell are you?"

"You wanted monsters." A form, claws digging deeper into both the front and back of Mike's shoulder, materialized before him. "You've got one."

It solidified into the shape of a gargoylesque demon, grinning a wide, malicious sneer full of jagged teeth. Spindly, bat-like wings slowly spread wide, darkening the room.

"W-what do you want?" Mike, on his knees, could barely ask the question. He felt the creature's sharp claws come together, tips meeting deep inside his shoulder.

"I want what you want," the thing said. It brought its pointed face down to Mike's, looking him in the eyes. Hot, dank breath washed over Mike as it spoke. "I want you to write."

Carolyn was bouncing when Mike opened the door. "Tell me you're not joking," she said, nearly dancing into his house. "You really finished a screamplay?"

"I had a visit from my muse."

Carolyn chuckled. "And what did you talk about? Aliens? Dinosaurs?"

"Demons, actually." Mike shut the door and motioned to the chairs in front of the fireplace.

"Demons? Really? Not your usual style." Pointing to the sling around his arm, Carolyn asked, "What happened?"

"Ah ... I'd guess you'd say I walked into a door." He smiled wanly. "Can I get you something to drink?"

"Sparkling water would be great, thanks. So, you wrote a screamplay about demons?" Carolyn asked, settling into a chair as Mike disappeared into the kitchen.

"Kind of," he answered when he returned. He carried an open bottle in his good hand and an empty glass in the other. "It's more about a muse." He filled the glass and sat the bottle on the table next to Carolyn.

"A muse?" she asked, frowning as she took the drink. "Like the kind that gives writers ideas?"

"Yeah, kind of." Mike sat on the edge of the other chair and leaned forward.

"You didn't write another crappy story about a writer, did you? People are sick of that."

"I revisited the idea about a living writer's block monster that steals ideas from writers, and I reversed it. You know, like a muse that forces a writer to write."

"Sounds like something Stephen King already did. I think I liked the idea of a demon better."

"I haven't finished yet."

"Yeah, but where's the monster in a muse?"

"That was exactly what I asked myself. Where is the monster in a muse? So, I started doing research. Did you know the original myths about the muses are conflicting? It's kind of like they were different things to different people. And were there nine of them? Or only three? Or ... maybe there is only one who pretends to be all of them?"

"Okay. When do we get to the good part? The *monster*?"

"The interesting thing, to me, was that there were almost no good stories about the muses themselves. They were almost always catalysts in other stories."

"Right. Hence being a *muse*." Carolyn motioned for him to hurry up. "So, again, I ask, when do we get to the good part?"

"The motivation. That's what makes all good monsters good. You have to understand why they do what they do. Just like any other character."

"Okay. So why do they do it?" She sipped her water and then looked at her glass and nodded appreciatively.

"They feed on it. It's what they need."

"Mike, you lost me," she took another sip of her drink, savoring it this time. "Maybe we should talk about the demon instead?"

"Oh, I am." Mike's eyes were bright now. He stood, pacing the room in his excitement. "How's the sparkling water?"

"It's really good. It reminds me of something I can't quite put my finger on."

"That's funny," Mike said, but there was no humor in his voice. "I thought you'd recognize it right off."

Carolyn frowned. Mike drew a dagger from inside his sling, and her eyes went wide. She dropped the glass. Before it hit the floor, Mike stabbed her through the shoulder, under the collarbone, pinning her back into the chair.

She screamed.

When she gasped for breath, Mike snarled at her. "Hurts, don't it?"

Carolyn screamed again.

"Go ahead," Mike said. "I've had horror movies cranked up full volume for the last few days. The neighbors are used to it. They think I'm doing research." His face tightened. "Come to think of it, I guess I am." He twisted the knife, and Carolyn screamed again.

"That was probably uncalled for. I'm sorry." Mike sat on the arm of the chair, where he could keep pressure on the knife in her shoulder. "But you've weighed heavily on my mind for a while now. Let me know when you're ready. I'd like to talk for a few minutes."

Carolyn's breath came in quick pants.

"This water was really hard to come by," Mike said. "I'm sure you can appreciate that." He turned at the waist to gingerly pick up the bottle with his hand in the sling. "Turns out I had a fan in Delphi who was willing to go all the way up Mount Parnassus as a special favor to me. This came straight from the Castalian Spring. Can you believe it? Would you like some more?" He lifted the bottle to her lips. "I have plenty."

"Please ... please ..." Carolyn turned her head away.

"I really wasn't sure it would work, but I didn't have a better idea. How do you research a monster so old that no one remembers it's a monster?"

He sat the bottle back on the table. "Thank god for the internet. And for rabid fans."

Carolyn's tears flowed, but her breathing was slowing.

"Are you ready to talk?" he asked. "Okay. Good. First, I didn't like it when you did this to me." He wiggled the knife, making her flinch again. "It still hurts like hell. And it was totally uncalled for. It makes it hard to concentrate—and to type. You could have just appeared and scared the crap out of me. I'm sure that would have been just as effective. There was no need for violence.

"I probably would have even welcomed your presence. But you had to *threaten* me. You had to *hurt* me!"

"I don't know what you're talking about," Carolyn's voice was a scratchy whisper, "but I promise to listen to whatever it is you have to say. Please, just call an ambulance. I don't feel so well."

"Of course you don't, Melete. Or is it Aoide? Or Mneme?"

Carolyn winced. "Please, Mike, I don't know what you want."

"That's okay. You don't have to tell me anything. I figured it all out on my own." He leaned slightly to the side, moving to catch her gaze. "I don't know what other names you have carried over the centuries. I don't even know which one you are, or how many of you there are, but I know what you are. You're a muse."

She met his eyes, agony etched across her face. "You're delusional! You need help. I need help. Please call an ambulance ... *please?*"

"I also figured out you're actually some kind of demon. You live off people. Throughout the centuries you, or your sisters—how many of you are there? You inspired people and reveled in being worshiped for it. Just like any other god, you need people to believe in you, to need you, don't you?"

"Please, Mike ... I feel lightheaded ..."

"The thing is, you bastards don't really *give* people ideas, do you? You just *feed* off creative people somehow."

She shifted and made a weak effort to pull away from his blade.

"Oh, no you don't." Mike picked up the bottle and splashed water in her face.

She flinched and spat droplets from her lips, falling back into the chair.

"We can do this all night. I've got plenty of this stuff. I thought about trying holy water, which would have been much easier to get, but I didn't want to take any chances."

"Please, Mike. Please." Her head swayed, and she looked to the floor. "Please ..."

"Why did you change your rules with me, *Carolyn*? Why didn't you just move on when my inspiration ran out? Why did you *come into my home and threaten me?*" Mike shook as he tried to meet her eyes.

"I don't know what you're talking about!" she sobbed.

He twisted the knife, and Carolyn gasped. Her eyes rolled up, and her head fell forward.

Mike lifted her chin and looked into her slack face. "You're not getting away that easy."

"I've decided to kill you." Mike's voice was flat and distant. He sat at the breakfast nook table, staring at his untouched whiskey glass. The cone of light spreading down from the lamp over the table was the only light in the house.

"What? Oh my god. No. Please, Mike. Please." Carolyn had been duct taped to a chair in the middle of kitchen. Mike placed her there so she couldn't be seen from the windows. Blood soaked gauze covered the wound in her shoulder.

"I don't have a choice. Now that I know you for what you are, you would kill me as soon as I untied you. Well, as soon as the effects of the water wore off anyway. I still can't believe I guessed correctly it would be your weakness. I should be grateful the myths still mention the muses' affinity to the spring."

"Mike, I swear to you, you are making a terrible mistake." Carolyn was out of tears. Slick, dried trails reflected off her cheeks. "You're out of your damned mind! Help!" Her hoarse screams filled the little house. Mike didn't bother to silence her.

"I've thought about this a lot," he said when she quieted. "I don't know that I have it in me to outright kill you. I'm not sure I could live with myself if I did that. Paying you back for my shoulder was unsettling enough. It made me feel ... dirty. I don't think Glen would have approved of it."

"Oh my god, please, Mike. Let me go."

"The thing is, you hurt me. You threatened to kill me. But, on some level, I think you really did have my best interests at heart, even if only because they coincided with yours." He picked up his tumbler and swirled the golden liquid inside of it. "But now I know your secret. Now I am more risk to you than I ever was an asset, I am sure."

He held the glass up to the light, examining the amber contents.

"I lied to you, you know," he said. "I haven't written another scream-play. After you threatened me, all I could think about was you. But I did research like my life depended upon it. Because, you know, you said it did.

"In my research, I found your kind never drank wine." He chuckled. "That's part of what gave you away—that and your continued insistence that I write more and spread out into new markets. You were never satis-fied, always needing more."

"For god's sake, Mike, I'm your agent! That's what I'm supposed to do!"

"I put my mind to the whole situation, just like a good story doctor would. Who had skin in the game? Who were the main characters?

"Well, there's me, of course, and there's the muse who really, really seemed to want me to write. Which made this seem to be all about my writing. So, following that thought, who else cared if I wrote or not? Well, there was Glen. He cared. But he's gone. I have fans, but fans are fickle. Then there are all those people at the company who won't work if I don't write. But then, they seem to be working just fine while I haven't written. In fact, the company Glen and I created is doing pretty well without me—without us—despite what you said."

Mike tossed back the whiskey. "And then there's you, Carolyn."

"Mike, you need help. You're not thinking clearly. Please stop this before it's too late."

"You wormed your way into the game when I didn't need an agent. You've pushed and pushed for me to write, to sell to other places, to do more ..."

He stood and walked over to look down at Carolyn. "Wouldn't it be something if a shape-shifting, demonic, muse-thing decided to be my agent so that it could be closer to me? So it could control and manipulate what I did for some reason?"

"You've gone insane! I'm not a demon, Mike!"

He pulled a green bottle from a metal wine rack on the counter and absently wiped dust off the neck and label. It hadn't been touched since Glen died.

"I assume the reason your kind doesn't drink wine has something to do with Dionysus, the god of wine?" He popped the cork and poured a glass. "Something about how drinking wine invites him *inside* of someone? Allows him to take control of them?"

He held the glass of red wine under her nose.

"I thought," he continued, "it was strange the muses were so closely associated with Dionysus, the god of wine, yet they themselves never drank wine. While it seems to be fun for us mere mortals—blaming alcohol for our actions—I would guess it's probably not so exciting for a god to lose control of themselves to another god like that. It's probably much more literal for you, right?"

"Please, I'm allergic to the sulfites."

"And I'm allergic to demonic muses who come into my home and threaten my life to try to make me write more!" Mike held the glass to her lips. "Drink up, bitch."

"No!" Carolyn's face contorted. She pulled away from the glass, her features flickering, replaced by the craggy, pointed face of the demon.

"Throw yourself to the crows, mortal!" it roared, easily snapping the duct tape binding its wrists and shattering the chair. It rose to tower over Mike. "You should have paid more attention to how long the effects of the water lasted!" A salacious grin split its face. "I'd kill your lover all over again if I could, but I'll settle for torturing you to death as you have tortured me!"

Mike fell back as it stalked forward. "Y-you killed Glen?"

The demon laughed at the misery twisting across Mike's face. "He was a distraction. You should have been writing, but you were too busy fawning over his pathetic weaknesses."

"No!"

"Yes!" The demon lunged.

Mike threw wine into its face as it landed on him.

Mike's neighbors peeked out windows, many afraid to set foot outside. The screams and crashes coming from his house were no longer explainable by even the best sound system. A few braver souls met in the street, phones in hand, debating calling the police.

A *whump* reverberated deep in their chests, and the front door to Mike's house splintered outward. A dark shape, half again larger than a man, sailed out through the flying shards, soaring up into the night sky, roaring with demonic laughter.

A dog yelped convulsively. The bystanders scattered. A gaping hole in Mike's house revealed furniture upturned, if not outright destroyed, and broken glass everywhere. Mike, bloody, crawled through it all, trying to make his way back into the kitchen.

The winged thing dove from the night sky into the nearest house, shattering through the picture window. Landing, it tore open cabinets and pulled out drawers, searching. Screams echoed inside the house, and the gray, leathery creature threw back its head and laughed.

"Here!" Mike called from his ruined doorway. "Here! I have what you want!" He held four wine bottles, already opened, cradled in his arms as he swayed. Blood, from the slashes across his forehead and his shattered nose, ran down his face, dripping onto the cement steps.

Peeking back through the broken window, the demon saw Mike and beamed toothily. It leaped through the window, wings catching the air, and glided across the street to land in front of Mike.

"An offering!" the creature bellowed. "Wonderful!" It took the bottle Mike held out and guzzled the wine. As the monster drank, the world became eerily silent but for a dog whimpering in a nearby yard. When the bottle was emptied, the demon sighed deeply and tossed it aside.

Mike held out another bottle. "Dionysus?"

"Garnering favor! I approve!" Its voice was the echo of thunder. "Dionysus is but one of the many names I have been called." It took the second bottle and drank before looking back to Mike. "You honor me.

Searching the memories of this creature, I see you are not only responsible for granting me access to this parasite's mortal shell, but you are a creator of both tragedy and comedy, mixing them into these *monster movies* you make. Wonderful." It drank the rest of the bottle and looked at Mike expectantly.

Mike handed it another bottle. Somewhere in the distance a police siren started.

"I am pleased to take control of this body." Dionysus, a bottle in each gnarled fist, indicated its form. "It was a disparate creature, garnering power by leeching from *my* followers. I also see it has done you a wrong. Killing your lover was an unkindness." The monster swilled more wine. "Fear not, we shall find you a new one! We shall find many!"

Two empty wine bottles flew past Mike and shattered against the house. Dionysus held out a clawed hand and Mike put the fourth bottle into it.

"Dionysus is reborn yet again!" The creature laughed and surveyed the neighborhood.

People hid behind cars and peered through windows up and down the street.

"Come my children! Come!" Dionysus raised his arms and people began walking toward him, jerkily, against their will. "We will celebrate, and you will be reborn free of fetter!"

Dionysus pointed to a woman shambling near the yard with the whining dog. "Fetch the beast!"

The woman, terror on her face, did as he compelled. The dog yelped and bit at her, tearing her arms open, but forced to disregard the injuries, tears streaming down her face, she carried the kicking animal into the semicircle of people forming around Mike's doorstep.

"Let the feast begin!" Dionysus cried.

Like zombies, people stumbled forward to tear at the dog in the woman's arms. Its horrid squealing was cut mercifully short. Mike turned and retched as people feasted on raw, fur-covered flesh.

The arriving police car splashed red and blue lights across the scene. The officers stiffly stumbled from the car to join the growing mob.

"Let the orgy begin!" Dionysus commanded.

Compulsion pulled Mike. He took steps he did not want to take. He approached a woman he did not want to approach. "Allow me to fetch more wine!" he cried out.

"Yes! Yes! More wine!" came the guffawing response.

Mike felt the geas release him, and he ran into the house. Taking the final bottle of wine from the rack, he poured half into the sink. Then he added Castalian Spring water into the bottle, mixing it with the remaining wine.

Returning, he held the bottle out to Dionysus. The winged creature took it without taking eyes off the forced Bacchanalia and downed it without hesitation. When Mike plunged his knife into Dionysus' chest, the newly risen god fell without a whimper.

People, suddenly released, screamed and scattered in shock and panic. Most ran for their homes. None seemed to note the ash pile at Mike's feet.

Mike sipped whiskey in front of his fireplace as he listened to the speakerphone.

"The effect of the media coverage about the attack on you by a crazed fan has been unbelievable," his new agent was saying. "We got another offer for the rights to the story. I think you really need to consider this one."

"I think," Mike said, his eyes rising to the portrait and meeting Glen's kind smile, "I'll write this one myself." His gaze flickered down to the two urns on the mantle. Between them, they represented the best and worst in his life, his muse and his monster.

Sam Knight has worked for three different publishers, curated four anthologies, authored six children's books, four short story collections, three novels, and nearly five dozen short stories, including a Planet of the Apes story and a Wayward Pines story, both co-authored with Kevin J. Anderson.

A stay-at-home father, Sam attempts to be a full-time writer, but there are only so many hours left in a day after kids. Once upon a time, he was known to quote books the way some people quote movies, but now he claims that having a family has made him forgetful—as a survival adaptation.

TOAD MAN, TOAD MAN

HAILEY PIPER

TOAD MAN, TOAD MAN

T oad Man, Toad Man, hoppin' along,
     Best hope he don't look at you wrong.

Almost to the front of the concessions line, a pointed finger prodded Sandy's shoulder from behind.

"How dumb is this going to be?" Colette asked. Melanie nodded beside her.

"Licorice dumb," Sandy said. Her friends didn't push the point, it being her parents' money that bought their tickets, sodas, popcorn, and candy. They just wanted to escape summer's oppressive heat.

Sandy came with purpose. Magic lived at the antiquated Johannesburg Cinema in a way that it was dead everywhere else in town. The lobby's velvet ropes, scarlet carpet, and old-fashioned marquee radiated glamor that lay distant in both space and time, but she pretended that glamor was present, that the four-screen, has-been cinema was a special place. Movie posters old and new drew her eyes with mystery and intrigue, haunting the walls with the promise of story.

One poster promised *Blood-Curse of the Toad Man,* ringed in golden lights outside Auditorium 2. She'd spotted it last week, an ad for today's one-time screening. Despite the hokey title, its dark painting had a spell-binding aura. Against a marshy horizon pockmarked by mangrove trees and brush, a dark figure loped from the water toward Sandy. His lumpy silhouette was pitch black except for two mustard yellow eyes.

191

The movie was rated R and the girls were only fifteen, but the boy at the ticket counter was sixteen and easy. Sandy had convinced him with nothing more than a smile. It helped that apparently no one else had yet bought a ticket. The scent of faux leather seating mixed with popcorn as she ushered her friends down the aisle to the best seats—close to the front, but not too close.

"Fingers crossed that nobody else pops in," Colette said, propping her feet atop the seats ahead. "Just us gals and a Toad Man."

Sandy and Melanie began to dance in the aisle, their sneakers making smacking noises each time they left the sticky floor. They had done this on a bridge last July. Colette hissed for them to stop goofing off that day, too, in case someone showed up, but no one did. They'd only quit when the wind grew fierce enough to tear the girls away, never to return.

Some nights, listening to her parents shout at each other through the walls, Sandy wished it had. Perhaps the movie would carry them off instead.

Lights dimmed, she and Melanie scrambled into their seats, and the projector ticked behind them. The Johannesburg Cinema kept its trailer reel short. No point previewing more movies than it could show.

Colette's finger again jabbed Sandy's arm. "Take a sweet straw." She offered a fistful of licorice and had dunked several into hers and Melanie's paper cups. Sandy took a couple and sucked up fizzy cola as the movie began.

Darkness circled a boy and his dad, who sat in a bobbing wooden boat, a dim lantern between them. They chatted how their night fishing was going, their dialogue hardly audible under the chorus of crickets and frogs.

Or toads, Sandy supposed.

A fishing line snagged. The dad reached into the water to untangle it, only to be yanked under by hands unseen. "Pa?" the boy called a few times. Unanswered, he dipped his oar into the water, perhaps to row for help. The water tugged the oar underneath and the boy with it.

He could've let the oar tear out of his hands, Sandy knew, but this was the movies. Nonsense was part of how they worked.

The pond's surface stilled. The title card appeared, *Blood-Curse of the Toad Man*, with red rain dribbling down each letter. A synthesizer ticked out the rhythm of a heartbeat, and children chanted over the opening credits.

Toad Man, Toad Man, a nest of bones,
Best hope Toad Man leaves you alone.

Their chanting faded as the auditorium door swung shut. Sandy glanced back.

The girls weren't alone anymore. A stranger nestled into a seat several rows behind, his frame bundled in thick clothes. Why the layers? No sense escaping summer's heat only to fight the air conditioning.

A slender ice cube fragment slid up Sandy's sweet straw and across her teeth, making her shudder. Maybe the stranger had it right after all. She returned to the movie.

A detective, the lead, arrived in a swamp village to investigate a series of murders that were holding up a construction project. Real estate businessmen swore it was a conspiracy. The village madman ranted about a curse. Cut to night, something dragged a villager and construction worker underwater to the chant of unseen children.

Toad Man, Toad Man, he won't wait long,
When it's your turn, you'll hear our song.

Colette shifted impatient legs. "But when do we see the Toad Man?" Melanie shushed her.

Panning shots followed the detective across indistinct swampland as another day faded to night, the world nothing but lightning bugs, moss-coated trees, and odd footprints in the mud. He and a village woman became romantic too fast.

A sticky rhythm began at the back of the auditorium, someone pacing the soda-stained floor. Sandy tried to ignore it, but when it kept going she looked over her shoulder to the stranger.

He was still seated. Was he lifting his shoes up and down? The sound came again, wet lips smacking shut and open. Melanie looked over with Sandy and shushed at the stranger. He wriggled in his seat, but the smacking stopped. The girls glanced at each other, shook their heads, and turned again to the screen.

The movie cut to the village and panned a black pond. Footsteps trudged through water, coming ashore, each louder than the last.

Sandy clenched her teeth. She knew when to expect a jump scare.

But the timing was off, and the clumsy Toad Man waddled from off-screen. He was nothing like the poster's loping shadow, steeped in mystique and dread. His blood-curse was to have rubbery, fake-looking skin and white plastic eyes, a cheap Halloween costume in place of a special effect.

Colette and Melanie screamed laughter. Sandy sank low, her face burning. She'd wasted her mom's money on this '70s B-movie of all things? She tried to join in the laughter, but the children's chant drowned her out.

Toad Man, Toad Man, comin' at night,
Before that, pray you die of fright.

The chanters sounded like they believed it. They must not have seen the costume before recording the audio.

Colette and Melanie were still laughing when that wet smacking came again behind them, only once this time, but that was enough to kill their good mood. On-screen, the Toad Man's mouth smacked open and shut, the noise almost identical.

Sandy leaned forward, transfixed as the Toad Man assaulted the swamp village. The costume didn't look so funny anymore. It didn't look realistic either, but she would've rather it had. Everything else in the movie—acting, sets, props—at least passed for Hollywood genuine, the most kind of real she would ever hope for in a movie.

The Toad Man wasn't genuine or even Hollywood passable. His unreality shambled through the scene, a child's dreamlike creation somehow manifested from crayon into an R-rated movie. He did not belong in this world. Every clumsy step threatened to throw him through the screen where he'd plop into a theater seat, its leather fake as his flesh.

Why was he here? He had no right. A better costume must have been thrown aside for this uncanny abomination. Sandy chewed a licorice whip down so fast that her teeth nicked her fingernails

Toad Man, Toad Man, closer he be,
Best he gets you and won't get me.

When the nocturnal massacre ended, Colette sprang out of her seat. "Need to use the restroom. Mel, too." Melanie nodded.

Sandy started to stand. "I'll go with you."

"Then who's going to tell us what we missed?" Colette jogged up the aisle, Melanie close behind. Their purses knocked their sides as they ran.

Sandy watched them slip out the door and eyed the bundled-up stranger four rows back. He watched them too. Had he moved? She hadn't counted the rows dividing them before, but he seemed closer. His shadowy, indistinct head turned from door to screen.

To Sandy. She looked to the movie before he could notice her stare.

The detective wanted to evacuate the village, but the local madman said everyone had to pay for the curse and blew up the bridge to the highway. The only escape was to hike through the swamp. Between scenes, the

Toad Man waited for nightfall. Plastic eyes peeked through the pond's surface as if watching all who watched him.

Sandy caught her teeth at her nails again and sat on her hands. It was just a movie. At the end credits, she would find out what poor guy had to crawl into that Toad Man costume and traipse through mud and pond scum. All this was fiction.

But she already knew that. That it was fiction didn't comfort her this time. His being a costume meant the surreal Toad Man was only a skin that anyone could put on and bring to life.

Wet smacking started again, louder now. Sandy hoped it was Colette and Melanie crossing the sticky floor, but the auditorium door hadn't opened. What was taking so long? She glanced at their seats, where red licorice poked out of soda cups. Usually she could make out every row once her eyes adjusted, but fingers of darkness coated the far seats, shrouding patches of the auditorium in false night. Her friends were the smart ones. They had probably abandoned her, realizing it was a mistake to leave the safety of warm daylight for hours of silence with strangers in the dark.

Toad Man, Toad Man, nowhere to hide,
Locked your doors, but he got inside.

Had Sandy wanted to be alone and miserable, she would've stayed home. Let her parents keep the bribe money that sent her out on the town where she couldn't find divorce papers left on the kitchen table, the stuff of genuine chills that thankfully no movie could replicate.

Except she wasn't really alone. Another wet smack forced her to glare over her shoulder. She couldn't see four rows back anymore, only the distant projector's white glow and the shape of the bundled-up stranger, now three rows behind. She hadn't heard him get up. Shadow added another layer across him, thick as his clothing.

The darkness deepened when the movie again turned to night. Villagers, construction workers, the detective, and his love interest waded single file into the stagnant black swamp. Chanting rang through the trees, but there were no children among the fleeing survivors. The chant was in the wind.

Toad Man, Toad Man, what does he find?
Don't you look back; he's right behind.

Sandy tried not to look but couldn't help it. The stranger sat two rows back. She could almost make him out, but the flickering projector flashed in her eyes, casting a ghostly circle on her sight. Clearer came a stench that overpowered popcorn. She recognized it for putrid, algae-coated pond water, undisturbed unless this stranger had washed his stinking clothes in it.

The auditorium door swept open. Shoes kissed the floor, Colette and Melanie dropped into their seats, and Colette leaned over with a whisper. "What'd we miss?"

Sandy couldn't look at them. "They can't get out."

Melanie leaned over to ask a question, too, but gurgling drew her eyes to the screen, where the Toad Man snatched another victim. Watery screams rattled the auditorium speakers. Sandy smelled the broken pond surface and recoiled against her seat.

Weight pressed at her back. She didn't look over her shoulder again, didn't need to. The stranger now sat behind her. Clouds of swampy stink rolled out of his clothes. Didn't the others smell that? Colette should've been whining about it by now, but she and Melanie only slurped soda through licorice, clueless and content. They had been out of the auditorium too long to sense the danger.

Victim after victim went to watery graves. The survivors dwindled until only the detective and his lover remained. He aimed his pistol this way and that, while she clung to his arm and shrieked at every shadow.

Just a movie. Not real. But what did that make the bundled-up stranger? Sandy couldn't escape reality into movie magic and hide from the movie at the same time. If there was a third category between reality and fantasy, it had spawned the Toad Man.

Bubbles climbed her throat. She was sinking into the pond with the dead, algae pressing inside her lungs. The stench wafted from her soda when she tried to take a sip. Someone had replaced it with brew from the movie's swamp. Wet smacking echoed through the auditorium, but this time it came from her sticky lips.

Toad Man, Toad Man, there's one way through.

Offer your friends instead of you.

She glanced at Colette and Melanie. If they looked at her, what would they see just behind? A man bundled in clothing, a rubbery costume, or something worse, an avatar of swamp and decay? Their eyes never left the screen, no matter how badly Sandy fidgeted. She tried to focus, but the weight on her back grew heavier.

The detective and his love interest neared the shore, but chanting and croaking chased them. Water bubbled nearby, the Toad Man about to strike. "I'm sorry," the detective said. He aimed his pistol, shot his lover in the knee, and trudged toward shore. The camera followed him, abandoning his lover as the Toad Man came for her.

Colette clicked her tongue. "So chivalrous." She didn't understand.

Hot breath clouded the rows. Sandy squeezed her eyes shut, but the back of her eyelids brought no relief. The projector light's ghostly after-image had transformed into the mustard yellow eyes of a creature wholly separate from the world. It was neither part of real life nor the product of human imagination, a thing impossible and yet absolute.

Best he gets you and won't get me. Offer your friends instead of you.

The stink was inside her, infectious. Vomit threatened the edge of her throat. She stood sharp from her seat and charged toward the aisle.

"It's almost over," Colette said. "You'll miss the end."

Melanie must have spilled soda after they returned; the floor was stickier than before and sucked at Sandy's shoes like mud. Smacking sounds stalked her, but she didn't dare glance at the stranger now. She made it out the auditorium door and darted for the ladies' restroom.

There was no one inside. Swamp stink traded for the chemical sting of cleaning supplies. Sandy hunkered over a dingy sink and splashed water in her eyes and mouth. It tasted muddy. She spat and stared at her reflection in the stained, cracked mirror. She didn't mean to blink, fought the urge hard as she could, but it was a losing battle.

Brown eyes gave way to yellow. She forced her eyelids open. Familiar eyes. Blink. Alien eyes. Chanting floated at the edge of earshot, the words no longer distinct but muffled by the wall between restroom and auditorium.

Her voice came hoarse. "What do you want?" she asked but already knew. Her eyelids shut, locking her in with a sickly, inhuman glare. "I'm sorry."

She tried not to think of Colette, Melanie, and the bundled-up stranger, instead thought of home and the hell that brewed there. It was solid, real, broke no rules like the movie had broken, promising fantasy but giving something that was neither fact nor fiction but Other.

The movie had to be getting loud, its screams piercing clear through the wall. Smacking came again, quieter now. Sandy was surprised there was anyone left for the Toad Man to kill. Her eyelids slid up and down again, and at each blink the phantom yellow gaze shrank into blackness.

Toad Man, Toad Man, hoppin' away,
You get to live a few more days.

When the chant faded, Sandy left the restroom. Ten minutes must have passed inside, but eons had worn through Johannesburg Cinema. New posters appeared muted, as if years had drained all their color. Lights still bordered the poster for *Blood-Curse of the Toad Man*, but now several bulbs flickered or had gone out. Sandy avoided looking at the loping figure as she pressed open the door to Auditorium 2.

A glistening yellow eye filled the movie screen, wide as the auditorium. It was not the costume's plastic, nor was it a real toad's eye, but deep and ethereal in a way known only to nightmares. Liquid slid between its pupils and iris. It seemed almost human.

Then the movie cut to black, the synthesizer soundtrack repeated its heartbeat rhythm, and children again sang the Toad Man's chant.

Sandy trudged down the aisle toward her row, shoes going *smack, smack* on the floor. Purses and soda cups lingered at the seats, but Colette and Melanie weren't there. Neither was the bundled-up stranger who'd sat just behind them. The auditorium once more smelled of popcorn.

Glancing back at the door, Sandy wasn't sure how to leave. What waited out there, real life or something alien? She looked to the screen instead, read the credits.

They named no one for playing the Toad Man. Maybe no one had. Synthesizer music faded as the last of the unseen children's chant overtook the soundtrack, ringing in the credits' end.

Toad Man, Toad Man, he'll have sweet dreams,
Of hands and hearts and skin and screams.
Toad Man, Toad Man, he needs his rest,
But don't forget he likes you best.

Hailey Piper is the author of horror novellas *Benny Rose, the Cannibal King* and *The Possession of Natalie Glasgow*. An active member of the Horror Writers Association, her short fiction appears in *Daily Science Fiction*, *The Arcanist*, *Tales to Terrify*, *Blood Bath Literary Zine*, and many other publications. Her debut dark fantasy/epic horror novel, *The Verses of Aeg*, will be published by Bronzeville Books in late 2020. She lives with her wife in Maryland, where Hailey haunts their apartment making spooky noises. Haileypiper.com.

FALSE BAY

RICK WILBER

FALSE BAY

C hloe Cary, she of the Emmy nomination for her shoot-em-up role in the *Annie Oakley* series of the same name, she of the two golds and a silver in the pool at the Paris Olympics in '24, she of the Pac 15 champion women's soccer at Stanford in '25, she who seemed to have it all just a year ago but is now reduced to the female lead in the straight-to-freestream *Colossal III* where she's a frightened teenager (the wonders of de-aging technology!) who becomes a big ol' monster kaiju, is in her trailer. She's prepping for the second day of trying to get the scene right where she slowly emerges from the shallow water of the Gulf of Mexico and then, as she wades in toward the beach, she changes and grows and morphs into the eponymous colossal monster that stomps its way toward the city to thwart the attack from that *other* monster that threatens our very way of life. Twenty takes yesterday and no one's happy. She doesn't have the intensity the scene demands. She can't seem to summon up the blinding anger necessary to make it work.

Maybe today she'll get it right, find the right internal anger and fear to channel into her acting. She sighs. It's a stupid movie. There's not much of a plot and she hates this scene, but *Colossal III* will make her a few bucks and keep her name out there. It's been a rough year.

So now she's working on her physicality, trying to look tough, when her smarty dings. It's set on silent and block while she works, so the ding means a top priority override. "I'm focusing, myBetty. I said no calls," she says to her helpmate, her always-there companion who resides in a tiny bowl amp in her right ear and has all the answers to all the questions all the time.

"Sorry to break in, Chloe, but it's all over the clouds," says myBetty. "A S'hudonni ship has landed in the Salton Sea and Twoclicks is on it. He's alive."

"What!?" Twoclicks is the roly-poly alien overlord of the whole damn planet who was, or is, either a cuddly comedian or a stone-cold ruthless killer and profiteer, take your pick. He and his pals, a couple hundred of them, showed up a couple of years ago, landing their ships in warm, shallow estuaries worldwide, full of promises and, in Twoclicks's case at least, a jovial and gently disarming charm that was backed up by those deadly screamships that dealt death when it was necessary. Twoclicks always expressed his deep regrets after thousands died in each of those early uprisings. Earth got the message, and after that the dissenters went underground, staying quiet and biding their time and making plans.

Which seemed to have worked, a year later, when Twoclicks died, two weeks into a trip to the home world where he brought along Earthie emissaries. The whole side of his screamship blew out and sent Twoclicks and his cabinet and all the Earthies—the ambassadors and directors and presidents and papal emissaries and under-secretaries—all of them and more, spinning away into the nothing, arms and legs flailing, mouths open in screams that were terrible and sad one second and then gone the next, because you couldn't hear a thing in that sudden vacuum.

And all of this went live to everyone on Earth who was wearing a sweep receiver, or watching on old-school television or their smarties, or their new wavescreens or whatever the hell they used. All of them were watching and hearing as three dozen died, including Twoclicks, who'd brought them all together to sign the treaty he'd worked so hard for. Peace in our time! Under the benevolent guidance of mother S'hudon!

Benevolent, sure, but with the occasional reminder of who was in charge. The porpoisy S'hudonni, the friendly and slightly squishy and moist aliens from Out There who'd brought Earth the chance to trade and learn from a dozen worlds in their system. There were some adjustments to be made here and there, of course. But the science! The technology! The access to all those other worlds!

And the screamships. Ah, yes, those purveyors of power, those enforcers of calm. Those three examples as the Russians and the Chinese and the Americans all watched in dismay as their best weaponry, the hypersonic drones, the ghostships, the pulse weapons, the laughable lasers, the silly B-1s and 2s and creaky old F-35s and Russian Stingrays and French Dasaults and all the rest. Puddled. A quick flick from that beam from the screamships and that was it. Dissolution.

So it was the end of war, and peace reigned, rather gently enforced really. Surely the medcots and the free energy and the hypertubes and the travel for Earth's elite were all worth a little humility, right? Visit distant planets! Learn the hidden secrets of the universe! Sign me up!

Not everyone thought the New Order was the best possible future. There were dissidents, a lot of them, but they were underground and powerless now, so who cares?

And then that tragic blowout meant the dissidents had proven they weren't powerless at all, and when Earth woke up the next morning the aliens were leaving. The S'hudonni don't stay where they aren't wanted. And just like that, in forty-eight hours, they were gone. And with them went all the wonder, all the future, all the promise of membership in a galactic empire.

Oh, and there also went Chloe's career, into a tank, an actual very large water tank ultimately, where Chloe/kaiju roamed as a disappointed Hollywood tried hard to forget about her. She'd taken a gamble with Twoclicks and she'd lost. She was lucky to be a part-time kaiju.

Until now! Twoclicks is alive! And he's back! A ship, all spindly legs below that huge egg-shaped hull, landed this morning in the Salton Sea—the S'hudonni do love warm, shallow water—and, first things first, Twoclicks came out onto the landing platform to wave at all the flyeyes and drones and choppers and all the rest that had it on live and then he dived off the landing platform and into the shallow water. Hardly a ripple!

After the swim he popped back up on the platform, a meter or so above the water line, and disappeared back into the ship. Later, the usual platform opened at the top of the egg and an Earthie chopper landed. Twoclicks and another, smaller S'hudonni came out onto that platform while the world watched, and climbed into the helicopter and off they went, with dozens, then hundreds, of drones and other choppers and satellites high in orbit and cameras on the ground and Earthies with their phone cams on building tops, all getting it live as the chopper landed on the roof of the famous S'hudonni Consulate on Pershing Square.

So Chloe took that call from Twoclicks, for sure, and now here she is on her way to the consulate, coming to pay her respects. She's his very first visitor! Before the new governor or any of the new presidents or popes or supreme leaders or secretary-generals or anyone else. Chloe Cary, his favorite Earthie!

And why would that be? Well, it was Chloe Cary that brought Twoclicks here in the first place. She'd been the host of *Space Chicks* two years before, when her career was in a major slump and she took the job to keep her name out there. Her Stanford bachelor's in physics finally paid off when she got the offer. She'd always felt guilty about earning that bachelor's and then doing nothing with it, but there she was, asking the right questions of women who were space scientists, physicists and science writers, exobiologists ready to rave about the Mars bugs, and many more. Twenty-two weeks of classy pop science with plenty of CGI to dress it up fancy. They'd even done a three-parter on what aliens might look like if they ever came to Earth.

They'd guessed wrong. No one had figured on porpoisy, aquatic, jokesters, eager to help Earth along on the road to Shambala. Yep, no one had called that shot, but sure enough, up there in orbit around it, looking us over, undetected, was Twoclicks, who liked the show and loved Chloe Cary, so when they finally landed, the first thing he did was ask to see her. Take me to your actor! Wow, did her career take off. It went stratospheric, you might even say. She was everywhere! And that's how you make it in Hollywood, boys and girls. Have an alien overlord as your pal.

Then a year later he died, assassinated in an act of terror was the general belief. One of those three dozen Earthies was a bomb who came in peace and died in violence, along with everyone else in that ship. And suddenly no one would take Chloe's agent's calls, and that high-flying career came back down to Earth. Months later, she finally got the *Colossal III* gig, and was happy to have it. That's how bad things got.

But now Twoclicks is back. How had he survived? Why did he return? What were his plans for the future now? There were a lot of questions, and it seemed to have fallen to Chloe Cary to ask them, get some answers and clue us all in. Twoclicks wasn't talking to anyone else.

So here comes Chloe! She's heading straight from the studio to the consulate in a human-chauffeured limo, no lowly self-drive for Chloe Cary.

The paparazzi are following her with their ebikes and their drones and flittercams and spyeyes. All that whirring and humming right outside the smoked glass of her window in the back seat of the limo from the time she left the studio's arched entrance right through the half-hour drive down Sunset and then Rodeo and then a left on Wilshire, past Louis Vuitton and Spago and all the rest of that, all the way past the Children's Museum and the Tar Pits and MacArthur Park and on to Pershing Square and the ornate deco of the S'hudonni Consulate, three floors of quiet grandeur.

"Chloe! Chloe! Chloe!" they shout at her as she exits the limo when her human driver steps around the limo to open her door. She's back at the top of the cycle! There's nothing better, nothing bigger, than Chloe Cary!

And then, when the consulate's door opens and the most powerful being on planet Earth steps out, "Twoclicks! Twoclicks! Twoclicks!" they shout, and he waves at them as he steps toward Chloe and gives her a big damp hug and says "Dear friend Chloe, we are sso, sso happy to see you!"

Twoclicks is really back! And he's hugging Chloe Cary! The air is alive with buzzing and whirring and humming drones and the smaller flitter-cams and the pricey new spyeyes. Great stuff! Fabulous!

And then the door shuts and that's that. Time to save some battery and bring back the cams and sit and relax for a while. And then wait, and wait some more if that's what it takes.

Inside, Twoclicks takes a step back, holds Chloe out by her shoulders and seems to size her up. Then he smiles hugely and exclaims, "I knew it! You are a wonder!" and he brings her in for another hug.

It seems a little creepy, to be honest. Chloe can feel the oddly cold and slick, dark skin of his arms against hers and as if that isn't weird enough, he then leans in to kiss her on the left check.

What's the damn protocol here? myBetty wasn't helping at all. Where is her helpmate's advice when Chloe needs it?

Enough is enough, so Chloe gently pushes him back and extricates herself from those spindly arms, then forces herself to smile and say, "It's a great pleasure to see you again ..." and she hesitates, waiting for help from myBetty, who finally speaks up in her ear, "I'm having connectivity problems, Chloe. But he's First Consul Twoclicks," and Chloe says that, "... First Consul," and adds, "We all thought you were dead. We watched you die, didn't we?" It would be nice, she thinks, to get some explanation for how this is happening. Hell, the whole world wants to know, and she's the one who's here.

"First Consul?" Twoclicks says, "That iss too sserious! I am Twoclicks! We are great friendss! There is much to ssay and much to do!"

"Well, okay, then," says myBetty, and "Sure, Twoclicks" says Chloe, smiling despite how creepy this is getting to be. She does have a lot of questions, starting with what the hell really happened out there. How did Twoclicks survive?

"So," she tries again, "What happened out there?"

Twoclicks waves the question away. "Firsst things firsst, dear friend Chloe," he says as he walks next to her down the long, ornate hallway toward the dining room.

"We will eat! Sso much to ssay for one meal, but we will try, dearest friend Chloe. Come, come, and I will tell you all about our adventuress. Sspace ssaga! Amazing! Astounding!"

Not for the first time, Chloe has to wonder just how goofy is this character. Our newly returned great alien overlord, our self-styled First Consul, is, at heart, a clown? A deadly clown, to be sure; but a goof, yes, and a charming one at that.

She hears from myBetty in her ear. "Breaking news, Chloe, S'hudonni ships, at least a dozen of them, are landing all over the planet. Nothing hostile. Seems our friends are back."

Twoclicks waves his other hand at her to say, "Yess, yess, all are returned, dearest friend Chloe. Back! All will be answered ssoon! For now. Food!" And he takes her by the hand to walk into the dining room.

Chloe knows this room from the last time around with Twoclicks. There are long curtains that are always closed over the tall, narrow windows, and the long banquet table centers the room. There are settings for three at one end of the table. One at the head of the table, one on each side. Very cozy. But who is the other setting for?

Twoclicks walks over to a side table and pours two glasses of wine. He brings them over to Chloe, hands her one, says "Nice wine!" and when she takes her glass he reaches out to touch hers for a toast. "To our great friendship!"

"Friendship," says Chloe, and smiles even as she wonders where the hell this is going.

She finds out. Twoclicks whistles and clicks something in S'hudonni and in through a side door at the back of the room waddles a S'hudonni child, a happy one at that, fairly skipping into the room.

Twoclicks is beaming to see him, Chloe notes, and then he says why. "Dearest friend Chloe, I introduce to you The Perfection, my son Treble, prince of the House of S'hu!"

"Your son?" Chloe asks, stunned.

"My son and ssavior!" says Twoclicks, "the one who found my lifecraft after drifting for weeks. Near death!" Then he turns to whistle and click at the little one, who whistles happily back and then steps up to Chloe to say, in perfect English, "Chloe Cary, I am Treble, and I am very excited to meet you. My father has said so much about you. You are, he says, the nicest human on Earth! I will be delighted to travel with you!"

"Wonderful!" says Twoclicks, "now let uss eat!" And so they take their places as waiters—Earthies, all—bring in the first course, some kind of soup. Chloe is wondering as she sits just what the child meant by "travel with you"?

Treble to the rescue. As he sits, he chats, in perfect English, "A grand tour is being arranged, and my father would like you to escort me as we meet your people. Would that be all right?"

"A grand tour?" Chloe asks. What the hell?

"Yes, a global tour, to all those places where my father needs to revive his interests. London, Paris, Cairo, Mumbai, Cape Town."

Chloe shakes her head, blows out a breath. This is the worst idea she's heard all day, or all year, or ever. Travel with the S'hudonni overlord and his little alien kid who surely will have a huge target on his back, since the same dissidents who tried to kill his father will certainly take aim at him now, too. And Chloe right there with him. Wonderful. The three targets.

"No, no," Treble says, seeming to read her mind. "Father Twoclicks will stay home. There are important matters of state that he needs to take care of here."

Chloe looks at Twoclicks, who is busy spooning cream of mushroom soup into his capacious mouth. Big slurps off the spoon. A satisfied smile. He said "Thiss iss very tasty, dear friend Chloe."

So obviously the kid did better in the brains department than his father. And Chloe smiles and slides her bowl of soup over to Twoclicks even as Treble turns his attention to his soup, which he spoons with precision, bowl to mouth.

But Twoclicks! This goofy creature with little dribbles of cream of mushroom trailing down from his mouth as he slurps, is back in town and he is, no question, the most powerful being on Earth, the world's leader in fact if not in name. She wonders if he wants to get even for the assassination attempt. In a day or two he'll be attending to matters of state and heads, she suspects, will roll.

"Sso, dear friend Chloe," Twoclicks says as he lifts the spoon to his mouth and slurps again, "it will be you and The Perfection, dear sson Treble and some Earthie guardss and media and the ssuch. Oh, and in Cape Town your guide will be the wonderful Anodiwa Pinaar!"

Great, thought Chloe. She'd meet Pinaar, whose career was rising even as Chloe's fell. Sure, that'd be fun, hanging out with the next big thing. But she smiles as Twoclicks adds a bit of persuasion. "Great expossure, dear friend Chloe! Whole world will be watching you with my sson The Perfection, Treble."

Chloe thinks about things. It will be good, great even, for her face and name to show up all over the place. Her publicist will be very, very pleased, and so will the agent and the studio and all the rest of the hangers-on.

Plus, the truth is you can't really say no to the returned Scion of S'hudon, the Sultan Who Might Swat You, the Jovial Genius, the Man Behind the Curtain for Earth's Future. So, "Yes, sure, I'd be delighted," is her answer. And that earns her a hug from Twoclicks and another from the pint-sized Perfection, Treble, and then, some pretty decent chicken for dinner, which Twoclicks makes a mess of, but Treble carves and eats with aplomb.

So they're going to shoot around her for a few weeks on the set, and off she'll go with the kid to show him around, starting in L.A. at the S'hudonni Consulate and then heading east to D.C., then on to London and Paris and the rest. Social stops all the while, admiring the scenery and the weather, nothing political, visiting famous places from the London Zoo to the Eiffel Tower and finally, two weeks later, to Cape Town, where Treble will get a chance to frolic with some real Earthie wildlife.

Which, looking back, seemed like a good enough idea at the time, Chloe will tell famous rumormonger Gayle Gadfly three months later in a live interview from Chloe's home in Malibu on the very day of the very premier that recalls the excitement that went down like this:

"We saw these at the zoo in London!" Treble said in perfect English, excited to see the cute little Cape penguins waddle along a sandy path to the beach. He saw no resemblance between himself and penguins that ran along the path ahead of them, though in fact he was a little taller but otherwise, when he mimicked their walk, fit into their flock more or less perfectly.

Chloe laughed at that for the cameras and flyeyes and drones and the rest that were capturing it all live for the global billions, the Hollywood star and her little pal, traveling the world so everyone could meet and be charmed by the princeling, Treble.

Who had, in fact, turned out to be pretty darn charming.

Chloe really liked Treble, and he liked her. He'd taken to calling her Aunt Chloe and she'd smiled at that and didn't say no. Sure, traveling with him was wearing and while she was enjoying all the hoopla and appreciative of the numbers; really she just wanted it to end. She was nervous all the time, worried over who might be planning to kill or capture The Perfection and, oh by the way, make a major splash by doing away with Chloe Cary at the same time. A few more days and it would be over, Twoclicks had promised just this morning. He was in touch nearly hourly, fretting over his child apparently.

For now, here Chloe stood, on a boulder at the back of a beach near Cape Town, South Africa, with Treble holding her hand as Anodiwa Pinaar, the hottest item in the stable of Cape Visions, the fifth-largest media entity on Earth and a sister studio to Chloe's since both of them were owned by Totalcom, showed them around.

They'd started with a tour of Cape Visions, which made movies when it wasn't making military tech to export in the great tradition of South African arms merchants. Lots of studio tech, high and low, and then, the pièce de résistance, the BCI work with animals, where a human wearing a headset could direct thoughts to an animal wearing a receiver, and the animal reacted. They weren't ready to try it yet in moviemaking, but the military apps were all over it, said Anodiwa, and she showed why as she sent a tasty thought to a lab rat and it sped right over to its food tray for a nibble. She made the rat sit up, turn in circles, play dead, and then dash through a maze. Treble was duly impressed. Chloe could almost see the wheels turning in the kid's head. Maybe these humans weren't so backward after all. Thought control. Cool!

Most of the touring had been more ordinary, pleasing the crowds and signing autographs and waving at the flitterbys and spyeyes and the drones and the old-school paparazzi holding actual cameras. Chloe was glad to see it. After a year of no one caring about her, worrying over the paparazzi made her oddly happy.

Early in the day, Pinaar had stood with them on the bluffs overlooking False Bay and showed them where to look for whales. There were none in sight, to Treble's great disappointment. Then they'd come down off the mountain and driven for an hour to reach Cape Agulhas, the southern tip of Africa. There they'd stood next to the stone marker with the line down the middle and the words Indian Ocean in English and Indiese Oseaan in Afrikaans, with the arrow pointing left; and Atlantic Ocean and Atlantiese

Oseaan, with the arrow pointing right. You could look out from there and see where the lighter blue of the Indian Ocean met the darker Atlantic.

It was all too good to resist for Treble, so while Chloe and Anodiwa—not to mention the global audience—watched and worried, young Treble dived off the rocks at the end of Africa and took delight in the chance to swim in two oceans almost at once, swimming through the demarcation line between the Indian and the Atlantic, unworried about the great white sharks and orcas that hunted there and, instead, hoping to see and play with the humpback whales. No luck with the humpbacks, but no harm from the sharks or orcas, either, much to the relief of the watching two billion or more, not to mention Chloe and Anodiwa.

They'd seen plenty of other things in Cape Town, too. They'd taken the new zoom lift to the top of Table Mountain. The lift encased them in that glass bubble that rose up the side of the mountain. At the top they'd had lunch at The Table, the restaurant that seemed to be suspended out over the nothingness, with the city to the left, the ocean in front, and the shoreline curving away into the distance to the right. You could even see Cape Point from there.

Then, after lunch, they'd come down from the mountain to take the studio limo to the TruNature park entrance and walked into the interpretive center, where they'd helped Treble put on the modified sweep receiver so he could sweep a caracal, those handsome mid-sized cats with the upswept ears. The sweep helmet meant Treble could feel like he was inside the cat's sensory input as it stalked and hunted.

They'd slid the altered helmet onto Treble's conical head and attached the ear buds, the taste buds, the smell tips, and all the rest. It wouldn't be the same experience for him that it was for humans–his hearing extended into both higher and lower ranges, for starters–but it would give him a good idea of what Earthie animals sense and how humans received those sensory inputs, and that was the point. Chloe's myBetty helpmate turned out to be indispensable for the software connectivity. She was linked in with the Trebnet servers at Twoclicks' consulate in Los Angeles and those servers had the answers to myBetty's questions. In five minutes, Treble was hooked into one of the wandering caracal cats for the better part of an hour as it roamed the scrub brush and fynbos looking for a meal of guinea fowl or mongoose or, yummiest of all, a dassie, those chubby critters the size of a small groundhog. Chloe and Anodiwa both wore headsets, too, as spectators.

Somewhere along the way, sensing it all through her own headset,

Chloe realized that Treble wasn't just watching, he was guiding the cat's actions, turning it left and then right, having it sit, then getting it up and moving. It was fascinating, and worrisome, to watch. When the caracal stalked and killed a young dassie, tearing and chewing, tendons and muscles and bones all cracking and the blood flowing as the cat fed on the warm meat, it was hard to know whether cute little Treble had been at the controls or the cat had been acting on its own.

When it was over, Treble took off his helmet and said, "Aunt Chloe, that was awesome!" in his best colloquial American. Chloe laughed politely then looked at Anodiwa, who was looking back at her. They both knew what had just happened as they watched Treble walk off, hand in hand, with the park director, to see and do even more exciting things.

Anodiwa looked at Chloe and shook her head. "Not possible," she said. "That's a receiving set only that the kid was wearing. There is no possible way for that little princeling to have controlled that cat."

Sure, thought Chloe, absolutely no way. And yet he did. There was no question. "We both saw it, Anodiwa," she said.

Chloe had to wonder what Daddy Twoclicks thought about this. He was tuned into myBetty and no doubt to Anodiwa's helpmate, too. That was a constant live feed, so he'd seen it all. Wasn't he curious about his son's abilities?

"No," said myBetty, chiming in unbidden. "He's not curious. And he wants to talk with you."

It occurred to Chloe that she'd been thinking that the only time she wasn't being eavesdropped on by Twoclicks and probably the whole damn world on this epic journey with the princeling was when she was thinking to herself. And now, she realized, not even that was true.

"Ho! Dear friend Chloe!" said Twoclicks into the tiny bowl amp in her right ear. She walked away from the others for some semblance of privacy, as silly as that now seemed.

"Not ssilly at all, dear friend Chloe!" said Twoclicks with his usual exuberant lisp. "Right now almosst private!"

Oh Christ, she thought. "Almost" couldn't be good.

"All right, Twoclicks," she said. "Almost just the two of us? Good. So tell me, does Treble have this ability? To control things with his mind?"

"Yess!" Twoclicks said. "The Perfection is one ssmart cookie!"

"Sure," said Chloe, wondering for a moment what kind of cookie Twoclicks had in mind.

"Ssugar!" he said, with that throaty cackle that passed for a good laugh.

"Yess, dear friend Chloe. Treble has established linkss everywhere, it sseems. We are sso proud! For Treble, and for all of uss!"

Well, that's good to know, thought Chloe. But it didn't explain the mind-reading thing. Anyway, "Thank you, Twoclicks. I'll tell Anodiwa. She was wondering, too."

"She knowss now, too!" Twoclicks said, with a loud cackle of S'hudonni laughter.

Chloe looked up and there was Anodiwa, twenty feet away over by the viewing window for the huge main tank. She smiled, gave Chloe a thumbs-up, and Chloe shrugged and did the same. Damn Twoclicks. Damn S'hudonni. And what the hell was Anodiwa doing anyway? They hadn't needed to be squired around by anyone special at any of the other sites. Was this being done just to boost Anodiwa's profile? Yes, probably.

Chloe turned to walk back to the others, and noticed for something like the hundredth time that a total of four bodyguards seem to be involved in looking after them. And one of those was clearly a South African Special Forces type, so really watching Anodiwa.

Twoclicks, she thought, testing her newfound theory on who could read her mind, *shouldn't we have more security around us? The current level still seems very light to me. I've had more security than this for a trip to the drugstore in Malibu.* Which wasn't true, but made her point.

"Ho, good friend Chloe!" Twoclicks said in her ear. "We will keep you ssafe. We promise!"

"Thanks," she said, and then tried to not think the thoughts that might have been less than gracious.

And on they went.

Eventually the busy day brought them here in late afternoon, to Boulders Beach, in Simon's Town, some twenty kilometers south of Cape Town. To get here they snuck away from the usual gaggle of paparazzi and drones by renting their own car, a boxy Nistoy electric with tinted glass that they clambered into in Anodiwa's capacious garage and then drove down the back alleyway away from the house and headed down the bay.

Away from the media for a precious hour or so, Anodiwa felt free to pull over in the empty parking lot at the beach. Treble headed straight for the water, waddling along a path with the penguins and laughing before he, and they, dived in, while Anodiwa helped Chloe don a wet suit, a mask, and a snorkel. Carrying the fins, Chloe led the way as they wandered down between the house-sized boulders and onto the grainy sand. She wasn't worried about the swimming, she still did a morning swim often enough in Malibu, down the wooden steps to the beach, out and into the cold Pacific, and then straight out for a few hundred meters, left or right from there depending on the whim of the day, and then back for a good half-hour. Refreshing.

This was no Malibu, though. As she walked the path from the car park to the water, there were penguins all around, eyeing her suspiciously but unafraid. They were noisy as hell individually, and together they raised a great cacophony, calling to each with loud squawks. Chloe could barely hear herself think, and that seemed pretty damn ironic.

Anodiwa and Chloe worked their way through the penguins and then, as they reached the water, Chloe balanced on one leg at a time to reach down and slip on the fins and then stood to put on the mask and, five steps later, she was in the water.

It was marvelous. The water wasn't any colder than Malibu, and had a lot less wave action, so she had no trouble snorkeling. She could see about twenty meters underwater, not great but not too bad, either. Even in that range there were penguins next to her and around her and beneath her as she snorkeled out to deeper water. She paused once to float and look around. A number of boulders were big enough to rise out of the water and one had a large flat area just above the waterline, wet and sparkling in the sun, crowded with penguins. It was a playground, she thought, watching the penguins as they seemed to leap out of the water to land on their webbed feet, standing upright on the flat surface. Then they waddled around for a few paces, apparently to take stock of one another, and then dived right back in. It was comical to watch.

Treble surfaced just a few meters away, a huge smile on that round face. He was having fun, a lot of it. "Race you to that rock, Aunt Chloe!" he said, and dived back in.

"myBetty, you getting all this?" Chloe asked her helpmate.

"Absolutely, Chloe. Looks like fun," myBetty said.

"Okay, then. Here I go," Chloe said, and ducked down into the water, went down a meter or two, and started porpoising her fins to maximize her speed. She couldn't possibly beat Treble, who was already halfway there; but she'd give it her best shot. The penguins bumped her several times, which was somewhere between funny and frightening. But she worked her way through the crowded water to the flat rock and clambered up. Minutes later, sitting side by side on the rock, surrounded by pushy penguins, Chloe and Treble grinned at each other, then turned to wave to

Anodiwa, who was on the beach, watching through a binocular cam that was getting good video of the whole thing.

Together with myBetty's video through Chloe's mask and the sweep that caught the tang of the salt air and the warmth of the sun on a cool, South African day, and the feel of the wet rock beneath her, this made for a great segment, and for a few moments, at least, they had it all to themselves, the playful young prince from S'hudon, with Chloe Cary and her glamorous bestie, Anodiwa Pinaar, and all those funny penguins.

The water, the cute little penguins, the stunning scenery; their numbers were good, at more than two billion, myBetty whispered into Chloe's ear. That meant the paparazzi and the rest of the media knew where they were now and would be here in minutes, but, for the moment, it was peaceful and fun. All the world was paying close attention to charming little Treble and Aunt Chloe.

Treble hopped up to walk to the rock's edge and pop into the water and come back out, emerging with a laugh the same way the penguins did, coming out so fast that he was able to land upright on the rock surface just like they did. Fun!

It took all of a minute or two for him to do that a half-dozen times while Chloe watched and laughed and applauded, and then, sure enough, things got busy as motorcycles and then cars and then open boots on the cars and, voila, drones of all kinds headed their way: flitterbys and spyeyes and gnats and even, in the case of two very smart paps, drones that were water capable. Toss them into the surf and send them on their way, speeding along on the surface or diving down below it.

So they were all there watching, and Chloe was sweeping, and Anodiwa was live with her binoc-cam, when it all came down, a Zodiac rounding the headlands to the south and coming right at Chloe and Treble, three men aboard, one at the helm, another with a mask around his neck and carrying a speargun, another with a rifle. The outboard in the rear was pushing them along in a hurry, moving them from onethousand meters away to nine hundred, and then eight hundred in one damn hurry.

"Chloe, get the two of you off that rock!" myBetty commanded, seeing the feeds from the others; the paparazzi and Anodiwa and even one, incredibly, from the prow cam on the Zodiac. The bad guys were keeping their own cam going while they tried to assassinate the princeling and the Hollywood star!

Chloe started looking around, but Treble didn't seem to care and he popped into the water and back out again so everyone worldwide could see his new trick one more time. He even took a bow for the cameras. What a great kid, that Treble!

But then the frantic contact from myBetty and from Anodiwa finally fell on ears that were listening and Treble looked up as there came the pop of a rifle shot and a bullet struck the rock outcrop where they sat. The whole rock seemed to vibrate as it rang like a bell, and Chloe and Treble were, in an instant, in the water.

Chloe's decision was where to go. Into deeper water? Treble could stay down for hours if he needed to, but not Chloe. She couldn't protect him there, but he'd be able to swim away from any danger. Into shore? She could protect him there, and they would have help from Anodiwa. Yes, that.

But Treble didn't wait for Chloe to decide, so no, not that at all. He stayed above the water line just long enough to tell her "Aunt Chloe! Get to shore!" and then he dived, disappearing from view. Chloe, her decision-making over, struck out for the beach, which turned out to be the longest minute of her life as she ripped off her mask but left the fins on and swam like a demon for the sandy shore, where Anodiwa Pinaar stood there waving, foolishly perhaps, and yelling at her to "Swim! Swim!"

Which she did, and very well. Chloe had won those medals at the Paris Olympics ten long years ago. She'd quit competitive swimming the next year, when fame and fortune struck her in the form of a what-the-hell-why-not audition that turned into her first starring role as the young Annie Oakley. But the body remembers, and the muscle-memory kicks in when you need it to, and Chloe Cary most certainly had her personal-best time as she plowed right through the low swells and the shore break and reached the beach in one damn hurry.

There she stood and hurriedly waded in the last ten meters to the beach and then turned to look out toward the Zodiac as it slowed and a diver front-flipped over the side, holding onto what looked like a spear-gun. He was going after Treble, which in a long-short moment of utter clarity Chloe realized was thankfully stupid. The diver would never catch so much as a glimpse of Treble. Chloe had seen that kid swim.

But she couldn't worry about that at the moment. A bullet whizzed by and hit a large branch of driftwood behind her, spraying woodchips as she glanced back. Close. She turned to see the Zodiac again, hoping to see it turning away and instead it was coming straight on, and now two other Zodiacs had rounded the headland and were coming in fast.

"Chloe!" she heard from behind her, and "In my bag," said Anodiwa calmly, nodding toward the bag she'd brought to the beach. It was unzipped and Anodiwa had already pulled a pistol from it and was holding it in her right hand with the left hand bracing it as she let off a round. Hopeless, but worth the shot.

So security in Cape Town wasn't as lackluster as she'd assumed, thought Chloe.

Chloe reached down into Anodiwa's bag and there was another pistol, a Smith & Wesson Model Three with pearl grips. She laughed. Of course. This looked like the very gun she'd trained on for *Annie Oakley* and the only gun model she knew how to use. So all this was planned, start to finish. Hah!

She grabbed the revolver, turned to face out toward the Zodiacs, the first one now bouncing along over the outer edge of the low surf-line that Chloe had swum in through. The other two coming hard toward the beach. She needed to be closer. Too much movement. Too far away. She started wading out through the shore break even as Anodiwa, down the beach and up on a large boulder now, began taking pot shots from her vantage point.

Knee deep, Chloe took her first shot, and then another, missing badly both times as far as she could tell. While she was aiming for a third shot she saw one of the figures in the closest Zodiac spin and turn, grabbing at a shoulder. A shot from Anodiwa had found its mark.

But they were firing back now from all three Zodiacs, and bullets began splashing into the water around Chloe. She waded out deeper and fired again and then again, caught up in the moment, no thought of her own safety, just wanting to hit someone out there, when there came a hard punch to her left shoulder and she knew she'd been hit.

She spun down into the water and kept going, submerging to get away from the hail of bullets. Was she seriously hurt? She didn't know, but the left arm seemed to work all right as she tried to move it.

She tried to look around, but one of the many lies of Hollywood is that underwater shot when the swimmer looks around and sees something. You can't see anything, really, unless you're wearing a mask.

Bullets kept zipping into the water around her, and Chloe had the uneasy feeling, crouched on the bottom, that there were more of the damn bullets, and they were stronger as they zipped in, so maybe the Zodiacs were getting close?

And she needed some air. She was in a crouch and she'd have to stand soon.

And then she saw a dark figure coming near. She wished to hell she could see what it was. Not too big, so a penguin or, god forbid, a small shark.

It came right at her. And grabbed her hand. Treble? Yes, Treble! And he tugged on her, moving her away from where she was crouching, and she started to help herself by swimming on her own even as he tugged her. Ten meters away, then fifteen, then they surfaced, away from the bullets, and grabbed a mouthful of air and a quick look around.

The Zodiacs, all three of them, were going right past them and roaring toward the beach. Anodiwa had retreated into the boulders at the edge of the beach and was firing from behind one of them. The attackers were firing at her and looking around for Treble and Chloe.

"C'mon," said Chloe and held Treble by the hand and started wading in toward the boulders. If they could get behind cover there and hold out for just a few minutes there'd be help arriving. There were drones flying around showing it all live to the world. Flyeyes and gnats were everywhere, and as they waded one of the underwater drones surfaced and blinked its eye as it broadcast them live wading in. It had probably been watching all the underwater struggles the two of them had been through.

Chloe's left shoulder hurt like hell as they pushed through the water. She felt possessed of madness, a frenzy; filled with anger and anguish combined. She stumbled and fell face first into the water and that capped it. She was furious and determined as she came to her knees, then stood and slowly rose.

She was kaiju! She felt herself changing, morphing, stronger, bigger, faster, scaled and tailed and mean as hell! She stood, and in her mind all those thirty takes back in Hollywood served her well. Kaiju! She roared and raised her arms—ouch! from that left shoulder—and roared again.

Everyone stopped for a long few seconds. Much later, like five or ten minutes after the tubers and the appers and the dotters deepfaked it, there was actually a kaiju that seemed to rise up from the sea. Just like in the movie!

But right there, live in the moment, she was still Chloe, five-foot-seven, fit and muscular, blond hair in a ponytail, that perfect face with the Newman-like penetrating blue eyes. But still just Chloe.

And then a shot rang out, and then more shots, as the Zodiacers renewed the battle and, to be honest, it looked bad for the daring three-some, Anodiwa up in the boulders and Chloe and Treble scrambling out of the water.

Or Chloe scrambling alone, actually. Treble waited, and looked out to sea, and raised his arms and whistled and clicked and on came a dozen, two dozen, a hundred, penguins, all answering the call of The Perfection, the princeling, the mighty Treble.

In thirty seconds it was over, the twelve people from the Zodiacs swarmed by penguins until they couldn't be seen beneath the scrum.

And then there were chopper blades, and sirens, and police and soldiers and a most exciting time. The ratings were through the global roof: the first time anything had reached an audience of six billion, or three-fourths of the Earthies on the planet.

It is three months later and, look, here they are! It's Chloe Cary and her pals Twoclicks and the hero princeling Treble, and even Anodiwa Pinaar! Wow! The four of them getting out of the limo right there in front of you, if you were smart and got there early so you could be in the right spot, up close to the restraining ropes. Worth a six-hour wait? Heck, yes! "Kaiju! Kaiju!" you're yelling, along with everybody else. "Chloe! Treble! Twoclicks! Diwa!"

Now they're posing together in front of the movie backdrop poster, a huge thinscreen that shows it in 3D as Chloe emerges from the water and becomes that kaiju that saves the world from other monsters, foreign and domestic. It's the actual vid from the actual moment in the actual False Bay in the actual Cape Town. How cool is that?!

They built that moment right into the movie, which meant building Anodiwa Pinaar right into the movie as Chloe's sidekick, and figuring out ways to make sense of Twoclicks and Treble. It took extra weeks and cost millions, but will all the reshooting be worth it? You bet, a likely ten billion gross in the first weekend globally!

So there they stand, the fearsome foursome, the most popular actors and the most popular leader and his most popular Perfection, at the front of Grauman's Chinese Theatre on Hollywood Boulevard. *Colossal III* is huge. The biggest! The best!

Chloe is happy it's all worked out, and she's holding hands with Anodiwa and that's worked out fine, too, and she has an arm around her little pal Treble, too, and he's grinning as his father Twoclicks goes on and on for the media about how brave and wonderful they were and how great the movie is. Chloe wonders, as she stands there, if Twoclicks set this whole mess up? Did he risk his son's life, not to mention her life? Would he do that?

Yes, she thinks. Sure. Of course he would.

Rick Wilber's favorite alien, the jovial but deadly Twoclicks of the House of S'hu, has appeared often in stories in *Asimov's Science Fiction* magazine, as well as in the novels *Alien Morning* (Tor 2016) and *Alien Day: Notes from Holmanville* (Tor, forthcoming in fall 2020). Chloe Cary is a central figure in both novels.

Rick has also published novels *The Cold Road* (Tor, 2002) and *Rum Point* (McFarland), several college textbooks on writing and the mass media, and more than fifty short stories in major markets, including the Sidewise Award-winning "Something Real," and the poignant "Today is Today," reprinted in the *Best Science Fiction of 2019* (Prime Books, 2019). Both of those stories are in his new collection, *Rambunctious: Nine Tales of Determination* (WordFire Press, 2020). *The Wandering Warriors*, with Alan Smale, is also forthcoming from WordFire.

He is a visiting professor in the low-residency MFA in Creative Writing program at Western Colorado University, and he is director of the Dell Magazines Award for Undergraduate Excellence in Science Fiction and Fantasy Writing.

Z IS FOR ZOMBIE

STEVE RASNIC TEM

Z IS FOR ZOMBIE

L ee was ill for a long time. Then he felt good again. Then he felt sick
  again. This cycle went on for at least ten years. After a while he
couldn't always tell the difference, with all the time he spent in bed, and
living alone.

Eventually the casting people stopped hiring him. He'd gotten too old,
too crippled up with arthritis. He'd never been more than an extra, a background actor in zombie pictures and TV shows—more than a hundred
films and episodes. But he'd taken it seriously; he was good at that one
thing. He was expert at playing dead.

He tried to convince them his arthritis was an advantage—he argued it
made his living-dead stumble more convincing. But he would fall at unexpected times and ruin scenes. He was too unreliable, they said, an insurance risk.

The decayed face in his bedroom mirror wasn't perfect. Some of the
edges weren't glued down and the paint job was splotchy, and Lee didn't
know how to give his eyes that dead fish look, although the shadows he'd
applied did a pretty good job of making them recede. He'd had no training
in special effects or make-up, but he'd always watched the professionals
while they did their work. Filming always meant much waiting around, and
he'd had nothing better to do.

The scar above his left eyebrow rose worm-like off his forehead and fell onto the surface of the dresser. He scooped it up and put it in a tray. Later he would return it to one of the display cases with his other treasures.

He practiced zombie looks, alternating fierce, hungry grimaces with loose-lipped and sometimes zany expressions of brainlessness. He spoke a few lines, if a string of phlegmish gargles could be considered language. They had always been the extent of his permitted on-screen vocabulary.

Lee still rehearsed every day in case he ever got the call again. Lacking his old stamina he quit after an hour or so. His little bungalow had always been shadowy and dim, even when his mother was still alive. As his eyes weakened with age he found he could see very little after a certain hour and mirrors were especially challenging. They possessed depths of gloom he could make no sense of.

He gently transferred his bits of putty, silicone, and rubber to one of the glass cases in the living room. This particular case held make-up items from his early zombie pictures: "The Dead Are Alive," "The Dead Aren't Dead," and "The Dead! The Dead! The Dead!" All low-budget, all primitive in both their effects and working conditions. In each he'd been part of a group of zombie actors who wandered from scene to scene, occasionally changing a ragged shirt or a facial appliance in order to make it seem as if they had a cast of hundreds of undead instead of the twenty or so they could afford. The make-up had been hot and smelly under the summer sun. He'd been denied water and almost passed out more than once. On "The Dead! The Dead! The Dead!" he'd broken his middle finger when his cadre of zombies fell into a ditch. He'd suffered through all three films, but he'd loved the work. He kept the splint from the incident in the case along with whatever make-up bits he was able to squirrel away in his pockets at the end of filming.

That was wrong of course. Lee was fully aware it was wrong. But it didn't feel unfair. Those bits of zombie make-up—scars and wounds and simulated rotting flesh, decayed organs—were everywhere. Not infrequently they dropped off and you stepped on them during the midst of some rambling zombie advance. He wasn't paid much, and this was physical evidence of the most important work he'd ever done. His dream job. Still, his mother would have been so ashamed of him if she had known.

He caught a glimpse of something in the tall glass case against the wall. In the glass door or leaning against the bits of rotting wardrobe hanging inside. A skeletal hand maybe, some bony fingers trying to reach in and take what was his.

Lee went over to the case and peered inside. Everything looked to be there, but sloppily arranged, as if it had been rummaged through. Of course, he might have done it himself. He was always taking things out and wearing them, stumbling around the house as he choreographed his moves. He always resolved to put them back the way they had been, but he didn't always recall the original order. He'd never cataloged his collection, which was a mistake, but he'd never been much good at organizing things. His mother usually did that for him, but she wouldn't touch his zombie bits—they disgusted her.

Lee did the best he could, but more than once he'd wake up in bed with bits of make-up stuck to the sheets or his pillow. And it wasn't unusual to step on a make-up piece lying on the floor. He went barefoot around the house, not wanting to damage the delicate pieces with his shoes.

A dead face loomed in the cabinet by the front door. Lee smiled at it, too far away to tell if it smiled back.

He'd always worked hard on these roles and would ask some of the featured actors now and then for tips. Often they brushed him off, but some were nice. "What's your name again?" they would say, or "What do you want? An autograph?"

Once he'd asked a second unit director about his motivation for a scene. "You're a freakin' zombie," had been the reply. "You have no motivation."

Although the official line was that zombies were no longer "people," their souls and personalities gone, leaving only these strangely animated shells behind, Lee never played them that way. Maybe it made no difference in the end, but he never thought of them as dead. He just thought of them as really old people with some rare disease. And, after all these years of playing them, he was at that advanced age himself. Minus the disease, although he hadn't seen a doctor in a very long time. Even the teenagers and little kid zombies were just old people in his eyes. A bit empty, sadly alone, just walking out of habit because that's all they knew. Nothing ahead of them and everything behind. Their bodies did rot, the flesh fell off their bones, but that was just a symptom of their disease.

He heard something toward the back of the house. A scratching, or a rubbing. Maybe some shifting weight, poking and prodding, touching his things. Lee was always worried about mice. If a mouse got into one of the cases it could do tremendous damage. Most of the make-up appliances were soft and chewy, just the sort of thing to appeal to rodents.

But it could also be someone trying to break in. He started in that direction, thinking he should at least double-check the locks. He moved carefully. He knew how clumsy he could be and the space between cases was quite narrow with not even enough room to turn around. There wasn't a chair to sit in or a single piece of furniture unrelated to his career. Most of his house was like this, a museum devoted to his collection.

Lee kept hearing those noises, but his passing reflections in the glass doors and display tops continued to distract him. Sometimes he forgot some of the things he had. All these shredded zombie face masks, rotting cheeks and protruding tongues and broken teeth, staring out at him as he passed, breathing hard through their torn lips, glancing at him with nervous eyes, needing to scream when all they could do was growl.

He stopped in front of a framed article on the wall. The newsprint had yellowed, the edges frayed, but the print was still readable if he got close enough. Lee had always thought of himself as anonymous—zombies were intended to be anonymous for the most part, unless it was a featured player who had recently turned, because he or she wanted out of their contract or because they had become difficult to work with. But years ago he had been interviewed for the local paper, and he'd been proud of his small moment of recognition.

But it had come with a cost. Fame always came with a cost—he'd learned that from watching the better-known cast members in his various projects. It didn't matter whether it was the movies or the TV shows; once you became famous you became another sort of creature entirely.

After the article appeared people would show up at his door wanting to ask him questions and see the collection. Younger people mostly— teenagers and college kids. And him with no security in place whatsoever. He'd never put locks on the cases. He'd never thought he needed to. These young people with all their energy and their barely-controlled enthusiasm, they frightened him. What if they took something? He was too old and weak to stop them. He had no idea how to protect himself and his things.

More than a few times he had the urge to bite one of them. Crazy, of course, but biting was something he knew a lot about. A bite could turn an enemy into an ally.

So he started turning people away. And when he had the opportunity, and no one was watching, he went out front and took the house number off the door. He figured the postal carrier must know his house by habit and wouldn't need a number, not that he ever received any mail. Anyone else would be looking for a house number that no longer existed. But he figured there should be *something* on the door, some non-identifying identifier, so he took some black paint and wrote "Zed" by the doorknob, and felt pretty clever about it. And he liked the way it looked. If anyone ever asked him where he lived, which they never would, he would tell them "I'm at destination zed," and feel good about it.

He didn't go out anymore. He didn't need to. He could always have his groceries delivered, if he just remembered to do so. He hadn't had much appetite in a very long time. He supposed it was an age thing. Food just didn't taste the same.

Lee was headed toward the back door, but he couldn't remember why. That happened sometimes. He was a man with a lot of things on his mind. He had this huge collection to take care of, and all these memories to protect and organize. All the zombie reflections surrounding him growled their agreement. This made him smile, and he growled back his encouragement, or was he the one who had growled first?

He could hear those young fans at the back of his house trying to get in. Or maybe they were already inside. He wondered how they had gotten in—he had triple locks on the door, or at least he had intended to. And where were they all hiding now? His house was too small for anyone to hide anywhere.

But there were always mysteries in this world. Like what had started the zombie plague in the first place? They almost never explained that bit in the movies, and when they even bothered it was usually the silliest, most unbelievable sort of explanation. Zombies were simply inevitable— that was Lee's basic theory. Just like solitude. Just like dying.

His best display case was near the back door. He'd planned it that way as a grand reveal, his collection becoming progressively more interesting as you moved toward its end. In this case he had a variety of large latex prosthetic appliances simulating dead skin, deceased skin, burnt flesh, corrupted hands and fingers and chest pieces, all of it finely detailed so as to be suitable for extreme close-ups. These were major pieces the make-up artists guarded closely as each represented an enormous amount of labor. All of these, he was ashamed to remember, he had stolen off the set when his role was done.

The last piece was a full set of faked abdominal viscera, magnificent in its realism, although the colors had been brightened some so they would show up better on film. Lee had heard that a butcher, one of the investors in the original *Night of the Living Dead*, provided actual animal entrails for the effects in the film. Lee was grateful he'd only had to wear foam or rubber for his roles, and the occasional acrid smelling paint, although sometimes the effects were so realistic he still became nauseated.

A ravaged face leered at him, making him stagger, and his left arm came down so hard it shattered the glass top and his hand became tangled in the nest of latex and silicone organs, tearing several and scattering the rest. He snarled inarticulately, thinking all those young people had come back to steal his treasures, and he did a crazy little zombie ballet, a kind of Zydeco dance, thinking it might scare them away.

But he appeared to have almost no control over his movements. Arthritis had spread through his arms, hands, legs, feet, stiffening some joints and making others swing in the wrong direction. All the shambling and drunken stumbling he'd done through barren, dismal fields and post-apocalyptic wreckage over years and years—how many and how long ago? —must have done considerable damage.

He raised his arm and looked at it. The flesh was torn and ripped all the way to the bone, several inches of which gleamed nakedly through gaps in the meat and the rotted threads of fat and sinew. But oddly—he couldn't say luckily—there was no blood at all except for some rust-colored powdery debris, as if the pump attached to his special effects arm had run dry.

He turned his head to the glass wall cabinet beside him and stared at his reflection. When he grinned the zombie in the cabinet door grinned back, exposing its receding gums and enormous teeth, its missing lips and ears. The nose had rotted away to a pair of bone cavities. The eyes lay deep in the shadows of its skull, but clearly panicked.

Someone was beating on his front door. Lee dragged his feet through the broken glass, making his way past his precious display cases. He thought maybe he'd damaged his shoulders because one hung lower than the other, putting a labored twist into his ungainly stride. His hands seemed broken, the way they kept slipping off the doorknob, but he felt no pain at all, and was able to wedge them around the stem of the knob, twist, and pull open the door.

Two police officers waited on the porch. He saw the looks on their faces, and wasn't at all surprised when they raised their weapons.

"Jubst ..." Lee knew he had to enunciate as best he could, even though he had no idea how the words would come out. He struggled to contain his excitement for at last he had a speaking role. "Just aim for the head."

Steve Rasnic Tem is a past winner of the World Fantasy, Bram Stoker, and British Fantasy Awards. He has published over 450 short stories, with some of his best collected in *Figures Unseen: Selected Stories* (Valancourt). His latest collection is *The Night Doctor and Other Tales* (Centipede Press).

VINEGAR SYNDROME

BEN MONROE

VINEGAR SYNDROME

As Carlos Villanueva locked up the Coronet Theatre after a Friday night screening of the early '80s Italian zombie schlocker *Dead on Arrival*, his phone began to chirp. Not an unusual occurrence; the Coronet was on the outskirts of town, and cell phone signals could rarely penetrate the thick walls. A fact which thrilled the film fans who were the Coronet's lifeblood. No cell signals meant no annoying electronic interruptions during the screenings of the vintage and retro movies for which the Coronet was known. So usually as he was leaving the building, his phone alerted him to a few voicemails or text messages sent earlier.

But this was his incoming call ringtone. Who'd be calling him at midnight? He pulled his phone from his hip pocket and took a peek. *Brad Thompson*, the little iPhone screen displayed. He thumbed the answer button and raised the handset, trying to remember who that was. Carlos looked up and down the street. Was someone watching him? But no, it was empty; he was alone under the darkened theater marquis, his only company the yellow glow of streetlights glittering off sprinkles of a light rain.

"Hello?" Carlos said, cradling the phone between ear and shoulder as he fished in his pocket for his car keys.

"Hey, hi!" the voice on the other end of the line said, enthusiastically. "Is this Carlos?"

"Yeah, speaking," he said. *Brad Thompson?* Carlos thought again.

"Hey, Carlos, this is Brad, from ThriftGoods."

Ah! Carlos thought. *One of the thrift store guys.*

Brad continued, trampling over Carlos' train of thought. "You came in hella long ago, and told me if I ever got any old film equipment or reels or whatever, I should call you, right?"

"Sure, I remember," Carlos said. He'd stopped fishing for his keys. Carlos was always dropping his card off at thrift stores, junk shops, scouring yard sales for good deals on vintage film industry memorabilia. Calls like this were rare, but not unusual.

"Some came in today," Brad said, excitement in his voice.

"Yeah? Look, Brad, it's pretty late."

"I know, I know," Brad said. "Just that I thought this stuff was interesting and thought you'd want to know. Came in as part of an estate lot today. Like the son or nephew of some guy who used to work in movies or something. Bunch of old scripts, photos, a Movie-Mite projector, a few reels of film. The film stinks though, like someone spilled pickle juice on it."

"It's what happens when old film stock decays. Turns pink and starts to smell acidic," Carlos replied. "That's called vinegar syndrome."

"Oh, yeah?" Brad asked, a tinge of disappointment in his voice. "Well, maybe the projector or other stuff's worth some dough? You ever heard of George Bronstein? That's the name all over this stuff."

Bronstein? Brad sifted the name through the voluminous archives of his film trivia-saturated brain. *He edited for Universal or AIP or someone back in the day. Have to check IMDB later.* "Okay, color me curious. When can I come check the stuff out?"

"Groovy," Brad said. "Yeah, I thought you might be interested. I need to be at the store by noon tomorrow. But I took it all home."

"Oh, well that's great, then," Carlos said. "Well, mum's the word."

"Right, mum's the word," Brad said. "So come by before eleven tomorrow, and you can check it out."

Carlos was getting tired. It had been a long night, and he was getting the feeling that Brad was about to ask him over for breakfast. Still, a Movie-Mite projector might be worth a couple hundred bucks if it was in decent shape, or he could fix it up. The scripts piqued his curiosity, though. If Bronstein had owned them, they might be autographed, or collectible somehow. "Brad, I'm beat, but I'll come by in the morning."

"Okay, sounds great. Come over early enough I'll make you breakfast."

There it is, Carlos thought. "Well, we'll see. Text me your address and I'll let you know when I'm on my way."

"Groovy," Brad replied. "Okay, man. I'll see you in a few hours. Bring your checkbook!" and he laughed.

Carlos chuckled, but that's what all this was about, anyway. The whole reason he hit up the junk shops was to make connections and get the good stuff before anyone else did. Maybe this time his leg work had actually panned out.

Carlos slid into the driver's seat of his car, a dusty, green '90s Chevy hatchback that was held together with duct tape and prayers. He turned on the heater, let it idle for a moment, warming up the interior. "George Bronstein," he said to the night. "Hell, might be worth a buck to the right collector."

But while the haul sounded interesting, all he wanted right now was a decent night's sleep. He pulled away from the curb, leaving the Coronet silent, still, and dark behind him.

Carlos pulled up in front of the address that Brad had texted him the night before. A dingy multi-unit apartment building on the other side of town from the Coronet and Carlos' apartment. The building's brick facade had been painted over with a thick mustard yellow now caked with dust and grunge. The light rain had continued into the morning and had thickened the dirt into a grimy caul. Carlos pulled into a visitor spot in a covered part of the parking lot. When he approached the building, he saw an aluminum sign, metal bent into cursive script stating that this was the "McKay Arms" building.

Outside the lobby, Carlos had to buzz up to Brad's apartment for entry. He punched the apartment number—*3011*—into a metal keypad below a speaker. He had to push the *0* button three times though, as it stuck and wouldn't depress easily. Carlos waited a moment, watching cars speed by on Cox Road across the parking lot. A click and a tinny male voice asked "Yes, hello?"

Carlos turned back to the speaker. It took him a second to find the "Talk" button, as the paint had worn off from many finger presses over the years. He stabbed at it with his finger, holding it down and saying, "Hey, Brad, it's Carlos." He let the button go, but Brad was already talking.

"... wait for you by the elevator." And then a loud electric buzz, and a click as the front door unlocked.

Carlos stepped into the lobby of the McKay Arms. Instantly the smell hit him, a must of tobacco smoke and cleaning chemicals. Not overpowering, but an unpleasant smell. The lobby walls were floor-to-ceiling mirrors with an abstract pattern of gold paint splattered across them. He watched his reflection broken into jigsaw shapes as he crossed the lobby and pushed the glowing button to call the elevator.

The elevator doors slid open almost immediately, as if the car had been waiting for him. Carlos stepped inside and punched the "3rd Floor" button. The elevator doors closed slowly, and it began its ascent. The interior light flickered a few times as the car rose, and for a moment Carlos wondered if he would get stuck in the elevator, but then it slowed, a "ping" rang out, and the doors opened again.

He stepped into a dimly lit hall and looked around for Brad. The hall was empty aside from him and a dusty potted plastic ficus tree in the hallway's corner across from the elevator doors. Two of the six overhead lights were out, but enough morning light shone through the dusty windows at the far ends of the hall that he could see well enough. The door ahead of him was 3001, so Carlos walked down to the opposite end. There were twelve units in all on this floor, Brad's being at the farthest end away from the elevator.

Carlos was almost all the way down the hall when Brad's door opened slowly, and someone stepped out. It took Carlos a moment to recognize Brad. He'd only met him the one time at the thrift store, and that was six months or more ago. Brad was tall and unnaturally thin. Probably in his early 50s, he still wore a long ponytail at the base of his skull, but the dome of his head was bald.

"Oh, hey, Carlos!" Brad said upon seeing him. "Sorry man, nature called." He held out his hand.

Carlos nodded and put out his hand to shake Brad's. It was clammy, chill and moist. *Hope he washed,* Carlos thought. "No worries, Brad. How's things?"

"Good, man, good," he said, pumping Carlos' hand. "Hey, come in, look at this stuff, will you?"

Carlos practically had to pull his hand away from Brad's. "Can't wait," Carlos said. "Can't stay long, though. Gotta get to the Coronet and start setting up for tonight's show," he lied.

Brad stepped to the side of the door, sweeping his hand in a wide-open gesture and beckoning Carlos inside. "Groovy, man. Yeah, come on in."

Carlos walked into the small apartment and subtly looked around. Pale gray light came in through the dirty windows, and Carlos could see storm clouds thickening outside in the distance. Typical bachelor stuff filled the room, a TV sat atop a behemoth of a DVD/VCR combo on a small table against one wall, a recliner across from it. Carlos was amused to see a cinderblock and waist-high pine plank bookshelf against another wall, something he hadn't seen since college. It was littered with magazines, books, DVDs, and even a few VHS tapes. A kitchen across the room contained a table with a small, gray 16mm film projector on it, and a pair of metal and pleather chairs next to it. Dirty dishes filled the sink, and the window above the sink showed nothing more than a view of the road beyond. Next to the table were two cardboard file boxes, and he saw the familiar steely gray cylindrical shapes of film cans peeking over the edge of one. They were big ones, too. Carlos guessed they were 10" reels, meaning they'd hold about 45 minutes or more of film on each one.

"Sorry, man, I had breakfast before you got here. If you're hungry, I could whip up some eggs."

Carlos also noted the smell of the place. Not the musty odor from the lobby, but the sweet skunky funk of marijuana. The place was steeped in it. And underneath that just the faintest sour hint of lemon, or vinegar. "I'm good, thanks," he said. He pointed to the projector in the kitchen. "Is that the Movie-Mite?" He walked toward it.

"That it is, my man," Brad said. "What do you think?"

Carlos moved toward the objects on the table, noting that the vinegar smell was stronger as he approached the film cans. A musty, sour smell. Not as bad as some old film stock he'd come across, but still pretty foul. He leaned over the projector, getting a closer look. It was small, barely bigger than a large shoebox. Clean, though, hardly any dust on it at all. The base of brown dyed leather had an alligator-hide print to it. Brownish-gray powdered enamel coated the body of the machine and it was in altogether great shape.

"It's in decent shape, I guess," Carlos said. He was tapping his finger on his lip trying to act nonchalant but thinking a Movie-Mite in this good condition might fetch two hundred bucks if he could find the right collector. But if it really belonged to George Bronstein, it could be worth more.

Brad nodded enthusiastically. "I plugged it in last night, and the motor or whatever still works. Bulb's shot, though."

Carlos moved over to the cardboard boxes. "Bulbs are fragile and don't last forever, anyway. I'd have to look around, but it's probably not too hard to find a replacement." He lifted the first box onto the kitchen table and carefully sorted through it. A few old screenplays, a few boxes of magnetic tape reels, and some faded old black-and-white photographs. Carlos recognized Bronstein in all of them. A hefty fellow in a tweed suit, his eyes overly large from the thick glasses perched on his nose. He had an intense, angry look to him. Carlos recognized a few semi-famous faces from the '50s B-Movie film industry alongside Bronstein. "This is your guy Bronstein," he said, pointing him out to Brad.

"Yeah? What was his deal?"

"He was a film editor back in the day," Carlos said. "Worked for some big studios, lots of workhorse stuff. The war movies, Westerns, and beach party movies that were their bread and butter in the '50s."

"Wonder if I've ever seen any of his movies?" Brad said, suddenly regaining interest in the collection.

"Oh, probably," Carlos said. "It was the stuff they used to fill time with on local TV stations on Saturday mornings when I was a kid."

"Whatever happened to him?" Brad asked. "Did he ever make it big or anything?"

Carlos picked up a gray metal film can. "No, nothing so fortunate," he said, opening up the can. The smell of vinegar hit him like a wave. "Woah!"

Brad crossed over to the sink and opened the window over it. "Yeah, man, that's the smell I was telling you about."

Carlos waved the lid of the can over the film stock to disperse the stink. "It happens to old film stock. The chemicals used in the emulsion break down, and it gives off this smell."

"So what happened to Bronstein?"

"Nervous breakdown," Carlos said. "He was working on this film for ... crap, I can't remember. Some rinky-dink studio on the fringes of Hollywood. He'd fallen far from the glitz by then." Carlos put the film can down. He was in his element, and his excitement was palpable. "He was working on this monster movie. *The Dead of Night.* Ghosts or vampires, something like that. Nobody's really sure."

"Why's that?" Brad asked, turning back from airing out the fumes.

"Studio burned down before they finished it. Bronstein was in it. Supposedly an accident, but who knows?"

"Oh, yeah. There's always a story with those Hollywood types," Brad said.

"Right? I mean, the official report is that the studio office burned down and took the film with it. But then I read that working on the film unhinged Bronstein. Probably a lot of late hours for shitty pay and sniffing too much of the splicing glue they used to use. He started raving about the film, about how it was evil and should never be released."

"Oh, man, cool," Brad said. "Wonder what it was about?"

"Lots of people would love to know. Mind if I take a peek?" Carlos said, pointing to the film.

Brad nodded. "Go for it, man."

He picked up the film can again and gently removed the reel of film stock within. The outermost film was white double-perforated Kodak leader. The same sort of leader stock Carlos had spooled up a thousand times in his career. He picked at the yellowing paper tape holding it down. It came up easily, the glue long since dried up to flakes. The white leader strip slid free and slowly he unrolled the first few feet of the film. Then he stopped. Scrawled on the thin white plastic were three words written in grease pencil: DON: WP—R1.

Carlos looked over at Brad whose back was to him. Brad was opening the rest of the windows, trying to get a cross-breeze going. Quickly Carlos spun the reel around, rolling the leader strip back onto it, and placing it back in the film can. He looked at the boxes of magnetic tape, and saw them labeled "DON1," and "DON2." *Holy shit,* he thought.

Brad walked back over to him. "You think any of this is worth anything?"

Carlos' heart was beating hard in his chest. *This could be worth a fortune,* he was thinking, but what came out was, "Maybe a couple hundred bucks for the projector. The scripts aren't anything special but might interest a collector."

Brad nodded. "What about the film?"

Carlos paused. "Well, from the smell I can tell you it's probably ruined. I'd have to have an expert check it out, though. Restoration's really not my field."

"Oh, yeah, okay," Brad said, downcast. "So, do you want to buy any of this?"

Carlos breathed deep and slowly, pretending to think, but trying to calm his enthusiasm. "Yeah, I guess," he said. "Tell you what. I'll give you a hundred for it now, or we can split the fee if I can find anyone interested in any of it."

"Only a hundred?" Brad said, disappointment obvious in his tone. He was looking at the projector. "I looked online and the projector's worth a hundred fifty alone."

"It could be," Carlos said. "If you're sure the motor's working right, find a new bulb, clean it up a little." He waved his hand over the rest of the collection. "This stuff? I have no idea if anyone would want it at all." He watched Brad who was staring at the boxes. He could tell Brad was doing the mental math to see if half of maybe a hundred and fifty plus half of maybe nothing and not seeing any of that for a long time was worth more than a hundred bucks right now.

"Yeah, okay. Deal," Brad said, and stuck out his hand again to shake on it.

"Okay," Carlos replied and shook Brad's hand. "I'll probably end up tossing the film, but who knows?" He pulled his hand away, got out his wallet and handed over five rumpled twenty-dollar bills.

Fifteen minutes later he had tossed the projector in the trunk of his car along with the box of film scripts and photos. The film cans however, he kept in a box on the seat next to him where he could see them. No way was he letting those out of his sight.

Carlos blew through several stop signs on his way home. He had a few hours before he had to get to the theater for the evening shows. Carlos had lied to get out of Brad's grungy apartment and didn't have to work until later in the afternoon. Excitement was burbling in him to get that reel onto his own home projector and see what it was. Checking the film in the cans he'd found they seemed connected. The first reel's leader was marked DON: WP—R1, and the second's DON: WP—R2. Checking out the condition of the film he saw many bumps and ridges along the edge of the reel, the tell-tale signs of cement splices. From this he logically surmised the *WP* on the leader stood for "Work Print," and "Reel 1 & 2" if his luck held out. Not a final release print, but the version of the film Bronstein was working on before the studio would send it to the negative cutter.

Years ago, Carlos had installed a pull-down screen on the ceiling over one wall of his living room. He didn't own a TV, preferring to watch films projected on the screen via a digital projector from his laptop. Friends had long given up teasing him about being the consummate film snob, because he relished the label. He had covered the windows with blackout cloth and set his own little Victor-Kalart 16mm projector on a stand in the center of the room where his digital equipment normally roosted. If this was the film he thought it was, he would watch it in private. He was bursting with excitement that he'd be the first person to watch the film in maybe 60 years. Possibly the only other person to have ever seen it aside from George Bronstein. He'd worry about the restoration later. The vinegar smell was powerful, but he'd started to get used to it. Letting the can air out a bit seemed to have helped.

Carlos threaded the plastic leader through the aqua blue 16mm projector's gate, wrapped it around the spindles inside, and closed off the covering door. He'd bought the projector years ago when the local elementary schools were getting rid of their antiquated multimedia equipment. It was the same kind he remembered from his own youth, watching strange science films in class, and then begging the teacher to play them backwards as the reel spun out. He rarely ever used it, owning 16mm prints of only a handful of movies. The projector was a single-system job, unable to handle the magnetic tape sound reels, so he'd have to figure out a way to listen to them later. But he could at least watch the film.

Finally, he thumbed the remote in his palm to lower the lights, and flicked on the projector. White light suffused the screen, the projector clattered to life, rattled for a moment, then subdued to a mechanical purr. Countdown numbers did their job. 5 ... 4 ... 3 ... then 2 where Carlos imagined a phantom sync-beep.

And then on the screen a pink-tinged gothic castle, all spires and crenellations stood atop a ruddy hill, and faded pink dripping bold letters proclaimed, "The Dead of Night."

"Holy shit," Carlos whispered.

The film was definitely old stock. The print had lost all of its greens and blues, becoming a wash of red details and pinkish landscapes. The warmth of the projector bulb made the vinegar smell stronger. He watched enraptured for the next hour as the film unfolded. Without the soundtrack he couldn't make out the exact details, but the story was fairly straightforward as near as he could tell.

The inhabitants of the castle were a pair of aristocratic-looking siblings or spouses; a man and a woman who seemed to hold some disdain for each other, so it could go either way. They were clearly evil, as the stark make-up, and occult imagery in their costumes and the decor of their abode showed. Silver thread stitched into their robes described runes and arcane symbols. Pentagrams woven into tapestries hung from the walls, and human and wolfish skulls with dripping, smoking candles affixed to them illuminated the stone corridors of their strange abode. The pair looked down from their balcony overseeing the valley below where distant torches marched toward them. Soon a torch-wielding mob breached the castle's interior and put fire to it. It went up in a blaze, as the strange pair of inhabitants retreated to an underground lair via a clichéd secret door.

It transfixed Carlos. He sank into the sofa cushions, never taking his eyes off the screen. For the next hour he watched as time shifted a hundred years past the burning of the castle. A new owner bought the edifice, and had it moved brick by brick, all the furniture and trappings, to the United States, somewhere outside of New Orleans. Workmen went missing, and the neighboring family grew frightened. The new owner was too focused on his business to heed the concerns of the workers. The neighboring mother tried to warn him that something was wrong, but he ignored her. The man became obsessed over the slightest detail of construction but seemed to take a special interest in the two large, long boxes which he kept in the basement.

Carlos smiled when he saw the two coffin-like shapes. He could see where this was all going and enjoyed it immensely. He didn't recognize any of the actors, but with a little research he knew it wouldn't be hard to figure out who most of the players were.

The neighbor children went missing one night, lured away by a pair of shadowy figures in the woods surrounding their bayou home. Their mother was distraught, shaking her finger in blame at the owner of the castle. The police dragged her away while the abode's new owner shook his head and walked back into the castle, uninterested in her pleas.

Then the screen went white, and a rhythmic slapping behind him alerted him to the fact that the first reel had run out. Carlos rose to turn off the projector's motor and load up the second reel. As he did so, a pain stung his hand and he recoiled from the projector. A line of blood welled up along the back of his hand, where the film's end leader had spun around and slapped him, slicing a shallow wound.

He shut off the projector entirely, then raised the lights in the living room. Carlos went into the bathroom and gently washed his hands in the tap. He rinsed the wound with lukewarm water and shook it to get most of the moisture off. Opening the medicine chest behind the bathroom mirror, he got out some antiseptic ointment and a box of plastic bandages. When he used his injured hand to open the tube of ointment, he saw that the wound wasn't as bad as he'd originally thought. It was only a scratch, really. A pink weal, just an inflammation, no blood. He caught a whiff of vinegar coming from the scratch and thought that it must have rubbed off on him from the film. He washed it again with soap and water and returned to the living room.

As Carlos began threading the second reel onto the projector, he yawned. A deep, stretching yawn. His eyes were dry, and he was feeling tired. He must not have gotten enough sleep last night. Got up too early to go visit Brad and collect these treasures. He decided to watch the second reel and then take a nap before work.

The second reel picked up with the children's mother distraught, in jail. The police offered no succor as she took her place on the cot in the cold stone cell and went to sleep. But then she began acting strangely. Leaning up and craning her head around as if listening to distant sounds or voices. She removed a cloth belt from around her waist, placed it around her neck, tied one end to a cell bar and slid limp against it, choking herself to death.

Pretty dark for a '50s movie, Carlos thought. The story continued through the ruby haze of the decaying film print. The strange couple returned and led a dark ritual of Satanic splendor in the swamp beyond the castle. The dead rose from their graves and rampaged across the country-side. In time, they assaulted the castle itself, taking the new owner prisoner and dragging him off into the swamp. In the end, the awful pair reclaimed their home, and the dead sank back into the boggy earth. A final lingering shot of the bayou, fog drifting along the swamp, breezing between banyan trees as the lurching dead shambled into darkness. Then from out of frame the ex-new owner of the castle lurched into view, dead white eyes and ghastly pale skin. He shuffled along, and the film faded to darkness as he receded into the swamp.

Carlos's eyes were tired and heavy, his limbs sluggish. Looking at his watch, he found he still had a few hours before work. He reached over to the projector and flicked the switch to turn it off. The room went dark immediately, only a thin trace of ghostly blue light peeking around the edges of the blackout curtains covering the windows.

I'll take a nap, he thought. *Head in after that. Pick up some coffee on the way in, too.*

Carlos was too tired to get up and shuffle off to his bedroom. He turned over into the back of the sofa, drifting asleep instantly.

Later that evening, Carlos dragged himself in to the Coronet. The Saturday Night Feature was a repeat performance of *Dead on Arrival*, and the same could be said for him. Mary Barnes who ran the concession stand called out to him as he was climbing the stairs to the projection booth, "Feeling okay, Carlos? You look a little pale."

Carlos stopped and turned to her. He felt sluggish, dazed. "Yeah," he said, blinking. "Just tired is all. Didn't get enough sleep last night."

Mary nodded and then poured a measure of corn kernels into the popcorn machine. "I'll run you up a Coke in a few," she said. "Little sugar and caffeine will help you right out. Better get to steppin', though," she said, waving him off. "Showtime's in an hour."

Carlos smiled and waved to her. "Thanks, Mary. Appreciate it." He turned back to the stairway.

"Hey," Mary said as he turned away. "You smell something funny?"

He climbed the stairs, ignoring her and the art deco movie palace decoration that used to impress him so. He crossed a small lobby and went into the upstairs men's room to splash some water on his face. When he caught a glimpse of himself in the mirror, he noticed that he was looking a little pale. As he rubbed a wet paper towel over his face, he also noticed that his shirt was faded. The normal vibrant crimson was a dull, rusty red. It looked washed out, faded. He looked down and noticed the same about his jeans. "Weird," he said to no one. *Must've over-bleached them last time I did laundry,* he thought.

He tossed the wet paper towel into the trash bin, left the bathroom and crossed to the projection booth door. There was another flight of stairs behind that and Carlos groaned when he saw it. By the time he'd reached the top, his legs were tired and achy, his hands weak from holding the railing. He turned on the overhead light and then collapsed into one of the worn-out office chairs in the little room.

"Okay," he said to the empty room. "Just one show and I can go home."

Carlos came home with all the intentions in the world just to go to bed. But after he kicked off his shoes and sorted through the mail, he began to wonder if maybe watching the film one more time wouldn't be a bad idea. Soon he would have to look into finding a film restoration facility, and then he wouldn't be the only person on Earth who'd seen it in living memory. Besides, something about the film just intrigued him. Maybe it was the thrill of knowing he'd discovered something unimaginable. Or just plain old human greed of wanting to keep this treasure for himself.

Either way, he threw a frozen pizza in the oven, grabbed two cold bottles of beer, and sat down to watch the film again. He dimmed the lights but didn't bother closing the curtains this time. It was dark enough outside that no ambient light would disrupt the image. He cracked the windows a little to get some fresh air in the apartment as the vinegar smell had returned. He'd been smelling it all evening, actually. A few of his coworkers at the Coronet had even commented on it. Carlos assumed that the smell of the decaying film stock must've gotten in his clothes while he was watching the film or handling the boxes.

He set both reels to rewind on the projector while his pizza warmed up. By the time the oven was beeping for his attention, the film was ready to go. After replacing the first reel he wasted no time in turning it on. The projector hummed to life and it filled the screen against the far wall with light.

Carlos had a mouthful of pizza and was swigging from a cold bottle of pilsner when the titles came up. "The Dead of Night" in dripping blood-red letters against a cobalt blue sky, and a ghostly green castle on a hill. Funny, he remembered the colors being completely washed out, faded and pink when he watched it earlier. There must've been more light coming through the cracks in the curtains than he remembered.

This is great, he thought. *Doesn't need nearly as much restoration as I thought.* The film churned along just as he'd remembered, but the colors were much more vibrant, closer to the dreamlike glow of vintage Technicolor. As he watched, his eyes drooped, and he thought he couldn't remember ever having seen a 16mm film this old with color this good. The splices were a hassle, but a competent post production lab could deal with those in making a release print. This was about the best print possible short of miraculously stumbling across the original negative somewhere.

The weird couple lurked about the castle again. The villagers burned it down, and the workmen transported it to Louisiana. Everything progressed the way it had earlier, and Carlos decided that this was a film that was worth preserving. A little cleanup, and get the soundtrack married to it, and he could have the world premier at the Coronet in a month or two.

The dead rose, the swamp burbled, and the story marched to its inevitable conclusion. Carlos' head was lolling on his neck and he felt a headache simmering behind his eyes. He could barely keep his eyes open he was so tired. He reached for the beer on the floor by his foot and raised his hand to drink as the castle's new owner walked in from out of the frame.

Light shone through his hand. His skin was glass, translucent, shimmering in the light of the movie screen. He dropped the bottle in his lap, looked down and saw that his clothes and legs were vanishing. On-screen, the dead owner of the castle turned away from the swamp, and walked toward the camera. Then the strange original owners of the castle joined him, slinking in from off-screen. Their dark robes embroidered in shimmering, strangely shifting occult sigils. The ghastly trio's eyes glowed with dead, pale light. Like the glow of alien stars seen from a distant world.

They turned and walked toward the camera. Carlos tried to scream but no sound came. He tried to rise, but his muscles betrayed him. The three came closer, hands outstretched, eyes glowing, pulsing rhythmically. In unison they opened their mouths and took deep breaths. Every time they sucked in, Carlos felt a wave of fatigue, like whatever life remained in him was being drawn away. Streamers of color drew forth from Carlos and floated toward the sinister trio on screen like shimmering ribbons of light.

Again and again, they breathed, they sucked the very life away. The light drawing from Carlos to the screen lost its color, faded breath by breath until it was nothing more than dim pale gray. The final essence of Carlos drifted across the small room into the glowing image on the wall.

The image faded to black. The projector shut off of its own accord. The room was quiet, empty.

After a few days, neighbors began to complain of the strong scent of vinegar emanating from the apartment.

Ben Monroe grew up in Northern California and has spent most of his life there. He lives in the East Bay with his wife and two children. His most recent published works are *In the Belly of the Beast* and *Other Tales of Cthulhu Wars*, the graphic novel *Planet Apocalypse*, and a number of short stories. Benmonroe.com.

BEER WITH FRIENDS

CHARLES MACLAY

BEER WITH FRIENDS

R alph tossed peeled garlic into his mouth like peanuts. As far as Peter was concerned, this was just another oddity to add to the list of oddities surrounding his old high school friend, although this habit was alarmingly new. He'd brought a whole bag of the cloves. *Maybe it's a new diet.* One Peter hadn't heard of. He drained his beer and set it down with a thunk on the wooden table. Ralph had been away for months but was visiting town for the holidays. For Peter, it just felt good to relax and catch up after getting off a twelve-hour EMT shift.

Strangeness aside, Ralph was an entertaining friend. He liked to wargame the impossible and practice martial arts. At over six-foot, wide enough and muscled enough to look taller, Ralph was a mean sparring partner. Like Peter, he was in his early twenties and should not have drawn any particular notice in the bar, but the bag of garlic ruined the look. Around them, half a dozen larger tables were filled with patrons that drowned out everything softer than a half-shout. The bar itself was dark. The drinks, taps, and countertops only dimly lit.

Peter wondered if the gin Ralph had been drinking went well with garlic but decided not to ask. He'd rather know why Ralph's right arm moved stiffly—as though he'd injured it during some escapade. But they'd been catching up for hours and it hadn't come up. Peter figured Ralph had something on his mind and that everything else would be preamble. Ralph had been thoughtfully holding his chin most of the night. When Ralph held that pose, he made a habit of bending the truth at right angles. When the truth came out, it would either be profoundly fun or profoundly troubling.

Ralph's eyes roved the bar with a wild light. As he scanned the tables, he pulled an eight-inch blade from his left sleeve. The motion was so smooth it looked as if the knife had always been there. Ralph spun it once on his palm and slid it back into his sleeve as though it had never existed.

Peter's pulse raced as he checked if anyone had noticed. The bouncers would ban Ralph and possibly Peter. Blessedly, no one had shouted about the blade and Ralph would just heckle Peter if he brought it up. They were in the clear. He returned his gaze to Ralph, outraged, ready to say something. Only he stopped at Ralph's expression. The curly-haired fool's eyes were intent as he completed his own scan of the bar and ate another clove of garlic. *Was he trying to get a rise out of someone?*

Ralph spoke, and his voice barely registered over the bar's ruckus. "You hear about the Ester heist?"

"The jewelry store?" asked Peter. It wasn't what he'd expected. The heist happened the week before, and Ralph had only just returned to town.

"Yeah, that," said Ralph.

Peter frowned as he answered. "Not much. A little from the cops at an EMS meeting, but I shouldn't repeat it." They'd brought up anomalous diamonds and gold left in broken cases.

Ralph smiled knowingly. "I hear they only took the silver."

Peter choked. "Where'd you hear that?" The cops had told him, but it had specifically been left out of the news.

Ralph stroked his chin while scanning the bar again. "I swung by the store, heard it from someone."

Peter's blood went cold. Ester Jewelers had been closed since the heist. Ralph couldn't have visited it. To Peter's knowledge, Ralph had never turned to crime, but Peter had often wondered if he would. It wasn't just his fondness for knives. Ralph liked to free run, parkour, and prowl the night. In high school, he had always been up to mischief. For a while, Peter had figured Ralph would either turn to crime or end up in the CIA.

Finally Peter jokingly asked, "So, did you steal it and then hide out?" They'd gotten up to enough mischief together in high school, he almost figured Ralph would tell him straight out. Thievery would be a whole new level though. Ralph had to be playing at something.

Ralph smiled, drinking his gin. He set down the cup and lifted his hand to hold his chin thoughtfully. "No, I didn't."

Shit. No. No, I'm just paranoid. He—

Before he could ask further, Ralph continued, "So, do you think vampire hunters did it?"

The odd question snapped Peter's attention sideways. Then he sighed in relief. It was like old times. Ralph was war-gaming, only with nosferatu instead of zombies. It wasn't a big stretch, especially if he'd heard about the silver—somehow. Relieved that Ralph wasn't asking how to fence silver, Peter went to sip his drink but remembered it was empty.

"I don't think so," he said, "no such thing as vampires." *And thank god this is what this is about.* If Ralph wanted to talk vampires, the bit about the silver could have just been pretense.

Ralph nodded knowingly. "But what if there were? What would it take for you to believe?"

Peter pondered the question—not seriously, but as a logic problem. Proving the existence of vampires wasn't a topic he'd contemplated. But if he didn't give a passable answer, Ralph would keep pestering him until he did. It had been that way with the zombie questions—amusing and exasperating.

"Besides one living, breathing—well, not breathing, but lifting cars?" asked Peter. "Video maybe? Proof? Something that isn't cosplay." He laughed. "There's nothing out there, though. It would be all over the web."

"Ha, yeah," said Ralph, going quiet. This was where he would normally start war-gaming silver sources for vampire hunters or discussing how to prove that enlarged canines weren't fake. He didn't.

"C'mon," said Ralph. "Let's see if there are any videos. Head to my place. I got a short-term rental. The bar is about to close anyway."

Peter frowned, looking at his phone. The bar wouldn't close for another hour, not with the crowd. "You have beer there?" he asked. Crazy questions were better with beer.

"Of course," replied Ralph.

"Not the cheap stuff?"

Ralph gave Peter a pained expression and he remembered that Ralph never went for the cheap stuff.

"Right, drinks at your place then."

Outside the bar the air smelled fresh and the night felt impossibly quiet. The only noise came from the nearby river, a gentle sound, even as they approached a trail that ran along it. Peter chuckled, reflecting on his concerns. *I can't believe I thought he robbed the store. He's just looking for an excuse to talk vampires. Would he make up the silver detail?* It seemed possible.

As they reached the low rises where Ralph rented, Peter wondered if his friend would leave him alone in the dark to scale some building and do a parkour flip. Whether it was courtesy or the sore arm, Ralph stayed on the ground until they reached the apartment.

The place was a mess. Clothes and boxes lay scattered everywhere and a heavy smell of garlic permeated the place. Ralph had also driven nails into the walls to hang swords and knives. It always amazed Peter that people still rented to Ralph. Amongst the hanging weapons, Peter looked for Ralph's Japanese sword set. It consisted of three matching blades and scabbards. He spotted two of the three—the traditional katana and shorter wakizashi. The space for the tanto hung empty. It was more of an oversized knife, bigger than the knife he'd pulled in the bar, but still easily concealed. Peter looked at Ralph, trying to decide where the tanto hid.

As he did, Peter noticed a bit of fibrous tatami mat clamped horizon-tally onto a countertop. Normally tatami mats were rolled and positioned vertically for a martial artist to practice sword slices. This one was clamped horizontally onto the counter like an arm jutting forward. Within the mat he could see something else rolled up in the center, probably meant to simulate bone. He now noticed bits of the stiffer bone-core amongst the tatami slices. Ralph had cut the mat and bone-whatever into at least six pieces. Each time getting closer to the counter, until he'd cut a deep gouge into the woodwork. Peter leaned in to examine the cut.

"Come on," said Ralph impatiently. "Let's go to the computer."

Peter pulled back from the counter and threw up his hands. "But where's the beer?"

"In the fridge. Grab it yourself. Let's go."

Peter chuckled, took one last look at the counter, and went to grab two of the best bottles, just in case Ralph wanted one.

Ralph refused the drink when Peter proffered and instead pulled out a chair for Peter in front of the PC. Then he turned the room lights off before pulling up a file—not a web video, no search needed. The video player loaded up a crisp if oddly shaded image, a nighttime shoot with the camera working to compensate. It revealed city sidewalk, street, and low-rise buildings with few windows. Wherever it was filmed it was far from their hometown.

"Hey, Mia, who's the new boyfriend?" said a voice from the video.

Is that Ralph's voice? Is this a film project? Who is Mia?

The audio sounded scratchy, clipped, like it came from a bad microphone or rather a phone mic not shooting video. Garlic breath punched Peter's nose as Ralph leaned in to adjust the volume. Peter held back a nervous shudder. *Why do I let my tanto-wielding friend stand behind me in a dark room?*

The video shifted as the camera pivoted upward, taking in the low-rise buildings, a few windows dimly lit, a darker starless sky. What wasn't dark was overly bright and aglow as the phone tried to filter the odd contrast.

The frame shook from the amateur videographer's steps. Then the view pivoted to an alley, dark but for a light illuminating a business doorway. Two figures stood in the lamplight, then shuffled into the darkness beyond.

"Aww, come on," said the same voice as before. It sounded more like Ralph's anxious cousin than Ralph.

The camera shook violently, pointed at the ground briefly, and revealed jeans and yellowish Nike free runs. The view re-centered, moving down the alley toward the now-shadowed couple. A siren sounded in the distance, possibly from a fire engine. The camera passed through the lamplight into the darkness.

The view faded to black, then blue-green tinged illumination returned, revealing indistinct forms in an embrace. A girl with long black hair latched onto a young adult male's neck. He mouthed an 'O' and looked lost in ecstasy.

"Whoa, I guess this is a bit private," said the obtrusive voice behind the camera.

That's Ralph. Peter relaxed. Watching a home movie, even a bad one, was fine enough. *He just wanted to key me up with the vampire questions and garlic. Jeez.*

The siren blared louder and louder from the speakers. At the same time the camera moved down from the pasty-looking male toward the back of the girl's head. A dark stain grew across the male's shirt, away from the girl. *What am I watching? Blood?* It spread too slowly to be the carotid, but looked real enough. He'd seen plenty of bad special effects and too many real wounds as an EMT.

Ralph's voice came out of the speaker. "What the shit? Say something, dude. Mia, what is this?"

Ralph's concern sounded real. Peter's heart raced. *How real is this?*

The siren blared, filling the small dark room and drowning out all other sound from the video. The black-haired girl turned toward the camera, her face flashing white and red from passing lights. A thick red liquid dribbled from her mouth and down her chin.

Shit!

The camera suddenly pointed vertically into the night sky, revealing the brick walls. The view jumped towards the bricks like the camera had been thrown. Red and white lights played across the brick. A body—Ralph's body—flew airborne, separated from the camera.

How?

The camera dropped to the ground. Ground that now filled half the frame. The alley walls were more visible. The view shuddered, bounced, and then landed on its side pointing down the alley. Ralph crashed onto trash bags and rolled awkwardly. The lamp light, where he'd been thrown from, was twenty feet down the alley.

What the hell? Peter wanted to ask. There was no way that tiny girl could throw him. Did they have someone else working the camera?

She stood under the light and pivoted with her right arm outstretched; the other arm held the limp form of the young man. Blood dripped from where her right hand should have been. The red and white lights played across the alley, briefly illuminating it, then disappearing. The lamp was the only light remaining.

In his chair, watching the movie, Peter started to reach for the pause button but stopped himself. *I'll watch it straight through, once. It's just a scare project.*

A shaking left leg stepped into the camera's sideways view, bright yellow with a white Nike swoosh. It took another step forward, revealing Ralph's torso. His right arm dangled awkwardly askew. Peter looked away from the video, down and back at Ralph's yellow Nike shoes. Even in the shadows the color was distinct, only a dark stain covered the swoosh.

"Keep watching," snapped Ralph.

Peter's eyes snapped back to the video. The girl, Mia, dropped the boy limply to the pavement. It didn't move. The siren still overpowered all. Mia stooped, picking up something with her left hand. Her severed right hand, surprisingly clear under the lamp.

A prosthetic? He tried to think of how Ralph or some college kid could fake that, but the EMT had doubts. *It looked so real.*

Ralph's yellow Nikes took two steps forward. A short knife protruded from his left fist, glinting silver, then shifted from view.

The tanto.

Under the lamp, the girl casually placed the severed hand on top of the stump. Her formerly severed hand clenched stiffly. She jumped into the air.

The screen flashed with light as she broke the lamp. Peter gripped his seat. The view returned to green and blue-tinged blackness. The siren volume started to drop. Two sets of arms flickered in motion above the Nike shoes, parrying and counter-parrying. Something small flew past the camera. A left hand, pale white, delicate looking, and with green-painted nails had rolled into the bottom right of the screen. A black closed-toed sandal followed, knocking the hand out of the frame.

The siren decreased, its wail fading.

Mia's sandaled foot advanced, exiting to the left. Her right foot was bent forward, straining, pushing. There was a horrible slick and sliding sound, like a piece of meat being carved. Her leg buckled forward, and the siren sound vanished. *He won.*

He killed her!

Ralph stepped from behind the camera into view. His yellow Nikes almost stepped on the camera. The foot lifted from view. Something dark blocked the lens, rolling toward the camera, gaining definition, black hair, the girl's head.

Peter gasped, clutching the chair. Her decapitated head had rolled in front of the camera—eyes wide, pupils indistinct, mouth open, still bloody, teeth white and gleaming. Her canines jutted forward, much longer than her other teeth. The phone, helpfully, auto-focused on her severed neck.

Peter took a deep breath as his eyes roved to the stump. He saw the detail, the excruciating detail, and remembered when a car had crashed into a barbed wire fence where he'd been first on the scene. The head had fallen into the guy's lap, bone, windpipe, arteries all visible. No one could fake that.

It's real. Really real. He stared fixedly at the screen, not wanting to turn and see his friend, a murderer.

The video was silent. The room was silent. No siren played. Peter said nothing.

"Shit." The words sprang from the speakers. It was Ralph's voice, breathless.

Peter's eyes fixed on the girl's head. Her face did not shift or change, something he might see in cheap special effects that would indicate editing. Instead her canines just shrank. They didn't retract. Their bases widened and they drew into her head until they looked normal.

No. No. No. Peter clutched his chair.

More cursing sounded from the speakers. The camera lifted into the air and righted. It pointed down at the girl's head. There was a dark puddle where the neck ended. The frame shook with more violence and Peter felt bile rising in his stomach. Then the camera view tilted upward, revealing the narrow alley walls. The computer screen went black and a white play symbol appeared in the center of the screen.

Peter let out a breath he hadn't realized he'd held. *Ralph killed someone —Mia—whoever she is.* Bits of the movie flashed before Peter. The man— victim-lover—his vapid expression, the blood running down his neck. *She killed him. She—*

The blood running down her chin. Her hand, cut off, reattached, moving again. The fangs. The fangs shrinking. Garlic. Silver.

Ralph's voice intruded from behind Peter, the pungent garlic wafting forward with Ralph's words, "Do you believe?"

Peter exhaled, trying to pull every ounce of breath from his body. He didn't want to reply, but he finally took a deep breath and asked, "Where's the silver?"

Charles Maclay is an enthusiastic writer, gamer, hiker, and skier—when he has funds for skiing. He is earning his MFA at Western Colorado University, studying genre fiction and screenwriting.

While Charles grew up on his family's cattle ranch in Western Montana, he has also lived in a tiny Seattle basement and a surprisingly spacious apartment in Seoul. He's done everything from wildland fire-fighting to playing chess while answering billing questions in a call center.

Always a gaming enthusiast, Charles took second at the 2019 Montana X-wing Regional to an out-of-stater from Washington, making Charles the best pilot in Montana—at least for a little while. When he isn't flying squadrons of X-wings, he works on his writing. He lives in Western Montana with his girlfriend, their dog, and the cat.

MOTIVATING A MONSTER

IRENE RADFORD

MOTIVATING A MONSTER

R uffle," the make-up *artiste du jour* demanded. He brandished his airbrush as if it were a sword about to decapitate his prey.

Zillagon complied, filling the pockets beneath each of his scales with enough air to triple his size. "There!" he said with just a hint of disgust in his voice. A squiggle of natural sage green, more gray than green, showed beneath the first layer of paint. His natural coloring was perfect camouflage for desert living. Movie monsters need to be more colorful.

Five years and twelve movies in Hollywood had taught him that any deeper degree of menace in his voice would push his minions into quitting. He still needed this person to airbrush good color on him.

"If you want me to look like a damned bird, you need more red on that scale, and move the brush delicately so that it looks like a feather not a splotch of roadkill." He shuddered at the years he'd been reduced to eating squashed coyotes and roadrunners. That was in his youth, before he realized the necessity of killing and then flaming his prey before they ran for the hills.

The make-up *person*—Zillagon decided he wasn't worthy the designation of artiste—complied. He probably thought his life depended upon getting the effect just right. In a different lifetime, it might.

"Lookin' good, Zilly baby," Montrose, the director said, coming into the abandoned aircraft hangar that had become Zillagon's dressing room.

He was followed by his ubiquitous assistant, complete with glasses sliding down her nose, tablet in hand, and a stylus tucked behind her ear.

"You about ready? We've got the backdrop, sets, and special effects ready for you." Montrose waved his arms wildly to demonstrate the size of the backdrop, sets, and special effects.

"Is there enough room to fully spread my wings?" Zillagon asked politely. Ten of his twelve films since coming to Hollywood had been directed by Montrose (no other name, just Montrose, as if he were as iconic as he thought he was in his beige jodhpurs and chocolate-brown boots, cream-colored poet shirt and black beret. All he needed to complete the outfit was a monocle and megaphone). Montrose's films had earned Zillagon spectacular amounts of gold. His hoard was now almost as full as his belly. The first two movies with other directors had been enormous failures, soon to be consigned to Zillagon's internal fire as had the directors when they demanded money from *him* to cover their financial losses. They'd soon learned not to mess with a dragon's ire. (Add an 'f' to that and you got the real special effect of *fire*.)

Zillagon stretched his wing membranes a bit to emphasize the need for more room than this cramped hanger. The pen for milling sheep, goats, and a cow or six took up almost as much space as the pastry table—necessary supplies to keep his blood sugar stable.

"Of course, this studio is big enough. Ten stories high and as long and wide as a football field! No more wiping out the backdrop of New York City at sunset with the swipe of one wing. We want to burn that city to the ground this time," Montrose explained with wide gestures and a red gleam of excitement in his eyes.

Maybe that murderous glare came from the sun coming through the skylight and glinting off the thirty-five fire extinguishers scattered around the room.

"Burning New York," Zillagon mused flatly. "Why would I want to burn New York?"

"Because it's in the script! Best screenplay ever written for you. We'll make six fortunes this time."

Zillagon glared at the director. "What's my motivation?"

Montrose gulped and backed up, his throat working up enough moisture to reply. "Everyone wants to see the heart of the predatory financial institutions burn?"

"Oh, okay. Vicarious revenge on the banks that everyone thinks cheats them into the poorhouse." Anger boiled in Zillagon's fat belly. He'd been poor once, and starving. He'd been so angry at life he wanted to burn everyone.

Oooops. Did Montrose know about those wildfires the full length of the Interstate-5 corridor the year he'd made those first two awful movies?

"Yeah, yeah, now you got it Zilly baby. Let's go burn New York."

Zillagon waddled after Montrose, through the doorway big enough to accept a 747 with wings fully extended. He didn't even have to close his wings to get through. Not that he could really fly anymore. His wings couldn't support his weight. Maybe he should cut down on the pastries, a necessity on every set, not just the monster movie ones.

Cut down on his essential food stuffs, NEVER!

By the time he reached the filming studio, he was so angry at the banks that didn't pay enough interest to keep his flock of sheep fed he was ready to burn the entire city for real, not just a projected backdrop. He wanted his flames to be real rather than computer generated.

"Easy, Zilly baby, remember the cost of insurance. Less profit for us if we have to rebuild the sets more than once. Keep your fire under control. Dribbles of flame, not full infernos.

"But ... but ..."

"Do it!" Montrose yelled.

Zillagon dropped his head in meek compliance. He still wanted to burn something. Maybe he should indulge in a trip to the trash dump when they finished for the day. The city always needed help reducing the mountain of garbage and the nice methane pockets flared with extraordinary beauty.

Yeah, he'd get to flame something later. But first he had to destroy New York.

"Beautiful, Zilly baby. Beautiful." The director gazed fondly at the model skyscrapers outlined in flame by propane jets. "Now lift your snout and howl to the moon."

"Huh?" Zillagon had never howled at the moon in his life. That was for werewolves. "Why would I do that?"

"Oh, I don't know. Because it looks cool on camera."

"What's my *motivation?*"

"You want the audience to love you. You want them on your side so that when it takes a squad of Marines to kill you, all those screaming teenagers will shed a tear for you. That way they'll pay good money to see the movie again, and more money to see the next movie."

"But what am I mourning? I burned the bankers because they cheated me on interest for my hoard. Why do I mourn them now?"

"Oh, I don't know. Maybe because the bankers killed your girlfriend for her gold, and you can't ever have her as your mate."

"I don't have a girlfriend. And girl dragons don't have hoards. They sit on boy dragon's hoard while they incubate eggs." As big as Zillagon's hoard had grown from his successful movies, he still didn't have enough to attract a mate. But he would. One more film and he'd have enough. But he'd have to fly in order to mate.

He looked down at his sagging belly. It nearly touched the ground between his splayed feet. With a sharp snap he opened his wings as wide as they'd go and flapped, once, twice, three times while he ran toward the exit.

Air whooshed beneath his wings, caught the membranes and ... and dashed elsewhere.

He couldn't get off the ground.

Then he lifted his muzzle and roared—a decent dragon roar, not some puling wolf's howl. He stretched his sinuous neck until his nostrils brushed the light crane and pulled his anguish up and out until the tin roof rattled. Flame followed sound. And he screamed his regret that he let acting fill his life so much that he ate himself into a fat old man without enough gold to find a mate.

"And cut!" Montrose called in a voice that resounded and echoed and shook the sound boom. "Perfect, Zilly baby. We'll break for the night. "Everybody back here by six tomorrow morning, before six, not after. We've got the studio for one more day. We still have to stomp Tokyo and drown Detroit. So no delays and no tardiness!"

"Why would I do that?" Zillagon reached for one of the dragon-sized Danish pastries. His paw shook as he forced himself not to grab the delicacy and gobble it in one bite.

"Aren't you hungry, Zilly baby?" Montrose asked.

The thought of all the sugar melting on his tongue sent quivers of delicious anticipation through his body. Then he saw his belly making a barrier between him and the desert table.

"I'll be in my trailer." Cave actually. He lived in a cave carved out of the hillside behind the studio lot. His home was devoid of gold because the bankers had custody of his hoard. Why was he doing all this? "What's my motivation?"

Last month, Montrose had fitted out Zillagon's cave with electricity and Wi-Fi, and provided a desktop computer with a fifty-four inch monitor, so that far-sighted dragon eyes could focus on the screen while he streamed old monster movies. He liked the old prototypes of himself. The Japanese directors had done a good job of imitating him before they knew he really existed and that he loved making movies.

Zillagon had needed Montrose to find plastic tubing to sheath his talons so he didn't shred the keyboards and trackpads. A tiny bubble of foam on the end of each tube made each claw a perfect stylus. He could type one hundred ten words per minute when he needed to complain to mail-order houses when the latest tools and gadgets weren't up to his satisfaction. It seemed like he returned everything he bought. Human-sized tools never fit dragon-sized paws.

Out of curiosity, he checked the status of his hoard. Quarterly royalty payments from his previous movies should show up in his account today.

Three clicks brought him to the log-in. He typed a twelve character string of letters, numbers, and symbols that meant nothing in English but spelled out his name in Dragon perfectly.

January payment, check.

February interest, check.

March advance on signing new contract, check.

March deduction to Montrose as Media agent, *WHAT*? Fifty percent! That was not right. Never would Zillagon have authorized that kind of payment.

He opened a new file in the ether holding area. There was the contract that spelled out the percentage and his signature. He didn't remember signing that.

Carefully he opened a new window for his private files from his hard drive. There was the contract. He compared them side by side, word for word. The only difference was that obscene amount of money going back to Montrose as his agent.

Somehow, Montrose had hacked his ether account.

His blood boiled and his gut churned.

He marched out to the garbage dump south of his cave entrance and loosed a long blast of flame. The methane exploded, turning the red flares to blue and back to white. Heat charred his face, but his scales deflected any damage. The airbrushed make-up might look a little smoky, but that's what he paid the fumbling minion for.

Still not satisfied, he roared another bout of fire into the garbage. More methane exploded. Flames reached toward the dry hillside. Sparks shot toward the full moon.

Sirens erupted in the near distance.

Zillagon stomped back to his cave. Plans fermented in his brain as anger continued to distill in his gut.

He had lawyers and accountants to run errands for him. He began the slow process of converting all of his accounts to cash, then instructed people in five different cities to convert that paper money into gold bars, gold coins, gold jewelry, high-quality gems, and the gold toilet belonging to an orange muskrat.

Then he set about hacking into Montrose's accounts to see what else had been stolen from the accounts of a dragon.

Morning came and went. Zillagon continued selling real estate and stock and buying treasures. Everything was for sale for the right price.

About noon, Montrose's assistant, the pretty young woman with short and fluffy brown hair, no make-up, and tired walking shoes, arrived at Zillagon's cave. She pulled the rope connected to a big bell at the entrance.

"Sir, you are needed on set," she said in her squeaky and timid voice. What was her name? Tammy maybe. Tommie? Nattie, short for Natalia.

Zillagon ignored her. He was deep into recovering money that Montrose had stolen from him.

The bell rang again, longer and more insistently. "Sir, Mr. Montrose says that every minute is costing you money. We only have the rest of the day to shoot two destruction scenes before we wrap the whole movie. You have to come now, or he'll cobble together shots from other movies with computer special effects."

That penetrated Zillagon's mind. He'd done what he could remotely. Now he had to confront the perpetrator of the crimes. Nattie wasn't responsible. He wouldn't punish her, or risk Montrose abusing his power over her.

"I'm coming." He said simultaneously as he hit enter on the remote to roll up the metal door to his cave. The sun backlit little Nattie with her inevitable tablet and glasses resting atop her head like a headband. Meek she might sound, but her posture shouted that she was the true power behind Montrose. Without her determination and courage to face down even a dragon, the director would get nothing done.

She'd make a worthy mate if she weren't a puny human.

Much to his delight the same sun that created a halo around Nattie glinted around the metal trailers attached to semi-trucks coming up the long, graded gravel road between Zillagon's home and the studio. He gratefully counted six in today's convoy.

Six semis loaded to the gills with treasure. He was really looking forward to presenting an antique Russian Orthodox silver chalice to Nattie as a thank you for her years of dedication to Montrose and therefore also to himself.

"Miss Natalia." He bowed to the woman. "Would you please stay and organize the offloading of the coming cargo. I wish it to be arranged in the shape of a nest. When you are done, you may choose an item for yourself." He really hoped she'd take the chalice. He'd selected it from an auction house with her in mind.

Then he stalked toward the studio. He hadn't eaten since the day before and already felt lighter, less sluggish and surly. Fasting three days between meals was normal for a dragon. Why had he let Montrose convince him that gorging on donuts all day, every day, was what he needed?

He had chosen the right path. Now he just had to deal with Montrose.

"Zilly baby! You're right on time. We had some problems with our permits from the Fire Marshall. I finally bought him off with promises of no fire today. Today you are going to stomp on Tokyo."

"No, I am not."

"Zilly baby, what's wrong? We talked about this yesterday. You were fine with the idea of wiping out ..."

"You were fine with me crushing the finest city in the world, the city that gave us the first and best monster movies."

"Rubber puppets ..."

"Prototypes."

"Prototypes, smototypes. What's important is that audiences love mass destruction, blood, and gore. They love you and how you end the tyranny of politicians over ..."

"Politicians were the last movie. This script calls for the demise of bankers."

"Yeah, yeah bankers, same difference. So, let's get to it. The rest of the movie is finished. We just have these last two scenes ..."

Zillagon felt his stomach roil and grumble.

"Hungry? Have a chocolate éclair. Get your blood sugar up and you'll feel much more like the fine actor I know you to be."

Zillagon scooped up the director and held him in a cage of his talons.

"Zilly baby, put me down. We've got work to do." Montrose looked all around him with a degree of panic in his voice and the quivering of his chin. He dropped his megaphone on his way up to Zillagon's eye level—only about six feet above ground, not high enough to kill him if he fell. But he'd probably break something and hurt badly for a long time.

"Time is money, Zilly! Put me down so we can get to work."

That got the dragon's attention.

"How much money will you lose if you do not finish this film today?" He squeezed his fist a little tighter.

"Ulp. Um, quite a lot. You'll lose too. You invested heavily in the up-front production costs."

"I did?"

"Yeah. You and me, halvsies. When the box office receipts roll in, we don't have to share with anyone else."

"Did I invest as much money as you have stolen from me?"

"Stolen? I haven't stolen anything from you, Zilly baby."

"Aside from my name. I am 'Zillagon,' a proud dragon name from a proud dragon heritage. You may not call me 'Zilly baby.'"

"Okay, okay. A little familiarity. This is Hollywood, laid-back lifestyle and all. We're all casual here. Now put me down so we can start work."

"What about the change to my contract authorizing a fifty percent payment to you as my agent? I have the original contract. It specifies ten percent." He brought his eyes closer to the wriggling figure of the director.

"No, no, no. You read the contract wrong. It's a standard fifty percent." Montrose looked everywhere but into Zillagon's eyes ... er ... eye.

"I retained the original on my hard drive. Not subject to hacking by your internet robots. And ten percent is standard. I've filed a complaint with SAG."

Montrose's phone beeped an incoming email.

"And I've terminated the contract."

"Okay, okay. Since you only act in *my* movies, you don't really need an agent. Can we get back to work now?"

"I want to change the script."

"You can't do that!"

"I can or there will be no movie at all." He squeezed his talons a little tighter.

"Change. What change?" Montrose squeaked.

"We leave Tokyo unscathed and I take a dip in Lake Michigan to wash off the stink of burning New York. The waves from my splashing with joy threatens a few waterfront villages. With children in inner tubes splashing with me."

"But ... but ... stomping Yokato is ingorrig ... is iconic. Tokyo is iconic to the genre."

A little smoke leaked from Zillagon's nostrils.

"Eeeep!" Montrose squeaked.

"At the moment you are the only director with a real dragon for his movies. I can easily sign with someone else. Get more realistic scripts, Monty baby."

Montrose paled. Zillagon licked his lips.

"Okay, okay. But can you at least fly over Beijing and drop some heavy rocks? Make the Chinese think it's asteroids and God's judgment?"

Zillagon thought that over for a moment. Thinking that might be a good idea.

Then he thought again, and loosed his grip on Montrose. "Next film. I need to lose some weight in order to fly."

Montrose slipped within Zillagon's grip.

"Zilly ... Zillagon, don't drop me. We're partners. You have to work with me!"

Zillagon held up Montrose once again and asked quietly, politely, through gritted fangs, "What's my motivation?"

Irene Radford has been writing stories ever since she figured out what a pencil was for. Editing, under the name Phyllis Irene Radford, grew out of her love of the craft of writing. History has been a part of her life from her earliest childhood and led to her BA from Lewis and Clark College.

Mostly she writes fantasy and historical fantasy including the bestselling Dragon Nimbus series and the masterwork Merlin's Descendants series. She writes historical tales as Rachel Atwood. In other lifetimes she writes urban fantasy as P.R. Frost or Phyllis Ames, and space opera as C.F. Bentley. Lately she ventured into steampunk as Julia Verne St. John. Ireneradford.net.

TUNNEL VISIONS

JAMES A. HEARN

TUNNEL VISIONS

"[T]he only thing we have to fear is ... fear itself."

—Franklin D. Roosevelt, first inaugural address

"When the water's rising and the bombs are falling, it's sure as hell not fear you're afraid of."

—Anonymous survivor of the USS *Arizona*, Pearl Harbor

AUGUST 3, 1933: SOMEWHERE IN THE ITALIAN ALPS

Rachel Knox popped the blue pills into her mouth and chased them down with champagne. She didn't know what the blue pills were called—like most everything in her life, Frank J. Sloan had handed them to her and expected his biggest star to swallow them down without question. The owner of Sloan Film Studios was born to give directions, and it seemed to Rachel it was her fate to take them.

Memorize these lines, my dear. Take these pills. Stand over here, chin up. Kiss your co-star, he just saved your life. And always, always, smile for the camera. Frank was producer, director, and pharmacist all rolled into one overweight, licentious package.

Rachel refreshed her flute glass and sat down on the bed of the

271

sleeping compartment she shared with Frank. Outside the window, a blue sky blazed above forested mountains as the Adriatic Express Train barreled through the Italian Alps, bound for Greece.

A smile touched Rachel's lips, but her blue eyes were as vacant as a painted porcelain doll. If only her father could see how far his only child had come up in life. A movie star, traveling the world. Parties that lasted for days. The late Lukas Knox had expected his daughter to stay on the family's rice farm in the bayous of Louisiana, a farm that always teetered on the edge of bankruptcy.

On her eighteenth birthday—just days before the stock market crash of 1929—she'd escaped the farm's drudgery by hitching west to California. The world was plunging into an economic depression, but young Rachel had hardly noticed. She was poor but free, and Los Angeles seemed full of possibilities.

After six months of working in chorus lines, she was "discovered" by Sloan Film Studios. The discovery was made by Frank Sloan himself, the self-proclaimed Christopher Columbus to a slew of silent film starlets. Rachel thought of him more as a Cortés than a Columbus, as Frank had a ruthless penchant for despoiling virginal resources, especially girls with golden hair.

In her more lucid moments, in those days when she couldn't find her pills, Rachel reflected that she'd escaped the rice farm only to exchange one form of servitude for another. But surely the life of an actress was preferable to working her fingers to the bone on a farm she'd never own?

The train gave a lurch in its otherwise smooth ride, jolting her back to the present. The sleeping compartment was supposed to be the largest and most luxurious on the Adriatic Express, but she still felt like the walls were closing in on her. She fixed her eyes on the jagged mountains passing outside of her window, silent sentinels at the northern edge of Mussolini's Italy.

"Did you take your pills, my dear?" Frank Sloan asked as he slid open the compartment door. He sat heavily into the seat opposite her own, his girth swallowing the cushion.

"Yes, Frank."

"Good. They should keep your claustrophobia in check. Let me know if you need more." He patted the pocket of his suit vest with a fleshy hand, pills rattling in an unseen bottle.

Not to mention my nyctophobia, she said to herself. *And my depression, anxi-*

ety, and whatever else Frank's doctor said I had. "When do we reach Athens? I'm ready to get off this blasted train."

Frank assured her they were right on schedule. "Just picture it: Rachel Knox amid the splendors of ancient Greece, as Queen Helen." He took her chin in his fingers, turning it in the light as if she were a prized mare from his stables. "You certainly have a face that could launch a thousand ships. That blond hair is so lovely."

Rachel allowed herself a brief smile. The hair color Frank was so captivated by came in a bottle. Did everything that made life bearable come in one bottle or another?

Frank had taken her sardonic smirk for encouragement and was droning on about all they would see while filming his Trojan War epic. Rachel was playing Helen, the mythical beauty Paris had spirited away to Troy. She wondered again why it was necessary to film on location in Athens, when the "splendors" Frank spoke of were in ruins. She suspected the protracted trip to Europe was all a ploy to break down her defenses and get her to finally set a date for their wedding.

Why not get it over with? After all, she was contractually bound to Frank's studio for another six years. But the thought of possibly bringing a child into the world that was one-half of Frank Sloan chilled her to the marrow. Frank was sliding a hand up her strapless black dress when a gentle knock sounded at the door.

"Come in," Rachel said hurriedly.

The door slid open to reveal a tall man dressed in an immaculate gray suit. Her male co-star and best friend, Douglas McGregor, had a rugged face, with a thin mustache resting above an ever-present grin.

"How are you feeling, Rachel?" Douglas asked.

"Much better, thank you."

"Well, well," Frank said with a nasty frown, "if it isn't Paris himself paying a call to Helen? I warn you, I can be as jealous as Menelaus." He kissed Rachel's ear.

"Lay off, Frank," Douglas said, lighting a cigarette. "I've been sitting alone in that cramped second-class sleeping compartment for hours. Shall we go up to the dining car for a bite?"

Rachel almost smiled over Frank's jealousy. If only he knew Douglas as she did, the studio owner would know he had nothing to fear from his biggest male star, at least in that quarter.

"Why don't you go ahead of us?" Frank said, his eyes feasting on

Rachel's milk white shoulders. "I think Rachel wants to … rest for a few minutes."

Douglas glanced at his pocket watch. "Oh, she does, eh? Shall I expect you in, say, four minutes?"

Frank's face contorted in cold fury. "You go too far, Douglas. I made you, and I can break you just as easily."

"That's three times you've threatened to fire me on this trip alone," said Douglas, laughing. "What are you going to do, Frank? Tell the world that my real name is David Weiner? That your all-American cowboy from Arizona is actually a Jew from Brooklyn?"

"Keep your voice down," Frank said.

"Well, go ahead and tell them. I'm under contract for five more pictures, remember?"

Rachel's voice cut through the air like a knife. "Where did the mountains go?"

"Beg pardon?" Douglas asked.

"The mountains!" Rachel hissed, pointing to the window and rising from her seat. The Italian Alps were gone. In their place was a dark rectangle, devoid of all light.

Frank laughed derisively. "We're in a tunnel, my dear. Nothing more. These trains pass through many such tunnels as they traverse the mountains."

Rachel sank back into her seat, holding her forehead. Tunnels! She hated any enclosed space, ever since her father had locked her in the storm cellar when she was twelve. It was punishment for her first attempt to run away.

Rachel had gotten as far as the bus station in Lafayette before Lukas Knox had found her. A strange man in a straw hat was sitting next to her on a bench, asking questions. Where was she going? Was she hungry? The man's hand was on her knee when her father drove up. He'd beaten the stranger's face to a bloody ruin, then hauled her back to the farm and shut her into the storm cellar. Night had fallen by then, and her father had taken out the lanterns before locking her in.

Rachel had flung herself against the door, beating on it with her fists, but it wouldn't budge. In the darkness, rats scurried on clawed feet, their agitated squeals like mad laughter in her ears.

During the longest night of her life, sleep never came, though she occasionally slipped into a kind of paralysis, like a catatonic dread. Beyond the pounding of her heart in her ears and her fists on the door, Rachel thought she could hear something in the back of the cellar.

Something breathing. As the night stretched out, as her terror grew, the breathing seemed to get closer. Stronger.

Frank's psychiatrist, while exploring the subject with her years later, had told Rachel there was nothing in the cellar, and the breathing she sometimes heard in the dark of night was all in her mind. If anything, she was only hearing the sound of her own heartbeat and respiration in her ears, like the narrator in Poe's "The Tell-Tale Heart."

In the cold light of day, Rachel had agreed with Dr. Gothame. But when the sun went down, when the shadows deepened into darkness, the good doctor's rational words lost their power, and Rachel found herself more often than not sleeping with the lights on. She didn't hear the strange breathing when the lights were on.

As Douglas and Frank exchanged barbs, Rachel rubbed her eyes to banish her childhood memories. She was Rachel Knox, international film star, not some scared little girl.

When her eyes opened, she screamed to find the sleeping compartment was pitch black, save for the glowing tip of Douglas' cigarette.

A few moments later, the lights came back on. Frank was reaching for the pills in his pocket, while Douglas was eyeing her with genuine concern.

"What happened?" Rachel gasped. "Why did the lights go out?"

"How the hell should I know?" Frank said as he handed her two pills.

Douglas swore softly. "I thought you were going off those, Rachel. They cloud your judgment." He looked meaningfully at Frank.

Frank snorted in derision. "What're you, a doctor? Her pills are prescribed by a medical professional."

"One in your employ, no doubt."

Rachel held up a hand for peace. "I'll put them in my purse, in case I need them later."

"Excuse me," Douglas said to a passing porter. "Is there any trouble we need to be worried about?"

"Trouble, sir?"

Rachel caught sight of Douglas' surreptitious wink at the porter as her friend nodded in her direction. "About the lights and the tunnel, I mean?"

The porter seemed to take the hint. "There's no trouble, sir. We lost power for a few moments."

"So everything's under control, right Marco?" Douglas asked, glancing at the porter's nametag.

275

"I believe so," Marco answered. "The luggage car's still blacked-out and the radio's down while we're in the tunnel, but that's all."

"Is there power in the dining car?" Rachel asked.

"Yes. Only the last railcar is still blacked-out. The second- and first-class sleeping cars, the dining car, and the locomotive have power." The porter held up an electric torch. "If you'll excuse me, I need to check the luggage car. The porter on duty there isn't answering our pages."

"Might be hard to do, in the dark," Douglas observed.

"When will we be out of the tunnel?" Rachel asked.

The boyish porter consulted his pocket watch. "The schedule says eighteen minutes, but some of these tunnels seem to last an eternity. I have never timed it, I'm afraid. Excuse me." He disappeared down the aisle.

"My invitation still stands for the dining car," Douglas said.

Rachel got up and took her friend's arm. "I'm famished," she lied. The blue pills she'd taken earlier had made her nauseated, and she didn't want to be alone with Frank if the lights went out again. "Coming, Frank?"

The movie producer trailed behind them, his expression sullen.

"I tell you, there's nothing to fear from this Herr Hitler," said Frank, as he stabbed a slice of prime rib with his fork. "Mark my words: there'll be no war in Europe."

Rachel, Douglas, and Frank were seated at a table in the dining car. Rachel found that she much preferred its openness to the close quarters of the sleeping compartment. She felt like she could breathe here ... as long as she kept her eyes off the rows of black windows.

Outside, the darkness of the tunnel seemed to drink the train's electric lights. On occasion, light from the dining car would glint off some jagged edge along the tunnel wall. It caught Rachel's eye by instinct, like the movement of shadowy predators beyond the protective light of a night-time campfire.

"No war," said Frank again. "Mark my words."

Some diners had stopped their meals at Frank's intrusive voice, including a boy and a girl dressed in uniforms. The boy was wearing black shorts and a tan shirt, while the girl wore a brown jacket, white blouse, and a dark blue skirt. Both had black neckerchiefs tucked under their collars. They had ceased conversing in German and were openly staring at Frank and Douglas.

"Then what are the Germans re-arming for?" asked Douglas to Frank. "Why are they burning books?"

Rachel sat quietly, wishing they would talk about something else. She looked away from their table, shivering when her eyes caught yet another flash of reflected light from the tunnel walls.

The lights in the dining car flickered off, then came back on. Rachel bit back her scream. The blue pills in her purse were calling to her, but she forced herself to take a comforting sip of coffee instead.

"Don't be obtuse, Douglas," Frank said. He paid no attention whatever to the fact that the lights had gone off, however briefly. "Wouldn't you be arming yourself if you had Stalin on your doorstep? They deserve to defend themselves, just like we do. And what's the harm if they burn a few books, eh? More people will go to the cinema and see my pictures."

Rachel caught the attention of a porter. "Excuse me. What's going on with the lights?"

The porter swallowed nervously. "We're having some, uh, electrical problems with the rearward railcars. The lights are going out."

"Is that normal?" she asked.

"Your party should stay in the dining car until the situation is resolved. You'll be safer here."

"Safer? Safer from what?"

The porter muttered a goodbye and strode quickly to an exit.

"He didn't answer my question," Rachel said, watching the porter go. "Frank, did you notice that?" The movie producer ignored her as he continued his debate with Douglas on European politics.

In the meantime, one of the uniformed German youths had approached their table. *"Entschuldigung,"* said the boy politely. "I couldn't help but overhear your conversation. May I make some observations?"

The boy standing at Rachel's elbow was perhaps fifteen, with short-cropped blond hair and friendly blue eyes. His companion glowered at them from the other table, agitation written on her face.

"What's your name?" Rachel asked him, momentarily forgetting about the porter's strange behavior.

"Rolf Switzer. And you are the famous film star, Rachel Knox."

"Looks like you have a fan," Douglas said. He introduced himself and the members of his party to Rolf and invited the boy to join them. Rolf took the empty seat beside Rachel and accepted a small glass of wine from Douglas.

The girl got up from the other table, said something strident in German to Rolf, and left the dining car in a huff.

"Pay no mind to Johanna," Rolf said sheepishly. "My older sister mistrusts all *Ausländer*. Beg pardon, I mean non-Germans."

"No offense taken," Douglas said. "We cannot hold ourselves responsible for the behavior of our fellow countrymen." He said this while staring daggers at Frank.

"You said you had something to contribute to our conversation?" Frank asked, unaware of the cutting remark.

Rolf sipped his wine. "We Germans have no wish for war. At least, I don't. In fact, I've never been in a fight in my entire life."

"You're still young," Douglas said. "That might change in the near future."

"Rolf, no sane person wishes for war," Rachel said. "What do your new leaders want then?"

"The same thing every other nation wants: security."

"See what I was telling you?" Frank said. "War's bad for business."

Douglas rolled his eyes at Frank's last remark, but let it pass unchallenged. "Rolf, no one is begrudging your nation's right to defend itself. But what's happening is going beyond mere security. Why is your leadership organizing boycotts of Jewish businesses, or burning books, or putting political opponents into that prison in Dachau? It's the politics of fear."

Fear. Rachel closed her eyes, suddenly wishing she hadn't come on this trip. Douglas was right: this entire continent was roiling in fear. Who knew when it might coalesce into a tangible form and explode into open warfare?

Off to one side, she caught the sounds of a heated exchange between two train employees. Her Italian was rusty, but the men were obviously agitated.

"Marco è morto," whispered one to the other. He made slashing gestures across his body.

His companion made a shushing sound, but the man continued right over him. Despite his rapid speech, she picked out the words "darkness" and "blood."

Marco. Rachel remembered that was the young porter's name, the one with the electric torch who was going to check the blacked-out luggage car. And she was fairly certain that "morto" meant "dead." She set down her coffee. Had someone died ... or been killed?

"I think something's happening on this train," Rachel said. "Something bad they're not telling us about."

"You're right, my dear," Frank said. "The waiter hasn't been by in ages." He snapped his fingers in the air.

The train employees moved off, still whispering to each other. Rachel looked around. Other passengers in the dining car were eating and laughing. One young woman was bouncing a toddler on her knee. Everything seemed as it should as their train sped through the dark tunnel. Maybe the pills had made her jumpy?

"I don't know much about what happens in the cities," Rolf was saying, his back stiffening in response to something Douglas had said. "My parents are cheesemakers in a small village in Bavaria. My father says the Party is fulfilling its promise to restore Germany to its former greatness. And for the books, I would say books are like people: some are good and some are bad. Those without merit should be burned."

"Which should be burned up?" Douglas asked. "Bad books or bad people?"

"Books!" Rolf said, aghast. "And if people are being put into prison, I suppose they must have done something to deserve it."

"Like disagree with your leaders," Douglas muttered.

"Oh, who the hell cares what happens to a bunch of communists and malcontents?" Frank said. "The main thing is that no one wants to start another war. It's bad for business."

"I suppose, Frank," Rachel said, turning her attention back to her companions, "that would depend on the business. If you were selling bullets and bombs, war might be very good for your bottom line."

Frank sighed in exasperation. "My dear, ever since the advent of the talking picture, you've been very free to speak your opinion. Believe me, no one pays the price of admission to hear what you have to say. You're on screen to be admired, nothing more."

Rachel's right palm itched to feel the sting of slapping Frank's pudgy face. She reminded herself that she was a lady, and ladies didn't strike men for making pig-headed, chauvinistic comments. Douglas, however, had started to rise from his seat, but when Rachel laid a calming hand on his arm, he seemed to recollect himself. Frank continued devouring his prime rib, oblivious of the tension in his companions.

"I respectfully disagree, Herr Sloan," Rolf said. "I would buy a ticket to see and hear a beautiful and intelligent woman."

"Well said!" Douglas exclaimed.

Rachel kissed the boy's cheek, and Rolf blushed furiously.

Frank's retort was cut short when the dining car was plunged into darkness. Rachel gripped the armrests of her chair as confused and angry voices shouted out, Frank foremost among them. She heard the dining car's door slide open, and then something heavy slammed into their table. Dishes crashed to the floor.

When the lights returned after some moments, Rolf's sister was lying face down on the table, bloodied and moaning. Douglas and Rolf helped Johanna to a chair while Frank backed away from the girl's red-stained uniform. Other people ran into the dining car, shouting about a thing in the darkness.

Rachel's heartbeat pounded in her ears, and she cried out when a man in a conductor's uniform brushed past her. The man took a key from his belt, locked the railcar's door, and then ran toward the engine room. Outside the train's windows, the darkness of the tunnel seemed to press against the glass, searching for a way in.

Rolf gripped his sister's hand. *"Wer hat dich verletzt?"*

Johanna began rambling in German. Rachel took her other hand and said, "In English, please? From the beginning?"

"Auf Englisch, bitte," Rolf said.

"Is that door locked?" Johanna asked, still gasping.

Douglas gave it a firm tug. "Yes."

"Danke Gott." The girl sipped the water Rachel gave her, then spoke in a strained whisper. "I'd gone back to the second-class car, to my sleeping compartment. I'd drawn the curtain closed when the lights went off."

"The lights went off here, too," Douglas said. "But they came back on."

"The lights never came back on for me," Johanna said. "Then people in the car started screaming."

"Of course they screamed," Frank said with a nervous laugh. "The lights were off, and they were scared."

Other passengers were gathering around their table to listen. Douglas bade them be quiet, and the babble of voices ceased for the most part.

"Nein," Johanna said. "They were screaming at the—the thing—in the darkness."

"What thing?" Rolf asked.

"I don't know, brother. I pressed myself against the wall of the compartment, not daring to move. I heard a sound outside the curtain, a low whistling sound."

"Like something breathing?" Rachel asked, her voice filled with dread.

"*Ja*," Johanna answered. "Like a bear, or a tiger. Heavy footsteps passed by, claws clicking on the floor. Then the shrieks of passengers were silenced, one by one. I knew it would find me if I didn't get out. I threw the curtain aside and ran this way. I stepped on people, on bodies. Near the exit, I brushed against something cold, revolting. It slashed at me, tearing my clothes, but I got away. I ran into the first-class sleeping car, shouting for everyone to get out. Then the lights went off in there too, and some of us ran in here."

Rachel fell back into her chair, fear bubbling inside her like acid. This couldn't be real! Had Dr. Gothame been wrong about the storm cellar, and the sounds she sometimes heard in the darkness of her bedroom? Like an animal, breathing, waiting to kill her.

"What glorious fiction!" Frank said. "Young woman, you should come to work in my studio. But enough is enough. You're scaring my fiancée with your runaway imagination."

"This girl's blood isn't make-up," Douglas said.

"I'm not your fiancée," Rachel declared. She was scared out of her mind, but it felt good to say that.

In the meantime, the conductor returned and had been listening to Johanna's tale. Upon seeing him, Frank accosted the man about the quality of his railroad, and how the Adriatic Express had lost a very valuable customer. Douglas pulled Frank roughly away.

"Ladies and gentlemen," the conductor said, raising his hands for quiet. "My name's Petra Kanelos. I don't pretend to know exactly what's going on in the rearward railcars."

"I have a daughter back there!" the woman with the small child yelled. Others shouted angrily, speaking over one another.

"Quiet everyone, please!" Kanelos yelled. "Ever since we entered the tunnel, something has come aboard our train. Whether man or beast, I cannot say. Something ... evil, just like the young woman over here said." The passengers grew silent. "It began in the luggage compartment and is making its way forward, to here, killing in the darkness."

"What about my daughter?" the woman asked again.

"My brother is back there!" another said.

"I've lost three porters, good boys all," Kanelos said, voice rising above the others. "I sent them to their deaths, it seems. Do you want your other little girl to die, madam?" He pointed to the woman holding the child, and she fell silent. "Now then, I need two men to help me de-couple the train before the same thing happens to us."

"But we'll be out of the tunnel soon, won't we?" Rachel asked.

"We should have been out a long time ago, but I don't trust my watch. Two minutes, maybe? Who knows?" Kanelos answered. "But that thing is still on the train."

Douglas stepped forward. "I'll go."

Rachel grabbed his arm. "Don't go out there, in the darkness. Don't leave me."

"I'll stay with you," Frank said, voice quavering.

Rachel cursed the name of Frank Sloan. She felt revolted with both him and herself that she'd ever allowed him to control her life or touch her body. It was so unfair. Why did good men like Douglas have to risk their lives, while the Franks of the world hid in the corner, or made money off of war?

"Fraulein Knox, will you watch over Johanna?" Rolf asked. "I'd like to help the conductor."

The boy's bravery warmed Rachel's heart, banishing thoughts of Frank. "Of course, Rolf."

"Good men," Kanelos said to his two volunteers. As he unlocked the door and swung it open, the dining car was thrown into darkness once again. People scattered in confusion, screaming. Cold air rushed in from outside, followed by an even colder presence.

Rachel could sense, rather than see, the creature standing just inside the doorway, not six feet from her. Johanna collapsed in her arms like a dead weight. Rachel set her charge down on the floor, then fumbled on the dining table for something she might use as a weapon. Her groping fingers found the cutting edge of a steak knife. She held it in shaking hands, ignoring the gash that had opened across her right palm.

As Rachel stood alone against the darkness, the memories of her twelve-year-old self came gibbering out. She was back in the underground storm cellar, pounding on an unyielding door with bloody hands, crying to her father that she'd learned her lesson.

She heard the creature take a step toward her, claws clicking on the hardwood floor. In her mind's eye, it was her father, back from the grave. No, it was the solicitous stranger in the straw hat, the one who'd whispered in her ear of things she hadn't understood. No, it was Frank Sloan, offering her the bondage of money and blue pills. It was all of them and none of them, and every fear she'd ever known.

Johanna moaned at her feet, recalling Rachel to her senses.

"I'm not afraid of you." Some part of Rachel knew that was an utterly ridiculous thing to say. She held the knife at the ready.

The answering growl was a guttural, predatory sound that should have sent her chittering away like a frightened animal. But she stood firmly over the girl that had been placed in her care. "You may kill me. You may kill us all. But I'm not going to be afraid of you!"

There was a roar from the creature's mouth that sounded partly like a snarl and partly like laughter. Claws brushed against her cheek, ever so gently moving down to the jugular notch of her throat, the caress of a cat stroking the prey held between its paws. Warm breath, rank as death, filled her face.

Rachel thrust the knife upward with all of her strength, aiming just below the creature's mouth. The blade slid home, all the way to the handle, and a warmth gushed over her hands as an unholy scream split the air.

She'd found its throat, she knew. Powerful arms throttled Rachel's sides, but she didn't release her grip on the knife. She stepped closer and stabbed upward again, thrusting the blade higher until it hit bone.

At that moment, the train shot out of the side of the mountain, bursting into a bright, sunlit valley. Rachel blinked at the sudden light, temporarily blinded, and stumbled to the floor.

When Rachel regained her senses, she found Douglas and Rolf kneeling beside her. Nearby, she caught a glimpse of Frank's posterior sticking out from under a tablecloth. Some passengers, overcome with grief, were sobbing while a few others hugged and kissed their loved ones.

"Where's Johanna?"

"The girl is safe," said a familiar voice. Rachel looked up to see the conductor. "We all are, thanks to you. I've searched the train from top to bottom, and there's no sign of our killer."

"How many died?" Rachel asked.

"Eight dead, and three with minor injuries. It could've been much worse. Thank you again." He moved away to see to other passengers.

Rachel sat up abruptly. "Where did it go? The creature?"

"Creature?" Douglas said. "I didn't see anything. But something knocked the three of us aside when the door opened. Here, let me clean your hands." He took a napkin, dipped it in a pitcher of water, and began washing Rachel's hands. The blood caked on them was dark as midnight.

Rolf had removed his neckerchief and was binding a wound on Johanna's arm. "I saw something, Fraulein Knox. For just an instant. When the sunlight returned, there was a hulking blackness standing right in front of you."

"What did it look like?"

The boy shook his head. "I do not have the words for it, even in German. A blurry thing, indistinct around the edges. Clawed hands, like a predator. A few seconds before the train came out of the darkness, it screamed. Then the sunlight came through the windows, and the air around it turned, curved in on itself. And it was gone."

"Gone," she echoed. Somehow, on some instinctual level she didn't understand, Rachel knew the danger had passed. She got to her feet.

"You were very brave," Douglas said. "I heard what you said about not being afraid. When the lights went out, the only thing I could think to do was get away. But you stood your ground."

Rachel smiled weakly at his praise. "Thank you, Douglas."

"I want you to call me David from now on." She stared at him in disbelief. "That could've been the final curtain. I've decided that whenever I go, I'd like to go out as my real self. Or as close as I can get."

Rolf looked up in surprise. "I thought you were Douglas McGregor, the cowboy?"

"Stage name. My given name is David Aaron Weiner. I'm not really a cowboy from Arizona, either. I was born into a poor Jewish family from Brooklyn."

Rachel loved her friend more than ever at that moment. Douglas—no, David, she corrected herself—was incapable of reciprocating that love, at least not in the way she wanted. But it was enough.

She turned to the two German youths. "Are you okay, Johanna?"

"Yes." She looked at David, her eyes wet. "You were willing to face the darkness, *mein Herr*, and what did I do but faint dead away? And you were bravest of all, Fraulein Knox."

"You did better than most," Rachel said. "You tried to warn people of the danger." She threw a disgusted look at Frank. The movie producer had crawled out from under his table and was clutching a bottle of whiskey, far removed from his companions. She took Frank's blue pills out of her purse and threw them to the floor.

"It's hard to imagine," David said, "that there could be such evil in the world. Whatever it was."

Rachel glanced at the insignia on Rolf's red armband. "Not really, David. The evil is always there, waiting for the lights to go off."

The train rolled onward through the forested valley. In the distance, the Adriatic Sea churned below scudding dark clouds.

James A. Hearn is an attorney and author who writes in a variety of genres, including crime, science fiction, fantasy, and horror. He and his wife reside in Georgetown, Texas with a boisterous Labrador retriever. An amateur astronomer, James believes everything is better under a starry sky—a good book, time with friends, or Mexican martinis.

His crime fiction has appeared in *Alfred Hitchcock's Mystery Magazine, Black Cat Mystery Magazine, The Eyes of Texas: Private Eyes from the Panhandle to the Piney Woods, Guns + Tacos, Mickey Finn: 21st Century Noir,* and *Mickey Finn 2: 21st Century Noir.* James is a two-time finalist in the Writers of the Future Contest. jamesahearn.com.

OUR LADY OF CELLULOID

RYAN F. HEALEY

OUR LADY OF CELLULOID

Ben Mackey sat at a table the size of a swimming pool and tried not to look down at the dark wood, polished to a mirror. He didn't want to catch his own eye and lose all his nerve. He also didn't want to look out the window over Los Angeles, from hundreds of feet in the air. It was easy to believe this room didn't actually exist, and that didn't bode well for his attempts to feel like he belonged there.

The man sitting next to him, whose name and title he'd forgotten the moment they were spoken, wasn't helping. Instead, he was feeding Ben a constant stream of hot air about how, after this movie was released and broke all the box office records, everyone was going to know his name. But the man kept calling him Ted.

Very old and very young men filed into the room, laughing and pointing at each other, jockeying for seats and trading barbs. Gradually they began to quiet and turned their attention to the man sitting next to Ben. The man smiled with all of his teeth, put his hand on Ben's shoulder and took a deep breath.

"Before we start," Ben cut in, "I just wanted to say thank you for taking a chance on my script. I truly believe that there haven't been many action films with this level of heart or humor, and I've poured everything I have into it. I mean, just the fact that you're investing in a story where the two leads have a platonic and respectful relationship through to the end shows a level of integrity that I don't think most studios would even—"

The man next to him held up a hand and smiled apologetically to the rest of the room. "First off, Ted, I must inform you that the character of Barbara is now a dog. We think the emotional connection will play better with the audience than if she's a woman." He picked up the thick folder in front of him and waved it as if it held evidence that the decision was a winner. "So ... before we start ... any other questions?"

"Um ..." Ben looked at some of the papers and pictures sticking out of the folder. He chuckled and tried to save face. "Why are headshots still in black and white? This is the 1980s not the 1880s, right? Anybody ... know ... why?"

"You. Incompetent. Idiot." Ben spat as he waited at the bus stop outside the studio gates. He put his head between his knees and rocked on the bench like a man on the verge of a breakdown, muttering a stream of insults to himself.

"I have to assume you're talking to yourself, but either way you're being very rude to one of us," said a voice. Ben looked up, startled to see someone else on the bench with him. He was an old man, old enough that his face, his eyes, and what was left of his hair were all the same faded color. He wore a dark blue suit that must have fit his body once, but now hung around him in folds with his thin wrists poking out of the cuffs like the sticks of a scarecrow.

"Ah, sorry. Talking to myself."

"What, they didn't buy your movie pitch?" The man asked with a wry grin.

"Even worse: they did," Ben admitted miserably.

The man laughed and shook his head in sympathy, slapping against his thigh a trifold advertisement he clutched in his hand. Ben saw that it was for an exhibition of some old movies starring a bumbling detective. He knew the titles immediately.

"Hey, I love those old ..." Ben began to say, and then his head snapped up, shock and delight shining on his face. "*You're* Solomon Miscavige!"

The man's eyes grew suddenly cold, his mouth a brief underline. He nodded once, curtly. In his excitement, Ben ignored the obvious signs that the man was now closed for business. He barreled on, describing how his grandfather used to spend hours telling Ben about all his favorite old movies, the stars of the day, the stories that had charmed and delighted him. Even before he'd seen a movie screen, the boy had understood and appreciated the art of it.

Gradually, Ben realized that he was babbling and getting nothing back. He self-consciously pulled himself back into the mundane. "So, just a day at the studio, huh?"

Begrudgingly, the old man's face softened again, twitching several times before he replied. "I was here on behalf of my grandson, calling in a favor to one of the few people who remembers me."

"What?" Ben exclaimed, incredulous. "A big star like you?"

Solomon sighed. "Yes, a very big star. It's nice to know I have enough pull in this town to secure a studio job in the mail room. And the kid thinks he's made it, that he's on his way." He waved his fingers through the air as if gesturing to some future possibility, or maybe just to fan away an empty dream. "And who knows, maybe he is ..."

The old man lapsed into silence again, and after a minute Ben gave a nod toward the trifold in his hand. "So, you're going to see your movie?"

The young man watched the play of emotions, an argument the old man had with himself that carried back and forth until a vicious defeat left him to finally, painfully nod.

The bus pulled up just as Ben grinned in spite of himself. His excitement flared again, cavalier and impolite. "Great! I'd love to join you."

The film was one Ben had seen before, but on a television with busted rabbit ears in the middle of his grandfather's sun-drenched living room. Now here he was in the dark embrace of a proper theater, sitting next to the star himself, who in a few moments and four decades ago was about to bluster onto the scene of a crime and make several delightfully ridiculous pronouncements.

As that moment grew near, Ben felt a palpable tension coming from the man beside him, and looked over to see Solomon grimacing miserably in the flickering light of the screen. He was shaking and beads of sweat stood out on the dome of his forehead as though he was gripped by the flu. Ben was about to ask him if he needed to leave when, on the screen, the young Solomon Miscavige strolled through the open door in a trench coat and fedora.

When he turned his attention back to the old man, he found him flushed and grinning unabashedly at the sight of his dashing young doppelganger. In that smile, Ben saw the young man superimposed over the old, basking in his victories and swelling with pride. And in that moment, Ben Mackey's stupid, awful day became a good one. Suddenly he felt some hope for his future in Hollywood, which wasn't, after all, such a terrible place.

Solomon's good mood carried through to their goodbye outside the theater, where he generously offered his phone number without prompting, and told Ben to call if he wanted to talk about the "perils of outrageous success."

The next weekend, another film of his was on the exhibition schedule, so they met at a diner before they went and made an afternoon of it. As they dug into sandwiches and lukewarm fries, Solomon questioned Ben about his childhood in Iowa, and what brought him out to California.

"I guess I just wanted to go where someone might understand the things that excited me—and it might excite them, you know? I mean, I made a free throw in sixth grade basketball that my dad still talks about. Of course I was in a dozen school plays that I actually cared about, but whatever."

The old man smiled knowingly. "He didn't find them as memorable?"

Ben nodded. "He did admit that I had remembered a lot of lines. Once."

"Be careful who you let flatter you out here," Solomon said gravely. "This town is run by two kinds of men: old men who will never have enough money and young men who are defined by their haircuts and think they're responsible for all of human culture. You mean nothing to these people. Your dreams mean even less. I had some good friends and partners in this business, for a time. But people get used up quickly here. They burn out and blow away like that." The man said it with a force that made Ben think he was going to snap his fingers for emphasis, but instead he just stared into space. Ben thought better of interrupting the silence, and eventually the old man drifted back. They finished their lunch with small talk.

Later, in the theater, Ben felt a jolt of glee at the title card, *The Case of the Singing Bureau.* But when he ventured a sideways glance, he saw the same strange scene play out next to him: in the light of the screen, the man's grimace turned to an expression of mounting panic. He remained that way, sweating and panting until finally his character, Private Investigator Jack Mason, wandered into the scene with his over-confident swagger. At the sight of his young self, the old man slumped into his seat with obvious relief and even chuckled, shaking his head.

As they watched the escalating shenanigans of the clueless detective and his whip-smart secretary Marcy Grant, Ben kept stealing glances, completely distracted by his companion's strange behavior. But for the rest of the show, the man seemed only to enjoy himself.

The sun was crouching on the horizon when they exited the theater, both men blinking at the darkening street like disoriented time travelers. They took a taxi back to Solomon's house, where Ben made the driver wait until the old man had shakily mounted his front steps and closed his front door with a final wave.

They had only gotten a few blocks away when Ben noticed Solomon's jacket crumpled in the corner of the seat. He asked the driver to turn around, and when they got back to the house he bounded up the steps and gave the door several sharp raps. When a second round of knocking and waiting produced no answer, he tried the doorknob and found it unlocked.

The sunlight was waning but even that didn't account for the deep shadows inside the house. Every blind and curtain was shut tight, and the few beams of light that shone through gave the room a murky, underwater feeling.

Ben turned a corner into the living room, expecting to see Solomon there. Instead he found a shabbily furnished room, thick with dust. On one side of the room, stretched across a wall and blocking two windows, was a large canvas sheet. Across the room was a medium-sized movie projector, with a folding chair next to it. Resting on the seat of the chair was a gun.

Fingers closed on Ben's shoulder and he nearly screamed. He spun around to find Solomon, his eyes burning with rage. Even as he started to explain, Ben's gaze was drawn to the large black wheel in the old man's pale knobby hands. It was a film reel and written on the side of it in white marker was the title *The Case of the Singing Bureau.* Across the title was a large X made of two ragged strips of red tape.

The old man found his voice. "Get the hell out of my house!"

Ben brandished the limp jacket like a talisman, and the old man batted it aside. "No privacy ... I can't believe ... taking advantage of my generosity!" Solomon advanced on Ben, shouting him back down the hall to the door. Before Ben knew it, he was standing on the porch, hearing the deadbolt snap into place, with a forgotten jacket dangling from his hand.

The space was inside an enormous building the size of an airplane hangar. The ceiling and walls were painted black, and the ground was covered in snaking black cables. In the middle of the room, lit as bright as a summer day, was a set that consisted of one level of a house, bisected and open to cameras and lights. There were windows that looked out onto a giant poster of the outside world. There were doors that opened to nowhere. There were stairs that turned a corner and ended at the ceiling. It looked to Ben like a human ant farm.

He stayed close to a wall and kept out of the way, trying not to be noticed.

"Hey," a man called from a dozen feet away. He had to repeat himself a few times, hissing in Ben's direction, until Ben realized the man was talking to him. Ben pointed at himself and the man nodded, grinning and waving him over.

The man was also standing by the wall, accompanied by two identical dogs. One he was grooming and periodically handing treats. The other lay on a blanket nearby, unmoving except for its eyebrows, which it waggled up and down with slight interest every time a person hurried past.

"Hey," the man repeated, offering Ben a firm handshake. "You're the writer, aintcha? I'm Rico, animal handler. I thought you might enjoy meeting Rebecca." He indicated the dog he was grooming. Ben didn't know much about dogs but he knew their expressions usually meant the exact opposite of human ones. This dog was smiling at him.

"Rebecca?"

"Yeah, well really they're both playing Rebecca. This lady here is named Wanda and she'll be Rebecca in all the action scenes. That one is Princess, and she's better at dialogue."

Ben looked from one dog to the other. "What makes that dog better at ... dialogue?"

"She's very patient for treats. She knows she'll get more later if she can focus and hold for the shot. The talking effect will be added later."

Ben nodded, then said, "You know, Rebecca was actually supposed to be a woman. A human woman. She and Craig are best friends and she ends up saving him at the end."

"Oh." Rico gave a puzzled smile.

Ben nodded, then noticed the aluminum rack standing against the wall a few feet away. Hanging from it were a half-dozen outfits, one silver and futuristic, one pink and ringed by a tutu, one looking like business attire complete with a foreshortened tie stitched down the front of a faux-shirt and suit. All of the outfits had four leg holes and a slit in the back for a tail.

"Are these Rebecca's ... outfits?" Ben squinted as if he was succumbing to a migraine.

Rico brightened. "Yeah! Seems the men upstairs were worried the movie wouldn't be toyetic enough. That's a new word they love throwing around: TOYETIC. So, they ordered these nifty outfits and added a couple of scenes to, you know, justify the action figures."

Ben swayed on his feet and laughed a hollow, barking laugh. "Guess you could use a third dog, huh? Fashion dog?"

"Sure." Rico gave a polite smile.

One dog then the other turned to look at Ben. They both raised their eyebrows and stared until he turned and quietly left the set.

Ben called whenever he got the chance, whenever he thought of it. He called more than he should have, but Solomon wouldn't answer. When he was sitting in his dingy apartment, trying to write, wondering how long he should wait, asking his roommate to turn down his music again, he called Solomon. When he was finished tying his tie in the mirror, wearing his only suit and ready for a meeting where his agent would inform him of exciting new developments in the movie that vaguely resembled his script, he called Solomon. When he was eating an enormous salad because he got a good deal on produce, chewing endlessly on a mouthful of lettuce, he called Solomon.

"Hello? Will you help?" Solomon's voice was immediately too loud in his ear.

Startled, Ben choked on his lettuce.

"Hello please help will you help?" Solomon was slurring his words and for a moment Ben thought he might be drunk.

In the background was music, too loud and crackling like a television with the volume turned up all the way. There was a constant eardrum-itching hum.

Finally Ben managed to swallow his food. He had tossed his salad bowl in the sink and was already at the stretched limit of the phone cord, grabbing his key ring and stuffing his feet into his shoes. "Solomon? Solomon, are you okay? What do you need?"

"No, Marjorie." The old man whispered. And then, much louder, "Marjorieeeee, *please*."

There was a rasping exhale, like a sob, and then the sound of a gunshot punched through the receiver. The phone crackled senselessly on the carpet, and Ben was out the door.

Ben opened his eyes groggily, woken by a chorus of electronic beeps and the sound of peeling tape. Solomon was sitting up in his hospital bed, talking to a young man with slicked-back hair and a thick gold chain over his T-shirt. The boy kept peeling up the tape securing the IV in the old man's arm, then trying to smooth it down again.

"Now it's too tight." Solomon snapped at him. "And my skin's all pinched over here, just leave it alone." The young man threw up his hands and muttered while the old man picked at the tape himself, though it seemed a great effort just to reach across his own chest.

Ben's back gave several loud pops when he rose from the chair, and both men looked at him, startled.

"Benjamin!" Solomon exclaimed, giving him a wan smile. "Benjamin, this is my grandson Donny. Donny, this is my good friend Benjamin."

"Friend." Ben smiled. "Yeah, we're friends."

As he shook Donny's hand, the younger man lifted his chin and tried to convey meaning through his grip. "Friend, huh? And you, uh, found him? Brought him in? Just happened to come over, right when he was having a heart attack?"

Solomon waved his hand, dispelling the cloud of machismo. "Stop with the third degree. I phoned him for help and he came right over."

"Well actually, I called ..." Ben started, then stopped. "Right, he did call me."

Solomon patted Ben's arm affectionately and then told Donny to give him the list of items he wanted from home. Ben looked at the list: several specific outfits, a biography of Patton, a book of crossword puzzles from the bathroom, his toothbrush and toothpaste, his razor and shaving cream.

"C'mon, Pops, I can do it," Donny complained. "Let this guy go be wherever he needs to be."

"No," Solomon warned, his voice firm and imperious. "I trust him not to snoop around and start claiming my belongings before I even kick the bucket."

Donny sneered and clutched his chest dramatically. "Pops, you're breakin' my heart here."

"Yeah, yeah." Solomon grimaced and made a shooing motion with his hand. Ben took his leave, gladly.

Ben entered Solomon's house slowly, as though he were afraid of interrupting the carefully laid silence and dust. This was his third time in the house, but his first with the old man's consent. With a specific mission from the man himself, even. Still, he moved through the hallways and rooms haltingly, feeling decidedly unwelcome.

He only glanced into the living room, where he'd found his friend collapsed next to the projector, in the grip of a heart attack and barely conscious. The gun was still on the floor and sunlight shone through three bullet holes in the makeshift movie screen.

The large zippered duffel bag was in the hall closet where Solomon had said it would be. Ben punched the inside of it until it was the right shape, then began searching the house and filling it with items from the list.

The bedroom was as shuttered and murky as the rest of the house, but it smelled strongly of old man and chemicals. To Ben it wasn't unpleasant; it was the smell of afternoons at his grandfather's house, watching movies. He opened the closet door expecting to find clothes, and instead found shelves of large movie reels. He took down a couple, feeling the heft of the tightly bundled plates, and reading the titles scrawled on the side. All of Solomon's movies were there, lined up chronologically. And someone had x-ed out each title with two crossed strips of red tape.

With his curiosity finally surpassing his discomfort, Ben set down the bag and picked up several reels in a stack. He took them straight to the living room, set them on the metal folding chair, and switched on the projector. The film already spooled in the projector started to play again, the black-and-white image filling the stretched canvas from wall to wall, save for three white bullet holes.

The scene was of a small office: a tall file cabinet bulging with file folders, a desk littered with coffee-stained papers, and two empty chairs. Ben stared in confusion as the shot held. Nobody entered the room. If not for the jaunty score and the scratches on the film, not to mention the sound of the reels spinning near his elbow, he would've thought the projector was somehow stuck.

Then he noticed, in the way something is invisible until suddenly it's not, a darker shape in the shadow of the desk. It was the edge of a shoe, lying on its side. Only the shoe was visible, so either it was lying there discarded or there was a body behind the desk, just out of sight.

Ben stared a minute longer, watching for movement, then reached a shaky hand to the projector and fumbled with the switch. He wound up the reel, replaced it with another, and fed the ribbon of film through the projector. He started it again.

This one was the first they'd watched together, *The Case of the Screaming Telegram*. Again, the scene of a crime, the police officers questioning the witness, the cue for private investigator Jack Mason to enter and confound everyone with his clueless swagger. But the cue came and went, and Jack Mason did not enter.

Ben's mouth went dry. He was sure he must be mistaken; he was remembering it wrong. Then the other characters began reacting to empty space, talking to someone who wasn't there. In their eyelines and blocking, it was easy to see exactly where Jack Mason was supposed to be moving around the scene, exactly where he wasn't.

He stopped the film. Then, with growing dread, he queued up another. His hands were shaking so badly he nearly tore the film trying to feed it through the rollers. He started the film.

The first scene of this one was in a restaurant, where Jack Mason was treating his secretary to a dinner celebrating his success with a particularly dangerous mystery. Little did he know it was really Marcy Grant, his secretary and unrequited admirer, who made sense of all the clues and saved him from harm, time and again. Except Marcy wasn't in the seat across from him, and Jack Mason was slumped against the table, the hilt of a knife sticking out of his back.

Alone in the old man's living room, Ben gasped and sat heavily in the

298

folding chair. Reels of film scattered across the carpet. He watched a man in a waiter's uniform enter the scene and ask the corpse if he wanted more wine. He wrinkled his nose at an unheard comment, then proceeded to fill both wine glasses as blood continued to spread across one-half of the white tablecloth and drip onto his polished shoes.

The waiter left, and a moment later Marcy walked into the scene, wiping her hands on a stained white napkin. She didn't move the way Marcy was supposed to, with purpose and poise and a bright expression. Instead, she shuffled, meandered, and finally slumped into the chair opposite her dead boss, toasting him and draining her glass. Then she leaned across the table in a very unladylike way, plucked up his glass, toasted him again, and began to drink that too.

Ben was shocked by her appearance, her hair unkempt and wild, her lipstick smeared, dark circles of exhaustion around her eyes. She also looked like a different actress than the usual Marcy Grant, a less-delicate woman, not purse-lipped and swishy but still alluring in a strong and dangerous way.

He stood up and started to approach the screen, wanting to get a better look, but the moment he moved, she noticed him. She actually turned, smiled wryly, and stood up. Every motion was jumpy and unnatural, as if she were out of sync with the frame rate. She held his gaze as she tipped her head back and poured the last of the wine into her mouth. Then she spun on her heel and dashed the glass against the table. Broken glass sprayed across the motionless Jack Mason, sticking in his hair like snow.

She turned back with her teeth bared, making a sound that wavered between a laugh and a snarl. She stalked forward, stuttering and jumping closer. Her face grew larger and larger on the screen. Her eye was the size of a hubcap and expanding. She was a giant, coming to reach through the wall and pluck Ben up, perhaps to break him on the table.

In a panic he stumbled back, tripping over the chair and sending the projector crashing to the floor. The reel continued to turn, though the film ripped and flapped against the casing like an injured bird. White light shone across the room like a spotlight that might be occupied at any moment by a murderous ghost.

Ben wasn't hyperventilating by the time he returned to Solomon Miscavige's hospital room, in fact he was unnaturally calm. But the moment the man roused and looked him in the face, he knew.

"You saw something," he said simply. It wasn't a question.

Ben lowered himself into the chair by the bed, clutching the duffel bag in his lap. "What is she?"

Solomon grinned without humor. "A woman scorned."

He sat back in his bed and stared at the ceiling. "She was the love of my life, Marjorie Watterson. Well, the second love, after my love of the audience. Which I guess is love for myself, really. We were partners in theater, in writing, in ... every way. But she was the fire, the passion. She made it all happen. A brilliant writer, a shrewd judge of character, and a proud woman. When we started getting offers, when we started making deals, she could smell the rats. She came up with the hook: the private investigator who keeps getting saved by his secretary. It was all her. And as far as the studio was concerned, she could keep writing. But she didn't have a face or a figure for the big screen, not the way they saw it. So some doll would have to play Marcy Grant. She walked, and I signed."

Solomon sighed, a long deflating sound. "And as much as she loved me before, that's how much she hated me after. The fire of brilliance that burned in her, the passion, it burned her up. She hanged herself before the first film came out."

"But a few years ago ... she came back." The old man stole a guilty glance at Ben, and in that moment he didn't look like a man at all; he looked like a scared kid. When he spoke again, his voice was high and thin. "In the movies. She stalks me in my films, the copies I own, one by one, and I watch her murder me. And still the movie lives on, the rest of it plays out without me. I go to screenings when I can, just to be sure that I'm still there, but if I watch them at home, I get to see myself dead. And sometimes she comes to see me. To stare and taunt the scared old man."

His voice cracked and then he fell silent, sinking into his bed as though the confession had taken the last of his strength. Ben saw Solomon's outstretched hand shaking against the blanket and covered it with his own. The old man's fingers closed around his gratefully.

Solomon mounted the front steps without assistance, though Ben was at his elbow and prepared to steady him at a moment's notice. They entered the house together, turning on lights as they went, until they stood at the threshold of the living room.

The old man surveyed everything that now littered the floor: the tumbled chair, reels of film, the gun, and the projector itself. "I think it's time for me to get rid of my collection," he said heavily. "She's finally gotten me in all of them, but she only gets me for real if I let this obsession ruin my life. Hell, it nearly killed me already."

Ben nodded. "I think you're right. It's a good plan."

Solomon smiled. "I'm going to live what life I have left. And once I get a little stronger, I'll take the films out to a dumpster and burn them. Blaze of glory."

He continued down the hall as Ben crossed the living room and righted the projector, surveying it for damage. He removed the torn reel and returned it to its case, then collected the others from the floor and carried the stack through the house to the bedroom. He heard Solomon moving around in there and entered the room saying, "You know, it might not be a bad idea to have someone take a look at these, maybe—"

He stopped as soon as he saw the open closet, and the writhing mass on the floor. It looked like a black mummy, wrapped up alive by mistake, fighting to be free. As he dropped his armful and hurried to the bundle, he realized that it was all film, looped around the form of Solomon Miscavige over and over again, sliding and tightening like the coils of a snake. Even as he fell to his knees and stared in shock, the films he had been carrying slid from their containers and joined the scrum, wrapping themselves around the end that must have been the head.

Jolted into action, Ben dug at the film there, trying to uncover a face. But there were too many layers, and the film sliced his palms and fingers. Even as he tore faster, the film only continued to cover and consume. For a brief moment he saw skin, the edge of a lip peeled back in a rasping scream, and then it was covered again.

Sitting back, his bleeding hands hanging uselessly at his sides, Ben finally took in the tiny image on each frame of film before him. It was Marjorie's face, over and over, with her snarling laugh and an ember burning in each eye.

And as the bound feet drummed their last on the carpet and stilled, the face changed and softened. She didn't smile, and she didn't look happy, but in her expression was something very much like satisfaction.

301

RYAN F. HEALEY

Ryan F. Healey is a lifelong writer and illustrator who lives in Webster, NY with his wife, kids, and an emotionally unstable poodle. A mild-mannered IT analyst by day, he spent several years writing and producing the podcast *Tales from the Static*, which recounted and reviewed episodes of a fictional 80s horror anthology show. This is his first professional publication.

JOSIE'S LAST STRAW

KARINA FABIAN

JOSIE'S LAST STRAW

The moon shone through the cloudy sky, dappling the lone trailer in a patchwork of light and shadow. A man shambled toward it. With the ease of familiarity, he navigated the trip-traps of rusting car parts and garden gnomes, and the pitfalls dug by dogs. Then, his foot caught on a newly dug hole. He staggered into a plaster, birdshot-spotted deer. With an unintelligible roar, he smashed both fists into the fawn and shattered it. He continued to the porch, walked into the steps, backed up, and walked into them again. A pause, then right foot lifted, then left, and he ascended the rotting wood. He hardly noticed as he crashed through the screen door, leaving it hanging off one hinge.

Inside, the television blared reruns of *South Park* to no one. He snarled at the set, then slammed the channel button. It changed to Elvira as she introduced the next horror movie. He sat down on the Lay-Z-Boy to watch.

Josie woke up from yet another nightmare of Jebediah having one of his "fits." She always felt so guilty after a dream like that! Poor man, two days buried, and she had to think about him this way?

Not that the past few years had been kind, she reminded herself as she schlepped into the bathroom, one arm in her robe, only habit making her

305

wash up and get ready to face another day as Widow Gump. She sighed. No, not easy years at all. After that Conroy had shot him in the calf trying to kill that badger, Jeb hadn't been able to work much. He'd go out for the day, come home without a job, but always with something he'd killed for dinner. She didn't believe those people who said he was drinking in front of the Gaslight Inn. Then she took that job—

We were going to lose the trailer, part of her said, and she knew it was true, but she knew that was the last straw for him.

"No woman of mine is going to work! Your job is to stay home, cook my dinner and have my babies!" he'd declare. It was so cute when they were dating, how manly he'd act. 'Course, she'd failed him the baby department, too.

She looked into the mirror at a face dripping with water. "You're getting fat and ugly," he'd warned her, more than once, sometimes with a pull on her frizzy hair or a pinch of her stomach to prove his point. "Don't be thinking about leaving me now. There ain't a man in the world gonna take you!"

Now, as the tired, faded and *old* face stared back at her, she saw just how right he was. That was going to be the hardest part, too, she knew it. Living alone. She left the TV on all night and slept with the dogs, but it weren't no substitute for a man.

Their—her—retriever Buford and her toy poodle Pinkie scratched at the bedroom door. They nearly bowled her down as she opened it, dashing into the living room, barking furiously.

"What is it? Another coon?" She grabbed Jeb's shotgun and made her way down the hall. Her steps slowed as she realized the television was no longer playing the comedy channel, but one of those creepy shows Jeb had loved to scare her with. If one of his friends had come in and changed the channel as a sick joke ...

She recognized the back of the head she'd seen resting against that chair for twenty years. The shotgun slipped through her hands and crashed to the floor.

"Jebediah?"

Jebediah grunted and stuck out his arm in a way she recognized as well, and with shaking knees and trembling hands, she hurried to the kitchen and brought him his favorite beer.

It was him! It was a miracle!

"This is Dave Neilson, here with Josie Gump, whose husband, Jebediah, seems to be the first confirmed case of a zombie interacting safely with other humans."

Josie gripped her elbows and watched the camera as if the big lens might swallow her. She still didn't know if she'd done right by letting the reporter in, but she'd asked Jeb and he'd grunted that it was okay. At least she thought that's what he meant. He really only grunted anymore. Guess being dead takes a lot out of a guy.

Besides, after his grave had been found dug open from the inside, everyone from Momma to her preacher to the sheriff had come calling. He was a zombie – the murderous, shambling undead, they told her. She needed to take the dogs and get away fast, they told her.

They were worried about her, they told her.

They were always worried about her. Why couldn't they be happy for her? So she let them get a peek at him, and once they saw him drinking his beer, they were satisfied he wasn't some murderous shambling undead that was gonna rip her to shreds like in the movies he loved so much. She didn't let them talk to him, though. He wasn't ready. Besides, Jeb always hated visitors that weren't his friends. Not that any of them had come round, she thought bitterly.

Anyways, she needed to let folks know everything was okay, so they'd leave them alone to get on with life.

She was worried when the cameraman filmed him, even if he did so from the safety of the kitchen. Once upon a time, Jeb would have smashed the camera into the man's face or, at best, flipped him off. But he sat watching some vampire pull off his shirt and walk to the beach. Shoot. She liked that movie. At least Jeb was behaving peacefully enough. Even the dogs were behaving, snuggled together on the couch, giving their master forlorn looks. She'd been worried about that, too; Pinkie always protected her and never got along with Jeb. Things were going well.

Reporter Dave had asked her a question.

"'Changed'? Well, he don't talk about it much. Jeb was always the private sort. But, yeah, I think he has changed. He's a lot gentler now. Not that there's been any—you know. I just mean that he's a lot more content. He's a better listener, too." She blushed. Had she really just told the world about their ... you know? Not that there'd been any. Even alive, she could count on one hand ...

But that was my fault. I let myself go. I was so tired and angry all the time. Funny how anger made a person so tired. Still, he could have ...

"So how does he feel, physically? Is he stiff?"

Her eyes widened. Why had she ever brought it up? "Well, I think that's rather personal!"

Dave blushed. "I mean, like rigor mortis? Does he have a pulse? Is he warm? Does he feel alive?"

Actually, when she'd hugged him this morning, reaching around his back and squeezing into his arm, careful as usual to avoid getting in the way of the television, he'd felt kind of squishy under his skin. She forced a grin.

Dave continued, "And what about the smell?"

Suddenly she regretted ever having let this, this *reporter* into her home. "Now you listen here! I have been in mourning! And now my husband is back, and he has special needs! If I've let the housework slip—"

"No! Wait! I just meant—"

She didn't care what he meant. This was a bad idea after all! She blinked back angry tears as she stormed for the door and flung it open. She called for the dogs, and they rose from the couch, barking and snarling.

"Please! All I meant—"

"Buford! Pinkie! Sic!"

The reporter and cameraman ran past her. The cameraman remembered the quick turn and made it down the steps, Pinkie snapping at his heels, but Dave overshot and tumbled off the low railing. Buford jumped after him, teeth bared.

She slammed the door on their screams.

Jebediah grunted with more force than usual. Josie hurried to put a fresh beer in his hand.

"I'm sorry, Jeb! I'm so sorry. I won't ever let anyone intrude on us again!"

Jeb gave another grunt and poured beer into his mouth. Some spilled on his shirt. She wiped it off with a dish towel, then got a tissue for her eyes.

"Josie!"

Josie halted her cart from where she was about to enter the beer section and glanced past the detergent, stationery, and bargain aisles to where her best friend, Audrey Callahan, came rushing up from the

Hannah Montana clothing display aisle. It took a while, because Audrey was wearing those strappy heels of hers again. She outweighed Josie by 30 pounds, easy, but she always wore the latest fashions, always had a man looking her way. Some people was just born knowing how to "work it."

Audrey's smile clouded with concern as she approached. "Josie, oh, honey. You look so sad!"

Sad? "What? No, no. Just tired, I guess. Jeb's got a lot of needs these days, and I decided to spring clean ..." Her voice trailed off. After that reporter's rude comment, she'd taken a good look at her house and seen it for what it was. A sheer shambles. Plus, she'd found cockroaches near Jeb's chair! She'd decided she was going to spruce things up. She'd spent the past few days cleaning the house top to bottom. She'd come to Walmart to restock on cleaning supplies and buy some material for bibs. Jeb just didn't have the motor skills he used to, and when she mentioned that she'd make him something in camo and hunter orange, he'd grunted, which she took as a good sign.

Audrey peered into her cart with a gasp. "New curtains? He's letting you get new curtains?"

Josie shrugged. "I told you. He's changed." Actually, she'd gotten them for the bedroom, which he never went to anymore. He spent night and day in that chair. Still, she hoped that one day, he'd shower and rejoin her —and if he noticed the new curtains, he'd appreciate it. Besides, she needed something to cheer herself up, especially after the phone call from that Carol Lyffe, Zombie Exterminator Woman. Telling her that her husband was a reanimated corpse that would kill and infect her when given the right motivation. She'd even offered to come all the way from California and re-kill him for her!

After she'd hung up on her, she'd put the shotgun on top of the television set where Jeb could grab it fast and told him she was going shopping and to open the door for no one.

"That's a lot of Febreze," Audrey said.

Josie didn't want to admit the reporter had been right about that, too. "It ... was on sale."

Audrey dragged her to the in-store McDonald's and treated her to a biggie size McNuggets and chocolate shake. She chowed down on her own cheeseburger and fries while Josie told her about the very nice phone call she'd gotten from a woman representing the "Zombies Are People, Too" movement.

"They're really interested in Jeb and me joining—apparently, we're still the only case where an undead hasn't come back a murderous shambling monster. 'Course I don't see how we can. Jeb's got so many needs now, and ..."

Instead of smiling, Audrey asked, "Honey, are you really all right? 'Cause we're all worried about you."

How many times had Audrey stuffed her with fast food and asked her that question? The reply came automatically. "Oh, it's hard sometimes, but really, we're fine."

Then she laughed. "Actually, things are better. We sit and watch TV. Would you believe I'm getting a liking for that horror stuff he loves so? Guess after having my man come back from the dead, it's gonna take more to shock me. Plus, I talk to him—really talk to him. Like we used to when we was dating. He don't answer much—he can only grunt, still. If I can just find a way to break through—"

"Did you ask him about *her*?" Audrey demanded.

That evening, Josie tied the large square cloth around Jeb's neck, careful not to block his view. She'd already emptied a can of Febreze so that all she smelled was Lilac Summer. "There now! Do you like it? It's got little deer on it. Remember how you used to hunt deer?"

Jeb grunted and held out his empty can.

When she'd replaced it with an open cold one, she sat down on the chair beside him. She steeled herself. Audrey was right; if they were going to move on, they had to discuss this. She just had to find the right way.

"Jeb, honey, remember when we were dating? You were so handsome, and strong." She bit her lip, looking at how the lights from the television reflected off the pale, sickly color of his embalmed skin. The TV played some alien invasion movie, and the strobing lights highlighted more than the horror of the thing lurking in the shadows.

Maybe she shouldn't concentrate on his looks.

"And you were so protective of me! Remember? Remember when I cast flirty eyes on Carson Fielding? And you broke his nose?" And that night Jeb had shoved her hard against the back seat, screaming at her to stay away from that loser. She'd been so terrified—yet so drawn to his passion.

"'No one can love you like I do!' you told me. 'You're mine and mine alone.' Do you remember that? I do, like it was yesterday. And that's how it's always been, Jeb. I'm for you and you alone."

She waited for his reaction, but his eyes continued to stare dully at the TV as the scantily clad woman made a run for the airlock. Maybe she shouldn't have picked the most exciting scene to have this discussion. Too late now. She swallowed and steeled herself.

"Jeb. There was ... a woman at the funeral. Your funeral. She said that you and she were ... She wasn't nasty about it, either. Said that now that you were, well, were dead, we should comfort each other. But Jeb, I gotta know. Were you and she—did you and that woman ...?"

Jeb grunted and took a swig of his beer.

She took his hand in both of hers. She sniffled. "All right, then. I suppose it's enough that you chose to come home to me."

She felt a tickling on her palm. At first, she thought he was being frisky. Then she saw the cockroach.

Swallowing, she palmed it and rose to kill it outside. He didn't need to know. She didn't need him to know.

Josie glared at the mirror as she applied more blush. She puckered her lips and struck a pose. Last night, she'd washed her hair in mayonnaise and slept in rollers to tame her frizz into bouncy curls. So she wasn't the beauty she was thirty years ago; Audrey always said, "You have more confidence when you look good." She was going to look as good as she could.

She walked into the room, a rose-scented hankie up to her nose in part to calm her and in part to mask the smell of Lilac Summer and insecticide. She looked over to make sure Jeb was all right, and noted with disgust that the roaches had made it past the circle of Borax she'd put around his chair again. Well, she'd spray the area down with Raid in a bit. First, she was going to make that phone call. Now, while the TV was playing the quiet scene where the campers were about to have sex before the murderous madman broke through the door with a chainsaw.

I can't do this alone anymore, she reminded herself. *I need to get professional help. We need professional help.*

Still, her fingers trembled and hesitated as she dialed.

A warm, caring voice answered. "You're talking to Dr. Wilson. Who's this?"

Suddenly, despite her best intentions, the tears came. Oh, she so did not want to sniffle on the radio. She took a deep breath. "Josie Gump, doctor."

"The Josie Gump? Wow! How can I help you, Josie? Things not going so well with Jebediah?"

See? That's just why she chose to call the Relationships with Doctor Wilson show. He just knew how to zero in on a problem. *Now remember what you practiced. Be positive, like Momma always said.* "Well, I know I shouldn't complain, and I really am grateful to have him back. A house needs a man, if you know what I mean. But all he does is sit there and stare at the TV. Night and day, day and night, and—"

"Have you told him how you feel?" he interrupted, but now that she'd started, all the pain welling up in her wouldn't let her stop to answer.

"And it's grunt for a beer, and grunt for another. And I don't even know where they all go! Literally, Doctor. He never, never gets up from that chair—"

"Have you talked to him, Josie?"

Next, the guilt tumbled out. "And when that reporter talked about a smell, I thought he was criticizing me. He was trying to tell me about Jeb, and I sicced the dogs on him. I feel so bad about what Buford did to his—"

The doctor rose his voice without yelling. "*Josie!* Have you talked to him?"

"The reporter? I sent him a nice card." She kicked herself. Now she sounded like a twit. She glanced at the living room, but Jeb was absorbed in the make-out scene on the screen.

Dr. Wilson was kind enough not to laugh. "Jebediah, dear. Have you told Jebediah how his behavior makes you feel?"

"Well, I tried? All he does is watch TV. He don't even look at me anymore."

Wilson grunted, as if she'd said the most important thing. "You have to make him look at you, Josie. Didn't you turn his head once?"

Josie glanced at herself in the reflection of her steel sink. What was she thinking? "I'm not that pretty anymore."

"Every woman is beautiful to the man who married her. Get yourself dolled up, Josie. Get dolled up, turn off the television and remind him that you're his woman, and you need his attention, too."

Something in his voice made her think of evenings in the back seat at the drive-in. She'd certainly had his attention then. "Welllll, I thought you might say that, so I got prettied up before I called. But ..."

Did he hear her renewed uncertainty? He said, "Go, Josie. Set the phone down so we can hear what happens. I promise to hang up if it gets too ... attentive."

She giggled. He was as bad as Audrey had been senior year. *"Go for it, Josie-girl! I promise, Kenny and I will be too busy to watch!"*

She glanced at the TV. The girl on the screen had just pulled off her shirt. Perfect timing.

She set the phone down, let herself thrill in the sound of her heels clacking against the linoleum. She was young, beautiful and in love—and she would remind him of what he was missing. *That Woman* didn't have anything on her—and if death wasn't going to stop him from returning to her, death wasn't going to keep him aloof from her either! Besides, some of their best times had been when she got tired of watching the make-out scenes and took charge before the madman crashed through the door. How had she forgotten that? No more.

"Oh, Jebbers ... how about some real entertainment for a change?" she purred as she trailed her arm across his back and chest while she circled his chair. He grunted dully as she passed between him and the TV. She leaned forward, twitched her shoulders the way that used to drive him wild. Then she threw her head back and reached for her shirt.

He lolled his head to one side, trying to see around her.

Sudden irritation spiked her sexy mood. Who cares if the guy was sliding off the girl's shorts? Wouldn't Jeb rather do that with her for once? If she could put up with the smell of Raid, he could put up with a few minutes without the TV. Probably all he was up for, anyway.

She turned, sticking her butt out invitingly, and reached to snap off the television.

Jeb opened his mouth and let out a bellow worthy of a Lovecraftian horror film.

Josie spun back to glare at him, hands on hips. On the TV, the couple had embraced, but the music was turning suspenseful. "Now don't get so mad! I just want a little of your—no! No!"

Jeb rose.

He opened his mouth to bellow again, but this time, intoxicated cockroaches spilled out of his mouth and staggered at his feet.

Josie screamed and backed up fast, spilling the TV off its stand just as the madman broke through the door with a chainsaw. The girl's screams blended with her own. The dogs leaped from the couch and started barking, unsure what to do. Over the radio, she heard Dr. Wilson telling someone to call 9-1-1.

Jeb took a step toward Josie, and Pinkie made up his mind. He leapt at the master that had hated him, knocking him to the ground. Jeb hit the corner of the TV stand, and his nose fell off.

Again, Josie screamed, but this time, it was rage, not fear. He really was dead! Her momma, her preacher, that exterminator woman—they had all tried to tell her, and she didn't listen. Oh, sure! He'd come back to her, just like nothing had happened, like all he needed was a little attention. And she fell for it, too, taking care of him, guarding his pride ...

He'd duped her again!

As Jeb swung awkwardly at the toy poodle, which jumped on him and snapped at the roaches on his chest, Josie grabbed the shotgun from where it fell beside the TV. She took aim.

She screamed, "This is the last straw, Jeb! The. Last. Straw! You're not the man I married. You're not even a man! You're a *corpse*! You lied to me for the last time! Pinkie, heel!"

The dog bounded to her feet, and she emptied both barrels into Jebediah's dead and decaying head. Not like there'd been much of a brain in there, anyway.

Then she snatched up her keys and pocketbook, called for the dogs and got into the car.

She'd go to Audrey's, but just long enough to borrow some shoes. Then, maybe she'd drive to California, meet up with that exterminator woman. People had to know, when the dead died—they didn't come back. All the love in the world wouldn't make them come back. They were just dead!

And if Jeb hadn't come back a murderous shambling monster, it was because he was too damn lazy to make the effort!

Karina Fabian does not actually like zombies, except as a vehicle for humor. Her unique take on zombies as just another pest needing extermination is the basis of her Neeta Lyffe, Zombie Exterminator series, in which Josie plays a minor role. Karina writes science fiction parodies and humorous fantasy novels. She also writes serious science fiction. To pay the bills, she writes freelance articles on software and edits a local magazine. fabianspace.com.

THE LAST DRIVE-IN MOVIE

B.D. PRINCE

THE LAST DRIVE-IN MOVIE

Howard Pierce rushed through the front door, ignoring his arthritic knees screaming at him. The screen door slammed behind him. "Ellie ... I've got a surprise for you!"

His wife wasn't in her chair reading one of her sci-fi or mystery novels like he expected. He shouted into the kitchen. "Ellie?"

The kitchen was vacant, too.

Howard's heart sank. *No. Not today. Don't let this be the day. Please, Lord, just one more day with her.*

He hurried to the bedroom, his aching knees forgotten, half-expecting to see the love of his life lying on the floor. *Please, not today.*

The room was still, the air stifling. The bed was made, each corner tucked neatly. But no napping Ellie. He quickly checked the floor on both sides of the bed. Empty.

The bathroom door sat ajar. When he reached the doorway he heard her retch. "Ellie? You all right?"

"Don't come in—" Her words were interrupted by another loud retch and the sound of vomit splashing in the toilet. The door slammed shut before Howard could enter.

"I'm sorry," she said from the other side of the door. "You know I don't like you to see me this way."

Howard wrung his hands. "Can I get you anything?"

"No. It's just that darn pain medication. I'll be out in a minute."

Howard paced in front of the bathroom door, listening to the toilet flush and Ellie gargle. Finally, the door opened. His wife of fifty years emerged, her bones holding up her cotton nightgown. Her face was drawn and ashen, a kerchief tied over her head.

"Sorry, honey. I look dreadful enough without you having to see me like that."

Howard shook his head and smiled. *Not today.*

"I promised you for better or worse. Besides, you're still cute as a button." He tapped the tip of her nose.

"And you're still blind as a bat." She grinned and walked into his waiting embrace. "So, what's all the excitement about?"

"I got tickets to the drive-in!" Howard held them up, grinning from ear to ear.

"I thought they were going to tear it down and build more condos ..."

"It's their last week. I thought it'd be fun to go one last time. Be just like our first date!"

Ellie laughed. "I was so nervous that day. I think I threw up then, too!"

"You? I accidentally put my aftershave on twice. I rolled down the windows and drove around the block a few times before I picked you up to reduce the smell."

"It didn't help," Ellie chuckled. "Lucky for you, I'm a sucker for an Aqua Velva man!" Her musical laughter devolved into a coughing fit.

She wavered on her feet. Her knees buckled and Howard caught her before she hit the floor.

He helped her to the bed. As her energy drained the coughing slowed. She struggled to catch her breath. Howard fumbled with the portable oxygen tank next to the bed. He helped her get the canula affixed to her nose and breathed along with her until she was breathing normally again.

"Are you sure you're up to going to the drive-in, dear?"

She gave him a sly grin. "Just try and stop me."

Resting in her favorite recliner, Ellie set her paperback copy of Jack Finney's *The Body Snatchers* on the end table next to her Bible so Natalie, the large African-American hospice nurse, could strap a blood-pressure cuff around her arm.

"Make sure you give me a clean bill of health, Natalie. I have a hot date tonight!"

The hospice nurse threw her head back and laughed with her whole body. "I'm afraid I'm fresh out of B-12 shots, honey." She turned to Howard and pointed. "And don't even think about asking me for any of those little blue pills."

Howard raised his hands in surrender.

After the hospice nurse finished taking Ellie's vitals, she checked her oxygen canister. "How's your O2 supplies, Mrs. Pierce?"

Howard answered for her. "I just picked up a couple fresh canisters yesterday."

Natalie leaned over and looked Ellie in the eye. Her jovial tone turned serious. "And how's your pain level, dear?"

Ellie shrugged and grimaced. "Seeing it's been seven months since the doctors gave me six months to live, I suppose it could be worse."

Natalie shook her head. "Ain't no pride in sufferin', honey. You know I got the good stuff."

"Thanks, Natalie, but it tears my stomach up something awful. And it makes me downright loopy." Ellie sighed and gazed longingly at Howard. "Besides, I want to be at my best for that hot date."

The hospice nurse let loose another one of her full body laughs. "Guess I better finish up here and leave you two alone."

Howard stood before the bathroom mirror and wiped the shaving cream residue from his face with a hand towel. He rubbed his hand across each cheek. Smooth as a baby's bottom. Just the way Ellie liked it.

Opening the medicine cabinet mirror, he retrieved the aftershave. He uncapped the bottle and gave it a sniff. *There's something about an Aqua Velva man.* Howard chuckled and shook his head. Careful not to splash too much aftershave into his palm, he rubbed his hands together and patted his cheeks. The alcohol stung.

Ellie appeared behind him in the mirror holding a selection of wigs. "What shall it be tonight? Sassy redhead? Then again, I hear blondes have more fun ..."

"How about the bookish brunette I fell in love with?"

"You got it, handsome."

Howard winked. "Nothing like the original."

Ellie returned to the bedroom mirror and removed her head scarf. The chemo had taken all but a few wisps of white hair. Howard turned away, his throat tightening. He closed his eyes, trying to hold onto the image of the lively girl he first saw at the malt shop so many years ago.

Howard dabbed his eyes with his handkerchief and blew his nose. He inhaled deeply and released a shaky breath. Turning back he found Ellie wearing the brown wig, the ends curled under at the shoulders. In his mind's eye his love looked just as she did on their first date.

Howard opened the car door for his wife as he had every time since their first date. "Madame ..."

"Thank you, kind sir." Ellie noticed the single red rose on the seat and clasped her hand to her chest. She brought the bloom to her nose, closed her eyes, and imbibed its scent. She smiled and gave her husband a kiss on the cheek. He took her by the hand and helped her into her seat.

Howard closed the door and shuffled around to the driver's side and got behind the wheel. When he started the car the seatbelt chime complained. Ellie gave him *the look*.

"I know, I know. Don't think I'll ever get used to wearing a seatbelt." Reluctantly, he buckled up.

Howard switched the radio from AM talk radio to an oldies music station. The perfect soundtrack for their date.

As they drove, Howard was struck anew how much the town had changed since their first date. The diner they used to frequent had a *For Lease* sign out front. The old bowling alley had been demolished and replaced by a strip mall populated with a cellular phone store, a dry cleaner, a sushi restaurant, and another place serving *shawarma*, whatever the hell that was.

Fruit and vegetable stands were replaced with coffee shops and fast-food restaurants. The woods Howard and his friends used to play in became a subdivision. Memory lane sure had changed.

"Remember when this all used to be farmland?" Ellie asked, gazing out the window.

"I remember old man Tillman chasing me and my buddies out of his watermelon patch with his shotgun! Marty got a butt full of rock salt. Never seen him run so fast!" Howard laughed. "Howled like a cat in heat!"

Ellie laughed too but it degenerated into another coughing fit. Howard dug in his pocket for his handkerchief, but it was hard to retrieve while sitting. He wrestled with his pocket when a horn blared. Howard cranked the wheel, steering back into his own lane.

"Howard!" Ellie shouted breathlessly, pointing as they barreled toward a parked car.

He had overcorrected. The parked car seemingly came out of nowhere. Ellie put her hands in front of her face, bracing for the collision.

Howard swerved and barely avoided sideswiping the parked car.

The light ahead turned red.

He stomped on the brake and came to an abrupt stop, the seatbelt digging into his chest.

His heart pounded. Ellie continued hacking. He finally dug his handkerchief out of his pocket and handed it to his wife. The light changed and Howard pulled over at the next opportunity.

Ellie's coughing slowed. She gasped for breath. Howard put his hand on her shoulder.

"Breathe, Ellie. Just try and relax."

She closed her eyes and finally got her breathing under control.

"Are you okay?"

Ellie took a deep breath through her nose, inhaling from the oxygen tube. She nodded. "I'm fine." She wiped her mouth and returned the handkerchief to her husband.

Howard took it from her shaking hand. Blood spotted the handkerchief.

"Do you need to go the hospital?"

"No, I'm fine, really. Just need to catch my breath."

Howard's heart sank. He wanted tonight to be perfect. *Doddering old fool.* He'd nearly gotten them killed. He glanced at the bloody handkerchief. "Maybe we should just head home."

"No!" Ellie coughed again then pleaded with her eyes. "Tonight ... is *our* night ... Not the cancer's."

Howard took her hand and kissed it. She smiled. He wanted to say something but he feared his voice would crack. Instead he shifted into drive and held her hand all the way to the drive-in.

The blood-red sun settled atop one of the last remaining tree lines in the area. A slim crescent moon appeared amongst the amassing black clouds. It boded well for the drive-in movie screen. The darker the better.

Up ahead, the marquee sign flickered to life displaying tonight's double feature.

THE GLOB—3D:
AND
THE THING FROM PLANET X

Ellie gasped. "It's a creature feature!"

Howard grinned. "Just like on our first date."

They drove up to the ticket booth and Howard handed the middle-aged woman in the window their tickets. The woman smiled and leaned over to see who Howard had with him.

"Are you sure you two are old enough to see these movies?" She gave Howard a wink.

"Just barely," Howard said. "And I promise we don't have any friends in the trunk."

Ellie giggled and Howard put his hand on her leg.

The woman reached out the window. "Here's your 3D glasses. And no funny business in there," she said. "I'm gonna keep an eye on you two!"

Ellie giggled again and whispered, "Good luck once the windows get steamed up!"

Howard pulled into the drive-in lot and found a spot in the center, near the front. Just like on their first date. He prayed this wouldn't be their last.

By the time Howard reached the concession stand his knees ached something terrible. Spotting the *Restrooms* sign, he decided to make a pit stop. With his enlarged prostate and arthritic knees, he should've parked closer to the concession stand than the screen.

Howard got in line at the concessions counter and ordered the same thing he did on their first date—two hotdogs with mustard (no onions), a large bucket of popcorn, and a large drink with two straws. His friend Josh said if you can get your date to drink from the same cup, then kissing was only a few more inches. And no onions in case it actually worked.

Wedging the popcorn bucket under his arm, Howard grabbed the cardboard food tray and headed back to the car, careful not to trip and fall on the uneven gravel lot. His balance wasn't what it used to be.

Howard grinned as he passed some teenager's hand-me-down Ford with its windows already fogged up. Back in his day, the windows didn't get steamed until the second feature.

Squeals came from the playground as children climbed and ran and chased each other without a care in the world. Pleasant memories flooded back of his and Ellie's children climbing on giant fiberglass elephants, hippopotamuses, and giraffes on this very same playground.

Howard glanced around, disoriented. Why couldn't he find his car? He meandered from row to row. So many cars. *Ah, finally.* Howard walked up to the car and a strange face scowled back at him. He jumped back, spilling some of the popcorn.

"Sorry!"

Damn newer cars all look alike. Howard wandered for several minutes before finally spotting his car.

Approaching the passenger-side door, Howard held the food next to the window to get his wife's attention but her eyes were closed. He fumbled the food tray and popcorn bucket in an attempt to rap on the window but his arms were too full and he feared he'd dump their entire dinner on the ground. He sighed and shuffled around to the driver's side and set the food on the hood.

As he reached for the door handle a spike of fear pierced his chest. *No. Not today. Not now. God, please, not yet!*

Howard jerked open the car door and dropped into the seat with a grunt. Her eyes were still closed. She looked ... peaceful.

Howard reached for her, his hand trembling. Then stopped. He wanted to know—needed to know—but the answer terrified him. Taking a deep breath he steadied himself and felt her wrist. Her arm felt cold.

Wait, was that a faint pulse? Or just wishful thinking?

"Ellie?" He could barely speak her name.

She didn't respond.

Howard's heart beat hard enough for both of them. He held his shaking hand in front of her slack mouth to feel for respiration. Her breathing was either too shallow or ...

His throat clenched. Again, he called her name but nothing came out but a choked whisper. His eyes blurred.

Mustering every ounce of courage he had, he checked her carotid pulse.

Ellie's eyes sprung open and she gasped, startling Howard.

"What? Where?" Her chest heaved as she tried to get her breath under control.

"It's okay, Ellie. I'm here."

She glanced around, confused.

"I'm right here, honey."

Seeing Howard, her breathing slowed. She placed her hand on Howard's cheek and smiled.

Ellie's smile faded. She looked confused. "Weren't you going to get us something to eat?"

"I did but I thought you were ..." *Dead?* Howard shook the horrible notion from his head. "... asleep. And I didn't want to wake you."

Ellie looked around confused. "Then where is it?"

"I left it on the hood."

Ellie raised an eyebrow.

"To keep it warm. Until you woke up." Howard chuckled nervously. "I'll go get it."

Storm clouds obscured the moon. Lightning flashed somewhere in the distance. A moment later a low rumble of thunder resonated, setting the mood for the creature feature.

A test pattern flashed on the drive-in screen and counted down from five to one before an animated band of popcorn, soda, and candy danced across the screen singing, "Let's all go to the lobby."

Ellie laughed and slapped Howard's leg. "Boy, does that bring back memories!"

"Do you want me to go get you anything else?"

Ellie gazed at Howard and smiled. "I have everything I need right here."

Howard put his arm around his wife and pulled her close. She felt so small. So fragile. He wanted to squeeze her but he feared she might break.

The credits rolled and a message displayed on the screen cuing them to don their 3D Glasses. It took some effort to get them to fit over their bifocals but they managed just in time to see the title card zoom at them ...

THE GLOB! ... In 3D!

324

Thunder rumbled, as if on cue.

The movie opened at the La Brea Tar Pits in Hancock Park. Oil derricks pumped away with the Santa Monica Mountains in the distance.

An archaeology professor and a handful of his students clad in khaki shorts and pith helmets chipped away at the asphalt walls of an excavation pit. A female student dislodged a saber-toothed cat fang and cried out with excitement. Her fellow students gathered around as the professor verified her discovery.

Their excitement turned to screams when the earth began to rumble and shake. The archaeology students stumbled, fighting to stay on their feet but the earthquake was too violent.

The ladder fell into the pit, preventing their escape. A fissure split open the ground releasing plumes of steam. One of the students cried out as he fell into the chasm up to his armpits.

When the shaking subsided, the students rushed to help the young man hanging on for dear life over the steaming crevasse.

Suddenly, a viscous, black liquid oozed out of the hole.

Two students each grabbed an arm and dragged him from the bubbling sludge as his bottom half melted away. They quickly dropped him and backed away as The Glob continued to ooze out of the fissure, its oily black surface steaming as it engulfed the student's remains.

One of the female students screamed and fainted.

Panicking, the others scrambled to climb out of the excavation pit but there was nowhere to run. The pit's walls were too steep to climb out.

The gelatinous black substance spread across the pit floor, miring them down in its tarry morass. The bare legs of those it trapped blistered and popped as The Glob dissolved their flesh down to the bone. Their tortured cries were mercifully silenced as the molten sludge absorbed the rest of their bodies.

The professor managed to raise the ladder. But before he could climb out of the pit, the amorphous creature shot out a black tendril that lassoed his leg and pulled him down into the oily quagmire.

The Glob oozed up the ladder, freeing itself from its earthly confines, seeking to satiate its unquenchable appetite.

Ellie watched the scary parts through splayed fingers as she and Howard crunched their popcorn, losing themselves in good old-fashioned, B-movie nostalgia. The closest thing to heaven on earth.

Lightning flashed above the drive-in, quickly followed by a powerful thunderclap. The storm drew closer. Lightning continued to spider-web across the ominous purple sky. Howard had never seen an electrical storm quite like this. The speaker hanging from his window crackled with static each time lightning lit up the sky.

He hugged Ellie tight, knowing how fearful she got during thunderstorms, especially since they were surrounded by metal.

On the screen The Glob oozed down Main Street, consuming everything in its path—cars, lampposts, and people too slow to outrun it. The more it consumed, the bigger it got. Downtown was in complete chaos.

Police blocked off Main Street with their cruisers. The Glob rushed toward the barricade. The officers opened fire but the creature absorbed their attack without slowing. The Glob surged like an ocean wave, swelling high above the squad cars. The crowd gasped and screamed as it crested above them.

Suddenly a bolt of lightning struck the drive-in theater screen. Electricity arced and popped across the screen sending showers of sparks raining down. Electricity surged through The Glob as a wave of black sludge poured out of the screen and into the drive-in.

Howard couldn't believe his eyes. It must be a 3D optical illusion. He took off his 3D glasses and looked again.

Molten sludge continued to spill out of the screen. How was this possible?

"Ellie, do you see what I'm seeing?"

Flashes of lightning provided snapshots of The Glob amassing and oozing toward the drive-in patrons' cars. Brake lights flared as others discovered the approaching threat. Muffled screams erupted from the other cars. A handful of patrons got out of their vehicles to investigate.

A terrified mother ran toward the playground, yelling for her kids. The children continued to climb on the equipment, oblivious to the imminent danger behind them. Their mother frantically waved them toward her, but her children didn't want to stop playing.

The Glob swelled as it reached the playground.

Finally reacting to their mother pointing behind them and the rising chorus of screams, the children glanced back, but it was too late. A wave of black sludge engulfed the playground set along with the screaming children. Their mother dropped to her knees and released a tortured wail.

Headlights flared and cars sped in reverse, spraying gravel and ripping the speaker wires from their posts. Cars crashed into each other, horns honked, people screamed.

The creature continued to advance.

As the Glob reached them, drivers abandoned their vehicles and ran for the exits. Some weren't as lucky. The dark, hungry mass engulfed their cars, dissolving metal, glass, vinyl, and any flesh trapped inside.

Howard couldn't believe his eyes. He finally snapped out of his shock and slid behind the wheel. As he reached for the keys in the ignition, Ellie leaned on his shoulder.

He said, "Don't worry, sweetheart. I'll get us out of here."

Starting the car, he reached for the column shifter to put the vehicle in reverse. Ellie slumped forward, her head thumping into the dash.

Howard stiffened. His heart pounded. Because he knew.

He gently leaned Ellie back. Her head lolled.

Howard turned off the ignition, sat back, and held Ellie tight as the insatiable black mass rolled toward them, consuming everything in its path.

B.D. Prince was born in Michigan, a dark fiction and comedy writer who credits these proclivities to growing up near a cemetery and being endowed with a freakishly long funny bone. He ultimately moved to California to pursue screenwriting and get a tan. Prince has written everything from screenplays to one-liners for Joan Rivers. After completing several screenplays and publishing numerous short stories, Prince is currently working on a full-length horror novel and developing a project for television.

WELCOME TO THE UNDERHILL CINEMA

FRAN WILDE

WELCOME TO THE UNDERHILL CINEMA

11/1/19 1:05 pm—Cambell Stevens: 5 PM, UNDERHILL CINEMA, MEET ME THERE?

11/1/19 1:08 pm—Virginia Bell: I LOVE THAT PLACE. IT'S A MESS. WE GOING IN?

11/1/19 1:09 pm—Cambell Stevens: YOU KNOW IT. WEAR SOMETHING NICE? FOR THE FANS.

Cambell stared down the length of broken sidewalk beside the chain link fence and NO TRESPASSING signs outside The Underhill before he ducked beneath the fallen marquee. The rent-a-cop was watching Magnum-PI on his phone again, same as when Cambell did recon on the old theater the day before.

He was early, sure, but Ginny was usually earlier. For this episode of Ghost Town Caving, Cambell needed the extra time to set up lights and perch the drone cams just right without spoiling the surprise.

He cleared the plywood boards beyond the marquee, though it was a tight squeeze. Dust streaked his pawn-shop tuxedo jacket, and he had to use his GTC gear bag—with the glow-in-the-dark logo that Ginny had designed—to part the thick cobwebs. The drone rode his shoulder like a simplified crow, recording everything from the fading light to the pop of the webs as they parted.

He and Ginny had spent weeks researching the building for their season finale. When Ginny had gotten the call from Hollywood, they'd had to move the episode up. Rented a cheap car out of Portland and drove up US 5 until they found the place. Planned two days for recon and filming together, then she'd take the train down the coast to L.A.

"Can you imagine what this old building remembers?" Ginny had stage-whispered wide-eyed to the camera when they'd pulled the records from archives at Portland State University. "More than we could ever forget." The building's blueprints were torn and damaged, but they showed enough for Ginny to locate multiple entrances and exits, just in case. Ghost Town Caving, unlike newcomers Urban Spelunking and Olde Towne Caverns, did the work of getting to know a place, not merely abseiling through it.

Cambell let his eyes get used to the darkness before crossing the damp carpet to the concession stand. His footsteps squelched. Above, winged masks held back torn swaths of rotting velvet and dust swirled in the glimmer of a broken window somewhere high up.

The back of Cambell's neck prickled with anticipation. He'd been right. The Underhill was the perfect place to propose.

11/1/19 4:52 PM—GOING TO BE A COUPLE MINUTES LATE, CAMBELL, OK?

Cambell breathed relief. DEFINITELY OK. GLAMMING UP?

YOU KNOW IT.

Cambell pushed through the theater's heavy doors and walked between rows of seats. With a penlight in his fist, he scanned the floor, looking for danger. Where would be best? Up on stage, where Vaudeville singers had once performed, and a giant screen now sagged? Or down in the seats? The box seats, paneled in peeling commedia dell'arte masks and elaborate scrollwork, to the left of the stage had the best angle to catch Ginny's reaction. Would she scream? Be surprised? Then happy? He hoped for the last one.

The box to the right had partially collapsed. So had several rows of chairs, falling through a hole in the floor like a trailing tentacle into the basement.

So, really no choice then.

"All right, friends, let's do this." Cambell sent the drone up to the left-hand box, where it perched on the railing, its red eye focused on the scene below. He grinned up at it, as he walked down the middle aisle. He sifted through his gear bag for the LED throws.

Water dripped onstage and had been doing so for long enough that the screen had a scrim of mold. It looked like what happened to Ginny's mascara after she'd had a good post-scare cry. Had it been raining when Cambell came in? He didn't think so.

When he heard the voice, he froze. "Welcome to The Underhill Cinema," the recording had deepened with moisture and age. "A Landmark property." The last part wobbled and faded, so that it sounded more like "a large majesty."

"Thanks," Cambell replied. It was always nice to get on a building's good side before you went exploring.

"We'd love your feedback after the show," the voice continued, a garbled whisper.

"So far, so good," Cambell whispered back.

Outside, sounding muted by the doors, boards, and the chain link fence, the rent-a-cop yelled, "Who's in there? Get out, whoever you are."

A dispatch radio crackled. Cambell shut off his penlight and stood still in the dark as a beam breached the outside door, which he'd left ajar. "Damn kids wouldn't know what to do if they got hurt, treat for rabies or tetanus first? Or should I let you rot in there, you and the building both?" The guard slurred his words. "Place gives me the creeps."

After a moment of silence, the radio crackled again. "Nah, some rats. Probably triggered the motion sensors. Not worth worrying about." The light receded and Cambell texted Ginny: *security by the marquee.*

Okay, almost there, she texted back.

The rent-a-cop wouldn't come in a place like The Underhill unless he had to. Nor would Urban Spelunking or Olde Towne Caverns. Chickens.

Not like him and Ginny.

Cambell touched the ring in his pocket for luck, then tossed nine sticky LED throws at the stage and the walls, then a couple more. The tiny glitter lights made the whole place look even more romantic. A piece of velvet curtain beside the giant screen tore a little from the weight and swung slowly, making the screen look like it blinked from the dazzle. Between that and the way the fallen marquee had resembled nothing so much as a set of teeth, chewing the pavement, he knew Ginny was going to love this place more than she already did.

"Can you believe this?" She'd asked at the archives. "So much history. And weird shit too." She waved the multiple resurrections of the property as evidence: Vaudeville hall turned silent film stage, with a full orchestra pit. Then the 90s renovation, preserving the elaborate carvings and velvet seats, which had made it, briefly, the place to be seen for local-artist premiers.

When Cambell had scouted, some long-faded palm prints and signatures of forgotten stars had still been visible, beneath the bite of the marquee.

A dark wave skittered beside Cambell's foot, a ripple of fur and carpet. Rats, indeed. He coughed and whatever it was scattered.

"Actress vanishes during premiere," Ginny had read aloud to their GTC fans for the pre-show. "In at least the second occurence, The Underhill is home to a mystery." She'd wiggled her eyebrows, looking smart and cute in her glasses. Even though it turned out that the actress had been fleeing the law, an outstanding warrant, and everyone knew she'd evaded the cameras and escaped out the back, the disappearance had added to the building's legacy. Same for the violinist who'd vanished from the orchestra pit during a performance of *The Wind*, an old silent film. She'd reappeared decades later, supposedly none the worse for wear. Except that had been a scam, for publicity, the woman, her daughter.

Ginny ate things like that up, then talked through them during the show, wondering if this was where the violin section was; if that was the exit the actress had left by. "Learning a building's secrets," she winked at the camera, and at Cambell himself, "was a bit like falling in love, from the inside out."

Where are you? He texted. His palms were clammy, now that he'd gotten everything ready.

He reached in the pocket of the blue tuxedo pants again and spun the ring twice. He hoped she'd say yes.

11/1/19 5:05 PM—OKAY! I'M HERE! WHERE ARE YOU?

11/1/19 5:05 PM—IN THE THEATER. FRONT ROW, CENTER.

11/1/19 5:05 PM—REALLY? I CAN'T SEE YOU AT ALL. I'M RIGHT HERE.

Cambell looked at the message on his phone and then gazed around wildly. No shadows, no squeaks of footfalls on floorboards. Was she playing a trick on him?

11/1/19 5:05 PM—OH YOU MONSTER, YOU GOT THE PROJECTOR WORKING. WHAT A WONDERFUL SURPRISE.

In the darkness, with the LEDs twinkling like bee lights at a picnic, Cambell had most certainly not gotten the projector working. He hadn't even thought of it.

The screen was blank, concrete gray, rippling with a few LED shadows. That didn't constitute working. WHERE ARE YOU?

11/1/19 5:05 PM—FRONT ROW, CENTER, LIKE YOU SAID. OH THIS IS WONDERFUL. I LOVE THIS MOVIE. HOW DID YOU KNOW. AND WHERE ARE YOU FILMING FROM? WHAT'S MY ANGLE?

A chill ran down Cambell's spine, from the base of his skull to his feet. Ginny was not in the front row. He was alone.

Then the projector flicked on, and a black and white film, silent, began.

On it, he saw Ginny, watching a movie, wearing a glittering black dress. She'd done her hair up like a movie star, and had found full-length white gloves. Behind her, the velvet chairs, fallen into the floor, began to ripple. Her eyes looked right into his as she was embraced by the seats, then drawn down into the basement of the building. No chance to scream; she'd been so surprised. Her face had framed a panicked laugh before she disappeared, while the film continued to roll.

"Ginny!" Cambell shouted. Then, when his voice echoed through the empty cinema, he texted: GINNY?

Somewhere, deep within the movie theater, a slow sound rumbled. Like bricks and mortar, grinding together. Almost like laughter.

Breathing in panicked busts, Cambell signaled the drone, which left the balcony box and came to settle on his shoulder. He ran through the aisles, looking for the hole down to the basement.

"Ginny! Virginia Bell!" He shouted until he heard the security guard outside, daring himself to come into the theater and haul Cambell out.

Did he want the guard's help? Maybe?

Cambell hesitated, on the edge of asking.

He looked at the drone. The thing's red eye still held firm. Still recording. "Did you see that? What the heck's happening?"

His viewers wouldn't like it if he asked for help. Not one bit.

A board fell. A flashlight lit up the concession stand's glass front, and sent glare into the theater. "Projector's running," the guard slurred. "Kid, you'd better get out of there, before I haul you out."

Cambell wasn't about to get hauled out.

"Whatever's happening," he whispered to the drone, "I'm not leaving Ginny." If he left the Underhill, he felt certain he'd never find her. Maybe no one would.

He ran to the theater's farthest exit, opened the door, and tossed a broken arm from a chair into the hallway. The arm clattered against the floor, loudly.

Cambell crouched down, near the stage. The smell of damp and rot was overwhelming.

"He's getting out the back," the rent-a-cop shouted into his radio. The radio replied with a burst of static, and then the guard, breath heaving against the weight of cheap body armor, ran through the theater, and out the other side.

Cambell relaxed, but only a little bit. "Weird shit," Ginny had said. Her face had lit up, blue eyes dancing. The Underhill *was* behaving strangely, and he was catching it all on film.

That was great for ratings. But Cambell's stomach churned. It was super bad for him personally. If Ginny really had disappeared, people were probably already on the chat logs saying he'd planned it. Because she'd been getting ready to leave him.

If she hadn't disappeared, people were *definitely* going to say he'd planned this, and faked it all.

They wouldn't care about the truth: that he loved her. That he'd wanted to surprise her.

Either way, the only good outcome was for him to find out what was happening, and to find Ginny. He shivered as he recalled her face on the screen, so trusting.

So convinced this was part of the show.

Once he was sure the guard was gone, Cambell shone his penlight down into the hole in the floor of the theater. Light rippled back at him. Water. He heard the drip-drip-drip, again, and something swimming down there.

"Ginny?" He whispered as loud as he could.

"Ginny." The basement echoed back.

He dropped an LED throw down into the water, and it took a long time to splash. Then it disappeared, fast. The basement must be huge.

He'd have to go down there, alone. He reached into his equipment bag for the ropes. Ghost Town Caving recommended at least two climbers for safety when exploring structures, and Cambell wasn't excited about going alone. He was even less excited about the prospect of tying a rope to any of the theater chairs nearby, which could fall into the basement at any time.

Maybe there was another way. He tried to think of the blueprints. There'd been a door to the basement behind the stage. "Ginny, I'm coming okay?"

When he stood, his shadow stretched long behind him, falling into the hole with the seats. On the screen, which was still lit, the opposite set of seats looked like a wide mouth, an open throat. Ginny had disappeared inside those rotting, crimson guts.

Cambell stuck both hands in his pockets, feeling the ring press hard against his fingertips. Then he put the ring in a sealed plastic bag in his equipment kit and buckled the bag over both shoulders.

This was not the kind of surprise he'd planned, but urban caving meant be ready for anything, and Cambell was. Most of the time.

In his scramble to get up onto the stage, he triggered the motion detector again. The voice returned, deep and slow now, but stuck on a few words of the tape. "Love your feedback," blurred and became "love you back," as if the recording was water damaged.

After seeing the basement, Cambell couldn't imagine how it was still playing at all. He shivered. He hadn't planned on swimming in a tuxedo. Or at all. Neither had Ginny, though, and that's all he was thinking about now.

"Ginny?" Cambell kept calling as he pushed apart the backstage curtains and found the door to the basement.

337

His fingers punched right through the fabric, but he got the door open, on the first try.

"Hold up there, mister!" The drunken security guard lunged from the wings and tried to grab his arm. "Gotcha, you punk kid!"

Cambell jerked away, plowing through the stage curtain—what was left of it—and slamming the door behind him. He threw the latch and could hear the guard pounding against the door all the way down the stairs. But when he reached the bottom of the stairs, the pounding stopped, and the only thing Cambell could hear was water dripping and the welcome tape's drone: *Love you back. Love you back.*

"Ginny? *Ginny!*" The basement echoed her name back to him.

He pushed through piles of boxes, knocking over several. Reels of film spilled out into the water, snaking around his ankles. Cambell shook free and kept moving deeper into the basement. She wasn't answering him. *Was she even down here?*

Wait a minute. Cambell stopped again. *Had she even been in the theater? Or had she been punking him?*

The idea that maybe Ginny would have set up a last-minute goodbye surprise for him had never crossed his mind. He'd always been the genius of the Ghost Town Caving operation. Even if, over the past thirteen months, Ginny had done far more than the ad she'd answered had specified. *Actress wanted, 25% of net for popular YouTube & GetNow vodcast,* was what he'd written. But she'd helped him ramp up. Logos, advertising revenue, everything.

She could totally plan a gotcha reel.

Cambell sighed and made sure the drone was still filming. "Ginny, game's over. Knock it off."

11/1/19 5:05 PM—CAMBELL? I CAN HEAR YOU, BUT I CAN'T SEE YOU.

STOP KIDDING AROUND OKAY? IT'S GETTING COLD DOWN HERE.

WHERE ARE YOU?

SOMEWHERE IN THE BASEMENT. I CAN'T GET OUT OF THIS CHAIR.

All right, so she wasn't punking him. Or at least Cambell didn't want to risk it. He stepped deeper into the basement, into the water.

A beam of light caught him directly in the eyes. "Got you, punk-assed

338

kid. You know how hard it was to get down here through that hole? I'm taking it out on your hide."

Cambell backed up, splashing. The guard grabbed for him, but stumbled and dropped his flashlight into the water, where it shorted out. The guard cursed. "I can tase you, you know."

The guard wasn't much older than Cambell or Ginny. He had curls like hers, and long dark lashes. He could have easily been Ginny's cousin. Distant cousin. Except the guard was a pasty white, and paler now with fear, and Ginny's skin was olive hued. She was a classic beauty, in the old-movie kind of way. Plus, she was a good foot taller and her eyes—Cambell couldn't think about how beautiful her eyes were right now.

"If you're going to tase me, do it. It will look great on camera. If not, help me, I need to find my girlfriend," he shouted.

The guard smirked. "I'm only here to help you get your ass out of the building, son. Your pretty girlfriend's already with my partner. We drew straws."

Cambell knew the guard was lying. That the guy wasn't willing to help him find Ginny, wasn't even willing to listen to him, fueled his frustration.

He pushed the guard into the water and ran again, through a hole in the basement wall, that looked like it used to have a door in it. "Ginny?"

When he emerged, it was into sub-basement half flooded with something darker than water. Something that smelled like the contents of a drunk's stomach.

He saw pieces of foam cushions and old film reels floating in the brine. "What the hell is this?" Had the river nearby broken through? That wasn't likely but it wasn't impossible. If so, he knew the building's foundation was really unstable, not just the floors.

11/1/19 5:45 PM—GINNY IF YOU CAN HEAR ME, YELL, OK?

For a moment, he stared at his phone, waiting for the sound of her voice. Willing it to echo through the basement.

Then he looked at her messages. The timestamp was wrong on every single one. Somehow, Ginny was still there, messaging him, but from forty minutes ago. He could see the cursor blinking as she typed.

11/1/19 5:05 PM—IT'S DARK AND I CAN HEAR YOUR VOICE. BUT I CAN'T SEE YOU. AND YOUR VOICE IS STRANGE ... LIKE IT'S ALL AROUND ME. CAN YOU SAY SOMETHING ELSE BESIDES LOVE YOU? PLEASE?

Cambell froze.

He almost typed "That's not me," but he knew Ginny would freak at that and he needed her to stay calm, to tell him where she was. JUST GIVE ME A MINUTE. CAN YOU SEE ANYTHING?

Splashing behind him. The rental cop.

11/1/19 5:05 PM—JUST THE MOVIE. AND YOUR HAND. YOU'RE HOLDING ON TO MY SHOULDER, RIGHT? THAT'S YOU?

The next few words were garbled.
Cambell took a deep breath.

I'VE GOT YOU, GINNY. I'M GOING TO GET YOU OUT OF THERE.

11/1/19 5:05 PM—OKAY. THE MOVIE'S ALMOST OVER. THE LIGHTS WILL COME UP SOON.

She sounded so scared, and for a moment, Cambell worried he had left her upstairs in the theater, but then the building moaned and he knew he hadn't.

The security guard's footsteps echoed in the damp sub-basement. "Something tried to grab me!" The guard shouted.

Beside Cambell, a ripple in the water. An eyeball. The size of a whale's.

It blinked slowly, like it was thinking. Then an arm reached past Cambell for the rent-a-cop. Slowly. "Love you," the recording whispered, louder now. Echoing in the room.

"Get out! Run!" Cambell yelled at the guard. He wanted to run too, but he wasn't going to leave Ginny. If he could find her.

The security guard laughed. "You think I'm that stupid, kid?"

But then tentacles emerged black and slick from the fetid water. Torn movie tickets stuck to them. They looked, Cambell realized, like power cables, thick ones. And the eye had been one of the big, elaborate letters from the building's marquee.

He watched in horror as the guard was pulled under.

But then the eye closed and another hole in the wall opened, above the floodline. He heard the closing music of *The Wind*.

I'M COMING, GINNY. HOLD ON.

11/1/19 5:05 PM—OKAY CAMBELL HURRY. IT'S STILL DARK, EVEN
THOUGH THE MOVIE'S ENDED.

Then he heard her yelling his name. Following the sound, Cambell ran
back through the sub-basement, and beneath the Underhill Theater. He
felt as if he was running through the building's guts, until he found the
auditorium again. But this one had all its chairs intact, and there was a
movie showing. A real one. And there sat Ginny, in a seat that had curled
neatly around her, as if keeping her warm.

She looked up at him, drowsy. "Did you get the shot," she asked.

Cambell realized she was pointing at the drone, still perched on his
shoulder. "I'm pretty sure I did."

He pulled her from the chair, which didn't resist, and dragged her out
the far exit.

"How did you know I loved *The Wind*? I never mentioned that to you."

Cambell held her tighter. He nearly carried her down the hallway, her
long dress dragging behind them on the carpet. When he heard the
recording begin again—*love you back, love you back*—he moved faster.

"And all those things you said, about wanting me to stay, about
rebuilding the cinema, together," Ginny's voice trailed off. She looked
around her as if for the first time in a while when Cambell pushed the
emergency exit and they nearly fell out onto the sidewalk. They crawled
beneath the chain link, onto the street. "Did you say those?"

When they emerged, it was raining, and the marquee for the Underhill
was lit up bright as day, still biting into the concrete. The O for the word
movie was missing. Cambell shivered. "I didn't say those, Ginny."

"How did that—Cambell, you're soaking wet. And that tux!" Ginny
said. She frowned and shook her head. Her voice shook. "If that wasn't
you? What happened?"

"We got out," Cambell said. He put his hand against the building's
side. He checked the drone. It played back only a few moments of tape,
the bit in the under-basement, where the eye rolled at him, the guard
chasing him, the shot of Ginny on the screen, getting sucked into the
building's belly. The shot hadn't uploaded. He erased it. "What happened
is that we got out."

In Cambell's bag was the ring he'd wanted to use to surprise Ginny.
Back in that other time, before the cinema.

Now, thinking about her expression as the chairs grabbed her, Cambell thought he'd wait a bit, to see whether she'd even want to be surprised. "I don't know what we do from here, though, Ginny," he finally said.

They found a diner near the theater and tried to clean up from their escape through the building. Ginny somehow emerged from the restroom with her hair tucked back into place. Her dress brushed clean of cobwebs and dust. She looked beautiful.

Cambell's tuxedo was ruined. He couldn't get the smell of the Cinema out of his hair.

They ordered coffee and Ginny grinned, a little shaky still. "I was going to ask you something tonight, before everything."

Cambell held his breath.

Ginny leaned on him. "Want to go Hollywood with me and be there for the start of something amazing? It would mean leaving GTC for a while."

Cambell thought for thirty seconds, then he was grinning too. "Yeah. I'd like that."

"There's a rental car around the corner," Ginny pointed down the road. "That someone needs to take back to Portland. Then there's a train that goes all the way to California. Want to ride together?"

"All the way to California? You bet I do."

On their way out of town, Cambell stared at the Underhill, daring it to follow them.

He swore the letters on the marquee blinked at him as they left.

Fran Wilde's novels and short fiction have won the Nebula, Compton Crook, and Eugie Foster awards, and have been finalists for six Nebulas, three Hugos, two Locii, a Dragon, and a World Fantasy Award. She writes for several publications, including *The Washington Post*, *The New York Times*, *Asimov's*, *Nature Magazine*, *Uncanny Magazine*, *Tor.com*, *GeekMom*, and *io9*. Fran is Director of the Genre MFA concentration at Western Colorado University. FranWilde.net.

ABOUT THE EDITOR

Kevin J. Anderson is the author of more than 160 books, 56 of which have been national or international bestsellers, best known for his work in the Dune, Star Wars, and X-Files universes, as well as his original series The Saga of Seven Suns, Terra Incognita, and Spine of the Dragon. He has edited numerous anthologies, including the Blood Lite series, the Five by Five series, and the Star Wars: Tales series, which are the three best-selling science fiction anthologies of all time, He and his wife Rebecca Moesta are the publishers of WordFire Press. Anderson is the Director of the Publishing MA program in the Graduate Program in Creative Writing at Western Colorado University. This anthology was compiled by his grad students as part of their thesis work.

For more information on the Western Colorado GPCW Publishing MA program western.edu/mfa

IF YOU LIKED ...

If you liked *Monsters, Movies & Mayhem*, you might also enjoy:

Undercurrents: An Anthology of What Lies Beneath
edited by Lisa Mangum

Selected Stories: Horror and Dark Fantasy
by Kevin J. Anderson

Fantastic Holiday Season: A Gift of Stories
edited by Kevin J. Anderson

This book was produced as part of the Publishing MA program for Western Colorado University's Graduate Program in Creative Writing.

OTHER WORDFIRE PRESS ANTHOLOGIES

A Game of Horns

edited by Lisa Mangum

Dragon Writers

edited by Lisa Mangum

One Horn to Rule Them All

edited by Lisa Mangum

Our list of other WordFire Press authors and titles is always growing. To find out more and to see our selection of titles, visit us at:

wordfirepress.com

Made in the USA
Monee, IL
03 October 2020